GOING
AFTER
CACCIATO

by the same author

IF I DIE IN A COMBAT ZONE
NORTHERN LIGHTS

GOING AFTER CACCIATO

a novel by
Tim O'Brien

JONATHAN CAPE
THIRTY BEDFORD SQUARE LONDON

First published in Great Britain 1978
Copyright © 1975, 1976, 1977, 1978 by Tim O'Brien

Jonathan Cape Ltd, 30 Bedford Square, London wc1

Portions of this book appeared in different form in
*Shenandoah, Esquire, Redbook, Ploughshares, The
Massachusetts Review, Gallery, Denver Quarterly,
O. Henry Prize Stories 1976, The Best American
Short Stories 1977,* and *The Pushcart Prize 1977.*
The author wishes to thank the editors of those
publications and to express gratitude for support
received from the National Endowment for the
Arts and the Massachusetts Arts and Humanities
Foundation.

British Library Cataloguing in Publication Data

O'Brien, Tim
Going after Cacciato.
I. Title
823'.9'1F   PS3565.B75G/
ISBN 0-224-01626-1

Printed in Great Britain
by the Anchor Press Ltd
and bound by Wm Brendon and Son Ltd
both of Tiptree, Essex

For Erik Hansen

Soldiers are dreamers.

— SIEGFRIED SASSOON

Going
After
Cacciato

1
Going
After
Cacciato

IT WAS A BAD TIME. Billy Boy Watkins was dead, and so was
Frenchie Tucker. Billy Boy had died of fright, scared to
death on the field of battle, and Frenchie Tucker had been
shot through the nose. Bernie Lynn and Lieutenant Sidney
Martin had died in tunnels. Pederson was dead and Rudy
Chassler was dead. Buff was dead. Ready Mix was dead. They
were all among the dead. The rain fed fungus that grew in the
men's boots and socks, and their socks rotted, and their feet
turned white and soft so that the skin could be scraped off with
a fingernail, and Stink Harris woke up screaming one night
with a leech on his tongue. When it was not raining, a low mist
moved across the paddies, blending the elements into a single
gray element, and the war was cold and pasty and rotten.
Lieutenant Corson, who came to replace Lieutenant Sidney
Martin, contracted the dysentery. The tripflares were useless.
The ammunition corroded and the foxholes filled with mud
and water during the nights, and in the mornings there was
always the next village and the war was always the same. The
monsoons were part of the war. In early September Vaught

caught an infection. He'd been showing Oscar Johnson the sharp edge on his bayonet, drawing it swiftly along his forearm to peel off a layer of mushy skin. "Like a Gillette Blue Blade," Vaught had said proudly. There was no blood, but in two days the bacteria soaked in and the arm turned yellow, so they bundled him up and called in a dustoff, and Vaught left the war. He never came back. Later they had a letter from him that described Japan as smoky and full of slopes, but in the enclosed snapshot Vaught looked happy enough, posing with two sightly nurses, a wine bottle rising from between his thighs. It was a shock to learn he'd lost the arm. Soon afterward Ben Nystrom shot himself through the foot, but he did not die, and he wrote no letters. These were all things to joke about. The rain, too. And the cold. Oscar Johnson said it made him think of Detroit in the month of May. "Lootin' weather," he liked to say. "The dark an' gloom, just right for rape an' lootin'." Then someone would say that Oscar had a swell imagination for a darkie.

That was one of the jokes. There was a joke about Oscar. There were many jokes about Billy Boy Watkins, the way he'd collapsed of fright on the field of battle. Another joke was about the lieutenant's dysentery, and another was about Paul Berlin's purple biles. There were jokes about the postcard pictures of Christ that Jim Pederson used to carry, and Stink's ringworm, and the way Buff's helmet filled with life after death. Some of the jokes were about Cacciato. Dumb as a bullet, Stink said. Dumb as a month-old oyster fart, said Harold Murphy.

In October, near the end of the month, Cacciato left the war. "He's gone away," said Doc Peret. "Split, departed."

Lieutenant Corson did not seem to hear. He was too old to be a lieutenant. The veins in his nose and cheeks were broken. His back was weak. Once he had been a captain on the way to becoming a major, but whiskey and the fourteen dull years between Korea and Vietnam had ended all that, and now he was just an old lieutenant with the dysentery.

2

He lay on his back in the pagoda, naked except for green socks and green undershorts.

"Cacciato," Doc repeated. "The kid's left us. Split for parts unknown."

The lieutenant did not sit up. With one hand he cupped his belly, with the other he guarded a red glow. The surfaces of his eyes were moist.

"Gone to Paris," Doc said.

The lieutenant put the glow to his lips. Inhaling, his chest did not move. There were no vital signs in the wrists or thick stomach.

"Paris," Doc Peret repeated. "That's what he tells Paul Berlin, and that's what Berlin tells me, and that's what I'm telling you. The chain of command, a truly splendid instrument of . . . Anyhow, Cacciato's gone. Packed up and retired."

The lieutenant exhaled.

Blue gunpowder haze produced musical sighs in the gloom, a stirring at the base of Buddha's clay feet. "Lovely," a voice said. Someone else sighed. The lieutenant blinked, coughed, and handed the spent roach to Oscar Johnson, who extinguished it against his toenail.

"Paree?" the lieutenant said softly. "*Gay* Paree?"

Doc nodded. "That's what he told Paul Berlin and that's what I'm telling you. Ought to cover up, sir."

Sighing, swallowing hard, Lieutenant Corson pushed himself up and sat stiffly before a can of Sterno. He lit the Sterno and placed his hands behind the flame and bent forward to draw in heat. Outside, the rain was steady. "So," the old man said. "Let's . . . let's figure this out." He gazed at the flame. "Trick is to think things clear. Step by step. So. You said Paree?"

"Affirm, sir. That's what he told Paul Berlin, and that's—"

"Berlin?"

"Right here, sir. This one."

The lieutenant looked up. His eyes were bright blue and wet.

Paul Berlin pretended to smile.

"Geez."

"Sir?"

"Geez," the old man said, shaking his head. "I thought you were Vaught."

"No."

"I thought he was you. How . . . how do you like that? Mixed up, I guess. How do you like that?"

"Fine, sir."

The lieutenant shook his head sadly. He held a boot to dry over the burning Sterno. Behind him in shadows was the cross-legged Buddha, smiling from its elevated stone perch. The pagoda was cold. Dank from a month of rain, the place smelled of clays and silicates and dope and old incense. It was a single square room built like a pillbox with stone walls and a flat ceiling that forced the men to stoop or kneel. Once it might have been a fine house of worship, neatly tiled and painted, but now it was junk. Sandbags blocked the windows. Bits of broken pottery lay under chipped pedestals. The Buddha's right arm was missing but the smile was intact. Head cocked, the statue seemed interested in the lieutenant's long sigh. "So. Cacciato, he's gone. Is that it?"

"There it is," Doc said. "You've got it."

Paul Berlin nodded.

"Gone to gay Paree. Am I right? Cacciato's left us in favor of Paree in France." The lieutenant seemed to consider this gravely. Then he giggled. "Still raining?"

"A bitch, sir."

"I never seen rain like this. You ever? I mean, *ever?*"

"No," Paul Berlin said. "Not since yesterday."

"And I guess you're Cacciato's buddy. Is that the story?"

"No, sir," Paul Berlin said. "Sometimes he'd tag along. Not really."

"Who's his buddy?"

"Nobody. Maybe Vaught. I guess Vaught was, sometimes."

"Well," the lieutenant murmured. He paused, dropping his

nose inside the boot to sniff the sweating leather. "Well, I guess we better get Mister Vaught in here. Maybe he can straighten this shit out."

"Vaught's gone, sir. He's the one—"

"Mother of Mercy."

Doc draped a poncho over Lieutenant Corson's shoulders. The rain was steady and thunderless and undramatic. It was midmorning, but the feeling was of endless dusk.

The lieutenant picked up the second boot and began drying it. For a time he did not speak. Then, as if amused by something he saw in the flame, he giggled again and blinked. "Paree," he said. "So Cacciato's gone off to gay Paree—bare ass and Frogs everywhere, the Follies Brassiere." He glanced up at Doc Peret. "What's wrong with him?"

"Just dumb. He's just awful dumb, that's all."

"And he's walking. You say he's walking to gay Paree?"

"That's what he claims, sir, but you can't trust—"

"Paree! Jesus Christ, does he know how far it is? I mean, does he *know?*"

Paul Berlin tried not to smile. "Eight thousand six hundred statute miles, sir. That's what he told me—eight thousand six hundred on the nose. He had it down pretty good. Rations, fresh water, a compass and maps and stuff."

"Maps," the lieutenant said. "Maps, flaps, schnaps." He coughed and spat, then grinned. "And I guess he'll just float himself across the ocean on his maps, right? Am I right?"

"Well, not exactly," said Paul Berlin. He looked at Doc Peret, who shrugged. "No, sir. He showed me how . . . See, he says he's going up through Laos, then into Burma, and then some other country, I forget, and then India and Iran and Turkey, and then Greece, and the rest is easy. That's what he said. The rest is easy, he said. He had it all doped out."

"In other words," the lieutenant said. "In other words, fuckin AWOL."

"There it is," said Doc Peret. "There it is."

The lieutenant rubbed his eyes. His face was sweating and

5

he needed a shave. For a time he lay very still, listening to the rain, hands on his belly, then he giggled and shook his head and laughed. "What for? Just tell me: What the hell for?"

"Easy," Doc said. "Really, you got to stay covered up, I told you that."

"What for? Answer me one thing. What for?"

"Shhhhhh. He's dumb, that's all."

The lieutenant's face was yellow. He giggled. He rolled onto his side and dropped the boot. "I mean, why? What sort of silly crap is this—walking to gay Paree? What's happening? Just tell me, what's wrong with you people? All of you, what's wrong?"

"Relax."

"Tell me."

"Shhhhhh," Doc purred, picking up the fallen poncho and shaking it and then arranging it around the old man's shoulders.

"Answer me. What for? What's wrong with you shits? Walking to gay Paree, what's *wrong*?"

"Not a thing, sir. We're all wonderful. Aren't we wonderful?"

From the gloom came half-hearted applause.

"There, you see? We're all wonderful. It's just that ding-dong, Cacciato. That's the whole of it."

The lieutenant laughed. Without rising, he pulled on his pants and boots and a shirt, then rocked miserably before the blue Sterno flame. The pagoda smelled of the earth. The rain was unending. "Shoot," the lieutenant sighed. He kept shaking his head, wearily, grinning, then at last he looked up at Paul Berlin. "What squad you in?"

"Third, sir."

"That's Cacciato's squad?"

"Yes, sir."

"Who else?"

"Me and Doc and Eddie Lazzutti and Stink and Oscar and Harold Murphy. That's it, except for Cacciato."

"What about Pederson?"

"Pederson's no longer with us, sir."

The lieutenant kept rocking. He did not look well. When the flame was gone, he pushed himself to his feet, coughed, spat, and touched his toes. "All right," he sighed. "Third Squad goes after Cacciato."

Leading to the mountains were four klicks of level paddy. The mountains jerked straight out of the rice; beyond those mountains and other mountains was Paris. The tops of the mountains could not be seen for the mist and clouds. Everywhere the war was wet.

They spent the first night in laager at the base of the mountains, a long miserable night, then at dawn they began the ascent.

At midday Paul Berlin spotted Cacciato. He was half a mile up, bent low and moving patiently against the steep grade. A smudged, lonely-looking figure. It was Cacciato, no question. Legs much too short for the broad back, a shiny pink spot at the crown of the skull. Paul Berlin spotted him, but it was Stink Harris who spoke up.

Lieutenant Corson took out the binoculars.

"Him, sir?"

The lieutenant watched Cacciato climb toward the clouds.

"That him?"

"Oh, yes. Yes."

Stink laughed. "Dumb-dumb. Right, sir? Dumb as a dink."

The lieutenant shrugged. He watched until Cacciato was lost in the higher clouds, then he mumbled something and put the glasses away and motioned for them to move out.

"It's folly," Oscar said. "That's all it is. Foolish folly."

Staying in the old order, they climbed slowly: Stink at point, then the lieutenant, then Eddie and Oscar, then Harold Murphy, then Doc Peret. At the rear of the column, Spec Four Paul Berlin walked with his head down. He had nothing against

Cacciato. The whole thing was silly, of course, immature and dumb, but even so, he had nothing against the kid. It was just too bad. A waste among infinitely wider wastes.

Climbing, he tried to picture Cacciato's face. He tried hard, but the image came out fuzzy. "It's the Mongol influence," Doc Peret had once said. "I mean, hey, just take a close look at him. See how the eyes slant? Pigeon toes, domed head? My theory is that the guy missed Mongolian idiocy by the breadth of a genetic hair. Could've gone either way."

And maybe Doc was right. There was something curiously unfinished about Cacciato. Open-faced and naïve and plump, Cacciato lacked the fine detail, the refinements and final touches, that maturity ordinarily marks on a boy of seventeen years. The result was blurred and uncolored and bland. You could look at him then look away and not remember what you'd seen. All this, Stink said, added up to a case of gross stupidity. The way he whistled on guard, the funny little trick he had of saving mouthwash by spitting it back into the bottle, fishing for walleyes up in lake country. It was all part of a strange, boyish simplicity that the men tolerated the way they might tolerate a frisky pup.

Humping to Paris, it was one of those crazy things Cacciato might try. Paul Berlin remembered how the kid had spent hours thumbing through an old world atlas, studying the maps, asking odd questions: How steep were these mountains, how wide was this river, how thick were these jungles? It was just too bad. A real pity. Like winning the Bronze Star for shooting out a dink's front teeth. Whistling in the dark, always whistling, chewing Black Jack, always chewing and whistling and smiling his frozen white smile. It was silly. It had always been silly, even during the good times, but now the silliness was sad. It couldn't be done. It just wasn't possible, and it was silly and sad.

The rain made it a hard climb. They did not reach the top of the first mountain until late afternoon.

After radioing in position coordinates, they moved along the summit to a cluster of granite boulders that overlooked the Quang Ngai plain. Below, clouds hid the paddies and the war. Above, in more clouds, were more mountains.

It was Eddie Lazzutti who found the spot where Cacciato had spent the night, a gently recessed rock formation roofed by a slate ledge. Inside was a pile of matted grass, a can of burnt-out Sterno, two chocolate wrappers, and a partly burned map. Paul Berlin recognized the map from Cacciato's atlas.

"Cozy," Stink said. "A real nest for our pigeon."

The lieutenant bent down to examine the map. Most of it was burned away, crumbling as the old man picked it up, but parts could still be made out. In the left-hand corner a red dotted line ran through paddyland and up through the first small mountains of the Annamese Cordillera. The line ended there, apparently to be continued on a second map.

Lieutenant Corson held the map gingerly, afraid it might break apart. "Impossible," he said softly.

"True enough."

"Absolutely impossible."

They rested in Cacciato's rock grotto. Tucked away, looking out over the wetly moving mountains to the west, the men were quiet. Eddie and Harold Murphy opened rations and ate slowly, using their fingers. Doc Peret seemed to sleep. Paul Berlin laid out a game of solitaire. For a long while they rested, no one speaking, then at last Oscar Johnson took out his pouch of makings, rolled a joint, inhaled, and passed it along. Things were peaceful. They smoked and watched the rain and clouds and wilderness. Cacciato's den was snug and dry.

No one spoke until the ritual was ended.

Then, very softly, Doc said, "Maybe we should just turn back. Call an end to it."

"Affirmative," Murphy said. He gazed into the rain. "When the kid gets wet enough, cold enough, he'll see how ridiculous it is. He'll come back."

9

"Sure."

"So why not?" Doc turned to the lieutenant. "Why not pack it up, sir? Head back and call it a bummer."

Stink Harris made a light tittering sound, not quite mocking.

"Seriously," Doc kept on. "Let him go . . . MIA, strayed in battle. Sooner or later he'll wake up, you know, and he'll see how nutty it is and he'll—"

The lieutenant stared into the rain. His face was yellow except for webs of shattered veins.

"So what say you, sir? Let him go?"

"Dumber than marbles," Stink giggled. "Dumber than Friar Tuck."

"And smarter than Stink Harris."

"You know what, Murph?"

"Pickle it."

"Ha! Who's saying to pickle it?"

"Just stick it in vinegar," said Harold Murphy. "That's what."

Stink giggled again but he shut up. Murphy was a big man.

"So what's the verdict, sir? Turn around?"

The lieutenant was quiet. At last he shivered and crawled out into the rain with a wad of toilet paper. Paul Berlin sat alone, playing solitaire in the style of Las Vegas. Pretending ways to spend his earnings. Travel, expensive hotels, tips for everyone. Wine and song on white terraces, fountains blowing colored water. Pretending was his best trick to forget the war.

When the lieutenant returned he told them to saddle up.

"Turning back?" Murphy said.

The lieutenant shook his head. He looked sick.

"I knew it," Stink crowed. "Can't just waddle away from a war, ain't that right, sir? Dummy's got to be taught you can't hump your way home." Stink grinned and flicked his eyebrows at Harold Murphy. "Damn straight, I knew it."

Cacciato had reached the top of the second mountain. Bareheaded, hands loosely at his sides, he looked down on them through a mix of fog and drizzle. Lieutenant Corson had the binoculars on him.

"Maybe he don' see us," Oscar said. "Maybe he's lost."

The old man made a vague dismissive gesture. "He sees us. Sees us real fine."

"Pop smoke, sir?"

"Why not? Sure, why not throw out some pretty smoke?" The lieutenant watched through the glasses while Oscar took out the smoke and pulled the pin and tossed it onto a level ledge along the trail. The smoke fizzled for a moment and then puffed up in a heavy cloud of lavender. "Oh, yes, he sees us. Sees us fine."

"Bastard's *waving*."

"Isn't he? Yes, I can see that, thank you."

"Will you—?"

"Mother of Mercy."

High up on the mountain, partly lost in the drizzle, Cacciato was waving at them with both arms. Not quite waving. The arms were flapping.

"Sick," the lieutenant murmured. He sat down, handed the glasses to Paul Berlin, then began to rock himself as the purple smoke climbed the face of the mountain. "I tell you, I'm a sick, sick man."

"Should I shout up to him?"

"Sick," the lieutenant moaned. He kept rocking.

Oscar cupped his hands and hollered, and Paul Berlin watched through the glasses. Cacciato stopped waving. His head was huge through the binoculars. He was smiling. Very slowly, deliberately, Cacciato was spreading his arms out as if to show them empty, opening them up like wings, palms down. The kid's face was fuzzy, bobbing in and out of mist, but it was a happy face. Then his mouth opened, and in the mountains there was thunder.

"What'd he say?" The lieutenant rocked on his haunches. He was clutching himself and shivering. "Tell me, what'd he say?"

11

"Can't hear, sir. Oscar—?"

And there was more thunder, long-lasting thunder that came in waves.

"What's he saying?"

"Sir, I—"

"Just tell me."

Paul Berlin watched through the glasses as Cacciato's mouth opened and closed and opened, but there was only more thunder. And the arms kept flapping, faster now and less deliberate, wide spanning winging motions—flying, Paul Berlin suddenly realized. Awkward, unpracticed, but still flying.

"A chicken!" Stink squealed. He pointed up the mountain. "Look it! See him?"

"Mother of Children."

"Look it!"

"A squawking chicken, you see that? A chicken!"

The thunder came again, and Lieutenant Corson clutched himself and rocked.

"Just tell me," he moaned. "Just tell me, what's he saying?"

Paul Berlin could not hear. But he saw the wide wings, and the big smile, and the movement of the boy's lips.

"Tell me."

So Paul Berlin, watching Cacciato fly, repeated it: "Goodbye."

In the night the rain became fog, and the fog was cold. They camped in the fog, near the top of the second mountain, and the thunder lasted through the night. The lieutenant vomited. Then afterward he radioed back that he was in pursuit of the enemy.

From far off, a radio-voice asked if gunships were needed.

"Negative on gunships," said the old lieutenant.

"Negative?" The radio-voice sounded disappointed. "Tell you what, how about some nice arty? We got—"

"Negative," the lieutenant said. "Negative on artillery."

"We got a real bargain going on arty this week—two for the

price of one, no strings and a warranty to boot. First-class ordnance, real sweet stuff. See, we got this terrific batch of 155 in, a real shitload of it, so we got to go heavy on volume. Keeps the prices down."

"Negative."

"Well, geez." The radio-voice paused. "Okay, Papa Two-Niner. Tell you what, I like the sound of your voice. Honest, it's a swell voice, really lovely. So here's what I'm gonna do. I'm gonna give you a dozen nice illum, how's that? Can you beat it? Find a place in town that beats it and we give you a dozen more, no charge. Real boomers with genuine sparkles mixed in . . . A closeout sale, one time only."

"Negative. Negative, negative, negative."

"You're missing out on some fine shit, Two-Niner."

"Negative, you monster."

"No offense—"

"Negative."

"As you will, then." The radio-voice buzzed. "Happy hunt-ing."

"Mercy," the lieutenant said into a blaze of static.

The night fog was worse than the rain, colder and more saddening. They lay under a sagging lean-to that seemed to catch the fog and hold it like a net. Oscar and Harold Murphy and Stink and Eddie Lazzutti slept anyway, curled around one another like lovers. They could sleep and sleep.

"I hope he keeps moving," Paul Berlin whispered to Doc Peret. "That's all I hope, I just hope he's moving. He does that, we'll never get him."

"Sure thing."

"That's all I hope."

"Then they chase him with choppers. Planes or something."

"Not if he gets himself lost," Paul Berlin said. His eyes were closed. "Not if he hides."

"Yeah." A long silence. "What time is it?"

"Two?"

13

"What time you got, sir?"

"Very lousy late," said the lieutenant from the bushes.

"Come on, what—"

"Four o'clock. Zero-four-hundred. Which is to say a.m."

"Thanks."

"Charmed." There was a soft warm glow where he squatted. After a time he grunted and stood up, buttoned his trousers and crawled back under the lean-to. He lit a cigarette and sighed.

"Feel better, sir?"

"Smashing. Can't you see how smashing I feel?"

"I just hope Cacciato keeps moving," Paul Berlin whispered. "That's all. I hope he uses his head and keeps moving."

"It won't get him anywhere."

"Get him to Paris, maybe."

"Maybe," Doc sighed, turning onto his side, "and where is he then?"

"In Paris."

"Nope. I dig adventure, too, but you can't get to Paris from here. Just can't."

"No?"

"No way. None of the roads lead to Paris."

The lieutenant finished his cigarette and lay back. His breath came hard, as if the air were too heavy or thick for him, and for a long time he twisted restlessly from side to side.

"Maybe we better light a Sterno," Doc said gently. "I'm pretty cold myself."

"No."

"Just for a few minutes maybe."

"No," the lieutenant said. "It's still a war, isn't it?"

"I guess."

"There you have it. It's still a lousy war."

There was thunder. Then lightning lighted the valley deep below, then more thunder, then the rain resumed.

They lay quietly and listened.

Where was it going, where would it end? Paul Berlin was

14

suddenly struck between the eyes by a vision of murder. Butchery, no less: Cacciato's right temple caving inward, silence, then an enormous explosion of outward-going brains. It scared him. He sat up, searched for his cigarettes. He wondered where the image had come from. Cacciato's skull exploding like a bag of helium: boom. So simple, the logical circuit-stopper. No one gets away with gross stupidity forever. Not in a war. Boom, and that always ended it.

What could you do? It was sad. It was sad, and it was still a war. The old man was right about that.

Pitying Cacciato with wee-hour tenderness, pitying himself, Paul Berlin couldn't help hoping for a miracle. The whole idea was crazy of course, but that didn't make it impossible. A lot of crazy things were possible. Billy Boy, for example. Dead of fright. Billy and Sidney Martin and Buff and Pederson. He was tired of it. Not scared—not just then—and not awed or overcome or crushed or defeated, just tired. He smiled, thinking of some of the nutty things Cacciato used to do. Dumb things. But brave things, too.

"Yes, he did," he whispered. It was true. Yes . . . then he realized that Doc was listening. "He did. He did some pretty brave stuff. The time he dragged that dink out of her bunker, remember that?"

"Yeah."

"And . . . and the time he shot that kid. The teeth."

"I remember."

"You can't call him a coward. You can't say he ran out because he was scared."

"You can say a lot of other shit, though."

"True. But you can't say he wasn't brave. You can't say that."

Doc yawned. He sat up, unlaced his boots, threw them off, and lay back on his belly. Beside him the lieutenant slept heavily.

Paul Berlin felt himself grinning. "I wonder . . . You think maybe he talks French? The language, I mean. You think he knows it?"

"You're kidding."

"Yeah. But, geez, it's something to think about, isn't it? Old Cacciato marching off to Paris . . . it's something."

"Go to sleep," Doc said. "Don't forget, cowboy, you got your own health to think about. You're not exactly a well man."

They were in the high country.

Clean, high, unpolluted country. Quiet country. Complex country, mountains growing out of hills, valleys dropping from mountains and then sharply climbing to higher mountains. It was country far from the war, rich and peaceful country with trees and thick grass, no people and no villages and no lowland drudgery. Lush, shaggy country: huge palms and banana trees, wild flowers, waist-high grasses, vines and wet thickets and clean air. Tarzan country, Eddie Lazzutti called it. Grinning, thumping his bare chest, Eddie would howl and yodel.

They climbed with their heads down.

Two days, three days, and a single clay trail kept taking them up. The rain had mostly ended. The days were sultry and overcast, humidity bending the branches of trees, but now and again the clouds to the west showed a new brightness. So they climbed steadily, stopping when the old man needed rest, waiting out the muggiest hours of the afternoon. At times the trail would seem to end, tapering off in a tangle of weeds or rock, and they would be forced to fan out in a broad rank, picking their way forward until the trail reappeared.

For Paul Berlin, who marched last in the column, it was hard work but not unpleasant. He liked the silence. He liked the feel of motion, one leg then the next. No fears of ambush, no tapping sounds in the brush. The sky was empty. He liked this. Walking away, it was something fine to think about. Even if it had to end, there was still the pleasure of pretending it might go on forever: step by step, a mile, ten miles, two hundred, eight thousand. Was it really so impossible? Or was there a chance, even one in a million, that it might truly be done? He walked on and considered this, figuring the odds, speculating on how Cacciato might lead them through the steep country, beyond the mountains, deeper, and how in the end they might reach Paris. He smiled. It was something to think about.

They spent the fourth night in a gully beside the trail, then in the morning continued west. There were no signs of Cacciato.

For most of the day the trail ran parallel to a small hidden stream. They could hear it, smell it, but they never saw it. Still it was soothing to climb and listen to the rush of water, imagining from the change in sounds how the stream would be breaking over rock, or curving, or slowing at a level spot, or tumbling down to a deep pool. It was wilderness now. Jagged, beautiful, lasting country. Things grew as they grew, unchanging. And there was always the next mountain.

Twice during the day there were brief, violent showers, but afterward the sky seemed to lift and lighten, and they marched without stopping. Stink Harris stayed at point, then the lieutenant, then Oscar, then Harold Murphy and Eddie, then Doc, then Paul Berlin at the rear. Sometimes Eddie would sing as he marched. It was a good, rich voice, and the songs were always familiar, and Doc and Harold Murphy would sometimes come in on the chorus. Paul Berlin just climbed. It was an anatomy lesson. The way his legs kept going, ankles and hips, the feel of a fair day's work. A good feeling. Heart and lungs, his back strong, up the high country.

"Maybe," he murmured, "maybe so."

An hour before dusk the trail twisted up through a stand of dwarf pines, leveled off, then opened into a large clearing. Oscar Johnson found the second map.

The red dotted line crossed the border into Laos.

Farther ahead they found Cacciato's armored vest and bayonet, then his ammo pouch, then his entrenching tool and ID card.

"Why?" the lieutenant muttered.

"Sir?"

"Why? Tell me why." The old man was speaking to a small

pine. "Why the clues? Why don't he just leave the trail? Lose us, leave us behind . . . Tell me why."

"A rockhead," said Stink Harris. "That's why."

Liquid and shiny, a mix of rain and clay, the trail took them higher. Out of radio range, beyond the reach of artillery.

Cacciato eluded them but he left behind the wastes of his march: empty ration cans, bits of bread, a belt of gold-cased ammo dangling from a shrub, a leaking canteen, candy wrappers, worn rope. Hints that kept them going. Luring them on, gulling them. Once they spotted him far below, plodding along the bed of a valley; once they saw his fire on a distant hill. Straight ahead was the frontier.

"He makes it that far," Doc said on the morning of the sixth day, pointing to the next line of mountains, "and he's gone, we can't touch him. He makes the border and it's bye-bye Cacciato."

"How far?"

Doc shrugged. "A klick, two klicks. Not far."

"Then he's made it," Paul Berlin said.

"Maybe so."

"By God he has!"

"Maybe."

"By God! Lunch at Maxim's!"

"What?"

"A cafeteria deluxe. My old man ate there once . . . truffles heaped on chipped beef and toast."

"Maybe."

The trail narrowed, then climbed, and a half hour later Stink spotted him.

He stood at the top of a small grassy hill, two hundred meters ahead. Loose and at ease, smiling, Cacciato already had the look of a civilian. Hands in his pockets, patient, serene, not at all frightened. He might have been waiting for a bus.

Stink yelped and the lieutenant hurried forward with the glasses.

18

"Got him!"

"It's—"

"Got him!" Stink was crowing and hopping. "I knew it, the ding-dong's givin' up the ghost. I knew it!"

The lieutenant stared through the glasses.

"Fire a shot, sir?" Stink held up his rifle and before the lieutenant could speak he squeezed off two quick rounds, one a tracer that turned like a corkscrew through the morning haze. Cacciato waved.

"Lookie, lookie—"

"The son of a bitch."

"Truly a predicament," Oscar Johnson said. "I do think, ladies and gents of the jury, we got ourselves impaled on the horns of a predicament. Kindly observe—"

"Let's move."

"A true predicament."

Stink Harris took the point, walking fast and chattering, and Cacciato stopped waving and watched him come, arms folded loosely and his big head cocked aside as if listening for something.

There was no avoiding it.

Stink saw the wire as he tripped it.

There were two sounds. First the sound of a zipper suddenly yanked up. Next a popping noise, the spoon releasing and primer detonating.

There was quiet. Then the sound of something dropping; then a fizzling sound.

Stink knew it as it happened. In one fuzzed motion he flung himself down and away, rolling, covering his skull, mouth open, yelping a trivial little yelp.

They all knew it.

Eddie and Oscar and Doc Peret dropped flat. Harold Murphy did an oddly graceful jackknife for a man of his size. The lieutenant collapsed. And Paul Berlin brought his knees to his belly, coiling and falling, closing his eyes and his fists and his mouth.

19

The fizzling sound was in his head. Count, he thought. But the numbers came in a tangle without sequence.

His belly hurt. That was where it started. First the belly, a release of fluids in the bowels, a shitting feeling, a draining of all the pretensions and silly little hopes for himself. The air was windless. His teeth hurt. Count, he thought. But his teeth ached and the numbers were jumbled and meaningless.

First the belly, the bowels, and next the lungs. He was steeled, ready. There was no explosion. Count, he thought. But he couldn't get a grip on the numbers. His teeth had points in his brain, his lungs hurt, but there was no explosion. Smoke, he thought without thinking, smoke.

He felt it and smelled it, but he couldn't count.

Smoke, he said, "Smoke," and then the lieutenant was saying it, "Smoke," the lieutenant was moaning, "fucking smoke grenade."

And Paul Berlin smelled it. He felt the warm wet feeling on his thighs. His eyes were closed. Smoke: He imagined the colors and texture. He couldn't bring his eyes open. He tried, but he couldn't do it. He couldn't unclench his fists or uncoil his legs or stop the draining. He couldn't wiggle or run.

There was no explosion.

"Smoke," Doc whispered softly. "A booby's booby trap."

It was red smoke. The message was clear. Brilliant red, acid-tasting, all over them. The numbers were coming now, and he counted them as they came. It was easy. Red smoke, spreading out over the earth like paint, then climbing against gravity in a lazy red spiral.

His eyes had come open.

Stink Harris was bawling. He was on his hands and knees, chin against his throat. Oscar and Eddie hadn't moved.

"Had us," the lieutenant was chanting to himself. Senile-sounding. "Could've had us all, he could've."

"Smoke."

"All of us. The dummy could've—"

"Just smoke."

But still Paul Berlin could not move. He heard voices. He heard Stink weeping on hands and knees along the trail, saw him, saw red smoke everywhere. The numbers kept running through his head, and he counted them, but he could not move. Dumb, he thought as he counted, a struck-dumb little yo-yo who can't move.

There was just the silliness and astonishment. The foolishness. And the great folly that was just now beginning to come.

He was vaguely aware of being watched. Then keenly aware. He felt it beyond his vision, over his left shoulder: some gray-haired old goat chuckling at the sorry fix of this struck-dumb ding-dong at the moment of truth. His teeth hurt, his lungs hurt. He wanted to apologize to whoever was watching, but his lungs ached and his mouth wouldn't work. He wasn't breathing. Inhale? Exhale? He'd lost track.

You asshole, he thought. You ridiculous little yo-yo.

"He won't come," said Oscar Johnson, returning under a white flag. "Believe me, I tried hard, but the dude just don' play cool."

It was dusk. The seven soldiers sat in a circle.

Oscar spoke from behind sunglasses. "Strictly uncool. I told him all the right stuff, but the man just won't give it up. Won't. Told him . . . I told him it's buggo. Sure enough, I says, you bound for doom. Totaled beyond repair. I told it clear, how he'd end up court-martialed to kingdom come, an' how his old man'd shit molasses when he heard the story. All that. Told him, I says, maybe things don' come down so hard if you just abandon ship right now. *Now,* I says. An' what's he do? He smiles. Like this . . . the man smiles. He just don' be cool."

The lieutenant was lying prone, Doc's thermometer in his mouth. It wasn't his war. The skin on his arms and neck sagged around deteriorating muscle.

"All that good shit, I told it all. Whole spiel, top to bottom."

"You tell him we're out of rations?"

"Shit, yes, I told him that. An' I told him he's gonna starve his own sorry ass if he keeps it up, and so what's he do—?"

"The light of the world."

"There it is, man. The happy-assed light of the world."

"You tell him he can't walk to Paris?"

Oscar grinned. He was black enough to be indistinct in the dusk. "Well, maybe I forgot to tell him that. Can't add injury to insult."

"You should've told him."

"He's not all that dumb."

"You should've told him."

"Dumb, but not all that dumb."

Lieutenant Corson slid a hand behind his neck and pushed against it as if to relieve some spinal pressure. "What else?" he asked. "What else did he say?"

"Nothin', sir. Said he's making out okay. Said he was sorry about the smoke."

"The bastard."

"Says he's real fuckin sorry."

Stink laughed bitterly and kept rubbing his hands against the black stock of his rifle.

"What else?"

"Nothing," Oscar said. "You know how he is. Lots of smiles and stuff, real friendly. He asks how everybody's holdin' up, so I says we're fine, except for the scare with the smoke, and so he says he's real sorry for that, and I say, shit man, no harm. I mean, what can you do with a dude like that?"

The lieutenant nodded, still pushing against his neck. He was quiet awhile. He seemed to be making up his mind. "All right," he finally sighed. "What'd he have with him?"

"Sir?"

"Musketry," the lieutenant said. "Firepower. Ordnance."

Oscar thought a moment. "His rifle. That's it, I guess . . . the rifle and some ammo. The truth is I didn't pay much attention."

22

"Claymores?"

Oscar shook his head.

"Frags?"

"Don't know. A couple probably."

"Swell recon job, Oscar. Real pretty."

"Sorry. The man had his stuff tight."

"I'm a sick man."

"Yes, sir."

"Goes through me like coffee. You know? Just like coffee. What you got for me, Doc?"

Doc Peret shook his head. "Nothing, sir. Rest."

"That tells it. What I genuinely need is rest."

"Why not let him go, sir?"

"A sick, sick man."

"Just let him go."

"Rest," the lieutenant said, "is what I need."

Paul Berlin did not sleep. Instead he watched Cacciato's small hill humped up in the dark. He tried to imagine a proper ending.

The possibilities were closing themselves out, and, though he tried, it was hard to see a happy end to it.

Not impossible, of course. It might still be done. With skill and daring and luck, Cacciato might still slip away and cross the frontier mountains and be gone. He tried to picture it. Many new places. Villages at night with barking dogs, people whose eyes and skins would change in slow evolution and counterevolution westward, whole continents opening up like flowers, new tongues and new times and all roads connecting toward Paris. Yes, it could be done.

He imagined it. He imagined the many dangers of the march: treachery and deceit at every turn, disease, thirst, jungle beasts crouching in ambush; but, yes, he also imagined the good times ahead, the sting of aloneness, the great new quiet, new leanness and knowledge and wisdom. The rains would end. The trails would go dry, the sun would show, and, yes, there would be changing foliage and seasons and great expanses of silence, and songs, and pretty girls sleeping in straw huts, and, where the road ended, Paris.

The odds were poison, but it could be done.

He might even have tried himself. With courage, he thought, he might even have joined in, and that was the one sorry thing about it, the sad thing: He might have.

Then in the dark it rained.

"The AWOL bag," Oscar whispered from beneath his poncho. "There's the weirdness. Where in hell did he come up with the AWOL bag?"

"Your imagination." Eddie's voice, deeper than the others.

"No, man, I saw it."

"You say you saw it."

"I saw it. Black vinyl, white stitching. I speak truth, I saw it."

Quiet beaten by rain. Shifting sounds in the night, men rolling.

Then Eddie's voice, disbelieving: "Nobody. Not even the C. Nobody uses them bags to go AWOL. It's not done."

"Tell it to Cacciato."

"It's not *done.*"

And later, as if a mask had been peeled off, the rain ended and the sky cleared and Paul Berlin woke to see stars.

They were in their familiar places. It wasn't so cold. He lay on his back and counted the stars and named those that he knew, named the constellations and the valleys of the moon. He'd learned the names from his father. Guideposts, his father had once said along the Des Moines River, or maybe in Wisconsin. Anyway—guideposts, he'd said, so that no matter where in the world you are, anywhere, you know the spot, you can trace it, place it by latitude and longitude. It . . . it was just too bad. Too bad, a pity. Sad, it was. Dumb and crazy and, now, very sad. He should've kept going. Should've left the trails, waded through streams to rinse away the scent, buried his feces, swung from the trees branch to branch. Should've slept through the days and ran through the nights. Because it might have been done.

Toward dawn he saw Cacciato's breakfast fire. It gave the grassy hill a moving quality, and the sadness seemed durable.

The others woke in groups. They ate cold rations, packed up, watched the sky light itself in patches. Stink played with the safety catch on his rifle, a clicking noise like the morning cricket.

"Let's do it," the lieutenant said.

And Eddie and Oscar and Harold Murphy crept off toward the south. Doc and the lieutenant waited five minutes and then began circling west to block a retreat. Stink Harris and Paul Berlin stayed where they were.

Waiting, trying to imagine a rightful but still happy ending, Paul Berlin found himself pretending, in a wishful sort of way, that before long the war would reach a climax beyond which everything else would seem bland and commonplace. A point at which he could stop being afraid. Where all the bad things, the painful and grotesque and ugly things, would give way to something better. He pretended he had crossed that threshold.

He wasn't dreaming, or imagining; just pretending. Figuring how it would be, if it were.

When the sky was half-light, Doc and the lieutenant fired a red flare that streaked high over Cacciato's grassy hill, hung there, then exploded like a starburst at the start of a celebration. Cacciato Day, October something in the year 1968, the Year of the Pig.

In the trees at the southern slope of the hill Oscar and Eddie and Harold Murphy each fired red flares to signal their advance.

Stink hurried into the weeds and came back zipping up his trousers. He was excited and very happy. Deftly, he released the bolt on his weapon and let it slam hard into place.

"Fire it," he said, "and let's move."

Paul Berlin took a long time opening his pack.

But he found the flare, unscrewed its lid, laid the firing pin against the metal base, then jammed it in.

The flare jumped away from him. It went high and fast, rocketing upward and then smoothing out in a long arc that followed the course of the trail, leaving behind a dirty white wake.

At its apex, with barely a sound, it exploded in a green dazzle over Cacciato's hill. A fine, brilliant shade of green.

"Go," whispered Paul Berlin. It did not seem enough. "Go," he said, and then he shouted, "Go."

2
The
Observation
Post

CACCIATO'S ROUND FACE became the moon. The valleys and ridges and fast-flowing plains dissolved, and now the moon was just the moon.

Paul Berlin sat up. A fine idea. He stretched, stood up, leaned against the wall of sandbags, touched his weapon, then gazed out at the strip of beach that wound along the curving Batangan. Things were dark. Behind him, the South China Sea sobbed in against the tower's thick piles; before him, inland, was the face of Quang Ngai.

Yes, he thought, a fine idea. Cacciato leading them west through peaceful country, deep country perfumed by lilacs and burning hemp, a boy coaxing them step by step through rich and fertile country toward Paris.

It was a splendid idea.

Paul Berlin, whose only goal was to live long enough to establish goals worth living for still longer, stood high in the tower by the sea, the night soft all around him, and wondered, not for the first time, about the immense powers of his own imagination. A truly awesome notion. Not a dream, an idea. An idea to develop, to tinker with and build and sustain, to draw out as an artist draws out his visions.

It was not a dream. Nothing mystical or crazy, just an idea. Just a possibility. Feet turning hard like stone, legs stiffening, six and seven and eight thousand miles through unfolding country toward Paris. A truly splendid idea.

He checked his watch. It was not quite midnight.

For a time he stood quietly at the tower's north wall, looking out to where the beach jagged sharply into the sea to form a natural barrier against storms. The night was quiet. On the sand below, coils of barbed wire circled the observation tower in a perimeter that separated it from the rest of the war. The tripflares were out. Things were in their place. Beside him, Harold Murphy's machine gun was fully loaded and ready, and a dozen signal flares were lined up on the wall, and the radio was working, and the beach was mined, and the tower itself was high and strong and fortified. The sea guarded his rear. The moon gave light. It would be all right, he told himself. He was safe.

He lit a cigarette and moved to the west wall.

Doc and Eddie and Oscar and the others slept peacefully. And the night was peaceful. Time to think. Time to consider the possibilities.

Had it ended there on Cacciato's grassy hill, flares coloring the morning sky? Had it ended in tragedy? Had it ended with a jerking, shaking feeling—noise and confusion? Or had it ended farther along the trail west? Had it ever ended? What, in fact, had become of Cacciato? More precisely—as Doc Peret would insist it be phrased—more precisely, what part was fact and what part was the extension of fact? And how were facts separated from possibilities? What had really happened and what merely might have happened? How did it end?

The trick, of course, was to think through it carefully. That was Doc's advice—look for motives, search out the place where fact ended and imagination took over. Ask the important questions. Why had Cacciato left the war? Was it courage or ignorance, or both? Was it even possible to combine courage and ignorance? How much of what happened, or might have happened, was Cacciato's doing and how much was the product of the biles?

That was Doc's theory.

"You got an excess of fear biles," Doc had said one afternoon beneath the tower. "We've all got these biles—Stink, Oscar, everybody—but you've got yourself a whole bellyful of the stuff. You're oversaturated. And my theory is this: Somehow these biles are warping your sense of reality. Follow me? Somehow they're screwing up your basic perspective, and the upshot is you sometimes get a little mixed up. That's all."

Doc had gone on to explain that the biles are a kind of glandular substance released during emotional stress. A perfectly normal thing. Like adrenaline, Doc had said. Only instead of producing quick energy, the biles act as a soothing influence, quieting the brain, numbing, counteracting the fear. Doc had listed the physical symptoms: numbness of the extremities in times of extremity; a cloudiness of vision; paralysis of the mental processes that separate what is truly happening from what only might have happened; floatingness; removal; a releasing feeling in the belly; a sense of drifting; a lightness of head.

"Normally," Doc had said, "those are healthy things. But in your case, these biles are . . . well, they're overabundant. They're leaking out, infecting the brain. This Cacciato business —it's the work of the biles. They're flooding your whole system, going to the head and fucking up reality, frying in all the goofy, weird stuff."

So Doc's advice had been to concentrate. When he felt the symptoms, the solution was to concentrate. Concentrate, Doc had said, until you see it's just the biles fogging things over, just a trick of the glands.

Now, facing the night from high in his tower by the sea, Paul Berlin concentrated.

The night did not move. On the beach below, the barbed

wire sparkled in moonlight, and the sea made its gentle sounds behind him. The men slept peacefully. Now and then one of them would stir, turning in the dark, but they slept without stop. Oscar slept in his mesh hammock. Eddie and Doc and Harold Murphy slept on the tower floor. Stink Harris and the lieutenant slept side by side, their backs touching. They could sleep and sleep.

Paul Berlin kept the guard. For a long time he looked blankly into the night, inland, concentrating hard on the physical things.

True, he was afraid. Doc was right about that. Even now, with the night calm and unmoving, the fear was there like a kind of background sound that was heard only if listened for. True. But even so, Doc was wrong when he called it dreaming. Biles or no biles, it wasn't dreaming—it wasn't even pretending, not in the strict sense. It was an idea. It was a working out of the possibilities. It wasn't dreaming and it wasn't pretending. It wasn't crazy. Blisters on their feet, streams to be forded and swamps to be circled, dead ends to be opened into passages west. No, it wasn't dreaming. It was a way of asking questions. What became of Cacciato? Where did he go, and why? What were his motives, or did he have motives, and did motives matter? What tricks had he used to keep going? How had he eluded them? How did he slip away into deep jungle, and how, through jungle, had they continued the chase? What happened, and what might have happened?

3
The
Road
to Paris

YES, THEY WERE IN jungle now. Thick dripping jungle. Club moss fuzzing on bent branches, hard green bananas dangling from trees that canopied in lush sweeps of green, vaulted forest light in yellow-green and blue-green and olive-green and silver-green, algae multiplying in still waters. It was jungle. Growth and decay sweating green, the smell of chlorophyll, jungle sounds and jungle depth. It was true jungle. Soft, humming jungle. Everywhere, greenery deep in greenery, earth like sponge. Itching jungle, lost jungle. A botanist's madhouse, Doc said.

Single file, they followed the narrow trail through banks of fern and brush and vine. There was weight in the air. Smells came together, and the final smell was of rot. They moved slowly. The heavy grind of the march: Stink still at point, then Eddie, then Oscar and the lieutenant, then Harold Murphy toting the big gun, then Doc, then, at the rear, Spec Four Paul Berlin, whose each step was an event of imagination.

For two days they had moved through simple jungle. Cacciato had escaped—a trap sprung on a small grassy hill, flares in the dawn sky, but the trap was empty. A few empty ration

cans, some Hershey bar wrappers, Cacciato's dog tags. That
was all. So, regrouping, they pressed on. They crossed the last
mountains. They followed the lone clay trail as it slowly descended, narrowed, twisted westward into the jungle.

And now it continued. They marched steadily, stopping only
for water or to cut vines or to give the lieutenant time to rest.

In the early afternoon, when the heat became impossible,
they stopped along a shallow creek that ran parallel to the trail.
They drank, filled their canteens, then removed their boots
and lay back with their feet in the stream. No one spoke. Paul
Berlin closed his eyes, thinking it would be nice to have a cold
Coke, or a tray of ice from the freezer, or an orange, or . . . He
told himself to cut it out. He sat up, checked his feet for blisters, then rinsed out his socks.

"Another klick," Doc said. He spoke softly, showing the map
to the lieutenant. "Where these elevation lines drop . . . these
little lines here? That's Laos. One more klick."

The lieutenant nodded. He was on his back, looking up at
where the trees opened to a sliver of sky. He looked dazed.

"Then what, sir? At the border?"

Sighing, the old man closed his eyes. He lay still a long time.

"I don't know," he said slowly. "I don't. That's one bridge we
might've already crossed."

"Turn back," Harold Murphy said. He leaned against his
machine gun, left hand absently tapping the barrel. For a big
man his voice was very high. "The border, that's where we
turn back. Right, sir?"

Lieutenant Corson did not answer. His face flushed. The
cheek bones looked as if they had once been broken and had
never mended properly, too high and knobby.

"Isn't that right, sir?" Murphy said. "I mean—you know—we
can't cross the border, can we? That's—" He let it trail off.

"Desertion," the lieutenant said. "That's what it is. It's desertion."

"I tell you this," Harold Murphy said. "I don't like it. I say
we turn our butts back right now. Let him go."

Stink laughed.

"I just don't like it."

They rested another ten minutes. Then, without speaking, the lieutenant got up, put on his rucksack and helmet, and motioned them forward.

The jungle kept thickening. All afternoon the squad plodded through banyan and neem trees, and trees they couldn't name, vines and deep brush, soft country. They trudged along slowly, painfully, stopping often while Stink or Eddie went to work with a machete. Hacking, sometimes crawling. Once, late in the afternoon, the trail gave out entirely. It simply ended. Taking turns, they chopped through blunt jungle for nearly an hour. It was hard, awkward work. The machete handle turned slick. There was no room for leverage or full swinging at the tangled thickets, and the air was heavy with a kind of heat Paul Berlin had never known before. He measured his breathing: inhaling, holding it for two counts, swinging the machete and exhaling at the same time, pausing, inhaling, holding it, swinging. Twenty strokes left him exhausted.

Flopping down next to Oscar Johnson, he felt the sweat leaving his body as if through a tap.

"Smoke 'em if you got 'em," Oscar said softly. "Pooped?"

Paul Berlin nodded. He wanted to smile, to show he was holding up. He watched silently as Eddie took up the machete and began hacking away at the jungle.

"I'll say one thing," Oscar murmured. "Cacciato ain't passed this way. Not through this shit."

"Think we lost him?"

Oscar shrugged. "All I know's what I see, an' I see he ain't been here. That's all." He glanced at the lieutenant. "And I know this, too. The old man, he's ready to fall out. The man's sick."

Harold Murphy made a bitter hooting sound. "Turn back, then," he said. "Right now, while it's still possible."

Oscar pushed his sunglasses tight against his eyes. "We do what we do," he said. "No use thinkin', just do it."

He got up and went over to relieve Eddie.

It took another half hour to cut through to the trail. They rested a time, concentrating on their fatigue, then again they began moving. The earth was damp now, springy with crushed ferns and mushrooms, ancient smells, and there was the dank hush that comes before a summer storm. The heat came in layers. It was a sucking heat, the sort that draws moisture out of living things, and they filed through it with the dull plodding motions of men who move because they must.

Near dusk the trail began to widen. The trees thinned out, and the trail slipped down into a gully which, after a time, brought them to a wide, dark river.

There they stopped.

"Laos," Doc said. He hitched up his pack and pointed to the far side of the river. "Over there, that's Laos."

They gazed across at it. The same sheer jungle. Trees grew to the river's edge, their roots snaking down the bank and into the slow water. Things were very still. The river was like a pond without currents. Dusk gave it a murky brown color.

"No bridges," the lieutenant finally said. He stood slightly apart from the others, blinking as if trying to decide on something. Then he sighed. "I guess that's one good thing. No bridges to burn behind me."

They crossed the river.

The lieutenant went first. He stepped into the slow water, paused a moment, then began wading. The others followed. It was easy. They waded across single file, holding their weapons high. The warm feeling of passage. They regrouped on the far side.

"I don't like it," Harold Murphy whispered, but it was done.

For six days they marched through jungle. Once they skirted a deserted village. Once they crossed a spindly man-made bridge. Once, in the heat of early afternoon, they passed through an ancient tribal cemetery. But there were no breaks in the ongoing rain forest. And there were no signs of Cacciato.

34

It was a routine. They would rise at daybreak and march until midafternoon, when the heat seemed to click on like a furnace. Then they would rest, spinning out the hot hours in petty conversation or sleep. Later, as the shadows appeared, they would resume the march until dusk. The fatigue played heavily on all of them. Mostly, though, it showed on the lieutenant. Partly it was his age, partly the dysentery. But it was something else, too.

One afternoon as they were fording a shallow creek, the old man lost his balance and teetered and fell back. He sat there, watching the cold water rush past. He did not move. Slowly, like a pair of logs, his arms bobbed in the stream. He watched them. Then his pack slipped off, his rifle sank, and he floated.

Doc and Eddie dragged him out.

They propped him against the bank, dried him off, retrieved the M-16 and rucksack. The lieutenant's eyes were open and his lips moved, but he did not speak.

"Sick," Doc whispered. "The old man's had it."

They spent the night there. When the lieutenant was asleep, Oscar convened a meeting around the fire.

"Democracy time," Oscar said slowly. He removed his sunglasses, inspected them, put them on again. "Decision time. Do we go on with this shit or do we call it quits? That's the question."

Stink flicked his eyebrows and grinned. "Speeches!"

"Spit on speeches. We're taking a vote, no bullshit." Oscar's face was hard. His sunglasses sparkled in the firelight. "Doc says the LT's probably got a case of sunstroke . . . nothing serious, anyhow. No temperature, the dysentery's clearing up. But he still ain' exactly in wonderful shape. So we got to consider—"

"Turn back," Harold Murphy said. "That's my vote. I say we turn back now."

"Tonight?" Eddie said.

"Now."

Oscar ignored him. He held up a hand for quiet. "On the

other hand," he said slowly, "we got certain responsibilities to consider. Catching Cacciato . . . we got to consider that. The mission is—"

Harold Murphy made a high mocking sound.

"Speech, Murph?"

"No speech. Screw mission, that's all. I vote we bag it up. It's nuts. Chasing after the dumb slob, it's crazy as hell. There's a word for it."

"A word?"

"Desertion," Murphy said. "That's the word. Running off like this, it's plain desertion. I say we get our butts back to the war before things get worse."

Stink Harris cheered. "Murph's my man! Elect Murphy, by God, and happy days is here again. Let's—"

"Cut it."

"Vote Irish. Stick a pope in the White House."

"Cut it out," Oscar said. "I don't need this crap."

Harold Murphy studied his hands. "Look," he said, glancing up at Paul Berlin. "I'm just saying how nutty it is. Running away, that's what it comes down to. No mission crap. You can't . . . you can't *do* this. Know what I mean? You can't."

The others were quiet.

"You just can't. It's not right." Murphy shrugged. "So there's my vote."

"More speeches?"

No one moved.

"Okay, then," Oscar said. "Time to cast ballots."

It went quickly. Harold Murphy and Eddie voted to turn back. Oscar and Stink and Doc voted to continue.

"Berlin?"

"Okay."

"Okay what?"

36

Paul Berlin looked at Murphy, then looked at the fire. The possibilities were endless.

"Keep going," he said. "See what happens."

"That's your vote?"

"Yes," Paul Berlin said. "I vote to move on."

In the morning, Harold Murphy and his big gun were gone. They continued west without him.

4

How They Were Organized

EVEN BEFORE ARRIVING at Chu Lai's Combat Center on June 3, 1968, Private First Class Paul Berlin had been assigned by MACV Computer Services, Cam Ranh Bay, to the single largest unit in Vietnam, the American Division, whose area of operations, I Corps, constituted the largest and most diverse sector in the war zone. He was lost. He had never heard of I Corps, or the American, or Chu Lai. He did not know what a Combat Center was.

It was there by the sea.

A staging area, he decided. A place to get acquainted. Rows of tin huts stood neatly in the sand, connected by metal walkways, surrounded on three sides by wire, guarded at the rear by the sea.

A Vietnamese barber cut his hair.

A bored master sergeant delivered a Re-Up speech.

A staff sergeant led him to a giant field tent for chow, then another staff sergeant led him to a hootch containing eighty bunks and eighty lockers. The bunks and lockers were numbered.

"Don't leave here," said the staff sergeant, "unless it's to use the piss-tube."

Paul Berlin nodded, fearful to ask what a piss-tube was.

In the morning the fifty new men were marched to a wooden set of bleachers facing the sea. A small, sad-faced corporal in a black cadre helmet waited until they settled down, looking at the recruits as if searching for a lost friend in a crowd. Then the corporal sat down in the sand. He turned away and gazed out to sea. He did not speak. Time passed slowly, ten minutes, twenty, but still the sad-faced corporal did not turn or nod or speak. He simply gazed out at the blue sea. Everything was clean. The sea was clean, the sand was clean, the air was warm and pure and clean. The wind was clean.

They sat in the bleachers for a full hour.

Then at last the corporal sighed and stood up. He checked his wristwatch. Again he searched the rows of new faces.

"All right," he said softly. "That completes your first lecture on how to survive this shit. I hope you paid attention."

During the days they simulated search-and-destroy missions in a friendly little village just outside the Combat Center. The villagers played along. Always smiling, always indulgent, they let themselves be captured and frisked and interrogated.

PFC Paul Berlin, who wanted to live, took the exercise seriously.

"You VC?" he demanded of a little girl with braids. "You dirty VC?"

The girl smiled. "Shit, man," she said gently. "You shittin' me?"

They pitched practice grenades made of green fiberglass. They were instructed in compass reading, survival methods, bivouac SOPs, the operation and maintenance of the standard weapons. Sitting in the bleachers by the sea, they were lectured on the known varieties of enemy land mines and booby traps. Then, one by one, they took turns making their way through a make-believe minefield.

"Boomo!" an NCO shouted at any misstep.

It was a peculiar drill. There were no physical objects to avoid, no obstacles on the obstacle course, no wires or prongs or covered pits to detect and then evade. Too lazy to rig up the training ordnance each morning, the supervising NCO simply hollered *Boomo* when the urge struck him.

Paul Berlin, feeling hurt at being told he was a dead man, complained that it was unfair.

"Boomo," the NCO repeated.

But Paul Berlin stood firm. "Look," he said. "Nothing. Just the sand. There's nothing there at all."

The NCO, a huge black man, stared hard at the beach. Then at Paul Berlin. He smiled. "'Course not, you dumb twirp. You just fucking *exploded* it."

Paul Berlin was not a twirp. So it constantly amazed him, and left him feeling much abused, to hear such nonsense— twirp, creepo, butter-brain. It wasn't right. He was a straight-forward, honest, decent sort of guy. He was not dumb. He was not small or weak or ugly. True, the war scared him silly, but this was something he hoped to bring under control.

Late on the third night he wrote to his father, explaining that he'd arrived safely at a large base called Chu Lai, and that he was taking now-or-never training in a place called the Combat Center. If there was time, he wrote, it would be swell to get a letter telling something about how things went on the home front—a nice, unfrightened-sounding phrase, he thought. He also asked his father to look up Chu Lai in a world atlas. "Right now," he wrote, "I'm a little lost."

It lasted six days, which he marked off at sunset on a pocket calendar. Not short, he thought, but getting shorter.

He had his hair cut again. He drank Coke, watched the

40

ocean, saw movies at night, learned the smells. The sand smelled of sour milk. The air, so clean near the water, smelled of mildew. He was scared, yes, and confused and lost, and he had no sense of what was expected of him or of what to expect from himself. He was aware of his body. Listening to the instructors talk about the war, he sometimes found himself gazing at his own wrists or legs. He tried not to think. He stayed apart from the other new guys. He ignored their jokes and chatter. He made no friends and learned no names. At night, the big hootch swelling with their sleeping, he closed his eyes and pretended it was not a war. He felt drugged. He plodded through the sand, listened while the NCOs talked about the AO: "Real bad shit," said the youngest of them, a sallow kid without color in his eyes. "Real tough shit, real bad. I remember this guy Uhlander. Not such a bad dick, but he made the mistake of thinkin' it wasn't so bad. It's bad. You know what bad is? Bad is evil. Bad is what happened to Uhlander. I don't wanna scare the bejasus out of you—that's not what I want—but, shit, you guys are gonna *die.*"

On the seventh day, June 9, the new men were assigned to their terminal units.

The Americal Division, Paul Berlin learned for the first time, was organized into three infantry brigades, the 11th, 196th, and 198th. The brigades, in turn, were broken down into infantry battalions, the battalions into companies, the companies into platoons, the platoons into squads.

Supporting the brigades was an immense divisional complex spread out along the sands of Chu Lai. Three artillery elements under a single command, two hospitals, six air units, logistical and transportation and communication battalions, legal services, a PX, a stockade, a USO, a mini golf course, a swimming beach with trained lifeguards, administration offices under the Adjutant General, twelve Red Cross Donut Dollies, a central mail detachment, Seabees, four Military Police units, a press information service, computer specialists, civil relations spe-

41

cialists, psychological warfare specialists, Graves Registration, dog teams, civilian construction and maintenance contractors, a *Stars and Stripes* detachment, intelligence and tactical planning units, chapels and chaplains and assistant chaplains, cooks and clerks and translators and scouts and orderlies, an Inspector General's office, awards and decorations specialists, dentists, cartographers, statistical analysts, oceanographers, PO officers, photographers and janitors and demographers.

The ratio of support to combat personnel was twelve to one.

Paul Berlin counted it as bad luck, a statistically improbable outcome, to be assigned to the 5th Battalion, 46th Infantry, 198th Infantry Brigade.

His sense of place had never been keen. In Indian Guides, with his father, he'd gone to Wisconsin to camp and be pals forever. Big Bear and Little Bear. He remembered it. Yellow and green headbands, orange feathers. Powwows at the campfire. Big Fox telling stories out of the *Guide Story Book.* Big Fox, a gray-haired father from Oshebo, Illinois, owner of a paper mill. He remembered all of it. Canoe races the second day, Big Bear paddling hard but Little Bear having troubles. Poor, poor Little Bear. Better luck in the gunnysack race, Big Bear and Little Bear hopping together under the great Wisconsin sky, but poor Little Bear, stumbling. Pals anyhow. Not a problem. Shake hands the secret Guide way. Pals forever. Then the third day, into the woods, father first and son second, Little Bear tracking Big Bear, who leaves tracks and paw prints. Yes, he remembered it—Little Bear getting lost. Following Big Bear's tracks down to a winding creek, crossing the creek, checking the opposite bank according to the *Guide Survival Guide,* finding nothing; so deeper into the woods— Big Bear!—and deeper, then turning back to the creek, but now no creek. Nothing in the *Guide Survival Guide* about panic. Lost, bawling in the big Wisconsin woods. He remembered it clearly. Little Elk finding him, flashlights converging, Little Bear bawling under a giant spruce. So the fourth day, getting sick, and Big Bear and Little Bear breaking camp early. Decamping. Hamburgers and root beer on the long drive home, baseball talk, white man talk, and he remembered it, the sickness going away. Pals forever.

A truck took him up Highway One, then inland to LZ Gator, where he joined the 5th Battalion of the 46th Infantry of the 198th Infantry Brigade. There, in a white hootch surrounded by barbed wire and bunkers, a captain jotted his name and number into a leather-bound log. An E-8 took him aside.

"You look strack," the E-8 whispered. "How'd you go for a rear job? I can fix it for you . . . get you a job painting fence. Sound good?"

Paul Berlin smiled.

"You go for that? Nice comfy painting job? No paddy humpin', no dinks?"

Paul Berlin smiled. The E-8 smiled back.

"Sound good, trooper? You get off on the sound of them bells?"

Paul Berlin smiled. He knew what the man wanted. So, only faintly, he nodded.

"Well, then," the E-8 whispered, "I fear you come to the wrong . . . fuckin . . . place."

Walking down the hill toward Alpha Company, he passed a wooden latrine built over two sunken barrels. The first truly familiar smell of the war. He stopped, dropped his duffel, went in, closed the door, unzipped and sat down.

And for a long time he sat there. At home, comfortable, even at peace. Flies played against the screened windows. Outside, far up the hill, stood a tall tower, and, behind it, the sandbagged tactical operations center. Down the hill ran a gravel road along which the various company areas sprawled, six in all—Headquarters, Alpha, Bravo, Charlie, Delta, and Echo. The 5th Battalion, 46th Infantry. Farther down the hill was the wired perimeter, bunkers, a steel-mesh gate draped with a hand-printed sign reading THE PROFESSIONALS. Beyond the gate was flat paddy. Beyond the paddies were mountains.

Yes, at peace, warm and wet inside, and he watched the flies and the clean sky and a black man raking trash and two officers moving slowly up the road.

At peace, he read what was written on the shitter's walls. *So short,* it was written, *I just fell through the fucking hole.* Below that, *Better off where you at.* Others, he read—*On Gator, the wind don't blow, it sucks,* and in a different hand, *So does PFC Prawn, when he gets the urge.* Another, *Where am I?* And beneath it, *If you don't know, better climb out before I drown your ass.* Names, dates, residue. *Hapstein's queer ... No, man, Hapstein's just good fun ... I'm so short, I'm gone —this is my answering service ... Cacciato ... Brilliant, ain't he?*

Paul Berlin took out a pencil.

Very carefully, he wrote: *I'm so short, I can't see the forest for the trees.*

When PFC Paul Berlin joined the First Platoon of Alpha Company on June 11, 1968, he found three squads manned by twelve, ten, and eight soldiers.

The squads were led by two PFCs and a buck sergeant, Oscar Johnson.

There were no fireteams, no SOPs for tactical maneuvers or covering fire. There was no FO. There was no platoon sergeant. Doc Peret was the only medic, and his training was at best eccentric.

The platoon leader, Lieutenant Sidney Martin, was almost as new to the war as Paul Berlin. His intelligence and training were clearly above average, but his wisdom was in doubt from the very beginning. He died in lake country—World's Greatest Lake Country, Doc Peret kept calling it—and after him came a much older lieutenant, Corson, who, though only average in intelligence and training and wisdom, was a platoon leader the men could finally love. He took no chances, he wasted no lives. The war, for which he was much too old, scared him.

They were organized around personalities, specialties of knowledge, and tradition. They were also organized around superstition.

It was not rank so much as superstition, for example, that made Oscar Johnson leader of the Third Squad. He was a sergeant, true. But he held that rank because he'd survived nearly nine months in the bush. Nine was a lucky number. And the coincidence of it, Paul Berlin learned, was the peculiar fact that Oscar Johnson knew very little about surviving. They were organized around luck.

Stink Harris walked point because he prided himself on his scouting abilities. Eddie Lazzutti carried the radio because he prided himself on his voice. They were organized around pride.

They were organized also around principles of trust. Ben Nystrom, who later left the war and wrote no letters, carried the radio until he could not be trusted with it, at which point Eddie was given the trust. Jim Pederson, in many ways the most trusted of all, was given the responsibility for triggering ambushes, and so the ambush formations were always organized around Jim Pederson.

Disobedience was sometimes organized and sometimes not.

When First Lieutenant Sidney Martin persisted in making them search tunnels before blowing them, and after Frenchie Tucker and Bernie Lynn died in tunnels, the disobedience became fully organized.

They were often organized around Standard Operating Procedures. The SOPs were of two sorts, formal and informal.

Formally, it was SOP to search tunnels before blowing them. Informally, it was SOP to blow the tunnels and move on, without a search, without risking life. Lieutenant Sidney Martin, who was trained at the Point, violated the informal SOPs, and the men hated him.

The routinization of the war, which helped make it tolerable, included even trivial things—what to talk about and when, the times to rest and the times to march and the times to keep the guard, when to tell jokes and when not to, the order of the march, when to send out ambushes and when to fake them. These issues were not debatable. They were governed by the informal SOPs, and these SOPs were more important than the Code of Conduct.

"How many days you been at the war?" asked Alpha's mail clerk, and Paul Berlin answered that he'd been at the war seven days now.

The clerk cackled. "Wrong," he said. "Tomorrow, man, that's your first day at the war."

And in the morning PFC Paul Berlin boarded a resupply chopper that took him fast over charred pocked mangled country, hopeless country, green skies and speed and tangled grasslands and paddies and places he might die, a million possibilities. He couldn't watch. He watched his hands. He made fists of them, opening and closing the fists. His hands, he thought, not quite believing. *His* hands.

Very quickly, the helicopter banked and turned and went down.

"How long you been at the war?" asked the first man he saw, a wiry soldier with ringworm in his hair.

PFC Paul Berlin smiled. "This is it," he said. "My first day."

5
The
Observation
Post

S PEC FOUR PAUL BERLIN tilted his wristwatch to catch
moonlight. Twelve twenty now—the incredible slowness
with which time passed. Incredible, too, the tricks his
fear did with time.

He wound the watch as tight as it would go. Facing east, out
to sea, he counted to sixty very slowly, breathing with each
count, and when he was done he looked at the watch again.
Still twelve twenty. He held it to his ear. The ticking was loud,
brittle-sounding. The second hand made its endless sweep.

Maybe it was the time of night that created the distortions.
Middle-hour guard, it was a bad time. First-hour guard was
better; the safest time, and surest, and once it ended you could
sleep the night through. Or last-hour guard. Last guard was all
right, too, because there was the expectation of dawn coming
upon the sea, and you could watch the water turn to color as
if paint had been poured into it at the horizon, and the pretty
colors helped sustain pretty thoughts.

Sure, it was the hour. Things shimmered silver in the moonlight, the sea and the coils of wire below the tower, the sand
winding along the beach. The night was moving now. He tried

47

not to look at it, but it was true—the night moved in waves, fluttering. The grasses inland moved, and the far trees. Middle-hour guard, it was a bad time for keeping watch.

Kneeling, he lit a cigarette, cupping it in his hand to hide the glow, then he stood and leaned against the sandbagged wall and looked down on the sea. The sea helped. It protected the back and gave a sense of distance from the war, a warm wash-ing feeling, and a feeling of connection to distant lands. His mind worked that way. Sometimes, during the hot afternoons beneath the tower, he would look out to sea and imagine using it as a means of escape—stocking Oscar's raft with plenty of rations and foul-weather gear and drinking water, then shov-ing out through the first heavy breakers, then hoisting up a poncho as a sail, then lying back and letting the winds and currents carry him away—to Samoa, maybe, or to some hidden isle in the South Pacific, or to Hawaii, or maybe all the way home. Pretending. It wasn't dreaming, it wasn't craziness. Just a way of passing time, which seemed never to pass.

He could make out the dim outline of Oscar's raft bobbing at anchor in the moonlight. They used it mostly for swimming. Sometimes, when boredom got the best of them, they would take it out to deeper water and fish off of it, spend the whole day out there, beyond the sight of land, separating themselves from the daily routine.

He watched the sea and the bobbing raft for a long time. Then he checked the watch again. Twelve twenty-two.

He tried to remember tricks for making time move.

Counting, that was one trick. Count the remaining days. Break the days into hours, and count the hours, then break the hours into minutes and count them one by one, and the min-utes into seconds.

He began to figure it. Arrived June 3. And now it was . . . What was it? November 20, or 25. Somewhere in there. It was hard to fix exactly. But it was November, he was sure of that. Late November. Not like the old-time Novembers along the Des Moines River, no lingering foliage. No sense of change or transition. Here there was no autumn. No leaves to turn with the turning of seasons, no seasons, no crispness in the air, no Thanksgiving and no football, nothing to gauge passage by. Inland, in the dark beyond the beach, there were a few scrawny trees, but these were mostly pines, and the pines did not change whatever the season.

November-the-what?

Oscar's birthday had been in July. In August, Billy Boy Watkins had died of fright—no, June. That was in June. June, the first day at the war. Then, in July, they'd celebrated Oscar's birthday with plenty of gunfire and flares, and they'd marched through the sullen villages along the Song Tra Bong, the awful quiet everywhere, and then, in August, Rudy Chassler had finally broken the quiet. That had been August. Then—then September. He couldn't remember September. He thought about it, but nothing came for the month of September. Keeping track wasn't easy. The order of things—chronologies—that was the hard part. Long stretches of silence, dullness, long nights and endless days on the march, and sometimes the truly bad times: Pederson, Buff, Frenchie Tucker, Bernie Lynn. But what was the order? How did the pieces fit, and into which months? And what was it now—November-the-what?

He extinguished the cigarette against his thumbnail and flipped it down to the beach.

Stepping over the sleeping men, he moved to the tower's west wall and faced inland.

He tried to concentrate on the future. What to do when the war was over. That was one pretty thought. Yes—when the war ended he would . . . he would go home to Fort Dodge. He would. He would go home on a train, slowly, looking out at the country as it passed, recognizing things, seeing how the country flattened and turned to corn, the silos painted white, and he would pay attention to the details. At the depot, when the train stopped, he would brush off his uniform and be certain all the medals were in place, and he would step off boldly, boldly, and he would shake his father's hand and look him in the eye. "I did okay," he would say. "I won some medals." And his father would nod. And later, the next day perhaps, they would go out to where his father was building houses in the development west of town, and they'd walk through the unfinished rooms and his father would explain what would be where, how the wiring was arranged, the difficulties with subcontractors and plumbers, but how the houses would be strong and lasting, how it took good materials and good craftsmanship and care to build houses that would be strong and lasting.

The night was moving. He concentrated hard, squinting, trying to stop the fluttering . . .

He would go to Europe. That's what he would do. Spend some time in Fort Dodge then take off for a tour of Europe. He would learn French. Learn French, then take off for Paris, and when he got there he would drink red wine in Cacciato's honor. Visit all the museums and monuments, learn the history, sit in the cafés along the river and smile at the pretty girls. Take a flat in Montmartre. Rise early and walk to the open market for breakfast. He would eat very slowly, crossing his legs and maybe reading a paper, letting things pass by, then maybe he'd walk about the city and learn the names of places, not as a tourist but as man who comes to learn and understand. He would study details. He would look for the things Cacciato would have looked for. It could be done. That was the crazy thing about it—for all the difficulties, for all the hard times and stupidity and errors, for all that, it could truly be done.

6
Detours on the Road to Paris

S O WITHOUT HAROLD MURPHY and his big gun they continued along the trail west, twice finding the ash of Cacciato's breakfast fires, once a neat pile of discarded ammunition. They found a broken penknife and tripflares and grenades, but they did not find Cacciato.

"War's over," Doc Peret took to chanting. "Peace and domestic tranquillity, a humble line from Marsilius. Translated it means this: Back on the block."

The jungle ended.

Descending, flattening as it dropped, the land opened to expose patches of sky. The rain forest turned scraggly. There were antelopes and deer. The trees thinned out to make meadows, and the meadows grew wider and fuller, and soon the meadows became open plains. At the crest of a small hill they stopped to look down on savanna that stretched to the horizon. They were quiet. Taking turns, they used the lieutenant's binoculars.

"Peace," Doc murmured. "World unto end, amen."

It was graceful, expansive country. To the north, barely visible even with the field glasses, a river ran down from the hills and wound off into a flat meadow filled with wild flowers. There were gazelles in the meadow. The sky was full of birds.

They marched easily now. The trail widened, turning north toward the river, and soon it became a real road. At noon Oscar found an empty Black Jack wrapper. Ten minutes later Eddie spotted a swirl of smoke just beyond the next line of hills.

"It's him," Stink said. His teeth rapped together.

Unslinging his weapon, Stink tapped the magazine to be sure it was engaged. He waved impatiently for the others to follow.

The road kept widening. For a time it ran parallel to the river, then it swung off sharply to the west, weaving through a stand of hunched banyan trees. The smell of smoke was strong now. Up ahead there was a strange new sound, a low groaning, something stamping. Stink dropped his pack and broke into an awkward half-trot, cradling his rifle.

The road made a final violent twist through the trees and emerged into a bright clearing.

It happened instantly.

There was a short, high squeal, then a shout. Stink fired. He dropped to one knee and kept firing. Paul Berlin stumbled, threw himself forward and rolled. Insane, he thought. Gone mad. A pair of old water buffalo stood at the center of the clearing, both yoked up to a large slat-cart.

Stink fired without aiming. It was automatic. It was Quick Kill. Point-blank, rifle jerking. The first shots struck the closest animal in the belly. There was a pause. The next burst caught the buffalo in the head, and it dropped.

That fast. Every time, that fast.

Someone was screaming for a cease-fire but Stink was on full automatic. He was smiling. Gobs of flesh jumped off the beast's flanks.

Paul Berlin, sprawled now in the center of the road, had the rare courage to peek.

Mad, he kept thinking. Gone to the zoo. No reason, no warning. He heard someone bawling. A woman's bawling. Mad, foaming-crazy. The clearing shimmied in a hazy white swirl. Chunks of meat and hide kept splattering off the shot-dead water buffalo. It wouldn't end. Behind him, in the weeds, the lieutenant screamed for a cease-fire, pawing at the sky from flat on his back.

It ended. There was quiet, then a clicking noise as Stink rammed in a second magazine.

The fierce bawling continued. Doc and Eddie were picking themselves up. Oscar was gone.

Grinning, Stink Harris posed on one knee.

"Lash LaRue," Stink kept chirping. "Lash L. LaRue."

Whoever was bawling was still bawling. It was like a baby's wail, high and angry.

"Lash L. LaRue. You see them reactions? You *see*?"

The clearing gleamed. The dead buffalo was bleeding. The living buffalo kept trying to run. It would get to its feet, stumble, struggle for a moment and then fall.

"Like lightning, man! Zip, zap!"

It was a woman's bawling. It came from somewhere behind the cart. The cart was splashed with blood.

Stink licked his lips and grinned.

"Stupid," Doc said. He was shaking his head. "Stupid, stupid."

The cart was piled high with lamps and rugs and furniture. Three women sat there. The two old women were bawling. The other was a girl. A girl, not a woman: maybe twelve, maybe twenty-one. Her hair and eyes were black. She wore an *ao dai* and sandals and gold hoops through her ears. Hanging from a chain about her neck was a chrome cross.

"Greased lightning," Stink said. "Hands like bullwhips."

"Stupid."

"Zingo, bingo, bang!"

"Criminal stupid."

All three women were bawling now. Madhouse sounds. The bawling flickered in and out, sometimes very high, other times seeming to tremble and fade. The dead buffalo kept bleeding.

"Fastest hands in the West," Stink tittered. He looked at Paul Berlin and flicked his eyebrows. "Zip, splash, totaled!"

They spent the night in the clearing.

Unbuckling the harness, Eddie and Doc dragged the dead buffalo off the road and covered it with branches. Oscar managed to quiet the other animal. Patting its nose, clucking, he led it to a tree and tethered it and brought it water. Stink built a campfire. Afterward, as dark came, the lieutenant began the interrogation.

"Refugees," said the young woman, the girl. She glanced nervously at Stink Harris. "You know refugees? My aunts, they take me away. But the war chases us."

As if on signal, the two old women began howling, their noses at the moon. The lieutenant waited. He rubbed his eyes.

"Look," he said softly, "I'm sorry about this. War's a lousy thing."

"And now poor Nguyen."

"Who?"

Sadly, moving only her head, the girl gestured in the direction of the dead water buffalo. "My aunts raised him from a tiny baby. Their own breasts. And now poor Nguyen—"

"Stupid," Doc Peret said.

Stink looked up. He shrugged, picked up his weapon and began cleaning it.

They were silent. Leaning back against his rucksack, the lieutenant stared for a time into the fire. Then he blinked and looked at the girl.

"Again, I'm sorry. I am. These things—you know—these things happen. But right now, why not just spill the facts? Who are you? Where you come from?"

"You will pay solace?" the girl said. "For Nguyen, you will pay reparations?"

"Maybe. Just tell the facts."

She sighed. Her name was Sarkin Aung Wan. For many

months now she had been a refugee, traveling west from Saigon with her two aunts. Home was Cholon. Many Chinese in Cholon, she said, many fine restaurants. Her father had once owned a restaurant, but now it was owned by her uncle. Her father had died in childbirth. A very sad thing. As her mother gave birth to twin babies, her father was led out of the waiting room and taken down many corridors and then shot. VC Number Ten, she said. VC, bad news. Her father, a dedicated and honest restaurateur, had been executed against a hospital wall for pilfering chickens from the cadre's Cholon slaughterhouse. Unjustly, for he had always paid his bills and taxes. Two years later her mother died of grief. The family dispersed, brothers going to live with cousins, sisters spreading out among uncles and aunts, and the war continued, and Cholon became a combat zone, and in the end there was no choice but to leave. So the pair of buffalo were yoked up and harnessed, a few prized belongings were packed, and early one morning the girl and her two aunts began the journey west.

"Those are facts," she said. "And now my aunts take me to become a refugee."

Paul Berlin watched: smooth skin, dignity, eyes that were shy and bold, coarse black hair. She was young, though. Much too young. She smelled of soap and joss sticks. The gold hoop earrings sparkled.

"So," the lieutenant finally said. "It's a sad story. You have my sympathy. But, look . . . where exactly are you headed? You *bic* destination? A place you're aiming for?"

The girl shrugged. "We go home."

"I thought you were refugees. Isn't—?"

"We are refugees to go home," she said, smiling for the first time. "It is a long road to become a refugee."

The lieutenant scratched his nose. "Yeah, okay. But what I'm asking is this: I'm asking where you and your aunties are headed. What's the destination?"

"West," she said.

"Yes, but *where?*"

She smiled. "The Far West."

The old man nodded at this, pausing, licking his lips. "I see. But—" He kept scratching his nose. "But *how* far? That's the question. How far into the Far West?"

"Oh," the girl said, "only as far as refugees go."

"Ah."

"To go farther would be stupid."

"Of course."

She smiled again. "So now you will lead us, yes? You have shot Nguyen, so now you will lead us to the Far West?"

The lieutenant leaned back wearily. He shook his head, muttered something, then got up and moved into the weeds beyond the fire.

Later they ate dried fish and rice. It was a warm, sweet night. Crickets, a breeze, the velvet sky. For a time the two old aunties moaned for their lost Nguyen, sobbing, rocking miserably on their haunches. Then they slept. A bright half-moon rose over the plain.

Paul Berlin went to the fire. Stoking it, adding a log, he pretended not to watch the girl. She was young. It was hard to tell—fifteen, maybe. Or twelve or twenty. Her eyes curved up like wings. He watched as she spread out her blanket, removed her sandals, brushed her hair, stretched, yawned, lay back. He liked this. He liked it when she smiled at him, nodding slightly, smoothing her robes about her legs.

A possibility. A thing that might have happened on the road to Paris. He looked into the fire for a long time.

In the morning, after burying the dead buffalo, and after waiting while the two old women laid down flowers, they prepared to move out. Eddie and Stink climbed aboard the cart to tie down the rucksacks and sleeping gear. Oscar harnessed up the surviving animal. The lieutenant studied his maps. When they were ready, Paul Berlin climbed up and took a seat next to the pretty young girl. He grinned. Oscar shook the reins, hollered gid'yap, and soon they were riding westward along the rolling plains to Paris.

7
Riding
the Road
to Paris

AND THERE WAS A LONG, gleaming time during which the riding was everything, the riding and the road and the grassy plains. The days were sunny. The nights were deep and still. They rode for ten hours a day, stopping only to water the old buffalo. They saw no villages. Curving with the flow of the land, the road was hard and dusty, completely deserted. The trees were bare. It was parched country, for the rains had not yet come north, and the streams ran nearly empty. In the evenings a cooling breeze would sometimes move in from the mountains. They would rest then, waiting for dark, enjoying the feel of having traveled many miles without once using their legs. Sleep came easy. Paul Berlin rode along quietly during the days. The cart's gentle rocking motions pushed him against the pretty girl named Sarkin Aung Wan. He liked it when they touched. Accidentally sometimes, and sometimes not quite by accident. He liked her smell, her smile, the way she seemed to be holding things back. She was pretty. That was part of it. In Quang Ngai, where poverty abused beauty, women aged like dogs. So, yes, it was curious to watch this girl, to imagine how it might have happened.

"And you," said Sarkin Aung Wan near the end of the second day. "You are soldiers, yes?"

"Yes," he said.

Frowning, the girl looked out over the distant blue hills. "It is a pity," she said. "I am sad to learn that the fighting has spread so far."

He shrugged, pretending not to look at her.

"Has it?"

"What?"

"The war. Has it followed us this far?"

Paul Berlin answered truthfully that he wasn't sure. Opinions varied. According to Doc Peret, no fool, the war was over; if you listened to the lieutenant, the war was still a war. It was hard to be sure.

"Well," the girl sighed. "We must go on then. We must keep going until you are sure."

At night, after the fire died, the girl's two aunts would wail for their lost Nguyen. Rocking, their leathery old faces pointed to the sky, they would start with low moans like an animal's breathing. The moaning would grow. An hour, perhaps two hours, and the moans would become sobs, and the sobs would go mournful and high, and in the deepest part of the night the sobbing would become wailing. They could not be consoled. Dark and tiny and wrinkled, swaying on their haunches, the old women would howl the whole night long. And in the morning, without speaking, they would climb aboard the overloaded oxcart and take their positions at the rear, facing backward, squatting silently with their eyes always east.

"Paris?" said Sarkin Aung Wan. "You are going to Paris!"

Only a possibility, he said. Only one possibility out of a thousand, just a notion. Anything could happen.

"But Paris!"

The girl's eyes were bright. She was riding on a pile of blankets, painting her toenails with a tiny brush.

"Paris! Churches and museums! Notre-Dame! Oh, I should dearly like to be a refugee in Paris."

She dipped the brush into the bottle of polish and began painting the nails on her left foot. The paint sparkled in the sun.

"You will take me along, yes? As a refugee? Paris! Oh, I shall love to see Paris—Pont Neuf and the Seine, all the windows full of pretty things. We shall see it together!"

Careful to choose his words, Paul Berlin tried to explain that it wasn't what it seemed. He told how Cacciato had walked away in the rain, a dumb kid with maps and candy and an AWOL bag. How they'd taken off after him: a dangerous mission, nothing easy. How already they'd lost one member of the search party, Harold Murphy, and how they had marched many weeks through jungle and rain. A thousand hardships lay ahead.

"But Paris!"

"It's only a possibility."

She looked at him, holding the brush to her nose and sniffing it. A dab of red paint gleamed on her cheek. "I am sure of it," she said. "Together we shall see Paris. Stroll through the gardens, visit all the famous monuments. Perhaps we shall fall in love there. Is that possible?"

The oxcart swayed and pressed them together.

"Paris," she whispered. Her eyes shifted to the horizon. "Yes, I should dearly love to see Paris."

The lieutenant shook his head.

"No," he said.

"But, sir, she speaks French. Terrific French."

"And?"

"And . . . well . . . she could sort of help out. Guide us, show us the ropes."

Again the old man wagged his head. He was stretched out on a rug near the front of the cart. His nose was peeling. "No way. I'll say it again: We're still soldiers and this here is still a war."

"But she's smart. She is. She could help out with—"

"Negative." The lieutenant looked away. "Say again, this is no friggin' party. No party, no civilians. Next ville, we drop them off and that's the end of it."

"Just dump them?"

"War's a nasty thing."

"Not even—?"

"No," the old man sighed. "No."

True, it was no place for women. True, it would be a dangerous journey, full of bad times and bad places, and, true, they could not be burdened by weakness or frailty. All true. But Paul Berlin could not stop toying with the idea: a mix of new possibilities. A whole new range of options. He wanted Sarkin Aung Wan to join the expedition. He wanted it badly, and he wanted it even more when, by the light of a midnight campfire, she showed him her many strengths. "Do you see?" she whispered. "Do you see that I am strong?" And she was. Fragile, delicate like a bird, but still strong. She lifted the robe. Her legs were brown and smooth and muscled. The skin was tight without lines or wrinkles.

"Feel there," she whispered as the others slept. "Do you feel it? I have endurance like a man. I walk as a man walks and I do not complain."

He tested her arms and shoulders.

"I shall carry my share. I shall keep pace. I shall show courage and stamina."

Once more he felt the great strength of her legs, then he

60

folded his hands together and squeezed. The fire made silver in her eyes.

"You can persuade your lieutenant," she whispered. "Tell him of my strength, so that I may join you to Paris."

"It'll be treacherous," he said. "Nothing easy."

"I am brave."

"Deserts and mountains and swamps."

The girl dismissed this with a wave. "To be a refugee is to know danger. I can guide you. Yes . . . I shall guide you! You will need me as a guide."

"Cacciato. He's our guide."

"Cacciato?"

"Yes, he's—you know—he's out there in front. A scout."

"No matter," Sarkin Aung Wan murmured. She smoothed the robe about her legs. "No matter, Spec Four, because you will need me. I am strong, and soon you will need me greatly. And I shall love to see Paris."

The land was luminous. Pink coral and ferric reds, great landfalls of wilderness, and they moved through it for twelve days at a buffalo's pace. No villages, no people. Only the road. The girl's two old aunties wallowed in their grief. They rode along silently at the rear of the cart, facing backward, showing no interest in the journey or the passing countryside. At night they wailed. Coyotes, Eddie laughed. Stink Harris did not laugh. Dinks, he muttered: Dinks from Dinksville, Damsels from Gooktown. Silent through the sunny days, the old women howled endlessly through the nights.

But the land was rich, the weather warm, and the slat-cart yawed and pitched its way up the widening road west.

Once they spent the night in an abandoned tribal shrine. Once they spotted smoke on a distant hill. Once they found M&Ms scattered along a fork in the road, the M&Ms taking the northwest fork, and they followed the M&Ms. They slept through a fierce tropical storm; they nearly lost the buffalo in fast river waters; they shot quail for a Sunday feast. Many things, once, but mostly they rode the road west.

Then they captured Cacciato.

It happened at night, in the dark of fifth-hour guard. A strange rustling in the brush. A familiar soft whistling.

Smoothly, like a cat, Stink Harris crept away from the fire, staying in shadows, moving in on the intruder from behind. Then he pounced. Screaming, he tackled Cacciato.

"Got him!" Stink yelped. And it was true, he had him.

8
The Observation Post

POSTED LUCID HIGH OVER the sea and shifting sand,
Spec Four Paul Berlin looked out on nighttime Quang
Ngai. Nearly one o'clock. Ordinarily it would be time now
to rouse the next guard. Time to pick through the sleeping
bodies, touch Doc's shoulder and whisper words of friendship,
wait, and then, when Doc was fully awake, hand over the
wristwatch and wish him well and curl at last into a warm
poncho. Changing of the guard, rules passed down by dead
men.

Ordinarily.

He did not wake Doc Peret.

Instead he felt his way along the tower's west wall to the
ladder. He climbed barefoot over the double layer of sandbags,
found the ladder with his feet, tested it, then went down fast.

It was his bravest moment.

Calmly, unafraid, he turned and walked to the sea. The
beach was clean. The sand was cool and wet-feeling and good.
Nothing moved. It was a gentle sea. The waves, broken by a
coral reef, came in like smooth unfolding mats, one draped
evenly over the next, spreading themselves out with the calm

63

repetitive motion of energy given and energy returned. Dimly, he could make out Oscar's raft bobbing at anchor fifty meters from shore. Beyond the raft was open sea.

He waded in to his knees, spread his feet, unzipped, and relaxed.

High up were the stars like lighted lanterns, constellations telling where and when. He felt brave. He felt good.

When he was empty he waded down to where the wire entered the sea. He stopped there, washed his face and hands and hair, then waded out.

For a time he stood in the tower's moon shadow. Just standing. Not moving and not thinking much. It wasn't much of a tower. From down below, a sapper's-eye view, it looked rickety and fragile and tottering, just a simple square of sandbags supported by thirty-foot piles. A Tinker Toy in Quang Ngai. He smiled, wondering whose idea it was. An observation post with nothing to observe. No villages, no roads or vital bridges, no enemy, not a dog or a cat. A teetering old tower by the sea.

He walked once around the tower, looking up at it from various angles, then moved back to the water.

No, it was not an ordinary night. This night, posted by the sea, he was brave and wide awake and nimbleheaded. His fingers tingled. Excited by the possibilities, but still in control. That was the important part—he was in control. He was calm. Clear thinking helped. Concentrating, figuring out the details, it helped plenty.

After a time he turned back to the tower, climbed up and resumed his post.

One twenty now.

Smoking quietly, he remembered what his father had said on their last night along the Des Moines River. "You'll see some terrible stuff, I guess. That's how it goes. But try to look for the good things, too. They'll be there if you look. So watch for them."

And that was what he did. Even now, figuring how things might have happened on the road to Paris, it was a way of looking for the very best of all possible outcomes. How, with luck and courage and endurance, they might have found a way.

At one thirty he moved to the radio, called in the situation report, then lit another of Doc's cigarettes.

Sure, it was swell advice. Think about the good things, keep your eye on Paris.

9
How
Bernie Lynn
Died After
Frenchie Tucker

"GET ME THE M&Ms," Doc said, and Stink got them, and Doc shook out two candies and placed them on Bernie's tongue and told him to swallow.

Sidney Martin, who had ordered Frenchie into the tunnel, and who then ordered Bernie Lynn to go down to drag Frenchie out, knelt on one knee and looked over Bernie's wound and then went to the radio to help Ben Nystrom make the call.

Nystrom was not yet crying.

Frenchie lay uncovered at the mouth of the tunnel. He was dead and nobody looked at him. He was dirty. His T-shirt was pulled up under the armpits, which was how they'd finally dragged him out. His belly was fat and white and unsucked in. Black clumps of hair were matted flat against the white skin. He had been shot through the nose. His face was turned aside, the way they'd left him.

"Swallow," Doc said.

"I heard it," Bernie Lynn said.

"Orphan Six-Three, this is Indigo One-Niner—" The lieutenant's voice, though he was new to the war, was calm and unbroken. "Request urgent dustoff, repeat, urgent, one KIA-friendly, one urgent friendly WIA . . . grid . . . wait on grid."

"Swallow," Doc said. "It's good stuff for what ails."

"Say again, One-Niner."

"Urgent," the lieutenant said without urgency. "Repeat, wait on grid—" He gave the handset to Ben Nystrom and sat down with his code book.

The earth was shaking.

"There, man," Doc purred. "Down she goes. There. Feel better already, huh?"

"I heard it," Bernie Lynn said.

"Sure you heard it. How's that? Better? We got a ship coming, so . . . so hold still now. Hang tight and we'll have you out of here pronto."

"Bang," Bernie said. "Bang! Just like . . . just like that, *bang!*"

"Hold still now. Wait'll that good shit medicine takes hold, couple seconds or so. You feel it? Feel it?"

As he spoke, purring, Doc unwrapped another compress bandage and pressed it tight against Bernie's throat and held it with his hand.

"Bang, like that. Dark as . . . but, geez, I swear to God I heard it . . . What's wrong? What's wrong here? I did, I heard it."

"I know, man."

"All the way. I swear."

Behind them, the radio made a static sound, then a voice demanded grid coordinates. "Say again, no dustoff till we get those coordinates. No grid, no chopper. Is that a good read?"

"Jesus!" Oscar screamed. He was on his hands and knees. The earth kept shaking.

The lieutenant still worked with a pencil, using his map and compass and code book to work up the coded coordinates. He worked calmly and without hurry.

Beside him, Frenchie's helmet and boots and socks were arranged neatly on a square of rock. Frenchie was always neat. Bernie Lynn's gear lay in a heap where he'd dropped it.

"Going home," Doc said. "It's the truth. Nurses and booze and all that good shit. Home, man. Feel better now . . . Some-

body get the juice . . . Sure, man, I bet you feel better already."
Doc removed the compress and applied another. The wound
was wet. It was a tunnel wound, just below the throat and
slanting steeply into the chest, the way men were always shot
in tunnels, and it was hard to believe Bernie was talking, but
he said, ". . . real loud, like *bang* . . ." and he coughed and shook
his head, clearing it, "just like that, *bang!*"

"Stick him," Doc said.

"Not me, man. You're the fucking medic."

"Somebody—"

The earth was shaking again. To the south and southwest
and west, the First and Second Squads were still blowing bunkers. The explosions made Bernie blink.

"Not me," Stink Harris said. "I don't stick nobody with that
shit."

"For God's sake, somebody do it."

"Not me."

The radio whined. "One-Niner, you want them ships, by
God, you get me some coordinates. We can't—"

"Give it to him," Oscar Johnson said. He'd lost his sunglasses.
He looked hard at Sidney Martin. "Forget the codes, just give
it to him."

"One minute."

"Give it!"

The lieutenant bent over his code book.

"Indigo One-Niner, this is Orphan Six—"

"Forget that code shit!" Oscar screamed. "Give the grids.
Just *give* it!"

"One second."

"Indigo—"

The earth shook again. Two black clouds rose over the far
hedges.

"Look," Stink whispered. "I ain't doing it. That's all, I just
won't."

"Oh, if that—"

"I ain't."

"Somebody do it," Doc said. "I don't give a shit who, just do it now."

Rudy took the needle, and Stink held the plasma and cord, and Rudy shoved the needle into Bernie's arm. Stink kept his eyes closed. He hated blood. Doc pressed the compress against Bernie's throat.

Behind them, Lieutenant Sidney Martin was on the radio again, calling in the coded coordinates. He gave each number precisely, pausing, very calm.

The needle slipped. Clear fluid spilled over Bernie's arm. A muddy puddle formed at the mouth of the tunnel. Quickly Doc exchanged places and reinserted the needle.

"Repeat," said Sidney Martin, "one KIA, one urgent WIA, both US types. Repeat, urgent. Grid—" And again he read off the coded coordinates.

Now Ben Nystrom was crying. He squatted at the lieutenant's feet, his hands holding the radio, crying.

The earth trembled again, rocking the heavy fluid in Stink's bottle. Almost immediately, like an echo, another explosion went off to the southwest.

"Affirm, LZ secure . . . Wait on ETA. Stand by."

The second explosion jarred the needle loose. Bernie sat up.

"Hold it, for—"

"Jesus! Get the guy down, can you do *that*? Can you just hold him down?"

"It slipped, man." Stink opened his eyes to find the bottle. "He keeps moving, what can I do?"

"The needle—"

"For Christ sake. *Hold* it."

Rudy held the needle in while Doc ran to his pouch and found the tape. The morning was still bright. Filmy clouds scudded below the sun, making shadows in the clearing. Bernie lay in the sun. His eyes were open but he didn't speak when Doc adjusted the needle and taped it to the arm. Stink looked away.

"Hey, man," Bernie said.

"Hey yourself. That better now?"

"Real nice . . . What time you got? I don't know. Bang, it went. Just like that, bang. Something . . . What's wrong? What's wrong with me?"

"Stay cool now. Just—"

"Jesus!"

"Get him down. Hold him."

Rudy pressed against Bernie's shoulders, easing him back. "Right there."

"Okay."

"Just hold him right there."

Bernie relaxed. His legs straightened and he lay flat. His head shook from side to side. A medium-sized, brown-haired kid with thin arms and tanned skin and wide-open eyes. He looked at Frenchie Tucker but did not seem to see him. He kept shaking his head. "I heard it," he said. "I did."

When the plasma had emptied into him, Doc took out a fresh bottle and spiked it and attached the cord.

"I heard it," Bernie said. "Honest."

"We read you, man. Take her easy now, be cool."

Bernie smiled.

"Codes," Oscar said. He'd found his sunglasses. "Man messes with *codes* an' . . . Codes." He looked at Lieutenant Sidney Martin and spat. "Codes!"

Bernie Lynn's mouth formed a small circle. A bubble appeared, then broke.

"More medicine, kid?"

Bernie smiled.

"Okay, cowboy. We'll see about another dose. Don't run away."

Doc found a fresh pack of M&Ms. Very carefully, like a pharmacist, he shook out three green candies and began feeding them to Bernie Lynn. The men understood this. Except for Rudy, who held the plastic bottle, and Doc, who kept changing compresses, everyone moved away.

10
A Hole
in the Road
to Paris

"I HAD HIM," STINK WHINED. "By God, yes, I had him
nailed."

"Sure, you did," Doc said, unwrapping the bandage. "At
ease now. This'll hurt a little."

"Right by the balls, I had the fat little—"

Stink yelped as Doc tore the bandage loose. It was morning
now, and they were preparing to move out. Oscar and Lieutenant Corson harnessed up the water buffalo, backing it into
its yoke, and Eddie was busy tying rucksacks and sleeping gear
to the cart. It had been a long, sleepless night.

"Like I could smell the dude's breath, that's how good I had
him. Onions! That's what it was—onions, stale fuckin onions. I
had him."

"Shit," Oscar said. He spat and gazed spitefully at Stink's
wound. "How'd you have him, man? By the teeth?"

"It wasn't—"

Oscar's lips made a nasty smile. "Looks to me you never had
him. Looks like he had you."

Doc held Stink's elbow out, inspecting it for infection. He'd stopped the blood flow the night before, wrapping it in a temporary bandage. Now it didn't look too bad. Just two neat rows of teeth marks.

"Hell, it was *dark*. What you expect in the dark?"

"Nothin'," Oscar said. "From you, I don' expect nothin'. Had him, couldn't hold him. So we spend the whole sorry night tramplin' the bush. From you, I don' expect nothin'."

"Wasn't *my* fault. I couldn't—"

Stink squealed, squirming to get away from Doc's iodine brush. His face was gray. He looked away as Doc sprinkled the wound with sulfa powder and began rebandaging it.

"Next time," he muttered. "Next time the sleazy little creep'll pay. I swear it."

"Easy now."

"I swear it."

Doc clipped the bandage and helped him up into the cart.

"Hey, Doc," Eddie called. "Maybe you better feed him some M&Ms. You need some M&Ms, Stinko?"

"Screw a monkey, man."

Eddie laughed and finished tying on the rucksacks. He helped the two old women into the cart, gathered up a bag of rations, and waved at Oscar. Then they were moving again.

"Next time," Stink murmured. "Next time he fries."

Eddie laughed. "No more Mister Nice Guy?"

"You got it," Stink said. "No more. Next time . . . next time the toad gets his fuckin teeth brushed."

At midafternoon they found another of Cacciato's maps, this one tacked to a log across the road. The red dotted line led into deep rubber country. Doc pointed it out on the map's legend. "See these symbols here? Country rich in rubber, tin, and magnesium. That's what these symbols symbolize."

The lieutenant touched the map. "What's this?"

"What?"

"Right here. On the map . . . What the hell is it?"

It was a precisely drawn circle. Within the circle, in red,

were two smaller circles, between them an even smaller circle, and beneath them a big banana smile. A round happy face. Underneath it, in printed block letters, was a warning: LOOK OUT, THERE'S A HOLE IN THE ROAD.

That evening after supper Lieutenant Corson explained the new plan.

"Way it looks," he said, "is that Cacciato's headed for Mandalay. Can't be positive, but if he keeps on to the northwest like this and then turns west, well, that'll bring him smack into Mandalay. Anyhow that's my guess."

The old man paused a moment, glancing down at Cacciato's map. In the light of the fire his skin glowed bright red. His eyes were bloodshot.

"Anyhow . . ." and he coughed, licking the corners of his lips, "anyhow, I figure our best bet is to cut him off. Get ahead of him. Follow me? Strike off diagonal-like, take the shortest distance between two points." With his thumb the lieutenant drew a straight line through an area on the map colored green to represent dense jungle.

"You mean leave the road?" Eddie said. "Start humpin' again?"

"It's the only way."

"Yeah, but . . . Geez."

Doc picked up the map. "Might work," he said. "The basic hypotenuse strategy, right? Cut straight through, head him off at the pass. It might work."

"Yeah. But *walk?*"

"Might work."

The lieutenant rubbed the bone between his eyes. "Hell, I don't like it either. It's thick stuff we'll be going through. Real jungle again. Lord knows, I don't like it a bit."

"But it's still a war," Eddie sighed.

"There it is. It's still a lousy war."

Paul Berlin raised a hand. "What about them, sir?"

"Who?"

"The old women. The girl."

"Sorry," Lieutenant Corson said. "I told you before, this here's no joy ride, no place for ladies." He tried to smile. "Sorry, lad, but the answer's no. We leave them behind."

"Not even the girl?"

"I'm sorry."

They spent the evening making preparations, mending packs and filling canteens and setting aside rations. Afterward, as the others slept, Paul Berlin sat quietly with Sarkin Aung Wan. There was nothing to say. He could not imagine a happy ending. He held her hand, a tiny childlike hand, and together they watched the fire grow tight like a fist.

Later she cried. He put his nose in her hair.

"Do something," she whispered. "Can't you do something?"

"I'm trying."

"Wish it. Close your eyes and wish we might see Paris together."

"I am," he said.

"Are your eyes closed?"

"Yes."

"Can you see it? Can you see us in Paris?"

He saw it clearly.

"You will find a way," she said, lying back. "I am certain of it. You will."

Then she slept. He watched her—clean and young, her eyelashes curled like the petals on an orchid. She was fragile. To touch her would risk destroying the whole thing. He did not touch her. All night he lay awake, searching for a happy ending. A riddle, he kept thinking.

At dawn, the pink sun surprised him. He sat up blinking. Eddie and Oscar were already building a fire.

The feeling was of departure. After breakfast, they helped the two old aunties into the cart. Oscar patted the buffalo's huge nose, whispering to it in a soft voice, and Stink and Doc secured the women's belongings to the cart. As if to delay it, everyone moved in slow motion, paying attention to all the small things—extinguishing the fire, tidying up the campsite, checking to be sure nothing was left behind. But at last there was no avoiding it. Paul Berlin took the girl's hand, led her to the cart and helped her into the driver's seat.

Sarkin Aung Wan smiled. Little tears made her eyes slippery. She reached down for the reins.

He kissed her hand, then her cheek.

"You will find a way," she murmured. "I know that."

He nodded dumbly. Then he turned away. The lieutenant, never a mean man, pursed his lips to show sympathy. Slinging his weapon, the old man moved slowly up to the buffalo and gave the beast a sharp swat on the flank.

Paul Berlin's eyes ached.

No solutions. A lapse of imagination, so it simply happened.

It came first as a shivering sound. Next, a great shaking sensation. The big buffalo began stamping. Nose aflare, the animal seemed to quiver. The road was shaking. The whole road. Instantly there came a great buckling feeling, an earthquake, a tremor that rippled along the road in waves, splitting and tearing.

"Yes," the girl was saying, "I know you will find a way. And in Paris—"

The earth tore itself open.

Snorting, eyes rolling, the big buffalo tried to run. It reared violently backward, stumbled, fell to its knees.

The road opened in a long jagged crack, tiny at first, then ripping wide.

"Holy God," Eddie whispered.

The lieutenant shouted. Stink's mouth opened and closed, but whatever he said was lost in another series of enormous shock waves. Sheer rock tore open. Dust seemed to swell from pores in the ground.

Then they were falling. Paul Berlin felt it in his stomach. A tumbling sensation. There was time to snatch for Sarkin Aung Wan's hand, squeeze tight, and then they were falling. The road was gone and they were simply falling, all of them, Oscar and Eddie and Doc, the old lieutenant, the buffalo and cart and old women, everything, tumbling down a hole in the road to Paris.

11
Fire
in the Hole

PEDERSON WAS A MESS. They wrapped him in his own poncho. Doc Peret found the broken dog tags and slipped them into Pederson's mouth and taped it shut. Later the dustoff came. They carried Pederson aboard. Eddie touched his friend's wrist, Harold Murphy signaled to the pilot, and the helicopter took Pederson away.

They waded out of the paddy. No one talked about Jim Pederson. Moving from man to man, the lieutenant made a list of the lost equipment, then he led them to a hill half a klick away. At the top, they threw off their packs and formed up in a loose perimeter. The day was very hot. Before, coming down into the paddy, the day had seemed cold, much too cold, but now the heat could be seen steaming off the land. There were no clouds. There were no farmers in the fields. Down below, tucked next to the paddy, was the village called Hoi An.

The men waited while the lieutenant went to work with his maps and compass.

Taking turns, they used a towel to wipe away the paddy stink. It was in their hair and noses and mouths. The weapons were filthy. Paul Berlin moved his tongue along his teeth, collecting spit, and when he spat it came out green. Bits of algae swam in the bubbles. His hands were caked with slime. He could feel the muck in his boots, the softness; he could see it like grease on the others. The smell was thick. Harold Murphy took off his trousers and used them to clean his big gun. Eddie wiped the radio, getting it ready for the lieutenant, and Oscar and Vaught and Cacciato began disassembling their weapons.

When the lieutenant was finished with his calculations, he moved to the radio and made the call. He spoke crisply. He read off the coordinates and asked for a marking round.

They waited. Looking down, Paul Berlin saw flat brown paddies stretching off in every direction. The village of Hoi An was dead. There were no birds or animals. The sun made the paddies seem clean. From high up everything seemed clean. He tried not to think about Pederson. The way the cold came, nightly cold, and then the incredible heat. He wiped his hands on his shirt and rinsed out his mouth and tried not to think about it.

The radio buzzed. There was a whining sound. The marking round opened high over the southeast corner of Hoi An.

The lieutenant called in an adjustment and asked for white phosphorus.

And again the whine. White phosphorus burned the village. "Kill it," Paul Berlin said.

The lieutenant watched the village burn. Then he went to the radio and ordered a dozen more Willie Peter, then a dozen HE.

The rounds hit the village in thirty-second intervals. The village went white. The hedges swayed. A vacuum sucked in quiet and a wind was made. Hoi An glowed. Trees powdered. There was the scalding sound of oxygen being used. Sitting on their rucksacks, the men watched black smoke open in white smoke. Splinters of straw and wood sprinkled down, and there was light in the village like flashbulbs exploding in sequence, and then a melting, and then heat. Even high on the hill they felt the heat. Something liquid seemed to run through the center of the village. The fluid boiled. It burned and ran off into the paddies.

"Kill it," Paul Berlin said, but without malice.

The lieutenant returned to the radio.

Next came alternating Willie Peter and HE, first white, then black. The men did not cheer or show emotion. They watched the village become smoke. Rounds pounded the smoke. The trees and huts and hedges and fences were gone. White ash fluttered down. Something gleamed in the smoke, as at the center of a furnace, and the rounds kept falling. There was very little sound. A light, puffy tremble. Oscar Johnson smiled with each explosion, but otherwise the men seemed blank. Then they began firing. They lined up and fired into the burning village. Harold Murphy used the machine gun. The tracers could be seen through the smoke, bright red streamers, and the Willie Peter and HE kept falling, and the men fired until they were exhausted. The village was a hole.

They spent the night along the Song Tra Bong. They bathed in the river and made camp and ate supper. When it was night they began talking about Jim Pederson. It was always better to talk about it.

12
The
Observation
Post

THE ISSUE, OF COURSE, was courage. How to behave. Whether to flee or fight or seek an accommodation. The issue was not fearlessness. The issue was how to act wisely in spite of fear. Spiting the deep-running biles: that was true courage. He believed this. And he believed the obvious corollary: the greater a man's fear, the greater his potential courage.

Below, the tower's moon shadow stretched far to the south.

Nearly two fifteen now, but he was not tired. Lightheaded, he faced inland and listened. He could recite the separate sounds—a roiling breeze off the sea, the incoming tide, the hum of the radio. The others slept. Stink Harris slept defensively, knees tucked up and arms curled about his head like a beaten boxer. Oscar slept gracefully, spread out, and Eddie Lazzutti slept fitfully, turning and sometimes muttering. Their sleeping was part of the night.

He bent down and did PT by the numbers, counting softly, loosening up his arms and neck and legs, then he walked twice around the tower's small platform. He was not tired, and not afraid, and the night was not moving.

Leaning against the wall of sandbags, he lit another of Doc's cigarettes. After the war he would stop smoking. Quit, just like that.

He inhaled deeply and held it and enjoyed the puffy tremor it set off in his head.

Yes, the issue was courage. It always had been, even as a kid. Things scared him. He couldn't help it. Noise scared him, dark scared him. Tunnels scared him: the time he almost won the Silver Star for valor. But the real issue was courage. It had nothing to do with the Silver Star . . . Oh, he would've liked winning it, true, but that wasn't the issue. He would've liked showing the medal to his father, the heavy feel of it, looking his father in the eye to show he had been brave, but even that wasn't the real issue. The real issue was the power of will to defeat fear. A matter of figuring a way to do it. Somehow working his way into that secret chamber of the human heart, where, in tangles, lay the circuitry for all that was possible, the full range of what a man might be. He believed, like Doc Peret, that somewhere inside each man is a biological center for the exercise of courage, a piece of tissue that might be touched and sparked and made to respond, a chemical maybe, or a lone chromosome that when made to fire would produce chain reactions of valor that even the biles could not drown. A filament, a fuse, that if ignited would release the full energy of what might be. There was a Silver Star twinkling somewhere inside him.

13
Falling Through a Hole in the Road to Paris

S O DOWN AND DOWN, pinwheeling freestyle through the dark. Time only to yell a warning, time to snatch for his weapon and Sarkin Aung Wan's hand, and then he was falling.

Far below he could make out the dim tumbling outline of the buffalo and slat-cart, the two old aunties still perched backward at the rear. He heard them howling. Then they were gone. His lungs ached. The blood stopped in his veins, his eyes burned, his brain plunged faster than his stomach. The hole kept opening. Deep and narrow, lit by torches that sped past like shooting stars, red eyes twinkling along sheer rockface, down and down. He held tight to the pretty girl's hand. She was smiling. Odd, but she was smiling as she fell.

Silly, he thought. For a moment he was back at the observation tower, the night swimming all around him, and, yes, even there he was falling, his eyes sliding slick over the surfaces of things, drowsy, pinching himself, but still falling. Silly! Something came plunging by—a peculiar living object, a man—and as it descended he saw it was the old lieutenant spread out full-eagle like a sky diver. Then a flurry of falling objects: weapons and ammunition and canteens and helmets, rucksacks and grenades, all of it falling. Stink Harris sped by. Then Oscar and Eddie and Doc. Doc waved. Graceful even in full flight, Oscar fell with his arms neatly overhead like a springboard diver. Eddie yodeled as he fell, and Stink Harris cackled like a little boy. Tumbling after them, Paul Berlin watched until they'd disappeared deep into the hole.

Falling, flickering in and out, he wondered briefly what had happened to his fine march to Paris. And then the fear came. Silly, he thought.

He squeezed Sarkin Aung Wan's hand. She was smiling. "Lovely," she whispered, her eyes half-shut and moist.

Wind in his ears, falling, he felt the fear fill his stomach. He had to pee. He crossed his legs, closed his eyes, but the pressure swelled and then came the wet leaking feeling. He wanted to giggle.

"Lovely," murmured the girl falling beside him. Her lips were parted. She was licking her upper teeth. "Isn't it lovely? I knew you'd find a way! I knew it!"

He couldn't control himself. Brain neatly divided, wet all over, arms and legs flailing as if jerked by strings, down and down he sailed.

He hit softly.

Mercifully, the roar in his ears ended. Succeeded by silence. Succeeded by the sound of someone laughing. It was an eerie, echoing sound. He sat up, shivering and hugging himself, looking for the source of the laughter.

Oscar Johnson struck a match.

It was a narrow tunnel with walls of hard red stone. Giggling bounced off the walls, high crazy giggling.

"It's okay," Doc whispered. "Quiet down, man. It's over now."

But Paul Berlin couldn't stop giggling. Like when Billy Boy took it, dead of fright. He couldn't stop.

"Easy," Doc purred, taking his arm. "Grab hold now. Up we go."

But he couldn't stop.

"Easy," Doc said. "Ease up. Nobody ever said there wouldn't be pitfalls along the way."

It was a tunnel complex lighted by torches every fifty meters, an interlocking series of passageways that they followed single file, taking great care to watch for bats and punjis and booby traps. Stink Harris led the way. Next came the old lieutenant. Then Oscar and Eddie and Doc Peret. Paul Berlin brought up the rear, holding tight to the girl's hand. The buffalo and slat-cart and two old women were gone.

The tunnel curved, widened, and emptied into a large lighted chamber.

Along the far wall, his back to them, sat a small man dressed in a green uniform and sandals, a pith hat on his head. He was peering into a giant chrome periscope mounted on a console equipped with meters and dials and blinking lights. The man hadn't noticed them.

Motioning for silence, the lieutenant crept across the chamber and leveled his rifle against the man's neck.

"Move," the lieutenant growled, "and it's auld lang syne."

But the man moved. Swiveling on his stool, he smiled and reached out with his right hand.

"Welcome," he said. "It is a pleasure you dropped in."

His name, he said, was Li Van Hgoc—just Van was fine—a major, 48th Vietcong Battalion. Standing, the man came just barely to the lieutenant's shoulder. His skin was sallow and he squinted when he smiled. The squinting produced wrinkles around his eyes.

Bowing, ignoring the leveled weapon, the man led them into an adjoining chamber where candles lit a large banquet table filled with pots of rice and meats and fish and fresh fruit.

"So," Li Van Hgoc smiled. He poured brandy from an amber decanter. "So now we shall talk of the war, yes?"

* * *

84

Again there was a falling feeling, a slipping, and again Paul Berlin had an incomplete sense of being high in the tower by the sea. It was a queazy feeling, a movement of consciousness in and out.

He had never seen the living enemy. He had seen Cacciato's shot-dead VC boy. He had seen what bombing could do. He had seen the dead. But never had he seen the living enemy. And he had never seen the tunnels. Once he might have: He might have won the Silver Star for valor, but instead Bernie Lynn went down, and Bernie Lynn won the Silver Star. He had never seen the enemy or the tunnels, or the Silver Star, but he might have.

Drowsy now, and yet still excited, he felt himself falling. The fear was gone.

How, he asked Li Van Hgoc, did they hide themselves? How did they maintain such quiet? Where did they sleep, how did they melt into the land? Who were they? What motivated them—ideology, history, tradition, religion, politics, fear, discipline? What were the secrets of Quang Ngai? Why did the earth glow red? Was there meaning in the way the night seemed to move? Illusion or truth? How did they wiggle through wire? Could they fly, could they pass through rock like ghosts? Was it true they didn't value human life? Did their women really carry razor blades in their vaginas, booby traps for dumb GIs? Where did they bury their dead? Which of all the villages were VC, and which were not, and why were all the villes filled with old women and kids? Where were the men? Did he have inside information on the battle at Singh In in the mountains? Had he been there? Did he see what happened to Frenchie Tucker? Was he present when Billy Boy Watkins expired of fright on the field of battle? Did he know anything about the time of silence along the Song Tra Bong? Was it really a Psy-Ops operations? Which trails were mined and which were safe? Where was the water poisoned? Why was the land so scary—the criss-crossed paddies, the tunnels and burial mounds, thick hedges and poverty and fear?

"The land," Li Van Hgoc murmured.

And sipping his brandy, the officer smiled.

"The soldier is but the representative of the land. The land is your true enemy." He paused. "There is an ancient ideo-graph—the word *Xa*. It means—" He looked to Sarkin Aung Wan for help.

"Community," she said. "It means community, and soil, and home."

"Yes," nodded Li Van Hgoc. "Yes, but it also has other mean-ings: earth and sky and even sacredness. *Xa*, it has many im-plications. But at heart it means that a man's spirit is in the land, where his ancestors rest and where the rice grows. The land is your enemy."

Stink Harris was snoring. The lieutenant and Oscar and Eddie and Doc Peret had moved to a row of cots, where they slept with their boots on.

"So the land mines—"

"The land defending itself."

"The tunnels."

"Obvious, isn't it?"

"The hedges and paddies."

"Yes," the officer said. "The land's own slough. More brandy?"

With Sarkin Aung Wan's help, they spent many hours dis-cussing the face of Quang Ngai, whose features told of the personality, but whose personality was untelling. The under-ground, the smiling man said, was the literal summary of the land, and of mysteries contained in it; a statement of greater truth could not be made. *Xa Hoi*, the party, had its vision in *Xa*, the land. The land is the enemy.

"Does the leopard hide?" asked Li Van Hgoc. "Or is it hid-den by nature? Is it hiding or is it hidden?"

86

And later, while the others slept their endless sleep, Li Van Hgoc led him on a tour of his tunnels.

Chamber to chamber they went, exploring the war's underground. Bats nested in beams like pigeons in a hayloft; the walls were lined with tapestries and mosaics of tile and stone; among winding roots and tubers were the makings of an army: kegs of powder and coils of fuse and crates of munitions.

The chambers were linked by narrow passageways, one to the next, and at last they returned to the operations center.

Smiling, Li Van Hgoc led him up to the chrome console.

"Wait," he said.

The little man pushed a series of buttons. The periscope whined and began to rise. When it clicked into position, he pulled up a stool and motioned for Paul Berlin to look.

"What is it?"

"Ah," said Li Van Hgoc. "You don't know?"

Peering into the viewing lens, squinting to see better, Paul Berlin couldn't be sure. Several men appeared to be grouped around the mouth of a tunnel. The forms were fuzzy. Some of them were talking, others silent. One man was on his hands and knees, leaning part way down into the hole.

"What?" Paul Berlin said. "I can't—"

"Look closer. Concentrate."

14
Upon Almost Winning the Silver Star

THEY HEARD THE SHOT that got Frenchie Tucker, just as Bernie Lynn, a minute later, heard the shot that got himself.

"Somebody's got to go down," said First Lieutenant Sidney Martin, nearly as new to the war as Paul Berlin.

But that was later, too. First they waited. They waited on the chance that Frenchie might come out. Stink and Oscar and Pederson and Vaught and Cacciato waited at the mouth of the tunnel. The others moved off to form a perimeter.

"This here's what happens," Oscar muttered. "When you search the fuckers 'stead of just blowing them and movin' on, this here's the final result."

"It's a war," said Sidney Martin.

"Is it really?"

"It is. Shut up and listen."

"A war!" Oscar Johnson said. "The man says we're in a war. You believe that?"

"That's what I tell my folks in letters," Eddie said.

"A war!"

They'd all heard the shot. They'd watched Frenchie go

down, a big hairy guy who was scheduled to take the next chopper to the rear to have his blood pressure checked, a big guy who liked talking politics, a great big guy, so he'd been forced to go slowly, wiggling in bit by bit.

"Not me," he'd said. "No way you get me down there. Not Frenchie Tucker."

"You," said Sidney Martin.

"Bullshit," Frenchie said. "I'll get stuck."

"Stuck like a pig," said Stink Harris, and some of the men murmured.

Oscar looked at Sidney Martin. "You want it done," he said, "then do it yourself. Think how good you'll feel afterward. Self-improvement an' all that. A swell fuckin feeling."

But the young lieutenant shook his head. He gazed at Frenchie Tucker and told him it was a matter of going down or getting himself court-martialed. One or the other. So Frenchie swore and took off his pack and boots and socks and helmet, stacked them neatly on a boulder, cussing, taking time, complaining how this would screw up his blood pressure.

They watched him go down. A great big cussing guy who had to wiggle his way in. Then they heard the shot.

They waited a long while. Sidney Martin found a flashlight and leaned down into the hole and looked.

And then he said, "Somebody's got to go down."

The men filed away. Bernie Lynn, who stood near the lip of the tunnel, looked aside and mumbled to himself.

"Somebody," the new lieutenant said. "Right now."

Stink Harris shrugged. "Maybe Frenchie's okay. Give him time, you can't never tell."

Pederson and Vaught agreed. The feeling of hope caught on, and they told one another it would be all right, Frenchie could take care of himself. Stink said it didn't sound like an AK, anyway. "No crack," he said. "That wasn't no AK."

"Somebody," the lieutenant said. "Somebody's got to."

No one moved.

"Now. Right now."

Stink turned and walked quickly to the perimeter and took off his helmet, threw it down hard and sat on it. He lit a cigarette. Eddie and Vaught joined him. They all lit cigarettes. Doc Peret opened his medic's pouch and began examining the contents, as if doing inventory, and Pederson and Buff and Rudy Chassler slipped off into the hedges.

"Look," Sidney Martin said. He was tall. Acne scars covered his chin. "I didn't invent this sorry business. But we got a man down there and somebody's got to fetch him. Now."

Stink made a hooting noise. "Send down the gremlin."

"Who?"

"The gremlin. Send Cacciato down."

Oscar looked at Cacciato, who smiled broadly and began removing his pack.

"Not him," Oscar said.

"Somebody. Make up your mind."

Paul Berlin stood alone. He felt the walls tight against him. He was careful not to look at anyone.

Bernie Lynn swore violently. He dropped his gear where he stood, just let it fall, and he entered the tunnel headfirst. "Fuck it," he kept saying, "fuck it." Bernie had once poured insecticide into Frenchie's canteen. "Fuck it," he kept saying, going down.

His feet were still showing when he was shot. The feet thrashed like a swimmer's feet. Doc and Oscar grabbed hold and yanked him out. The feet were still clean, it happened that fast. He swore and went down headfirst and then was shot a half inch below the throat; they pulled him out by the feet. Not even time to sweat. The dirt fell dry off his arms. His eyes were open. "Holy Moses," he said.

15
Tunneling Toward Paris

"SO YOU SEE," SAID Li Van Hgoc as he brought down the periscope and locked it with a silver key, "things may be viewed from many angles. From down below, or from inside out, you often discover entirely new understandings."

Bowing once, the officer escorted Paul Berlin into a brightly lighted chamber made up to resemble a patio at midmorning. Birds chirped and butterflies fluttered above wrought-iron tables. The others were there having breakfast.

Afterward Li Van Hgoc escorted the lieutenant through his deep fortress, beaming, answering questions about military matters, shop talk, explaining the functions of various dials and buttons and blinking lights on his chrome console. Corson was impressed. The two officers got along splendidly.

When the tour was over they took chairs in the sitting room. The lieutenant accepted a cigar.

"So," the old man sighed. He let the word linger. "So this is how the other half lives. Very enlightening."

The two men talked for a time, mostly of military matters, then the lieutenant glanced at his watch and carefully cleared his throat.

There was a pause.

"Yes, it's a nifty setup you got here," Lieutenant Corson said. "A real sweet BOQ." Again he looked at his watch. "But I hate to say it's time we were moving on. Miles to go and all that."

"You can't stay longer?"

The lieutenant shook his head. "Afraid not. Honest, I wish we had a week to—you know—to compare notes. But it's time we hit the dusty trail."

"Nicely said."

Corson nodded. "So maybe you'll show us the door? Point the way and we'll be off."

Li Van Hgoc still smiled, but he seemed troubled. "Difficult," he said. "It is not an easy thing."

"No?"

"I fear not. You see, there is a certain problem."

"I'm listening," the lieutenant said.

Li Van Hgoc removed his pith hat, rubbed his scalp a moment, then placed the hat back on his head.

"A very sticky problem," he repeated, groping for the right words. He gazed at the ceiling fan as if searching for something just out of sight. "You see . . . you see, according to the rules, I fear you gentlemen are now my prisoners. You see the problem? Prisoners of war."

Quiet fell in the room. Sarkin Aung Wan, her gunmetal legs tucked up on the sofa, stopped clipping her fingernails. Eddie made a light gasping sound. Stink Harris rose partly out of his chair then sank back again. Paul Berlin felt himself reaching for his weapon.

"I see," the lieutenant said thoughtfully. "Yes, I think I see."

He tapped his teeth with his index finger. The quiet returned. Bashfully, Li Van Hgoc studied his own hands.

"Yes," the lieutenant finally sighed. "Now I'm beginning to see the stopper. I think I see it. POWs, you say?"

Li Van Hgoc bowed.

"And . . . and I suppose the rules can't be stretched?"

"Not easily."

"Of course."

The little man smiled. "Elastic rules are a poor man's tools."

Paul Berlin had the odd feeling of breathing at the very top of his lungs, short little breaths that left him dizzy. One moment happily on the road to Paris, then buried back where it started, a prisoner of war. He was conscious of a clock ticking. A sense of compression and heat.

"POWs? Is that basically it? You're saying we're POWs?"

"I fear so."

Absently, as if playing with beads, the lieutenant fingered the safety catch on his weapon. He flicked it back and forth in rhythm with the ticking clock.

"Of course," Corson said gently, "we do have you outmanned."

"Of course," nodded Li Van Hgoc.

"Outmanned, not to mention outgunned."

"Again, sir, that is a clear piece in the overall puzzle."

"Outmanned, outgunned, and outtechnologized." Lieutenant Corson tapped his forefinger against the weapon's plastic stock.

"Well spoken," the enemy said. "A neat summary of the issues. *Very* well spoken."

The lieutenant tried hard to smile. "No summary," he said. "Just the facts." Getting up, he yawned and snuffed out the cigar. He motioned for Stink and Oscar to saddle up.

"Ah! Then you have found an answer?" Li Van Hgoc beamed. He looked genuinely relieved. "Our difficulty has been solved?"

"A piece of cake."

"Marvelous! Honestly, I cannot tell you how happy it makes me. Please, what is the solution to our puzzle?"

"This," the lieutenant said softly.

Li Van Hgoc frowned. "I must be mistaken. That appears to be a rifle."

"No kidding?" The lieutenant looked down at the leveled weapon. "By God, you're *right*. That's exactly what it seems to be." He waved at Stink Harris. "Tie the little bastard up."

"What?"

"Tie him."

"With what?"

"His shoelaces, for Christ sake. Who cares what? Just tie him."

"He's got sandals. I can't—"

"Tie him!"

So while Li Van Hgoc shook his head in a sad smile, Stink used strips of curtain to secure the little man's feet and hands and arms.

Moving quickly, they spread out through the underground chambers. The routine was familiar. They broke up into teams. Eddie and Oscar set charges in the supply arsenal. Doc Peret and Paul Berlin destroyed the generating and electrical systems. And the lieutenant, showing new energy and command, took personal charge of dismantling the huge control console and operations center. Tied to his chair, Li Van Hgoc looked on with an odd smile. He did not protest until the lieutenant went to work on the prized periscope.

"Please," he said. "As one officer to another, I ask that you desist."

"Cork it."

"Violence will not—" The man flinched as the lieutenant thrust his bayonet through the viewing lens. Bits of glass sprinkled to the floor. "Please! The puzzle, it cannot be solved this way."

The lieutenant ignored him. Unscrewing the lens mechanism, he pushed his rifle up into the sleek machine and pulled the trigger six times.

Li Van Hgoc shuddered. "Don't you see? This only makes more pieces. Each thing broken makes the puzzle more difficult. I urge you to cease."

"Cut it."

"Please!"

"I said to cut it." The lieutenant pulled up a chair and looked the man in the eyes. "No more mumbo jumbo. I only wanna hear one thing. The sound of a dink giving directions. Now how do we get out of here?"

"It's not—"

"How? Speakie straight."

Li Van Hgoc slumped against the bindings. The pith hat was cocked far back on his head.

He sighed.

"If I knew," he said wearily, "would I be here? Am I crazy?"

"Speak clear."

The little officer wiggled his head until the pith hat settled straight, then he squinted to clear his vision.

"The puzzle," he said, "is not yours alone. The simple answer is this: I don't know."

"Waste him," Stink said.

"I *don't* know."

"Feed him to the worms. A Chinese cookie."

"I *don't.*" Suddenly the man sagged. His smile was gone. He was sobbing. His pith hat fell to the floor and spun like a top. The man's hair was white.

"Victor Charles," Stink said scornfully. "There he is, the famous Charlie."

The man wept. He shivered against his bindings. The weeping came in gasps, as snow breaks from cliffs.

"Take a long look," Stink said. "The famous Victor Charles."

The lieutenant poured brandy and held it to the man's lips, gently patting his shoulder. Spittle dribbled down Li Van Hgoc's chin.

Later, Li Van Hgoc managed to tell his story.

Though he looked fifty, he was in fact only twenty-eight. Born in Haiphong, raised in Hanoi. A good family, the best party credentials. On top of it, he had been a brilliant student, a wizard in electronics. His future held promise without limit. Then war came. He was drafted. It happened like that, he said

—a notice in the mail. Frantic phone calls, visits to Lao Dong headquarters, letters from teachers and commendations from his priest and family doctor and headmaster. None of it worked. He was inducted, pushed through training, and seven months later he was given orders to travel south.

"A whole future destroyed," Li Van Hgoc murmured, looking at the lieutenant with moist eyes. "Ruined by a war I never cared about, never even *thought* about. Ruined."

The man took a deep breath. He blinked and looked at each of them. His eyes finally settled on Paul Berlin.

"So," he said slowly, "I decided to resist. I . . . well, I ran. Imagine it! Confused, angry, frustrated. How do I describe the emotions? But, yes, I ran. For a time I lived with friends in a hamlet outside Hanoi. Then I simply wandered about the countryside, living as a beggar. Hiding, skulking. Eventually, of course, I was captured. The trial lasted eight minutes. Guilty . . . guilty on all counts." Li Van Hgoc made an encompassing gesture with his head, a kind of rolling motion. "This was my sentence. Condemned to the tunnels. Ten years. And here I am."

There was a short silence. The man's eyes dropped.

Then Stink Harris grinned. "A deserter," he said. "A fuckin sissy!"

The lieutenant waved for silence.

"Look," he said softly. "That's a touching tale. Real sad. But it doesn't get us out of here. So I'll ask it again: Which way out?"

The small officer managed a bitter smile.

"Don't you see? Don't you see that's the whole *point?* No way out. That is the puzzle. We are prisoners, all of us. POWs."

"Stick him," Stink said. "Cut the miserable runt."

But Li Van Hgoc seemed in a trance. "Ten years," he murmured. "Ten terrible years." The man's lip trembled. "Ten years! An earthworm's existence. Snakes and maggots and bats, rats and moles, lizards in my bed. How do I describe it? Terrifying? Insane? A prison with no exit . . . a maze, tunnels leading

96

to more tunnels, passages emptying in passages, dead ends and byways and forks and twists and turns, darkness everywhere. Buried in this vast stinking . . . How do I tell it? Filth! Ten years, and for what? What?"

Again he was weeping. When finally the man gained control of himself, the lieutenant renewed the questioning. He was gentle. Patting the small man's arm, he urged him to talk about means of escape. But Li Van Hgoc shook his head. No way, he said. He'd tried. For the first year it was all he'd done—crawling through the tunnels, looking for light, searching for hatchways or doors or ventilation holes. Hopeless. A maze without end. He was resigned now to wait out his ten years.

"Give up?" Lieutenant Corson said. "Quit?"

Li Van Hgoc shrugged. "Accept it. The land cannot be beaten. Here, at least, I have some small comforts. A few livable chambers in hell."

The lieutenant examined his own hands. He kept turning them, studying first the palms, then the knuckles, then the fingernails. His mouth was formed in a loose frown, as though puzzled by something. The only sound was made by the slowly spinning ceiling fan.

Stink Harris had stopped grinning. Nervous, he began pacing, scratching at the ringworm on his scalp. Eddie and Doc and Oscar were silent. It was the sudden feeling of disaster. Not quite disaster—hopelessness. A caught feeling. The walls seemed closer now, tight; the air had a stale smell that hadn't been there before.

The land, Paul Berlin kept thinking. A prisoner of war, caught by the land.

No one spoke.

Again there was the sound of a clock ticking in another room.

Sarkin Aung Wan uncurled her legs and stood up.

"There is a way," she said.

The lieutenant kept studying his hands. The fingers trembled.

"The way in is the way out."

Li Van Hgoc laughed but the girl ignored it.

"The way in," she repeated, "is the way out. To flee *Xa* one must join it. To go home one must become a refugee."

"Riddles!" Li Van Hgoc spat. "Insane!"

Sarkin Aung Wan took Paul Berlin's hand. "Do you see?" she said. "You do need me."

The small officer swayed against his bindings. "The broad is mad! No exits, no light." He flicked his head to one side. "Out there . . . out there it is a stinking hell. Filth you can't imagine! You would be lost in an instant. Lost forever! Accept it—we are prisoners, all of us."

But Sarkin Aung Wan led Paul Berlin to a doorway.

"The way in is the way out," she murmured. "We have fallen into a hole. Now we must fall out."

"Fall out?" said the lieutenant.

"As easily as we fell in."

The lieutenant paused a moment, still studying his hands. Then he shrugged. He pushed himself up and motioned for the others to get ready.

"She prattles like a madman!" Li Van Hgoc cried. "Mystic nonsense! I warn you again, out there you will perish without hope. Lost forever. Accept it!"

But the lieutenant waved at them to saddle up, and they slowly put on their packs, picked up the weapons, adjusted their helmets. There was no more talk. Eddie and Oscar tied up sacks of rice and dried fish and candy. Doc helped the old man into his rucksack. Then, when they were ready, the lieutenant untied Li Van Hgoc.

"You're free to join us," he said. "Chieu Hoi?"

The man's face filled with terror. He grabbed an iron post.

"Never," he whispered. "Execute me, shoot me dead, but I won't step into that beastly hell. *Never.*" His voice shivered. "The land cannot be beaten. Accept it."

The lieutenant hesitated. He rubbed his eyes, then glanced

at Sarkin Aung Wan. She smiled. Moving across the chamber, she took the old man's hand and led him out the door.

Eddie followed. Then Doc, then Oscar, then Stink, then Paul Berlin.

"Accept it!" a voice called after them. But already they were lost in the immense dark. They had fallen out.

Down and down. Or up and up, it was impossible to know. Sarkin Aung Wan led them single file through the black tunnels. Bats fluttered in the dark. Rodents, snakes, cobwebs stretching like curtains. The stench of death. Strange creatures underfoot, the blindness of graves. They walked hand in hand. When the passages narrowed, they crawled. Like sappers, Paul Berlin thought—on hands and knees, on their bellies. At times the heat was unbearable. A molten, hissing heat that scorched his lungs. Then the cold would come. They would hug themselves, stamp their feet, stiffen their backs. Then heat again. Then cold. But Sarkin Aung Wan led them on with the sureness that comes of knowledge. She moved swiftly. When their spirits flagged, she smiled and urged them on. Hours? Days? They slept in shifts, someone awake at all times to shoo off the rats. A maze, Paul Berlin kept thinking. Lost, condemned. He wondered what had gone wrong.

16
Pickup Games

THEY MOVED THROUGH THE villages along the muddy Song Tra Bong. They cordoned the villages and searched them and sometimes burned them down. They never saw the living enemy. On the odd-numbered afternoons they took sniper fire. On the even-numbered nights they were mortared. There was a rhythm in it. They knew when to be alert. They knew when it was safe to rest, when to send out patrols and when not to. There was certainty and regularity to the war, and this alone was something to hold on to.

Then, in the first week of July, it ended.

There was nothing. The odd-numbered afternoons were hot and still. The even-numbered nights were quiet.

They relaxed. Frenchie Tucker and Rudy Chassler played endless word games on the march, Oscar found time to mend his hammock, Paul Berlin composed letters to his mother and father: things were fine, he wrote, a nice quiet time with no casualties and no noise, nothing but a river fat with dragonflies and leeches and a million kinds of bugs. A good time. Times were divided into good times and bad times, and this, he told his parents, was clearly among the good times. He saved the letters, tucking them away as he wrote them, and when a resupply chopper arrived on the eighth day of July, he quickly addressed the envelope and handed it to the starboard doorgunner. In return the young gunner tossed out a Spalding Wear-Ever basketball.

So in the hottest part of the afternoon, in a tiny hamlet called Thap Ro, they chose up teams according to squads. Eddie Lazzutti ripped the bottom out of a woman's wicker grain basket, shinnied up a tree, attached it with wire and slid down. No backboard, he said, but what the hell—it was still a war, wasn't it?

With Eddie as captain the Third Squad won handily. They beat Rudy's team 52 to 30, then came back to whip the Second Squad 60 to 12.

They played until dusk. Afterward, leaving Thap Ro and marching up to a sandy hill that overlooked the river, the talk was of rematches and revenge. They spread out on the hill, dug their holes, then sat down to wait for night. Things were very still. The mountains to the west gave off their red glow. The river below was solid and unmoving.

"The real trick," Doc Peret was saying softly to Eddie, "is deception. It's true in all your sports—con the other side into thinking one thing, expecting one thing, then, pow, you zap 'em with just the opposite. Basic psychology."

Eddie nodded. He leaned forward and began diagramming a play in the mound of dirt piled in front of his hole. When he was finished, Doc studied it for a time, frowning, then used his thumb to redraw some of the X's and O's.

"There, see what I mean?" Doc grinned. "They'll be looking for you or me to take the shot. That's what they'll be *expecting*. So we take advantage of that—make 'em overcommit, then, pow, you shovel the ball off to ol' Cacciato." Doc giggled at this. "See what I mean? Who'd expect *Cacciato*?"

The night passed slowly. They were not mortared. In the morning they continued the march east along the river. There were no signs of the enemy and the day was hot and empty.

101

Later that afternoon they tried out Doc's new play. Eddie took the ball at center court, dribbled off to his left as if preparing for a quick jumper. Rudy's team snatched at the bait. They sagged off to the left, every one of them, leaving Cacciato wide open under the basket. Eddie stopped, faked once, pivoted, then made the pass. Cacciato caught it easily. He smiled, turned, shot, and missed.

"Anyhow," Doc said afterward, "the principle was sound. You can't bitch about the basic theory."

Over the next week, as they made their way east along the river, they carried the basketball through fourteen villages that led down the Song Tra Bong toward the sea. The villages were the same and the routine was the same. They destroyed rice caches, blew tunnels, then played basketball until dark. Harlem Globe Trotters, Eddie kept saying. He got a bang out of it—Harlem Globe Trotters bring their traveling show to Bic Kinh Mi, Suc Ran, My Khe 3, Pinkville. Goodwill ambassadors to the World, Eddie said.

And the lull continued.

Paul Berlin was the first to feel uneasy. He couldn't quite place it. A milky film clouding the hot days. Lapping motions at night. Artificiality, a sense of imposed peace. A wrongness.

He didn't understand it but he felt it. He wondered how it would end, and the wondering made him nervous.

Still, there was always basketball. Games were won and lost, mostly won, and he found himself looking forward it. He liked reciting the final scores: 50 to 46; 68 to 40; once, in My Khe 2, a lopsided 110 to 38. He liked the clarity of it. He liked knowing who won, and by how much, and he liked being a winner. So with Eddie and Doc and Oscar Johnson, he spent time diagramming new plays, figuring strategy, diagnosing weaknesses and devising ways to correct them. At night he sometimes found himself replaying whole games in his head. He dreamed of fast breaks. The ball spinning endlessly through the night around the rim of Eddie's wicker basket. The game in the balance. Balls falling home with soft swishing sounds in his sleep, jumpers and hooks and dunks. He dreamed of stadiums and sleeping crowds. He dreamed once that his father was out there in the bleachers: a rooted-for dream, boosted by an old man who built houses. He dreamed of bad angles and crazy bounces, suspense, victory and loss, blocked shots at the buzzer.

The Third Squad kept winning. In Tan Mau they whipped Rudy's team 56 to 16; in Ro Son Shei, with a few women and kids on the sidelines, they blew out the Second Squad 83 to 50.

It went that way through July 12. On July 13, in a hamlet called Nuoc Ti, they were rained out.

"I smell something," Buff said. He was looking out at the river, a big guy with sweat on his face. The river was silvery in the rain. "Something weird . . . bad. You smell it?"

Doc shrugged. "You win some, you lose some."

"You don't smell it?"

They huddled together in a small mud hootch on the outskirts of the ville. The place was deserted. No people and no chickens and no dogs. It was emptiness, but it was lived-in emptiness, emptiness recently vacated, and this made them fidgety. It was an odd-numbered day.

"That fucking smell," Buff murmured. "I don't like it."

"You win some, you lose some."

"I guess."

"And some get rained out."

They waited through the afternoon. Oscar Johnson rigged up his hammock. Bernie Lynn tossed cards into his helmet. Vaught and Harold Murphy and Buff and some others played poker for pennies, squabbling over the rules, and Sidney Martin sat alone with his maps. In a corner of the hootch, Cacciato practiced his dribbling.

"Psy-Ops," Doc Peret mumbled. Nobody looked up. "That's what it is, the gook version of Psy-Ops. Slope Psych."

"Stuff it," Oscar said from his hammock. "I don' need that shit today."

Doc smiled. "I'm just explaining the concept. It's basic psychology—silence. Gets you feeling edgy, and then *bang!* But the trick is to—"

"The trick," Oscar said, "is to shut up."

"Psychology."

"Whatever. Jesus! Somebody tell Cacciato to stop bouncin' that fuckin *ball.*"

When dark had set in solidly, Sidney Martin sent them out to form a perimeter around the hootch. Paul Berlin found a notch in one of the high hedgerows. He squatted and tested the field of vision, then sat back. Cold already, he thought. Funny how in the hottest place on earth, hell itself, there was still such cold. Funny . . . he cradled his rifle close. He let his mind ease away and soon he was rehearsing plays: a pick-and-roll; slick feigns; clearing out for Doc; shovel passes and flea-flickers and fall-away jumpers. But he couldn't concentrate. His knees ached. He lay back. He thought about the difference between good times and bad times, and how funny it was that he could not state the difference, only feel it.

In the morning the sky cleared. The rain ended and by noon the ground was hard. The men were tense, and the afternoon game was full of stupid errors; afterward there was no hand slapping or razzing or bragging, and Sidney Martin immediately had them pack up for the march east.

The lull continued.

The days were the same. The grass turned brown. The paddies, bone dry even after rain, stretched out in great flat sheets to the horizon, and at the horizon there was only the certainty of more flatness, everything the same. The men complained. The heat, the stillness, Sidney Martin. Once, when Martin ordered them to search a small bunker complex, Stink Harris and Vaught began making pig noises, softly at first, then louder, and others joined in. It wasn't exactly mutiny, not quite, but it was close. The men walked away. After a time the lieutenant shrugged, threw off his pack and went down into the bunker himself. They waited quietly. No one cared much for Sidney Martin—too fastidious, too skinny, hair too blond and fine. The way he kept pushing. A believer in mission, a believer in searching tunnels and bunkers. Too disciplined. Too clear-headed for such a lousy war.

Over the next week they destroyed twelve tunnels. They killed a water buffalo. They burned rice and shot chickens and scattered jugs of grain. They trampled paddies. Tore up fences. Dumped dirt into wells, diverted ditches, provoked madness. But they could not drive the enemy into showing himself, and the silence was exhausting.

The men bickered and fought. Caution became skittishness. Irritability became outright meanness, then worse. They walked with their heads down, stiffly, thinking of land mines and trickery and ambush. Sluggish and edgy. Slow to rise from rest breaks, fitful sleep, quick to anger, wound up tight. Doc Peret catalogued the symptoms. Psychosomatic, he said when Harold Murphy's face puffed up in a rash of boils and open ulcers. Rudy's back began hurting. Stink Harris complained of numbness in his fingers and feet. Even Doc felt it. He kept saying it was all simple Psy-Ops, advanced behavior modification, but even so he popped Darvon and smoked too much and began walking near the rear of the column. His theories turned disjointed.

"What we have here," Doc said at the start of the fourth week of the peace, "is your basic vacuum. Follow me? A vacuum. Like in emptiness, suction. Can't have order in a vacuum. For order you got to have substance, matériel. So here we are . . . nothing to order, no substance. Aimless, that's what it is: a bunch of kids trying to pin the tail on the Asian donkey. But no fuckin tail. No fuckin donkey."

The morning was bright with white light seeming to rise from the earth itself. Doc lay on his stomach, looking listlessly out across a brown paddy that ended at the river. Beyond the river was more paddy.

"A vacuum. No substance, no conceptual matériel. Follow me? Bad logistics. We're getting short-changed on conceptual supplies. And, mark me, armies rise and fall on the packhorses.

105

When the supply channels fail . . . it happened for the Krauts in Russia. Kept stretching their supply lines till they snapped, crackled, popped—poof, down the Siberian drain. Got to have conceptual matériel, right?"

Paul Berlin nodded.

"It's the truth. Ask Napoleon. You can't win wars on a shortage of matériel. Can't win in a vacuum. You end up like Bonaparte, drifting in the drifts."

Sidney Martin kept pushing. Inland through My Khe 1 and 2 and 3, then south, then southeast, then straight north back to the river. The silence continued and they did not find the enemy. The afternoon games of basketball turned vicious. Cacciato lost a tooth; Harold Murphy's jungle sores popped open and bled; Ben Nystrom talked privately with Doc Peret about self-inflicted wounds: where were the best places—the hand, a foot, a finger? There were bitter quarrels over where to camp, when to rest, what to eat, whether to search the tunnels or just blow them and move on. Stink compulsively cleaned and oiled his weapon. Frenchie Tucker complained of respiratory problems, chest pains, a fluttering pulse. Vaught broke out in hives. And Paul Berlin dug deep holes for the night, working long, piling up stones and blocks of clay before the holes, carving grenade sumps and battlements out of packed mud. At night he slept in the holes, his back against the cold earth, dreaming of basketball and moles and tombs of moist air.

A bad time. In early August, Ben Nystrom collapsed and began crying. He wouldn't stop. He lay face-up on the trail and cradled his head and cried. He was limp. Doc helped him up and led him by the arm, but Nystrom could not stop crying.

And later, after a fierce afternoon of basketball, Stink and Bernie Lynn began fighting.

No words were spoken. They were simply fighting. Tangled together and falling, wrapped around each other. No one moved to stop it. Stink clawed at Bernie's face with fingernails and thumbs. Bernie fought with fists and elbows. They fought to hurt. They did not speak. Stink went at Bernie's eyes, and

Bernie's face bled, and Stink raked the bleeding parts. A slab of skin dangled free and Stink tore it away. They fought to cause pain. It was not a fight of strategy or quickness. Stink bit into Bernie's scalp, shaking hair in his teeth, and Bernie kept using his fists and elbows. Clawing and gouging and hitting. The men watched without moving. Stink pressed his thumb deep into Bernie's ear, and Bernie hammered at the gap between Stink's legs. Bernie's face was red. A flap of skin lay open and Stink kept clawing at the flesh. It ended that way.

But the lull did not end.

On August 12 they made laager along a narrow stretch of the Song Tra Bong. Across the river was the village called Trinh Son 2. And in the morning, Lieutenant Sidney Martin said, they would cross the river and enter the ville and search it. He looked directly at Oscar Johnson. If tunnels were found, he said, they would be searched. He said this plainly and without drama. The men looked away.

"Is it understood?" the young lieutenant said. "If we find tunnels, we'll search them thoroughly, by the book, and we'll do it right. I hope it's understood."

"Lovely," said Oscar Johnson.

"I just hope it's clear."

"Like the sun," Oscar murmured. "Like the man in the moon."

Full night came slowly.

The men ate supper and then dug their holes and waited. Unwilling to face the village directly, they would now and then glance across quickly, obliquely, watching without really watching. There was nothing much to see: the tops of a few thatched roofs, the deep hedges, a narrow clay trail that wound down to the river in shadow.

The talk was soft. Buff said he'd seen the place before, months ago. Bad business, he said, grim. A bad place. Stink Harris laughed. Big guy's spooked, Stink said, but Rudy Chassler shook his head and said maybe it was smart to be spooked, and Murphy nodded.

Oscar spat. He looked across at the lieutenant, who sat near the river with his maps. "And the man. The man says we gon' search the tunnels. You hear that?"

"I heard."

"The man. Some brave man."

Oscar absently removed a grenade from his belt and tossed it from hand to hand as though testing its weight.

"Diggin' hisself trouble," he said. "That's all I say, the man diggin' hisself some deep fuckin trouble."

"Tell it."

"I tol' it."

"Jesus!"

"Is that—?"

"Cacciato!" Eddie hollered, too loud. "Stop bouncing that damn ball!"

Cacciato smiled. He went to his hole, dropped the ball in, then climbed in himself. Later he began whistling.

"Trouble with a T," Oscar said softly. He still played with the grenade, rubbing it the way pitchers do when they get a new ball. "The man *wants* trouble."

They watched the river and smoked. Dead dragonflies drifted toward the sea. Live dragonflies and fishflies and other insects swarmed just over the face of the water.

"Listen to that quiet, man."

"I'm listening."

At the border of night, when the river turned a final shiny rose color, a dog came from the village to drink. It waded in to its belly. When full dark came, the dog limped back up the trail into the trees.

Paul Berlin did not sleep. He didn't try. He sat with his back to the river, deep in his hole, glad to have water behind him. Sure, the silence was scary, but even so he could not imagine dying beside a river. In thick forest, maybe, or on the slope of a mountain, or in one of the paddies. But not beside a river.

He tried for stillness. He counted aloud, passing time. He listened to the river. He tried to distinguish, as his father could,

108

the river sounds from those of the moving grass and trees. Darkness grew on itself. Well after midnight a warm fog groveled down the river, a great softness that drenched and covered him.

He dreamed of basketball.

When he awoke he heard Cacciato in the next hole over, bouncing the ball. After a time the bouncing stopped and again there was quiet.

Crouching deeper into a corner of his hole, Paul Berlin bowed his head and closed his eyes and listened hard. But there was nothing. Not the wind or the grass, not even the river now.

A bad place, Buff had said. Bad place, bad time. He tried not to think about it, which started him thinking. In the morning they would cross the river and enter the ville and search it, that was what Sidney Martin said, and . . . and still the quiet. The nerveless quiet. It was in his head now. Silence that wasn't silence. And in the morning they would cross the river and enter the ville and . . . He thought about basketball. Winning, that was the sweetest part. The moves and fakes and tactics were all fine, but winning was what made him warm. Warm where the silence hurt, that was where the winning felt so good. Right there, the same place exactly. Bad places and good places. Winning—you knew the score, you knew what it would take to win, to come from behind, you knew exactly. The odds could be figured. Winning was the purpose, nothing else. A basket to shoot at, a target, and sometimes you scored and sometimes you didn't, but you had a true thing to aim at, you always knew, and you could count on the numbers. And in the morning . . .

The fog rose.

The quiet was in his head now. It was swollen there, pushing out. It was all in his head.

Morning came and the men climbed from their holes, had breakfast, rolled up their ponchos.

Buff kept shaking his head. Stink Harris grinned, and Cacciato packed away the basketball, and Frenchie Tucker complained about his blood pressure. Paul Berlin felt it in his head.

They doused the breakfast fires.

When the gear was packed, Lieutenant Sidney Martin raised a hand and led them across the river. The water was warm. It warmed the legs and belly.

Then they were out of the water, regrouping, moving up the clay path into Trinh Son 2. Paul Berlin's head roared with quiet. Splitting—but he moved into the dark village. When Rudy Chassler hit the mine, the noise was muffled, almost fragile, but it was a relief for all of them.

17
Light
at the End
of the Tunnel
to Paris

S O, YES, SARKIN AUNG WAN led them through the westward tunnels. And then they were wading in sewage, through deepening sludge, and the tunnels gradually inclined upward, and they marched faster, pinching their noses, breathing through their mouths. The walls expanded and turned to cement, the ceilings rose. They waded past pipe terminals and pumping machinery and clogged filters, through oozing slime.

And at last they came upon a steel-runged ladder bolted to stone.

Sarkin Aung Wan led them up. They climbed fast, coming soon to an iron lid. Sarkin Aung Wan heaved up on it. There was the sound of grating iron; the manhole cover opened to show a deep night sky. They climbed out into the streets of Mandalay.

Three deft syllables trilling on the tip of his brain as he hurried after Sarkin Aung Wan. Mandalay, even the name was musical. He imagined it clearly: museums and golden statues,

hansoms drawn by white stallions in braid, white-coated wait-
ers serving spareribs, flowers and a clean soft bed.

Mandalay, he thought, and almost said.

They walked fast along a dirt road that wound through city
smells, past rows of mud shanties that soon gave way to concrete tenements. No people yet, but all the signs. Cats and
chickens battling in alleyways, gutters wet with matted trash,
a faint hum, the sound of traffic. The road was lined with
palmyra and toddy palms. Dogs roamed everywhere: lean and
hungry dogs rummaging through garbage, chewing their tails,
howling.

"Detroit," Oscar whispered. "Leave it to Cacciato. He'll
take a body home."

They passed through an arcade that opened into a market
square. The place was deserted. They crossed the bazaar and
turned down a cobbled street winding past shops fronted by
steel slide-guards. Paul Berlin kept hearing a hum. He couldn't
place it but he knew it. No single name, no single sound. A
hum.

The streets widened. The garbage smells turned to spice
smells. The humming sound suddenly exploded, and he knew
its name.

The street became a wide boulevard.

Yellow gas lamps. Fountains spraying colored water. Children romping on trimmed grass, old men on park benches and
lovers hand in hand, women pushing baby carriages, people
lingering, people chatting and laughing, bikes and Hondas and
carts and buses and donkeys, date trees in neat rows, hedges
trimmed and cut square.

"Civilization," Paul Berlin said.

The trolley rattled toward center city. Crowded with Bur-
mese and their dogs and children and chickens, no handholds,
the car lurched and jiggled and pressed them together. Sealed
windows, blinking lights, no air conditioning. Paul Berlin could
not stop smiling. He smiled and watched old women fanning

112

themselves with bits of cardboard, men singing, men cheering and shaking hands, men drinking rice wine from goatskins. The trolley rounded a curve into the bright city, jerked to a stop, doors sweeping open, fresh city air, honking horns and traffic and motion. Outside the night was silky under a huge red moon.

They were directed to the Hotel Minneapolis.

"Not the Hilton," Oscar grumbled. "The Hotel Minneapolis."

It was a teetering three-story clapboard building, leaning leeward, locked and dark. Oscar hammered until the doors were opened by a woman in leather sandals and a greasy brown robe and a moustache. The woman led them in. "Cheap-cheap," she said. "Number-One cheap-cheap hotel." A dozen children sat naked on the stairs and desk and floors. One, a brave little boy, touched Oscar's weapon. Then he touched Oscar's hand. Oscar knelt, and the boy touched his face. "Nigger," Oscar said. The boy lit up. "Nigger!" said the boy. The other children giggled, and the woman shushed them. She lit candles and beckoned the lieutenant to follow. Her face was bubbly with carbuncles. "Number One," she said, and led them up the stairs and down a winding corridor to their rooms. "Hotel Minneapolis, Number-One sleepy."

"Tan and strong," Sarkin Aung Wan purred from somewhere below his knees. The sound was brittle—snap, snap. "In Paris we shall walk everywhere. Shan't we? Oh, yes, we shall be tan and strong and walk everywhere. We shall learn the city like home, learn everything there is to learn."

"Everything," he said.

"And . . . and, oh, we shall visit monuments and hold hands and watch the Paris lights, and then walk to the river, walk to all the lovely shops and . . . and perhaps you will buy me something pretty." She stopped. "Wouldn't you buy me something pretty?"

"Everything," he said.

His feet tickled. Even as a kid he'd hated to have his feet touched.

The room was warm and the bed was soft. He couldn't get over it—the softness of things. He squirmed. She was holding the big toe on his left foot, pinching it to raise the nail, locking in the clippers, then—snap, snap. Her hair lay like seaweed on his legs. Everything so soft.

She worked patiently. Her lips were parted and her tongue would sometimes snake out to moisten them.

"Spec Four—?" she said.

He lay still. It was odd, the way she kept calling him Spec Four.

"Spec Four, are you awake?"

He moved his toes.

"Spec Four, how long . . . how long must we stay in this place? Before leaving again for Paris?"

He pretended to think about it as she used the blade end of the clipper to clean his toenails. Quiet and cushioned and warm, everything soft.

"Spec Four—?"

"I don't know," he said. "As long as it takes."

"For what?"

"To do the job. To look for Cacciato. However long it takes."

She stopped scraping.

When she spoke her voice was wistful.

"Is it necessary?"

"What?"

"To—you know—to pursue him so vigorously. Is it necessary?"

He shrugged. "Not necessary, I guess. But it's the mission. Missions are missions, you can't back away. We're still soldiers."

"And what happens if you find him? If you catch him? What happens then?"

"Back to reality," he said. "If we catch him, then it's back to the realms of reality."

114

Sarkin Aung Wan moved. It was a light, backing-away move-ment.

"And what about Paris?" she said. Her voice was very soft. "What about the bistros and adventures and beautiful gar-dens? Have you forgotten the gardens?"

"No," he said, "I haven't forgotten." He tried to smile. "Paris is still a possibility. It is. It's still a live possibility."

But she was moving away now. The long hair slithered over his shins. He watched as she went to the window, her back to him. A blinking blue-and-yellow neon sign lit the room. She was sobbing. So he pushed up and went to her. Mind over matter, he thought, and, awkwardly, letting his hands circle her belly and down, down, nose in her hair, he made amends and promises: Paris was still possible, Cacciato was too slippery to be caught, don't worry; insane promises strung on a ribbon winding toward Paris, where he'd buy her those pretty win-dowed things, take her to lunch at sunny cafés, stroll with her through the Tuileries, take a cab to Versailles, to Nice, to Mar-seilles to watch poppy products going to sea on sailing ships, all this. Paris was still possible, he whispered, still fully accessi-ble. It could be done. It could still be done, and might be done: amends and promises. She smiled. She hugged him. Then back to the bed, where she resumed chipping away at the war, using the clipper blade to scrape caked filth from beneath the nails, rubbing him with alcohol. Then to the tub again for a rinsing. Later they almost made love.

In the morning they began the search. With Sarkin Aung Wan on his arm, Paul Berlin went route step through Man-dalay, moving along bazaar fronts where men squatted to smoke their pipes, where women haggled with hawkers ped-dling fruits and colored silks and jewelry. Like practice for Paris. Practice for all the good things to come. Things sparkled. No helmet crushing his skull, no rucksack or armored vest, no grenades or flares or weaponry, and he went lightly through the streets. Everything was clean and fresh. On the Street of

False Confessions, Sarkin Aung Wan helped him pick out new clothes and a pair of hiking boots; on the Street of Sweet Pines she threw bread to the pigeons. They followed the Irrawaddy until they came upon a traveling zoo, where the girl made faces at the peafowl and geese and apes and pythons. She held his hand. She touched him privately, laughed, pointed at old men in their funny hats and baggy pants. He felt happy. There was order in the streets. There was harmony, there was color, there was concord and human commerce and the ordinary pleasantries. So following the river with Sarkin Aung Wan, walking now and not marching, Paul Berlin paid attention to detail. He saw sunlight that lasted until dusk. He saw grain unloaded from small river junks. He saw a monkey dancing at the end of a leather leash. He saw the river darken, the sky turning pink, the city beginning to light itself. And he believed what he saw.

18

Prayers
on the Road
to Paris

AGAIN THAT EVENING they searched. They ate fried fish at a high rooftop restaurant, the whole city lighted below, potted palms tinkling with wind chimes. Then they searched.

But first Eddie asked, "What exactly do we look for?"

Shaved, dressed in blue jeans and a striped T-shirt, Eddie looked thoroughly American, his black hair combed up slick and shiny. "I mean," he said, pausing while a waiter uncorked wine, "I mean, it's a huge place. We got to have a plan, don't we?"

Doc sipped the wine and pronounced it suitable. The waiter shuffled into the darkness beyond the potted palms.

"See my point?" Eddie said. "What's the mission order? Is this a straight recon job, a patrol, an ambush? What?"

"None of the above," said Oscar Johnson. He wore a silk shirt, the top two buttons open. In his lap was a large felt hat. He held up two fingers. "You want to find Cacciato? Okay, so then you got to concentrate on basics." He wagged the first finger. "Number one, you go where the booze is." He wagged the second finger. "Number two, you seek out womanhood.

117

Booze and broads, dig it? That's where you'll find Cacciato. No different than any other red-blooded Joe—booze an' bimbos."

Eddie puckered his eyebrows. "I don't know. That don't sound much like Cacciato."

"You doubting me?"

"No, man," Eddie said. "I'm just saying it don't strike a right note."

"The basics. Focus on the basic commodities."

"But he don't drink."

Oscar shrugged.

"And, look," Eddie said. "I doubt the guy knows women from french fries."

"French fries," Stink Harris sighed. "Geez, what I'd give for some."

The waiter appeared with seven thimble-sized glasses of orange liquid. Doc Peret rose, lifted his glass, called for quiet.

"A toast," he said. "To peace and domestic tranquillity. To companionship and good memories. To Eddie and Oscar and Stink Harris. To Harold Murphy, who deserted us. To all the memories, may they rest in peace."

They drank, and the waiter refilled the glasses, and Doc toasted the old days, the times of trouble, the bad times. Then he proposed a toast to the lieutenant. "To a man with twenty-five solid years of service. A man now leading his men on a mission of the greatest daring. And . . . and to the lovely young refugee, and to Oscar Johnson, and to Pederson and Buff and Billy Boy Watkins. To all those fuckers."

"To Cacciato," Paul Berlin said.

Doc shrugged. "Why not? Sure . . . to Cacciato."

They finished the toasts and paid the bill.

"One last question," Eddie said. "What if we find him? What then?"

The men were quiet. They looked at one another, then finally at the old lieutenant. He sat stiffly. Dark spots carved at the cheekbones. His eyes, which in the old days had always glowed bright blue, were now as dull and dry as two stones.

"What then, sir?" Eddie asked. "What if we find the dude?"

Lieutenant Corson made a vague, dismissive gesture with his hand.

Then they began the search.

It became a routine. Roaming the powdered streets until midnight, then back to the Hotel Minneapolis for sleep, then searching through the hot afternoons.

For Paul Berlin, it was a puzzle. Where would Cacciato have hung his big hat? What was he after? What drove him away and what kept him going, and which way, and for how long, and why? Paul Berlin searched for detail. With Sarkin Aung Wan beside him, he searched the tea shops and taverns and a hundred flophouses, tested the restaurants, played the horses under floodlights at a track outside the city. Violet evenings were the best time. He liked watching night flow down from the Shan Plateau, the purply shades growing on one another. He liked moving through crowds, the street-corner talk, the hum of traffic. Yes, the search was for detail. What, in all that passed, was Cacciato interested in, and what would have drawn him here? He searched for clues. He remembered Cacciato fishing in World's Greatest Lake Country. He remembered how the kid used to carry a tattered photo album at the bottom of his pack. The album was covered by gray plastic. On the front cover, in red, it said VUES OF VIETNAM. And inside, arranged in strict chronological order, were more than a hundred pictures that somehow stuck better to memory than Cacciato himself. On the first page, like a preface, the kid stood with four solemn people identified below as MY FAMILY. Posed before an aluminum Christmas tree. A gray-faced father, a worried man. A salesman of some sort, or maybe an actuary. Twin sisters, both pretty. A pretty mother, too, slim and hipless and well dressed, dressed for XMAS EVE, printed below the snapshot in red ink. Deeper into the album were pictures of a stucco house with yellow trim, a blunt-nosed 1956 Olds, a cat curled in someone's lap, Cacciato smiling and shoveling snow, Cacciato with his head shaved white, Cacciato in fatigues, Cacciato home on leave, Cacciato and Vaught posing with machine guns, Cacciato and Billy Boy, Cacciato and Oscar, Cacciato squatting beside the corpse of a shot-dead VC in green pajamas, Cacciato holding up the dead boy's head by a shock of brilliant black hair, Cacciato smiling.

But who was he? Tender-complected, plump, large slanted eyes and flesh like paste. The images were fuzzy. Paul Berlin remembered separate things that refused to blend together. Whistling on ambush. Always chewing gum. The smiling. Fat, slow, going bald, young. Rapt, willing to do the hard stuff. And dumb. Dumb as milk. A case of gross tomfoolery.

Then he spotted Cacciato.

"That's him," he said. A bit of pastry clogged his throat. He looked again, swallowed—"That's him!"

Sarkin Aung Wan smiled. An outdoor café along the Street of Jewels, a calm violet evening. "That's who?"

"Him." Paul Berlin pointed. "Right there. That's him."

The girl turned, looked about in a puzzled sort of way, then smiled again. Cacciato passed directly behind her. Six feet away. She could have touched with a cane.

"Where?"

"There. Right *there.*"

She turned again and squinted and shook her head.

"There!"

He was dressed as a monk. A long brown robe gave him the look of Friar Tuck, the same round-faced piety. His hands were folded. He was smiling. Four other monks surrounded him like disciples, all dressed in the same tattered robes, all bald, all smiling Cacciato's vacuous smile.

Without hurry, they moved off into the dark.

"Him?" Sarkin Aung Wan said.

"No. That one. In the middle—*that* one."

"That one?"

"Jesus, no. *That* one. The dumb one."

Already Cacciato was nearly out of sight.

Quickly, Paul Berlin paid the bill, took the girl's hand, and hurried off in pursuit. They followed the street until it emptied into a large open park.

Sarkin Aung Wan stopped.

"Cao Dai," she whispered.

"What?"

"Most sacred. Cao Dai—the evening prayers." She pointed toward a crowd of monks gathered at the center of the park. Cacciato was just now joining the throng.

"Which one?" Sarkin Aung Wan said.

It was impossible to spot Cacciato in the growing herd. Another group of monks filed in from the east, several bearing lighted candles protected by glass. When the candles had been placed on a stone altar, and after a tramcar rattled by, the monks stopped milling and began to sway in rhythm, chanting softly in the violet evening.

More monks joined the crowd, hundreds of them now, and more coming, and the chanting grew fuller and deeper.

"I'm going after him," Paul Berlin said. "Now, before—"

"No!"

Sarkin Aung Wan reached out but already he was moving.

He paused at the edge of the gathering. For an instant he caught a glimpse of Cacciato, or what might have been Cacciato. He took a breath, ducked his head and plunged in.

There were thousands now. A mob. Bald skulls and empty smiles swaying under a calm seamless sky.

He pushed toward the center of the crowd. Smells of incense, pressure, the deep chanting, a rocking sensation. He pressed forward, using his elbows, but the crowd seemed to pin him down. He heard muttering and snarls. Then a flurry of shouts. Someone snatched him by the arm, tugging, and the shouting grew louder, the swaying ceased; he was being smothered. He twisted hard but two monks had him by the waist. Another grabbed him by the knees. As he fell, in the moment before disaster, he saw Cacciato's round face before him like a lighted jack-o'-lantern.

He couldn't breathe. He tried, but he couldn't.

He felt himself sinking. Vaguely, through a rush in his ears, he heard them shrieking.

His lungs burned. A dream: caught in an avalanche. They were all over him. He struggled, but it was hopeless. A monk with gleaming green eyes was screaming and bending his arm double. Two others bounced on his chest. He couldn't breathe. He kept trying, forcing it, but nothing came. Weight and incense and body sweat, pressure he'd never known before, a drowning feeling. Smothered, he thought. A dream crushed to death in Mandalay.

When he came awake the park was deserted.

Sarkin Aung Wan bent over him, gently licking his forehead. "Alive," he whispered.

He sat up, touched himself. His left arm wouldn't straighten. His lungs were full of cement.

"I'm alive."

She kept licking his forehead. In the dark he could see peonies in full bloom, a sky of amethyst, a single candle burning on a park bench. The monks were gone.

"What happened?" He tried to stand. "What was it?"

Sarkin Aung Wan stroked his face. "I tried to—"

"Tell me what happened." He got to his knees. He still couldn't straighten the arm.

"Such a hero," she said. "A brave hero disturbing Cao Dai. Disrupting evening prayer. Touching the untouchables. I tried to warn you, Spec Four, but, no, such a hero." Shaking her head, she bent down to lick his forehead. "Such a brave Spec Four."

He touched himself again. His ribs ached.

Then he felt the fear. He sat back in the grass. A fine evening in Mandalay. He sat for a long time, letting the girl lick his wounds, and when the fear had passed, and the humiliation, he felt the first anger.

He got up, brushed himself off.

"Which way?"

"What?"

"Cacciato. Which way did he go?"

It was real anger. It was Stink's kind of anger, killing anger.

Sarkin Aung Wan stood back and gazed at him. Her earrings gave off a soft glow. She sighed. Turning, she pointed to a large dark structure beyond the park.

"That way," she said gently. "He ran that way."

Paul Berlin rubbed his eyes. It was a huge building. Stone and cement and steel. Taxis lined a long driveway leading to the front entrance.

"What is it?"

Sarkin Aung Wan smiled. "The way to Paris," she said. "The railway station."

19
The Observation Post

THREE O'CLOCK, AND EDDIE'S homemade Jolly Roger fluttered at half-mast, blown now by a stiffening sea breeze. Amazing, how the nights turned cold. You could bake all day, fry, but then at night when you wanted heat you could never find it. Even the petty things never seemed quite right.

He found his poncho liner, wrapped himself in it, then lit another cigarette. The war had taught him to smoke. One of the lasting lessons.

Three o'clock, the darkest time. Two more hours till the first easterly pink. He decided not to rouse Stink for the next watch —tonight there would be no changing of the guard.

He moved to the north wall. The coast of the Batangan was a jagged silhouette that curved away until it swallowed itself. The moon was behind clouds. This was the dangerous time. He'd heard stories of how OPs were attacked: always during the darkest hours, whole squads blown away, men found days later without heads or arms. He tried to forget it. The trick was to concentrate on better things. The trek to Paris. All the things seen and felt, all the happy things. Average things.

Peace and quiet. It was all he'd ever wanted. Just to live a normal life, to live to an old age. To see Paris, and then to return home to live in a normal house in a normal town in a time of normalcy. Nothing grand, nothing spectacular. A modest niche. Maybe follow his father into the building business, or go back to school, or meet a pretty girl and get married and have children. Years later he could look back and tell them about the war. Wasn't that normal? To tell a few war stories—Billy Boy and Pederson, the bad time in lake country, the tunnels. And how one day Cacciato walked away, and how they followed him, kept going, chased him all the way to Paris.

He smiled. It would make a fine war story. Oh, there would be some skeptics. He could already hear them: What about money? Money for hotels and food and train tickets? What about passports? All the practical things—visas and clothing and immunization cards? Desertion, wasn't that what it boiled down to? Didn't it end in jail, the stockade? What about the law? Illegal entry, no documents, no military orders, no permits for all the weaponry? What about police and customs agents?

He stared inland.

Sure, there were always the skeptics. But he would explain. Carefully, point by point, he would show how these were petty details. Trivial, beside the point. Money could be earned. Or stolen or begged or borrowed. Passports could be forged, lies could be told, cops could be bribed. A million possibilities. Means could be found. That was the crucial thing: Means could always be found. If pressed he could make up the solutions—good, convincing solutions. But his imagination worked faster than that. Speed, momentum. Since means could be found, since answers were possible, his imagination went racing toward more important matters: Cacciato, the feel of the journey, what was seen along the way, what was learned, colors and motion and people and finally Paris. It could be done. Wasn't that the critical point? It could truly be done.

20
Landing Zone Bravo

THEY SAT IN TWO FACING rows. Stink Harris kept clicking his teeth. Next to him, Eddie Lazzutti moved his neck on his shoulders as if loosening up for a race. Oscar Johnson was sweating. Rudy Chassler smiled. Vaught and Cacciato were sharing a Coke, and, down the aisle, Jim Pederson sat with his eyes closed, holding his stomach with both hands. Flying scared him more than the war.

There was a long floating feeling as the Chinook fell. It dropped a hundred feet, rose, bounced, and cold air shot through the open tail section. Private First Class Paul Berlin could not understand how it could be so cold. He didn't like it. The smells were greasy and mechanical. On both sides of the ship, the door gunners sprayed down a drone of fire that blended with the chop of the rotor blades and engine, and whenever there was a slight change in the mix of sounds, the soldiers would jerk their heads and look for the source. Some of them grinned. Buff bit his nails, and Bernie Lynn coughed, but nobody said much. Mostly they watched their weapons or their boots or the eyes of the men opposite. Oscar Johnson sweated silver and Stink's teeth kept rapping together. Buff studied his right thumbnail. He would bite it, then look at it, then bite it again. Pederson, who hated noise and machines and heights, but who was otherwise a fine soldier, held tight to his stomach and pressed his thighs together. The others tried not to look at him. Cold air swept in as the ship dropped again, and Private First Class Paul Berlin hugged himself.

The door gunners squatted behind their guns and fired and fired.

They were not going down smoothly. The ship fell hard, braked, dropped again, bounced, and Paul Berlin shivered and held to the wall webbing, wondering how it could be so cold.

He tried to think better thoughts. He watched the door gunners do their steady work, hunched over their guns and swiveling and firing in long sweeping patterns, their mouths open, arms and shoulders jiggling with the rhythm, eyes dark under sunglasses and helmets. Spent shells clattered to the floor, rolling into piles as the Chinook banked and maneuvered down.

Paul Berlin rubbed himself against the cold. He watched the others. Buff was working on his left thumbnail and Bernie Lynn played with his pant leg. Pederson was curled inside himself. His eyes were closed and his tongue sometimes fluttered out to lick away sweat. Doc Peret sat next to him, and next to Doc was Buff, and next to Buff was Ben Nystrom. The lieutenant sat on the floor, leaning low and wiping dust from his rifle, his lips moving as if talking to it.

The door gunners leaned into their guns and fired and fired.

It was a bad feeling. The cold wasn't right, and Paul Berlin wondered if the others felt it too. He couldn't help watching them—all the faces composed in different ways, some calm and sure, others puzzled-looking. It was hard to tell. None of the faces told much, and the door gunners did not have faces.

The Chinook began to slide eastward, going slower now, then again it dropped sharply. Pederson's helmet popped up while his head went down, and the helmet seemed to float high a long time before falling to the floor. Pederson didn't reach for it. He kept licking his lips. It wasn't his fault or the church's fault that he feared heights; it wasn't a fault of faith.

"Four minutes," the crew chief shouted. He was a fat man in sunglasses. He moved up the aisle, rolled down the rear ramp and leaned out for a look. "Four minutes," he shouted, and held up four fingers, and then took a copy of *Newsweek* from his pocket and sat down to read.

Oscar Johnson lit up a joint.

The gunners kept firing. The Chinook trembled as the engines and blades worked harder now.

Oscar inhaled and closed his eyes and passed the joint down the row. The soldiers focused on it, watching its passage from mouth to mouth. When it reached the end of the far row, Harold Murphy got up and handed it to Vaught, and it came down the second row to Paul Berlin, who pinched the tiny roach and held it close to his lips, not touching, careful not to burn himself.

He drew the smoke deep and held it and tried to think good thoughts. He felt the Chinook falling. Pederson's face was waxy, and the cold swept in, and the gunners kept firing and firing.

The crew chief held up three fingers.

Immediately there was a new sound. The cords of exposed control wires that ran along the ceiling jerked and whined, and the ship banked hard, and Vaught started giggling. Doc Peret told him to hush up, but Vaught kept giggling, and the ship seemed to roll out from beneath them.

Working their guns left to right to left, the gunners kept firing.

"Two minutes," the crew chief shouted. Very carefully, he folded the magazine and put it in his pocket and held two fingers over his head.

The gunners leaned into their big guns, fused to them, shoulders twitching, firing with the steady sweeping motions of a machine.

The crew chief was shouting again.

128

The Chinook turned in a long banking movement, and for a moment Paul Berlin saw the outline of the mountains to the west, then the bland flatness of the paddies below. The ship steadied and the crew chief leaned out for another look. He shouted and held up both thumbs. Across the aisle the men were loading up. Oscar wiped his face and grinned. The lieutenant was still wiping his rifle, leaning close to it and whispering. Cold air shot through the hull and the gunners kept firing. Shivering, Paul Berlin patted along his chest until he found the bandolier. He pulled out a clip and shoved it into his rifle until it clicked, then he released the bolt and listened to be sure the first round entered the chamber. He just wished it weren't so cold, that was all. He didn't like the awful cold.

"Going in," the chief shouted. The fat under his chin was jiggling. "She's hot, kiddies. Everybody off fast, no dilly-dally shit."

He held up his thumbs and the men stood up and began shuffling toward the rear. They grinned and coughed and blinked. Buff balanced the machine gun on his shoulder, chewing on his cuticles now, going systematically over each finger, changing the gun to his other shoulder. It was hard to stand straight. The Chinook was bucking, and the men held to one another as they pressed toward the ramp.

"One minute," the chief shouted.

Then there were new sounds. Like dog whistles, high-pitched and sharp. Vaught was suddenly shouting, and Eddie and Stink were jumping up and down and pushing toward the rear. Harold Murphy fell. He lay there, a big guy, smiling and shaking his head, but he couldn't get up. He just lay there, shaking his head. Holes opened in the hull, then more holes, and the wind sucked through the holes, and Vaught was shouting. A long tear opened in the floor, then a corresponding tear in the ceiling above, and the wind howled in all around. Instant white light shot through the holes and exited through opposite holes. Bits of dust played in the light. There was a burning smell—metal and hot machinery and the gunners' guns. Harold Murphy was still on the floor, smiling and shaking his head and trying to get up, but he couldn't do it. He'd get to his knees, and press, and almost make it, but not quite, and he'd fall and shake his head and smile and try again. Pederson's eyes were closed. He held his stomach and sat still. He was the only one still sitting.

The gunners fired and fired. They fired at everything. They were wrapped around their guns.

"Zero-five-zero," the crew chief shouted.

Then there was more wind. The chief's magazine fell and the new wind snatched it away. "Damn!" the chief screamed.

The Chinook bucked hard, throwing the men against the walls, then a gnashing, ripping, tearing, searing noise—hot metal—then blue smoke everywhere, then a force that drove the men against the walls and pinned them there, then a fierce pressure, then new holes and new wind, and the gunners squatted behind their big guns and fired and fired and fired. Murphy was on the floor. Cacciato's empty Coke can clattered out the open tail section, where it hung for a moment then was yanked away. Pederson sat quietly. A gash opened in the ceiling, and the crew chief was screaming, and Harold Murphy kept smiling and shaking his head and trying to get up, and the gunners kept firing.

The chief's fat face was green. He pushed the men toward the ramp.

Pederson just sat there. The chief screamed at him, but Pederson was holding himself together, squeezing his stomach tight and pressing.

"Zero-one-zero," the chief screamed. "Pull that fuckin kid off! Somebody—"

The Chinook touched down softly.

The gunners kept firing. They hunched over their hot guns and fired and fired. They fired blindly and without aim.

"Out!" the chief was screaming, shoving the first soldiers down the ramp, and the gunners went mad with the firing,

firing at everything, speechless behind their guns, and the crew chief screamed and shoved.

Stink Harris went first. Then Oscar Johnson and the lieutenant and Doc Peret. They sank in the mush, but the gunners kept firing. Next came Buff, and then Eddie Lazzutti and Vaught. The paddies bubbled with the fire. Wading in the slush, falling, the men bent low and tried to run, and the gunners swayed with their firing, and the paddies were foam. Next came Harold Murphy, stumbling down, and then Ben Nystrom, and then Paul Berlin and Cacciato. The cold was gone. Now there was only the sun and the paddies and the endless firing, and Paul Berlin slipped and went down in the muck, struggled for a moment, and then lay quietly and watched as the gunners kept firing and firing, automatically, firing and firing. They would not stop. They cradled their white guns and fired and fired and fired.

The Chinook hovered, shaking, making froth in the paddies. Screaming, the crew chief dragged Pederson to the ramp and threw him out.

The gunners swung their fire in long brilliant arcs like blown rain. Pederson paused a moment, as if searching for balance in the muck, then he began wading with his eyes closed. He'd lost his helmet. Behind him, the gunners strafed the paddies, red tracers and white light, molded to their guns, part of the machinery, firing and firing, and Pederson was shot first in the legs.

But the gunners did not stop. They fired in sweeping, methodical rows. The barrels were white. Smoke hid the gunners' faces, but they kept firing, and Pederson was shot again in the legs and groin.

Slowly, calmly, he lay back in the slush.

He did not go crazy at being shot. He was calm. Holding his stomach together, he let himself sink, partly floating and partly sitting. But the gunners kept firing, and he was shot again, and this time it yanked him backward and he splashed down.

131

The big Chinook roared. It rose and turned, shaking, and began to climb. Clumps of rice bent double in the wind, and still the gunners fired, blind behind their sunglasses, bracing their guns to keep the fire smooth and level and constant. Their arms were black.

Pederson lay on his back. For a time he was rigid, holding himself, but then he relaxed.

Moving slowly, lazily, he raised his rifle.

He aimed carefully. The Chinook climbed and turned, and the gunners kept firing, but Pederson took his time, tracking and aiming without panic.

He squeezed off a single shot. The sound was different—hard and sharp and emphatic and pointed. He fired again, then again, carefully, and chunks of green plastic jumped off the Chinook's fat belly.

The gunners went berserk with their firing, and Pederson was shot again, but still he took great care, aiming and firing and tracking the climbing ship. One shot at a time, precisely and carefully. Bobbing in the slime, he tracked the Chinook and fired into its great underside. He rolled to follow the climbing machine, aiming, taking his time. Suddenly the door gunners were gone, but even without them their hot guns kept swiveling and firing, automatically, and the Chinook trembled as Pederson calmly aimed and fired into its plastic belly.

The Chinook's shadow passed right over him.

And the shadow shrank, and soon the Chinook was high and far away and gone, leaving the paddy soapy with waves and froth, but even then Paul Berlin could hear the ship's guns.

21
The
Rail Road
to Paris

TWO O'CLOCK ON A CLEAR December morning. Paul
Berlin sat up, scratched his throat, then moved to a window.

The country was the same. Huge, sunken fields of rice crept
by like sleep. There were no lights or towns. The moon hadn't
budged all night. In eight hours the Delhi Express had taken
them barely two hundred miles. The old train seemed to wob-
ble along—jerky, random motions followed by quick braking
followed by a feeling of suspension. Twice during the night
there had been long waits while the engineer and brakemen
sat outside drinking tea.

Paul Berlin sighed. For a time he gazed out the window.
Then he got up, stretched, and wandered back to where the
lieutenant was sleeping. The old man's face had the color of
bruises. He slept belly-up on the seat, legs bent. Paul Berlin
reached down and covered him with a poncho liner.

The lieutenant blinked.

"Sorry, sir. Go back to sleep."

The lieutenant nodded. "Dreaming," he whispered. "Where
. . . where we at?"

"Almost to Chittagong."

"Dreaming," Lieutenant Corson said. He didn't move. For several moments he was gone. Then again he blinked. "Chittagong?"

"A town, sir. A city. About an hour out."

"Chittagong," the old man sighed. "What's a Chittagong? What's ... I keep thinking I'll wake up and it'll all be over. You know? Poof, a bad dream. I remember once in Seoul. Time I first got busted. There was this Seabee, a great big mother named Jack Daniels. Arms like ... Jack Daniels, that was his real name. 'Who?' I say, and this big mother says, 'Jack Daniels,' real serious-like, so I ask him to prove it, and, sure enough, the dude pulls out dog tags and an ID and a flask with his name on it. Jack Daniels. A sorry bastard. But anyhow, I remember he takes me to this—you know—to this B joint. Half hour later I'm ripped, drunk like a skunk ... weird. And so's Jack Daniels. What happens? He starts this brawl, clubs and chairs, the whole thing. Thinks it's fuckin Hollywood or something. Then the MPs show up an' there I am, passed out, don't throw a single punch. Next morning I'm busted. 'What for?' I says. 'I didn't do nothin', I was sleeping like a baby.' But so what? I'm busted, right? Innocent, but I'm busted anyhow, and that's what started it. And ... and, Jesus, that's how I feel right now. Weird. That's exactly how I feel."

"Sure."

"Jack Daniels! I ever see that mother again, I'll—"

"Easy, sir. Lie back now."

Clucking softly, Paul Berlin pulled the poncho liner up to the lieutenant's chin. The train made its endless rumbling sound.

"You're a good lad, aren't you?"

"I'm swell."

"No, you are. You're a fine lad. Better than a whole pallet of Jack Daniels. Never drink that shit no more. And if I ever get hold of that ... But you're a straight-shooter, you are." Pushing himself up, the old man glanced behind him and let his voice drop to a confidential whisper. "Look, if I give you some inside poop, you think you can keep it quiet?"

"I think you should sleep, sir. Tell me in the morning."

"Bull. I trust you, kid. The others—screw 'em. You I trust." Again he looked behind him. Then he licked his lips. "We been kidnapped."

"Sir?"

"Kidnapped," the lieutenant said hoarsely. "Snatched. Bagged and nabbed, every one of us."

"I see."

"No shit, you see! It's the straight dope. We been kidnapped."

Paul Berlin couldn't help smiling.

"Any suspects, sir?"

"Not yet. Just stay alert."

"You think Cacciato—?"

"Shit." The lieutenant wagged his head scornfully. "You're dreamin' again. When you gonna stop dreamin'? Cacciato? Hell, he's small potatoes. There's bigger fish behind this thing."

For a time the old man lay quietly, rocking with the motions of the train.

"Chittagong!" He giggled and made fists. "I been a lot of places but I never been to Chittagong. Weird, isn't it? I mean . . . I been to Benning and Polk and Seoul and Hong Kong. I seen it all, but never . . . You ever see *Road to Hong Kong*?"

"Bob Hope."

"Lordy, they made movies then. Real movies." The lieutenant lay back. He laughed and then sighed. "But Chittagong? Who the hell'd ever pay to see *Road to Chittagong*? Know what I mean? Times changes, I guess. Lord, how times keep changing. Just change and change, don't they? Things never stop changing."

"I guess so."

"Chittagong!"

"Sleep tight, sir."

Corson shrugged. "Sure, kiddo, I'll play possum. But don't

135

forget: keep your eyes peeled an' when the chance comes, split. Me, too. I see a way out of this mess, pow, I'm gone. *Gone.*"

In thirty seconds the old man's breathing softened and he slept peacefully.

Kidnapped? For a moment Paul Berlin considered confessing. How it started as one thing, a happy thing, and how now it was becoming something else. No harm intended. But it was out of control. Events taking their own track.

He went up to the forward WC and locked himself in. Unbuttoning, he eased himself down onto the stool and used one hand to brace himself against the train's jerks and sways. The smell was incredible. He breathed through his mouth.

Kidnapped—the old man wasn't far wrong. Oh, he could confess, all right, but what would it bring him? Disgrace, the loss of his war buddies, the end of a budding romance, the end of everything.

He got up, buttoned his trousers, firmly pressed the toilet handle. There was a soft waterless swish.

The old man was right about Cacciato, too. A wild goose, the wrong donkey for the pinning of final responsibility. Responsibility. That was what was needed—somebody to take it as a solemn vow.

"Responsibility," he said.

He straightened his shoulders and looked into the mirror. The effect was unconvincing. "Responsibility," he said. He tried to make his voice firm. He slit his eyes, forced his lips into a straight line. "Responsibility," he said.

Then he saw it.

What else had he missed along the way? What other uncaught clues?

But this one, by chance, he did catch. It was there on the mirror, printed in pink lipstick so bright he blinked.

> Rozes are red
> Vilits are blue

Delhi is next
Then Timbucktwo

The feeling was all present tense.

Stink practiced Quick Kill in the aisle. He slammed the rifle butt to his shoulder, forced the muzzle low, fired. "Pow!" he yelped. "P-P-Pow!"

Doc Peret prepared his medic's pouch.

Eddie Lazzutti fidgeted, touching himself, licking his teeth.

Oscar Johnson worked up the battle plan. Cool and calm, Oscar had power. He had class. He had killed people. He had preserved the rules. Now he worked swiftly, drawing tactics onto a piece of yellow paper. When it was done he stood up and called for quiet and explained how it would be carried out.

"Standard search an' flush job," he said. "No frills, we do it by the numbers, understand?"

Eddie and Doc nodded. It was understood.

"Okay, then," Oscar murmured. He held up a diagram of the train. "Eddie an' me'll take the front part, Doc and Berlin take the rear. Stink stays here with the LT. That way—"

Stink wailed angrily.

"That way," Oscar finished softly, "we drive him right into Stinko's waitin' arms. Just like beatin' the bush for gobblers."

"A turkey shoot!"

"That's the plan. The trick's to do it systematic. No screwups, don' miss nothin'. If it moves, search it. If it's got a door, open it. Wiggles, pinch it. All SOP, by the numbers. Don' miss nothin'."

Then they moved out.

Through the cramped second-class coaches: kids staring with hollow eyes, babies bawling, dogs and chickens, women crouched before small fires in the aisles.

"Here it comes," Doc said. "One last time."

Paul Berlin remembered. It was the one truly shameful memory.

He avoided their eyes. They were dolls. Mechanically, he pressed through the crowded coach, checking IDs, testing for false beards and puttied noses and enemy infrastructure. Probing, sifting. Prying open baggage and kicking over jugs of rice. *Frisk 'em,* said Lieutenant Sidney Martin, and so he frisked them. Along the muddy Song Tra Bong. First the kids. Small ankles to bony shins to knees like bolts, thighs up to buttocks, avoiding the dark little eyes, along the waist and frisking upward to the shoulders and hair, then to the next kid, and then to the three old men squatting patiently beside the village well. *Sorry papa-san*—and he meant it truly, deeply, though he hadn't quite spoken it. But he meant it. Yes, he did. And he smiled at the first old man, showing how very much he meant it, then began the awkward frisking. Just a scrawny old man dressed in white shorts, nothing else, wisps of thin hair on his chin like Ho Chi Minh. *Sorry papa-san.* A caved-in chest, sores on his mouth. And hadn't the old guy smiled in return? Hadn't there been an understanding? *I don't like it either, nobody likes it, but we do what we do.* Hadn't that been the understanding? Hadn't the poor old goat smiled to fix it and seal it? So along the Song Tra Bong in August, a gorgeous day, he frisked the old man, helping him drop the white shorts for close inspection, a shriveled old guy without modesty. *Frisk him close,* Martin said. And the old coot clutched his arms as the frisking went private. Oh, yes, and then the women. *Frisk 'em all,* said Lieutenant Sidney Martin. *Make 'em smile.* So, sure, he frisked them all: one by one in a row, patting along the thighs and rumps and breasts without daring to look, not feeling but not unfeeling, no touch in his fingers. Then the babies, frisked them in their sleep, spilling out cradles at gunpoint. Cats and dogs, all frisked. The whole village was frisked. A technique called flame frisking, and then two hours later Buff floated with life after death in his big helmet.

He remembered it. It was a law of nature. A principle of human conduct.

Up the crowded aisles he went, Doc covering while he opened boxes and purses, checked beneath seats, ransacked the luggage car, searched the caboose.

Then back again, systematically, back through the third-class coaches, where whole families bawled in confusion, where chickens were loose, where women clutched infants like shields, where the trainmaster waved a huge wrench and screamed, *"Shame!"*

But they pressed forward, flushing their quarry.

"Shame!" the trainmaster thundered. Bearded, head wrapped in an oily linen turban, the man's face shined like varnish. *"Evil! Wicked!"*

Back through the second-class coaches, where the passengers cowered in their seats, where the smell of fear baked at high; then into the mail car, ripping open sealed bags, plunging bayonets into canvas sorting bins, jabbing at piled packages and cartons.

"Illegal!" the trainmaster screamed. He was dancing now, beside himself, waving his wrench like a sword. Doc wrestled it away from him, but the man kept screaming. *"Dishonor! Disgrace! Shame!"*

The passengers in the next coach seemed to sense his horror. In a wave that started at the front of the car and rolled toward the back, the women began to wail and moan, babies bawled, dogs barked, men shouted and began advancing.

Doc leveled his weapon and fired a burst into the ceiling, but the mob kept coming. He fired again, a longer burst that smashed windows and sent hot wind whipping through the coach, but still the mob advanced, led by the fierce trainmaster.

Paul Berlin countered with sympathy. He smiled. He composed himself, fixed a smile of understanding, neighborly good will. *I'm with you,* he was saying. *I don't like this either. I hate it. We do what we do.* But the crowd kept coming.

"Exit," Doc said. He grabbed Paul Berlin's arm.

And an instant before the final rush, they stepped into the next compartment, threw the door shut, locked it, and hurried back to first class.

Paul Berlin was shivering. "Savages," he whispered.

"Easy, man."

"World's crawling with madmen."

Later Oscar and Eddie came in. They looked unhappy.

"Goose eggs," Oscar said.

"Nothing?"

Oscar shrugged. "Just this." He held up a black vinyl valise with white stitching. It was Cacciato's AWOL bag. The bag was empty.

22
Who
They
Were,
or Claimed
to Be

EDDIE LAZZUTTI LOVED to sing. He sang marching songs and nursery ballads. Sometimes he sang folk songs, though he was not a radical and despised music created for a cause. Mama Cass was his favorite. "Man alive," he would say, "if I could ever sing like that . . . A new town every night, pussy on my tail and bucks in my pocket." The men in the Third Squad liked his melancholy songs best. Songs about going home, and families, and girl friends. He sang these songs with his heart. He pretended to hate classical music, but at six o'clock on Saturday evenings—which was how they knew Saturdays were Saturdays—he never missed a radio program called *The Master's Masters,* broadcast from Danang and narrated by Master Sergeant Jake Eames. When the program ended Eddie would be quiet for a time, looking out over the sweeps of land, and then he would begin to hum, and then he would sing, and the nights could sometimes be fine.

Clean and smooth like a tar runway, his forehead sloped sharply down and out. His nose was full but neither flat nor flared. An elevated chin. Ears tight against the skull, and the skull seeming to swell at the crown as if pushed out by excess pressure to form stiff protuberant veins at the temples. His sweat was silver. Black eyes and black skin, black brittle hair molded to emphasize the head's size and shape. A stiffness of neck. An aristocrat's way of turning the body to address a person or thing, a bearing signaling immense self-discipline. Sometimes seeming to dog it, but always fluid, always graceful. A faint smile, slit eyes, a vacant and almost inattentive expression in times of danger. Coldness. A distance that, whether natural or imposed, kept men from loving him, kept most from liking him. Hard and tough and cool and together . . . Oscar Johnson refused to back off from a claim that he was born and raised in center-city Detroit, where, he said, he first learned the principles of human diplomacy. He listed them in precise order—compromise, give-'n'-take, courtesy, magnanimity. "An' if you still don' get what you want," Oscar said, "then crack the sons of bitches with a sledgehammer." Diplomacy, he was fond of saying, is the art of persuasion; and war—never citing his source—is simply diplomacy continued through other means . . . He spoke of Detroit in affectionate generalities: Coonsville, MoTown, Sin City. He spoke with enthusiasm about the Lions and Tigers and Pistons, but, when pressed, he couldn't name a single modern player. Bobby Lane was still slinging passes. Yale Larry, best punter in the league. Norm Cash, a real badass bum . . . He talked of Detroit but his mail went to Bangor, Maine. The nigga from Ba-Haba, Vaught used to say. The Downeast Brother, the dude with lobster on his breath. But this left Oscar cold, no smiles and no explanations . . . True, his speech could be slurred and thick and spiked with all the grammar of modern invention, and it could turn surly with just the right inflection, dropping consonants and studding what was left with *mothers* and *dudes* and *cools* and *bads,* deep with the ghetto undercurrent of pending violence. All true. But to Paul Berlin it seemed somehow deliberate. Not an act, but not quite natural. More like a mimic absorbing too much of his own stage style. Still, it was hard to tell. With Oscar Johnson it was always hard to tell, and this gave him power.

"Cong Giao," Jim Pederson would say whenever he saw one of the villagers wearing a crucifix or carrying rosary beads. He would smile and say, *"Cong Giao, Cong Giao,"* and bow, and smile some more, and then go through his rucksack to find the pictures of Jesus Christ he carried in a brown manila folder. The pictures were supplied to him by the Church of Christ mission in El Paso, Texas. *"Cong Giao,"* he would say, finding the pictures, carefully pulling one out and inspecting it for dirt or damage, then handing it across with a deep bow. While he was not a Catholic, he considered it his duty to reinforce Christianity in any of its forms. Jim Pederson, Doc often said, had a Moral Stance. Once he stopped the Third Squad from burning down a village in Pinkville. Once he gave first aid to a dying VC woman. Once, when Billy Boy died of fright, he wrote to Billy's parents to tell them Billy Boy had been a fine man and a good companion and had often witnessed to his belief in Jesus Christ. The letter had never been answered, but this did not bother Jim Pederson.

The lewd flesh. Ringworm circling through his crew cut. Excitable, stewing with passions and depressions and petty angers, a taker of every small advantage, a believer in striking hard and fast and first. Daring when the odds looked good. Distrustful but still eager to place trust at the drop of a flattering word. Wiry and short and strong, wound up like a cuckoo clock . . . Stink Harris came from a family of seven. A brother among sisters. A mechanic, a tinker, Stink took immense pains to care for his rifle, oiling it and cleaning it and keeping it dry during the rains, sleeping curled around it like a boy with his teddy bear, always toying with the moving parts. His weapon, he said, was his best friend. So when Bernie Lynn acted kindly toward him during the first weeks of June, Stink Harris took it very seriously, even spoke to Doc about how in war a guy needs buddies, and how Bernie might make a pretty decent buddy. Wary at first, but then melting, he introduced Bernie by letter to his youngest sister, Carla, and took great pride when his new friend and his favorite sister began exchanging a daily correspondence. He viewed it solemnly. His inquiries were always discreet, hopeful. It ended on June 30, when Stink found Carla's snapshot in Bernie Lynn's wallet. Undressed, his best-loved sister faced the camera without the least embarrass-ment, high in a midair jumping jack. Stink Harris was made to be betrayed.

Widowed, Lieutenant Corson still wore his wedding band; twice busted from captain, once unfairly, he still carried the twin bars in his pocket; a lifer, he still loved the United States Army. Like Sidney Martin, he believed in mission. But unlike Sidney Martin, he did not believe in it as an intellectual imper-ative, or even as a professional standard. Mission, for Lieuten-ant Corson, was an abstract notion that took meaning in con-crete situations, and it was this that most separated him from other officers. Lieutenant Corson did not order his men into the tunnels. He simply ordered the tunnels blown, or blew them himself, and he saw no incompatibility between this and his mission as a soldier. The men loved him.

His eyes were mostly gray, but the gray was changeable. His nose was straight. His lips were thin and tight. He was tall. A chain-smoker, his teeth had a color that nearly matched the shade of his hair, and even his wire-rimmed spectacles devel-oped a smoky film. A theoretician, a pragmatist, Doc Peret believed deeply in science. But this meant many things. It meant a diagnosis of death by reason of fright, as in the case of Billy Boy Watkins, or it meant feeding M&Ms to Bernie Lynn, or it meant the rigorous verification of hypotheses by means of repeated empirical observation, which was the meaning whenever he engaged in debate with Jim Pederson or Frenchie Tucker. "The main thing," Doc once said, "is to find what works. That's real science—what works. Witchcraft, sorcery, I don't care what name you give it, if it works, it's good science." And this was enough for almost everyone in the Third Squad. While Doc rarely discussed his personal history, he once told Paul Berlin that as a kid he'd been intrigued by thunderstorms and fire and machinery. "A really curious kid," he'd said. "One day my old man brought home this new air-conditioner—one of the early models, a huge thing—and I kept looking at the damned thing, this way, that way, trying to figure out where the cold came from. You know? I mean, I was just a kid. I figured there was a little box inside where all the cold was stored up. A real dumbo. So I got out a screw-driver and started taking the thing apart. The aluminum tub-ing and the motor and stuff I didn't even know. The whole business . . . I tore out the damned guts. But no box. Couldn't find the cold. My old man, he went buggy when he saw the mess. 'You stupid so-and-so,' he says, 'there *isn't* any box. It's a machine, it *makes* the cold.' But I still didn't get it. I kept thinking there's got to be a place inside where all the cold was. Kept thinking they had to *put* the cold in there. A real dunce. My old man never did get the thing put back together. Still talks about it. And I still tell him, I say, if he'd just let me alone I'd have found that damn—"

A few names were known in full, some in part, some not at all. No one cared. Except in clearly unreasonable cases, a sol-dier was generally called by the name he preferred, or by what he called himself, and no great effort was made to disentangle Christian names from surnames from nicknames. Stink Harris was known only as Stink Harris. If he had another name, no one knew it. Frenchie Tucker was Frenchie Tucker and noth-ing else. Some men came to the war with their names, others earned them. Buff won his name out of proven strength and patience and endurance. He had no first name and no last name, unless it was to call him Water Buffalo, a formality which was rare. Doc's name was so natural it went unnoticed; no one

145

knew his first name and no one asked. What they were called was in some ways a measure of who they were, in other ways a measure of who they preferred to be. Cacciato, for example, was content to go by his family name; it was complete. Certain men carried no nicknames for the reverse of reasons that others did: because they refused them, because the nicknames did not stick, because no one cared. Other men were known only by rank. Lieutenant Corson, who came to replace Lieutenant Sidney Martin, was referred to only as the lieutenant, or as the LT. It was the way he wanted it. Some men were called by their first names, some by their last. Paul Berlin was almost always called by both names, first and last together, which suited him fine. Names brought men together, true, but they could also put vast distances between them. Ready Mix. No one ever learned his real name. Certainly no one remembered it. An Instant NCO, a pimpled kid with sergeant's stripes earned in three months of stateside schooling, Ready Mix was with them only twelve days. It was thought he would die quickly, and he did, and it was better not to know his full name. Easier to forget what happened, because, in a sense, it never did. Easier to talk about it: "Ready Mix? Cement City—gravestones."

23
Asylum on the Road to Paris

I N DELHI, IN THE TILED lobby of the Hotel Phoenix, the old
lieutenant fell madly in love.

They'd arrived at noon, changed their money, then
quickly searched the railyard before taking a cab through the
jammed lunchtime streets. It was the India that Paul Berlin
had always believed in: children running in barefoot gangs,
shrill voices, cattle browsing among bolts of cotton and madras.
An awkward embrace, want clutched close by riches, but for
Paul Berlin it was not unappealing. He wished he'd unpacked
his Instamatic.

Then, at the Hotel Phoenix, the old man fell in love.

She was behind the registration desk, riding an Exer-Bike.
Dressed in blue jeans and a gauze muslin blouse, the woman
instantly reminded Paul Berlin of his own mother. It was an
immediate thing, a total presence. Eyebrows plucked and repainted, bright carmine lipstick, streaks of auburn deftly
folded into black hair.

"Americans!" she cried.

Smiling, panting a bit, she dismounted the Exer-Bike and
signed them in.

She was breathless. "Americans!" she kept saying. Her eyes brushed over each of them before settling on the lieutenant. "Americans! Honestly, I had a *feeling* about today. A *premonition*, if you will. I honestly did. When I woke up this morning I looked outside and thought to myself, I said, today the Americans will come. Didn't I say that? Didn't I?"

She gazed at the lieutenant, who nodded and gazed back. He was in love even before dropping his rucksack.

Her name was Hamijolli Chand, which she spelled out on a postcard. Americans always called her Jolly.

That evening over cocktails she explained that she'd spent two years in Baltimore, studying hostelry under a scholarship at Johns Hopkins. The loveliest period of her entire life, she said. Memories of sailing ships, department stores and shopping malls, Fort McHenry, the Block, and Little Italy. America rang in her head like the golden bells of Masjid-i-Sulaiman.

"Corrupted," she said brightly. "That's what my husband contends—corrupted by hamburgers and french fries and Winston One Hundreds."

"You're a married lady?"

Jolly Chand nodded in a way that again reminded Paul Berlin of his mother, a way of acknowledging facts too painful for words.

Evening now, and they sat in an open courtyard tiled with mosaics of broad-winged birds on the ascent. Crickets chirped mildly in the grass beneath neem trees.

Relaxing, drinking from pewter mugs, they listened while Jolly Chand talked happily about her time in America.

"A land of genius and invention," she said. "Television, for example. You simply can't appreciate it. Television . . . it's one of those magnificent American inventions—and it *is* an American invention, I don't care what they say—an invention that, well, brings a country together."

She crossed her legs, lit a long cigarette and smiled at the lieutenant. Her eyebrows had been freshly drawn into great mobile vaults; her fingernails and lips glowed soft pink in the dusk.

"Yes," she said, "television is one of those unique products of the American genius. A means of keeping a complex country intact. Just as America begins to explode every which way, riches and opportunity and complexity, just then along comes the TV to bring it all together. Rich and poor, black and white —they share the same heroes, Matt Dillon and Paladin. In January the talk is of Superbowl. In October, baseball. Say what you will, but only Americans could so skillfully build instant bridges among the classes, bind together diversity."

The lieutenant, who had listened carefully, nodded at Doc Peret.

"That," he said gravely, "is one classy woman."

"Pass the gin," Stink said.

"Please." The lieutenant glared at him. "Pass the fuckin gin, *please.*"

Later, Jolly Chand led them into the dining room, where, as promised, the main course was blood-rare roast beef, a dish she fondly called "the sacred cow." Her husband served. He was a small man, barely half her height. When the food was served he disappeared behind a gauze curtain.

"Haques, I fear, disapproves of this." She gestured at the wine and beef. "In America—God bless it—one eats what one pleases, yes? Tradition be hanged. But here . . . here, a simple hamburger becomes a criminal offense. It's all so sad." As they began to eat, she explained how it was necessary to smuggle in beef from Ahmadabad at a hefty price and at great danger.

"A brave woman," Lieutenant Corson said. He had a habit of folding his arms when he was serious. "You're a brave, remarkable woman."

"Haques—my husband—he says I'm hopelessly corrupt."

"Yes?"

"Impure, he says. Tainted."

It was a long, extravagant meal, and Jolly Chand was charming. Over chilled herring, she questioned Doc about the future of socialized medicine, listening attentively as he discussed health-delivery systems and doctor-patient ratios, Medicare versus Medicaid. Over soup and salad, she complimented Oscar on his sunglasses and new hat, demanded to see snapshots of Stink's four sisters, listened with immense pleasure as Eddie recounted the final episodes of *The Fugitive*, clapped explosively to learn that Kimble had at last tracked down the one-armed man. Mostly, though, she concentrated on the lieutenant. Gently, using flattery as a probe, she urged him to talk about his life as a soldier, the places he'd been and things he'd seen. The old man was fast becoming drunk.

Only once, during dessert, did the woman's husband reappear. He was dressed in white, head wrapped in a turban, leggings to his knees. He stood quietly for a moment. Then without a word he turned and vanished through the gauze curtain.

The lieutenant hadn't noticed.

In Korea, he was telling Jolly Chand, ". . . In Korea, by God, the people liked us. Know what I mean? They *liked* us. Respect, that's what it was. And it was a decent war. Regular battle lines, no backstabbing crap. You won some, you lost some, but what the heck, it was a war."

He spilled some wine and stared down at it dispassionately.

"The trouble's this," he said slowly. "In Nam, you know what the real trouble is? You know? The trouble's this: Nobody likes nobody."

Slowly, shaking his head, he began wiping the spilt wine with a napkin.

"That's the trouble, all right. That's the difference. In Nam there's no respect for nothing. No heart. Nobody's got his heart in it, you know? Doves on their helmets. Faking ambushes. That's the real difference . . . no heart."

Jolly Chand touched his arm. Clucking, she led him out to the garden for brandy. The others followed.

150

The night was like felt. Olive-scented champac, crickets, neem trees and roses. Beyond the garden Paul Berlin could hear the far-off hum of traffic. They sat on wicker benches and soon a young boy brought out the brandy and glasses. They drank quietly.

Around midnight Doc went up to bed. Twenty minutes later Eddie and Stink and Oscar went inside for a game of billiards.

It was peaceful. Paul Berlin sat with his hand resting on Sarkin Aung Wan's lap. For a time he was blank, just sitting, then things began to tumble. The brandy, maybe. He sat straight until the slipping feeling subsided. He ran brandy across his teeth, letting it burn, letting the last drops evaporate in the hollow of his tongue.

"Heart," the lieutenant was mumbling. "Heart, that's one thing that shouldn't change. In Korea . . . in Korea there was heart. People liked people. Discipline and respect." He was drunk. His voice was quiet and sad. "What happened? What went wrong?"

Jolly Chand helped him up.

"Heart," the lieutenant said. "What happened to heart?"

As they left the garden the old man was sobbing.

Neither the lieutenant nor Jolly Chand came down for breakfast the next morning. It was all a little embarrassing. Sullen and tired-looking, the woman's husband served tea and bread in the small dining area overlooking the garden. He did not look up. He poured the tea, waited a moment, then slipped away.

Eddie eyed the food suspiciously. "You think it's safe?"

"Arsenic, I'd guess." Doc tested his tea, then shrugged. "But, hell, I wouldn't blame the poor guy. The LT should know better."

"Phony."

"Say again?"

"She's a phony." Oscar folded his arms. "All that crap last

night 'bout TV an' shopping malls . . . You ever hear such crap? The old man should . . . he should take some lessons in phoniness. Learn to recognize it."

"Puppy love," Eddie grinned. "It makes me tingle all over."

Afterward, while the others went out to see the city, Paul Berlin found a stuffed chair in the lobby and sat down to write postcards. It was hard to find the right words. He pictured his mother's face. *All is well,* he wrote. *Delhi is crowded and beautiful. I'm healthy. War's over and I'm heading home.* On the second card he said he'd met a girl, a young refugee, and with luck they'd be in Paris by spring.

Upstairs, Sarkin Aung Wan was still sleeping.

He found his camera, kissed her, then went out alone to mail the cards. It was still early but already the streets swirled with traffic and livestock and the smell of spices. A soft white dust seemed to cover everything.

After finding a mailbox, he wandered up through the bazaars of Chandi Chowk, stopping often to snap pictures of those things he might want to remember when it was over. Bloodstones, snake charmers, old men in their turbans and white shorts. A slide show: lights out in the living room, mom and dad in their chairs. Let the pictures explain.

He turned into a brick street that led to a younger, richer part of the city.

A residential area. Shade trees, broad green lawns, wooden shingles saying who lived where. The houses were modern and neatly painted. It was all familiar. Sundays in summer—his mother tending the garden up to her elbows, sprinklers and birdbaths and stone patios and trimmed hedges, a lawn mower buzzing in someone's backyard.

Home, he thought.

Beyond the houses was a wooded park. Beyond the park were tenements, and beyond the tenements were the shanties.

He did not go to the shanties.

It was late afternoon when he got back to the hotel. Jolly Chand and the lieutenant sat alone in the garden. He did not disturb them. At the desk was a note from Sarkin Aung Wan. It was printed in clean block letters and said: "Spec Four Darling. Went shopping for soap and creams. Others on ghastly bus tour. What ails Americans?" There were fifty rupees in the envelope.

He felt sad. He couldn't understand it.

He went to the room and showered and then lay on the bed. Home, he kept thinking. It seemed a long way off. He wondered if they would understand. It wasn't running away. Not exactly. It was more than that. He thought about his father building houses, and his mother, and the town. He thought about how young he was.

24
Calling
Home

IN AUGUST, AFTER TWO MONTHS in the bush, the platoon
returned to Chu Lai for a week's stand-down.

They swam, played mini-golf in the sand, drank and wrote
letters and slept late in the mornings. At night there were floor
shows. There was singing and stripteasing and dancing, and
afterward there was homesickness. It was neither a good time
nor a bad time. The war was all around them.

On the final day, Oscar and Eddie and Doc and Paul Berlin
hiked down to the 82nd Commo Detachment. Recently the
outfit had installed a radio-telephone hookup with the States.

"It's called MARS," said a young PFC at the reception desk.
"Stands for Military Air Radio System." He was a friendly,
deeply tanned redhead without freckles. On each wrist was a
gold watch, and the boy kept glancing at them as if to correlate
time. He seemed a little nervous.

While they waited to place their calls, the PFC explained
how the system worked. A series of radio relays fed the signal
across the Pacific to a telephone exchange in downtown
Honolulu, where it was sent by regular undersea cable to San
Francisco and from there to any telephone in America. "Real

wizardry," the boy said. "Depends a lot on the weather, but, wow, sometimes it's like talkin' to the guy next door. You'd swear you was there in the same room."

They waited nearly an hour. Relay problems, the PFC explained. He grinned and gestured at Oscar's boots. "You guys are legs, I guess. Grunts."

"I guess so," Oscar said.

The boy nodded solemnly. He started to say something but then shook his head. "Legs," he murmured.

Eddie's call went through first.

The PFC led him into a small soundproof booth and had him sit behind a console equipped with speakers and a microphone and two pairs of headsets. Paul Berlin watched through a plastic window. For a time nothing happened. Then a red light blinked on and the PFC handed Eddie one of the headsets. Eddie began rocking in his chair. He held the microphone with one hand, squeezing it, leaning slightly forward. It was hard to see his eyes.

He was in the booth a long time. When he came out his face was bright red. He sat beside Oscar. He yawned, then immediately covered his eyes, rubbed them, then stretched and blinked and lit a cigarette.

"Geez," he said softly.

Then he laughed. It was a strange, scratchy laugh. He cleared his throat and smiled and kept blinking. He pulled viciously on the cigarette.

"Geez," he said.

"What—"

Eddie giggled. "It was . . . You shoulda heard her. 'Who?' she goes. Like that—'*Who?*' Just like that."

He took out a handkerchief, blew his nose, shook his head. His eyes were shiny.

"Just like that—'*Who?*' 'Eddie,' I say, and Ma says, 'Eddie who?' and I say, 'Who do you think Eddie?' She almost passes out. Almost falls down or something. She gets this call from Nam and thinks maybe I been shot. 'Where you at?' she says, like maybe I'm callin' from Graves Registration or something, and—"

"That's great," Doc said. "That's really great, man."

"Yeah. It's—"

"Really great."

Eddie shook his head as though trying to clear stopped-up ears. He was quiet a time. Then he laughed.

"Honest, you had to hear it. 'Who?' she keeps saying. *Who?* Real clear. Like in the next . . . And Petie! He's in fuckin high school, you believe that? My brother. Can't even call him Petie no more. 'Pete,' he says. Real deep voice, just like that guy on Lawrence Welk—'Pete, not Petie,' he goes. You believe that?"

"It's terrific," Doc said. "It really is."

"And clear? Man! I could hear Ma's fuckin cuckoo clock, *that* clear."

"Technology."

"Yeah," Eddie grinned. "Real technology. It's . . . I say, 'Hey, Ma,' and what's she say? 'Who's this?' Real scared-soundin', you know? Man, I coulda just—"

"It's great, Eddie."

Doc was next, then Oscar. Both of them came out looking a little funny, not quite choked up but trying hard not to be. Very quiet at first, then laughing, then talking fast, then turning quiet again. It made Paul Berlin feel warm to watch them. Even Oscar seemed happy.

"Technology," Doc said. "You can't beat technology."

"No shit. My old man, all he could say was 'Over.' Nothin' else—'Weather's fine,' he'd say, 'Over.'" Oscar wagged his head. His father had been an RTO in Italy. "You believe that? All he says is 'Over,' and 'Roger that.' Crazy."

They would turn pensive. Then one of them would chuckle or grin.

"Pirates are out of it this year. Not a prayer, Petie says."

"I bleed."

"Yeah, but Petie . . . he goes nuts over the Pirates. It's all he knows. Thinks we're over here fightin' the Russians. The Pirates, that's *all* he knows."

"Crazy," Oscar said. He kept wagging his head. "Over an' out."

It made Paul Berlin feel good. Like buddies. Genuine war buddies, he felt close to all of them. When they laughed, he laughed.

Then the PFC tapped him on the shoulder.

He felt giddy. Everything inside the booth was painted white. Sitting down, he grinned and squeezed his fingers together. He saw Doc wave at him through the plastic window.

"Ease up," the PFC said. "Pretend it's a local call."

The boy helped him with the headset. There was a crisp clicking sound, then a long electric hum like a vacuum cleaner. He remembered how his mother always used the old Hoover on Saturdays. The smell of carpets, a fine powdery dust rising in the yellow window light. An uncluttered house. Things in their place.

He felt himself smiling. He pressed the headset tight. What day was it? Sunday, he hoped. His father liked to putz on Sundays. Putzing, he called it, which meant tinkering and dreaming and touching things with his hands, fixing them or building them or tearing them down, studying things. Putzing . . . He hoped it was Sunday. What would they be doing? What month was it? He pictured the telephone. It was there in the kitchen, to the left of the sink. It was black. Black, because his father hated pastels on his telephones . . . He imagined the ring. He remembered it clearly, both how it sounded in the kitchen and in the basement, where his father had rigged up an extra bell, much louder-sounding against the cement. He pictured the basement. He pictured the living room and den and kitchen. Pink formica on the counters and speckled pink and white walls. His father always . . .

The PFC touched his arm. "Speak real clear," he said. "And

157

after each time you talk you got to say 'Over,' it's in the regs, and the same for your loved ones. Got it?"

Paul Berlin nodded. Immediately the headphones buzzed with a different sort of sound.

He tried to think of something meaningful to say. Nothing forced: easy and natural, but still loving. Maybe start by saying he was getting along. Tell them things weren't really so bad. Then ask how his father's business was. Don't let on about being afraid. Don't make them worry—that was Doc Peret's advice. Make it sound like a vacation, talk about the swell beaches, tell them how you're getting this spectacular tan. Tell them . . . hell, tell them you're getting skin cancer from all the sun, all the booze, a Miami holiday. That was Doc's advice. Tell them . . . The PFC swiveled the microphone so that it was facing him. The boy checked his two wristwatches, smiled, whispered something. The kitchen, Paul Berlin thought. He could see it now. The old walnut dining table that his mother had inherited from an aunt in Minnesota. And the big white stove, the refrigerator, stainless-steel cabinets over the sink, the black telephone, the windows looking out on Mrs. Stone's immaculate backyard. She was nuts, that Mrs. Stone. Something to ask his father about: Was the old lady still out there in winter, using her broom to sweep away the snow, even in blizzards, sweeping and sweeping, and in the autumn was she still sweeping leaves from her yard, and in summer was she sweeping away the dandelion fuzz? Sure! He'd get his father to talk about her. Something fun and cheerful. The time old Mrs. Stone was out there in the rain, sweeping the water off her lawn as fast as it fell, all day long, sweeping it out to the gutter and then sweeping it up the street, but how the street was at a slight angle so that the rainwater kept flowing back down on her, and, Lord, how Mrs. Stone was out there until midnight, ankle-deep, trying to beat gravity with her broom. Lord, his father always said, shaking his head. Neighbors. That was one thing to talk about. And . . . and he'd ask his mother if she'd stopped smoking. There was a joke about that. She'd say, "Sure, I've stopped four times this week," which was a line she'd picked up on TV or someplace. Or she'd say, "No, but at least I'm not smoking tulips anymore, just Luckies." They'd laugh. He wouldn't let on how afraid he was; he wouldn't mention Billy Boy or Frenchie or what happened to Bernie Lynn and the others. Yes, they'd laugh, and, afterward, near the end of the conversation, maybe then he'd tell them he loved them. He couldn't remember ever telling them that, except at the bottom of letters, but this time maybe . . . The line buzzed again, then clicked, then there was the digital pause that always comes as a connection is completed, then he heard the first ring. He recognized it. Hollow, washed out by distance, but it was still the old ring. He'd heard it ten thousand times. He listened to the ring as he would listen to family voices, his father's voice and his mother's voice, older now and changed by what time does to voices, but still the same voice. He stopped thinking of things to say. He concentrated on the ringing. He saw the black phone, heard it ringing. The PFC held up a thumb but Paul Berlin barely noticed, he was smiling to the sound of the ringing.

"Tough luck," Doc said afterward.

Oscar and Eddie clapped him on the back, and the PFC shrugged and said it happened sometimes.

"What can you do?" Oscar said.

"Yeah."

"Maybe . . . Who knows? Maybe they was out takin' a drive or something. Buying groceries. The world don' stop."

25
The
Way It
Mostly
Was

THEN THEY WENT TO the mountains.

First, though, Sidney Martin said there would be no malingering. They would march fast and hard. They would
do their jobs; if a man fell out he would be left where he fell.

"Trouble," Oscar Johnson said before the choppers took
them to the foot of the mountains. "The man always looks for
more trouble. He want it? Is that the story—do the man *want*
trouble?"

Then they went to the mountains.

The road was red. It climbed the mountain at a bad angle
for the march, not winding with the mountain's natural contours but instead going straight up. For hiking or strolling it
would have been a good road. The view was magnificent, and
along the road grew many forms of tropical foliage, and everywhere it was wild country and pure. It would have been a fine
road for a botany field trip, or for a painter to paint, but it was
not such a good road for the march.

There had been no rain. The road was cracked like clay
pottery, and the grass alongside it was brittle. If the wind had
been blowing, the grass would have rustled like straw brooms

against an oak floor, but there was no wind and the afternoon was too hot even for birds. There were the sounds of the march. There were the sounds of boots against the red road, the metallic sounds of ammunition and matériel on the move, soldierly sounds. Altogether thirty-eight soldiers marched up the road, plus one native scout who was a boy of thirteen.

The thirty-eight soldiers and the boy marched with their heads down. They leaned forward against the day and the road and the side of the mountain. They were tired. Their thoughts were in their legs and feet. Some of the soldiers wore handkerchiefs tied about their necks. Several of them carried military radios with spindly aluminum antennas that bobbed and sparkled as they marched; others carried transistor radios. The strongest among them carried the machine guns, balancing the big guns on their shoulders and gripping the barrels with one hand while using the other for leverage against the grade. All of the soldiers carried fragmentation grenades and mosquito repellent and machine-gun ammunition slung in long belts over their shoulders. All of them carried canteens. Nearly all of them wore bush hats in place of helmets. Their helmets and armored vests were tied to their rucksacks, for it was late August and the battle was still far off. Straggled out along the red clay road, they formed a column that ran from the base of the mountain, where the Third Squad had just begun the ascent, to the top of the mountain, where the First Squad moved plastically along a plateau and toward the west and toward the much higher mountains where the battle was being fought. Most of the soldiers were shirtless. Those who had been longest in the war had the best tans. The most recent arrivals were pasty-skinned, burnt at the shoulder blades and clavicle and neck; their boots were not yet red with the clay, and they walked more carefully than the rest, and they looked most vulnerable; no one knew their names, for they had been hurried to the war for the battle in the mountains.

At the rear of the column, last of thirty-nine, Private First Class Paul Berlin felt the full labor of the march. He did not think of the mountains, or the coming battle, or what might happen there. He watched the road pass beneath his boots, the way the boots appeared and reappeared, the strain mostly in his hips. The road was very dry. It did not kick up dust as he climbed. Solid like summer cement. He did not want to think. The upward climb took energy from his thoughts and sent it to his legs and hips and back, and he climbed without thinking, just climbed, just kept climbing, then he was slipping. It happened first on the climb to the mountains, slipping out of himself, and, still climbing, he looked up at the summit of the small mountain, climbing but also slipping quietly out of himself, looked up to see the blond-headed lieutenant looking down.

Lieutenant Sidney Martin stood alone. His arms were folded as he watched the ascension of his men. He wore his shirt. It was dark under the armpits and at the hollow of his back, and the sleeves were rolled up over his elbows. In profile, his face was young; straight on, it was not so young. His lips moved as he counted to himself the number of soldiers still climbing. He counted to twenty-one, plus the scout.

His sergeants came to him, and they too wore their shirts. The sergeants conferred, then one of them faced west and took out the binoculars and surveyed the higher mountains where the battle would be. The sergeant with the binoculars then turned and spoke to the blond-headed lieutenant, who nodded but did not answer, then the sergeants left him and the lieutenant stood alone and watched his men climb. Once he looked west. The green of the mountains was splendid. Many shades of green, and colors not quite green but influenced by it, and the greens gave the impression, which the lieutenant knew to be false, of great coolness and removal and peace. He saw no signs of the battle. He knew he would hear the battle before he saw it, but he knew he would not hear it for many hours. He knew he must conserve the strength of his men for the fighting. He also knew he must get his men to the fighting before it ended. He had many problems to consider: whether to stay on the road, with its dangers of land mines but with its advantage of speed, or whether to move instead through the rough country, with less danger but with less speed. He had the problem of the heat. He had the problem of sending tired men into the battle. He had other problems, too, but he was a leader, working through his sergeants according to the old rules of command. That kept his sergeants happy, and it would eventually build respect for him among the men and boys. The lieutenant had been trained in common sense and military strategy. He had read Thucydides and von Clausewitz, and he considered war a means to ends, with a potential for both good and bad, but his interest was in effectiveness and not goodness. A soldier's interest is in means, not ends. So the young lieutenant prided himself on his knowledge of tactics and strategy and history, his fluency in German and Spanish, his West Point training, his ability to maximize a unit's potential. He believed in mission. He believed in men, too, but he believed in mission first. He hoped that someday the men would come to understand this; that effectiveness requires an emphasis on mission over men, and that in war it is necessary to make hard sacrifices. He hoped the men would someday understand why it was required that they search tunnels before blowing them, and why they must march to the mountains without rest. He hoped for this understanding, but he did not worry about it. He did not coddle the men or seek their friendship. And he did not try to fool them. Before starting the march, he had told them that he cared for their lives and would not squander them, but he also explained that he cared for the mission as a soldier must, otherwise every life lost is lost dumbly. He told the platoon he would not tolerate malingering on the march, even though the day was hot. "We will be soldiers," he told them, "and we will march steadily, and we will not be late for the battle. Any man who falls out will be left where he falls, even if it's sunstroke." The men hadn't cheered his speech, but this did not matter to the young lieutenant.

Standing bare-headed at the summit, Sidney Martin decided

to stay on the road. He spoke the decision as a declarative sentence, saying, "We'll stay to the road until I hear the battle," and when the decision was spoken he did not think about it again. Instead he looked up for clouds, hoping they would come to break the sun, but the sky was clear and unmoving and pure. All over, the country was baked still. The lieutenant folded his arms. He watched the remaining soldiers come up the road, counting them as they reached the top and moved off along the plateau toward the higher mountains.

On the road and still climbing, Private First Class Paul Berlin easily slipped back into himself, not losing a step. He was comfortable in his climbing, motion corresponding to the passage of time, a sense of continuity and purpose. He walked with his head down, bent forward to balance his pack an inch or so below the neck, at the top of the spine, distributing the weight evenly and high and transferring it to his legs and from his legs to the upward-going road. He did not think. Above him, he saw the blond-headed lieutenant standing with folded arms. The lieutenant's belt buckle sparkled and his lips seemed to move as if talking to himself, or as if counting, but counting what, or why? Private First Class Paul Berlin did not know. He knew the road. He knew the pull at his back, and the feel of the black rifle in his hands, and the weight of his gear, and the heat.

There were no villages along the road. It was not farming country, nor was it jungle. It was the country that connects the paddies to the jungle; poor, beautiful country. It was deep country. The grass grew thick and uncut, no wind to brush it, and the only motion was the steady marching of the thirty-eight soldiers and the scout, a boy of thirteen. He did not think. The march connected him to the road, and the climb was everything. An anatomy lesson, the feel of the tendons stretching, the muscles and fluids and gelatinous tissues moving like a machine. His body marched and his brain slept. He would climb until the machine stopped. And when the time came he would stop the way a machine stops, just stopping. He would simply stop, rest, tumble. He wiped his sweaty forehead with his sweaty forearm. When the time came, he told himself, he would stop. Slipping again . . .

The blond-headed lieutenant watched him climb. Though he did not know the soldier's name, this did not matter much, for the soldiers whose names he did not know he simply called Soldier or Trooper, whichever came to him first, and there was nothing impersonal or degrading about either word. He watched the boy's strange mechanical walk, the lazy obscurity of each step, the ploddingness, and he felt both sadness and pride. He saw the boy as a soldier. Maybe not yet a good soldier, but still a soldier. He saw him as part of a whole, as one of many soldiers pressed together by the force of mission. The lieutenant was not stupid. He knew these beliefs were unpopular. He knew that his society, and many of the men under his own command, did not share them. But he did not ask his men to share his views, only to comport themselves like soldiers. So watching Paul Berlin's dogged climb, its steadiness and persistence, the lieutenant felt great admiration for the boy, admiration and love combined. He secretly urged him on. For the sake of mission, yes, and for the welfare of the platoon. But also for the boy's own well-being, so that he might feel the imperative to join the battle and to win it.

The lieutenant did not enjoy fighting battles. Neither bloodthirsty nor bloodshy, he had not enjoyed the few battles of his career, nor the feeling that had come to his stomach when the fighting ended. But the battles had to be fought.

Watching the boy come up the road, the lieutenant felt urgency and pride, both. Though he was young, and though other officers of his age and rank often ridiculed him, the lieutenant was a serious man. Pride, for the lieutenant, was strength of will. And watching his men, watching the boy climb, the lieutenant felt proud. Though they did not know it, and never would, he loved them. Even those whose names he did not know, even Paul Berlin, who walked last in the column —he loved them all.

But he was not stupid. He knew something was wrong with his war. The absence of a common purpose. He would rather have fought his battles in France or at Hastings or Austerlitz. He would rather have fought at St. Vith. But the lieutenant knew that in war purpose is never paramount, neither purpose nor cause, and that battles are always fought among human beings, not purposes. He could not imagine dying for a purpose. Death was its own purpose, no qualification or restraint, and war was the way. He did not celebrate war. He did not believe in glory. But he recognized the enduring appeal of battle: the chance to confront death many times, as often as there were battles. Secretly the lieutenant believed that war had been invented for just that reason—so that through repetition men might try to do better, so that lessons might be savored and applied the next time, so that men might not be robbed of their own deaths. In this sense alone, Sidney Martin believed in war as a means to ends. A means of confronting ending itself, many repeated endings. He was neither stupid nor full of bravado. He was quiet. He had blue eyes and fine blond hair and strong teeth. He was a professional soldier, but unlike other professionals he believed that the overriding mission was the inner mission, the mission of every man to learn the important things about himself. He did not speak these things to other officers. He did not speak them to anyone. But he believed them. He believed that the mission to the mountains, important in itself, was even more important as a reflection of a man's personal duty to exercise his full capacities of courage and endurance and will power.

Still on the red road, now three-quarters of the way to the top, Private First Class Paul Berlin did not have the lieutenant's advantage of perspective and overview and height. Marching automatically, he had the advantages of motion and hard labor. He felt strong. He felt the muscles working in his thighs and stomach. He did not think about the mountains or the coming battle. For a time he did not think about anything —just the effortless coordination of the march. It was easy. It was not hard at all, for he was strong, and he did not think. And when the time came, when he made the decision, he would be able to stop. He would simply stop. But his legs kept climbing. He watched the road. He saw its color mottled by age and weathering. He watched the unmoving grass. He saw Stink Harris remove a belt of machine-gun ammunition and throw it into the weeds, then walk faster. He saw Cacciato using his rifle as a walking stick, muzzle down. He saw the shiny sweat like polish on the bare backs of Eddie Lazzutti and Pederson and Vaught, and the slow unfolding of events as the platoon moved up, the oddities of men close to the ground and weighted by gravity, foot soldiers with feet hardened, and the red road. Above him, he saw the blond-headed lieutenant standing alone and watching. "If we fight well," Sidney Martin had said before the march, "fewer men will be killed than if we fight poorly." Private First Class Paul Berlin had not analyzed that statement, but he knew it was both true and dangerous. He knew he would not fight well. He had no love of mission, no love strong enough to make himself fight well, and, though he wanted now to stop, he was amazed at the way his legs kept moving beneath him, climbing and climbing. Paul Berlin, who had no desire to confront death until he was old and feeble, and who believed firmly that he could not survive a true battle in the mountains, marched up the road knowing he would not fight well, knowing it certainly, but still climbing, one step then the next, climbing, seeing each thing separately, a wild flower with white blossoms, a pebble rolling, climbing, as if drawn along by some physical force, inertia or herd affinity or magnetic attraction. He marched up the road with no exercise of will, no desire and no determination, no pride, his muscles contracting and relaxing, legs swinging forward, lungs drawing and expelling, moving, climbing, but without thought and without will and without the force of purpose. He felt no drama. He felt a curious quiet. He felt he could stop climbing at any moment, whenever the time came, whenever he told himself it was time to quit. Then he decided: He would stop.

It came first as a dreamy, impossible idea, but then it became a decision, and he told himself that now was the time. He would stop. No more climbing. He decided it: He would let his knees collapse, go limp all over, topple, not even breaking the fall, just toppling and rolling to whatever spot he came to and not moving again. He decided it. He would fall. Fall out, fall down. If his eyes were open when he stopped falling, he would not close them. He would lie very still and watch the sky and then perhaps sleep, perhaps later dig out the Coke stored in his pack, drink it, then sleep again. All this was decided. But the decision did not reach his legs. The decision was made, but it did not flow down to his legs, which kept climbing the red road. Powerless and powerful, like a boulder in an avalanche, Private First Class Paul Berlin marched toward the mountains without stop or the ability to stop.

Lieutenant Sidney Martin watched him come. He admired the oxen persistence with which the last soldier in the column of thirty-nine marched, thinking that the boy represented so much good—fortitude, discipline, loyalty, self-control, courage, toughness. The greatest gift of God, thought the lieutenant in admiration of Private First Class Paul Berlin's climb, is freedom of will.

Sidney Martin, not a man of emotion, felt pride. He raised a hand to hail the boy.

But Paul Berlin had no sense of the lieutenant's sentiment. His eyes were down and he climbed the road dumbly. His steps matched his thoughts. He did not notice the heat, or the beauty of the country, or the lieutenant's raised arm. If he had noticed, he would not have understood. He was dull of mind, blunt of spirit, numb of history, and struck with wonder that he could not stop climbing the red road toward the mountains.

26
Repose
on the Road
to Paris

T HE TIME IN DELHI WAS a good time. Cacciato did not
show himself, and, except for a once-a-day stop at police
headquarters, they did not waste much time looking.
The days were hot. The evenings were warm. Eddie Lazzutti
spent the afternoons in an air-conditioned movie theater
across from the hotel. Oscar and Eddie sampled *nua dem*
houses in the new city, Doc Peret found a kiosk that sold
American magazines, and the lieutenant, whose health
seemed to be returning, spent his time with Jolly Chand, sometimes going off for day-long trips to the country, sometimes just
sitting in the Phoenix courtyard, where they talked in low
voices.

Paul Berlin passed the days with Sarkin Aung Wan. In the
mornings it often rained, and they would watch the rain from
the lobby windows, sitting quietly, then when it stopped they
would hold hands and go to the streets. Sometimes they
shopped for clothing or jewelry or special facial creams. Sometimes they visited the zoo. Often they walked just to make
themselves hungry, then they would eat, and then they would
walk again until dinner. When he was with her, having lunch

or walking or taking pictures in the old city, he did not think about the war or about Paris. He thought about the depth of the days, and the peace, and how fine it was to worry about where to stop for dinner. He felt normal. He felt fine. On the long walks Sarkin Aung Wan would talk about life in Cholon. How the district had its own special flavor, like a secret stew, and how her father's restaurant had once attracted all the important colonels and politicians. And then she would ask about Fort Dodge. Was it a true cattle town? Was it difficult to walk in spurs? He told her, no, it was mostly a corn town, but, yes, many people in Fort Dodge broke their legs and ankles trying to walk with spurs. Next to gunshot wounds, he said, it was the hospital's biggest business.

Most evenings they played cards in the lobby, then went to his room where they kissed. He pretended they made love.

They talked often of Paris. Sarkin Aung Wan wondered if together they might start a restaurant, or maybe a beautician's parlor on the Right Bank, where they would give skin care to the city's richest ladies. Her face brightened at this sort of talk, and it was then that he most liked to touch her. To put his hand on her calf and rub it to feel the smoothness of the skin and the short bristles of black hair at the spots she'd missed shaving. He liked putting the creams on her. All sorts of creams, a whole sack of them: "This one, it replenishes the facial oils," she'd say, and then explain how, after replenishing the oils, it helped close the pores to keep out bacteria. Then she'd laugh and dab some on his nose, and rub it in, and then rub more onto his chin and throat and chest and stomach, asking if he felt the replenishment, and he would say, yes, he felt greatly replenished.

He liked the evenings, and the afternoons, but the mornings were his favorite. He liked looking out at the wet streets and seeing the crowds huddled under awnings and umbrellas and newspapers. He liked waking Sarkin Aung Wan by putting his hand on her neck and then holding it there until she smiled. He liked, other times, watching her sleep like a child with the smells of creams and soap on her body, and he liked seeing her stretch and touch the corners of her eyes and do exercises on the floor.

Yes, he liked the mornings most, but he also liked the evenings. Jolly Chand served elegant dinners, always with an American staple and good wine and, afterward, plenty of brandy. One evening Doc Peret cooked hamburgers on a grill in the courtyard. Oscar made a bean salad, Stink and Eddie cut watermelon, and Jolly Chand, with great fanfare, produced a half bottle of Hunt's ketchup. She'd returned from America, she said, with forty-five bottles. This was the last. So everyone cheered her, and the lieutenant proposed several toasts, then after the picnic they sang folk songs and played charades until midnight.

But except for those occasions they saw little of the lieutenant and Jolly Chand. Doc Peret was worried. "Transferred loyalties," he said. "A case of gross overcompensation. I fear the old coot is gonna screw himself up good over this one."

Even so, the lieutenant showed signs of recovery. His skin turned tighter and more resilient, his spirits were high, and the dysentery had entirely disappeared. In Jolly Chand's presence he was subdued. Courtly, a bit awkward, he was always careful to hold the woman's chairs, to attend her empty glasses, to laugh or nod or make clicking noises in appreciation of her chatter about the wonders of America. He began taking care of himself again, dressing well and combing his hair into a neat old-fashioned part. He demanded that the men start showing the same good habits. "Garrison troops," he said loudly, for Jolly's ear, "are what make a wartime army." Twice in one evening he sent Stink upstairs to shave off the beginnings of a mousy moustache.

"A goner," Doc said one afternoon.

The lieutenant and Jolly Chand were sharing a pitcher of martinis in the garden. The woman's laughter drifted through the lobby.

"It scares me," Doc said. "I mean, look, the man's got certain obligations, right? Can't drop everything for some painted-up wench who's playing every angle in sight. Besides, it's not healthy."

Paul Berlin shrugged. "Maybe it's what the doctor ordered. If he—"

"No way." Doc winced and shook out a cigarette. "You're looking at the doctor, pal, and I never placed any such order. I tell you, it's trouble."

"You think so?"

"Trouble."

But there was nothing to do about it. The lieutenant was dazzled. One evening when Oscar said they should think about moving on, the old man giggled and took Jolly Chand's hand and led her away. He showed no interest in looking for Cacciato.

It turned into a waiting strategy. Oscar or Stink would sometimes lead a patrol out to watch the embassy or train station, and for a time they staked out the two major bus depots, but in the end there was no choice but to mark time. The momentum was gone. Restless, feeling a queer disquiet, Paul Berlin spent the days roaming the city with his camera. He liked the sense of peace, all the color and harmony, but even so he felt an urge to get back on the road. To finish things. Besides, there were times when he was struck with an odd sense of guilt. At night, playing checkers with Sarkin Aung Wan . . . pausing, everything seeming to dissolve: too quiet, too serene. A feeling of suspension. What the hell was he doing here? Why? Not guilt, exactly. A need to justify. A sense that someday soon he would be called on to explain things. Why had they left the war? What was the purpose of it? He imagined a courtroom. A judge in a powdered white wig, his own father, all the Fort Dodge townsfolk sitting in solemn-faced rows. He could hear snickers and hoots as the indictments were read. Shame, downcast eyes. He could feel himself sweating as he tried to explain that it wasn't cowardice or simple desertion. Not exactly. Partly it was Cacciato's doing. Partly it was mission, partly inertia, partly adventure, partly a way of tracing the possibilities. But it was even more than this. He couldn't put his finger on it, but he knew it had to do with a whole array of things seen and felt and learned on the way to Paris.

He was ready to move on.

Then early one morning Doc Peret showed him the newspaper.

"Cacciato," Paul Berlin said.

He held the paper up to better light. The photograph was grainy, partly blurred, but it was Cacciato's happy face.

"He's here, then. In Delhi!"

Doc shrugged. "Look closer. In the background. See there? What's that look like?"

"This?"

"Right. What is it?"

Paul Berlin studied a large dark smudge on the photograph. "It's . . . I don't know. A big machine or something."

"A locomotive," Doc said. He smiled, folded the newspaper and put it in his pocket. "That's exactly what it is: a locomotive. That picture was taken last night at the Tapier Station."

"And?"

"And the train's headed for Kabul. You can bet old Cacciato's on board." Doc smiled again. "So get packed. Haven't you always wanted to see Afghanistan?"

By noon they were ready.

Stink and Eddie carried the rucksacks down to the lobby while Oscar went out to hail a cab. The hotel was very quiet. Out in the garden, the lieutenant and Jolly Chand sat together in a wicker swing. They were drinking cognac.

"Time, sir," Doc said. He tapped his wristwatch.

The lieutenant smiled. With one foot he pushed the swing back and forth. There was a moist film on the surfaces of his eyes.

Doc glanced at Paul Berlin, then he gently touched the old man's shoulder.

"Sir? It's time—"

"No," the lieutenant said. The swing made a creaking sound. Sipping his cognac, he looked for a long time at Jolly Chand then shook his head. "All over for me. I'm officially retired."

"You don't mean it."

"Don't I?"

"No, sir, you don't." Doc stopped the swing. "Come on, now, we got twenty minutes to make the train. No more nonsense."

Lieutenant Corson laughed bitterly. "Nonsense!"

"Come on—"

"Nonsense!" The old man seemed to gag. Standing up, he refilled his glass and drank quickly. He was sweating. His face was red. "Nonsense? Chasing after some poor slob? Running away? Nonsense! I'm telling you, it's *over*. Not another step. Wasn't my war anyway."

"The war's over, sir."

"Ha!"

"It's over," Doc said, "and now we need you to lead us home."

The lieutenant waved his glass. "Cut the dumbness, Doc. Just cut it. The war's not over. We *left* the bloody war—walked away, ran. Understand that? No more crap about duty and mission. It's over."

"We need you," Doc said. "We do, we need you."

Paul Berlin nodded and tried hard to smile. He watched as the lieutenant sat on the swing and draped an arm around Jolly Chand's shoulder. She smiled meaninglessly.

Shaking his head, the lieutenant gazed into his cognac. "You need me? The way you needed Sidney Martin?"

Paul Berlin felt his eyes stinging.

"No," the lieutenant sighed, "you don't need me. Never did. Maybe I'm dumb. Behind the times. But, by God, I don't understand you guys. No heart, no respect. The whole business, I don't understand any of it. Should've retired ten years ago." He looked again at Jolly Chand. "So this is where I get off. Old soldier bids farewell."

"What about Cacciato? We can't—"

174

"Mercy."

Doc started to say something but stopped and sighed.

"That's it, sir?"

"That's it. Make your way, Rodneys. Send me a card from Paree."

They were quiet a moment. Then Doc reached out to shake hands. Paul Berlin's eyes ached. He blinked and tried to speak but couldn't.

There were no more words. The lieutenant clapped Paul Berlin's arm, held it briefly, then looked away. It was over. As they left the garden there was only the sound of the creaking swing.

Inside, Doc explained it to the others.

"A pity," he said. "A sick, sick man. A genuine pity."

Oscar Johnson shrugged. He removed his sunglasses and polished them and clipped them to his pocket. He was still grinning.

"What's the joke?"

"Wounded," Oscar said.

"What?"

"Wounded. The ol' man, he's among the walkin' wounded, right?"

Doc looked up. Then he smiled.

"Got the picture?" Oscar said. "You don' never leave your wounded behind. It ain't done."

When it was dark they slipped into the garden. Jolly Chand was gone. The lieutenant slept deeply, his head on an iron table. The cognac bottle was empty. Oscar and Eddie took the legs. Stink and Paul Berlin took the arms. Doc Peret opened doors. They loaded the old man into a cab, gave the driver fifty rupees and told him to make haste.

27
Flights
of
Imagination

I T WAS A NEWER, FASTER train. The coach was theirs alone.
They rolled out the ponchos and slept in the seats and
aisles, fine sleeping, the windows down and the fast rush
of night air and the smell of coal smoke and the feeling of
motion again, fast motion, fast through level country good for
speed, then graceful dark valleys, then climbing into higher,
colder country, into mountains, through Punjab and Peshawar
and Kabul, and beyond Kabul. The sun rose. The mountains
turned red, then white, then many colors mixed together. And
the train kept climbing.

There was snow in the mountains. Cliffs of snow. The lieutenant rubbed his eyes and gazed at the snow and shook his
head savagely.

"Where?" he kept asking. "Where the hell am I?"

The old man was wound up like a toy soldier. He threw off
the poncho, tapped out a Pall Mall, lit it, and asked again,
"Where am I?" Then he sighed. He smoked his cigarette and
stared out at the rushing plateaus, bleak windy November
country. The mountains in the distance were capped with

snow, and the snow looked permanent, and the wind was high and space-filling.

"Kidnapped," the lieutenant said. "That's where."

Flee, fly, flew, fled . . . down the high country, and up, rushing fast through snow flurries that hid the tracks. Mountains rose sharp out of the valleys, powerful old mountains that caught the snow and held it.

Flee, fly, fled, Paul Berlin thought, feeling the train's great pulling power.

It was bare, rugged country. A few goats, a camel stiff along a stone wall, rivers flowing with chunks of ice.

Like lake country, Paul Berlin thought. Like the World's Greatest Lake Country.

He did not want to think about it. High in the mountains, they had marched at last to the battle. Marching endlessly up the red road to the higher mountains, he hadn't stopped, hadn't been able to stop, and he'd gone to the battle where, as he knew beforehand, he would not fight well. And he did not. Twitching in his hidden little depression, hiding out during the one big battle of the war, he could only lie there, twitching, holding his breath in messy gobs, fingers twitching, his hands, his legs pulled around his stomach like a shell, but his legs twitching too, twitching, listening as the bombers came to bomb the mountains. For hours the bombers kept coming. The mountains burned from the bombing. Burning rock. Then Sidney Martin was up and hollering for the advance. Ready Mix was shot—Ready Mix, whose true name no one knew. They kept advancing. The mountains were taken. And in the mountains they found the dead. They found bomb craters full of the dead. The dead were tiny little men, many of them burned, and the stench was terrible. They found bunkers full of the dead. The dead knelt over their guns or lay in heaps. They spent the night among the dead, and in the morning they began counting the dead, who were countable only

177

by the heads. They stacked the dead. They counted captured weapons and crates of unexploded munitions and medical supplies. Paul Berlin could not stop the silly twitching. Then, late in the morning, it rained. The craters filled with gray water. It rained that day and the next day. On the third day, still raining, the craters were high with water, and the charred bodies of the dead bobbed to the surface, bloated now. It was then that Doc Peret named it lake country. "World's Greatest Lake Country," Doc said. They pulled out the bobbing dead and piled them up to be flown away in nets. They searched the tunnels and bunkers, because Sidney Martin ordered it, and in the bunkers they found more dead. They found canteens and the rubble of a hospital where the wounded were dead in their cots, and they found flakes of burned flesh, and orange peels, and helmets. All through the mopping-up operation the rain kept falling. "Lake Country," Doc would say, and soon it caught on, and the others began calling it Lake Country. They found more tunnels, a whole series of tunnels through deep mountain rock, and in each case Sidney Martin insisted that the tunnels be carefully searched. It was there, high in Lake Country, that Oscar Johnson began talking seriously about solutions.

Flee, fly, flown . . . down the granite country, and up, and the train carried them through central Afghanistan, where the rivers were hard and thick, where it was winter now, full winter, and the first-class coach swelled with the smells of man-made heat, dusty machine heat, and they played card games and slept and watched the strange, foreign country unfold like wings.

"Where?" asked the old lieutenant.
"Ovissil," said the town's mayor, in whose stone house they spent the night.
"*Where?*"

"Ovissil," said the mayor, laughing whenever the lieutenant or Oscar or Eddie tried to pronounce the name of the town. "With your tongue—Ovissil."

While the tracks ahead were being mended they spent the night in the mayor's warm stone house. His wife, a sturdy woman on wide hips, served mutton stew and biscuits and cups of milk. Later they watched fire dance in the huge hearth and listened to the wind. All night the storm was fierce. Snow piled high to the windows. The land was cold and frozen, but there was warmth in the mayor's house. He was a big man with moustaches drooping to his chin; his hair was black; he was a history-teller: "I speak only of history," he said, "never of the future. Fortune-telling is for lunatics and old women. History is the stronger science, for it has the virtue of certainty without the vice of blasphemy. God alone tells futures. God alone makes history."

As the blizzard wailed, the mayor of Ovissil smoked his pipe and told histories. He told his own history, and his wife's, and the lieutenant's. He told of how the lieutenant had once been an officer of high rank, a captain, and how all that had been ended because of indulgence and simple misfortune, and how God's will is always stronger than man's will. "We can live our lives," he said, "but we cannot shoo them like horses to a stable."

Later, while the others slept, Paul Berlin asked to have his history told. But the mayor smiled and shook his head. "You are young," he said. "Come to me when you have had time to make a real history for yourself. I cannot tell unmade histories."

"I'm not all that young."

The mayor squeezed Paul Berlin's arm. "Come to me in ten years. Then you shall have a history well worth telling."

They slept in ram skins.

In the morning the mayor of Ovissil led them to the train. "Travel well," he said. "Go safely and with God's blessing."

179

He presented a sack of dried lamb to the lieutenant. He kissed the old man on both cheeks and shook his hand and hugged him. There were tears in his eyes.

Then they boarded the train. Outside, in boots and a shaggy coat and cap, the mayor of Ovissil waved and smiled and cried as the train took them away.

28
The
Observation
Post

H E DID HAVE A HISTORY.
His father built houses, his mother buried strong
drink in her garden. He'd played baseball in summer.
He'd gone canoeing with his father. He'd gotten lost as an
Indian Guide in the Wisconsin woods. Sunday School and Day
Camp. A conscientious student: high marks in penmanship and
history and geography. A stickler for detail. He had thrown
rocks into the Des Moines River, pretending this would someday change its course, imagining how the rocks would accumu-
late to form new currents and twists, how large effects might
come from small causes. Pretending he might become rich and
then travel the world, pretending memories of things he had
never witnessed. A daydreamer, his teachers wrote on report
cards—standoffish and shy and withdrawn, but these would be
outgrown. In high school, Louise Wiertsma had almost been
his girl friend. He'd taken her to the movies, and afterward
they had talked meaningfully about this and that, and afterward he had pretended to kiss her. He had graduated from
high school. Enrolled at Centerville Junior College, earned
thirty-six credits, then quit. Spent a summer building houses

with his father. Strong, solid houses. Hard work, the sun, the feel of wood in his hands, a hammer, lifting and striking and waiting. Cruising up Main Street in his father's Chevy, elbow out the window, smoking and watching girls, stopping for a root beer, then home. He'd become a soldier at age twenty.

Sure, he had a history.

29
Atrocities
on the Road
to Paris

THEY TOOK ROOMS IN AN old-fashioned boardinghouse in Tehran. It was a quiet place with faded rugs and feather blankets and walls papered with pictures of donkeys and camels. The rooms were clean, and it gave the lieutenant a chance to wait out another bout with the dysentery.

There they celebrated Christmas. Doc and Eddie strung up colored lights in the parlor. Sarkin Aung Wan made candles while Stink brewed up a pot of eggnog. And on Christmas Eve, under cover of dark, they crept into the Shah's National Memorial Gardens, chopped down a fine long-needled spruce, placed it on Eddie's poncho and carried it back like a body through the city's ancient streets. They spent the night around the tree. Drinking, making awkward talk, they trimmed the spruce with medals and strings and grenades and candles. Later they tried a few carols, then smoked the last of Oscar's precious dope. It ended quietly. The lieutenant passed out on the parlor floor. Sarkin Aung Wan went up to bed. Stink and Eddie and Oscar rolled craps until dawn. No matter, Paul Berlin thought. It was a land of infidels anyway.

The old man's sickness persisted through New Year's and

into January. Lying in bed or sitting wrapped in blankets before the windows, he would spend whole days curled inside himself without eating or speaking. It had gone that way since Delhi. Shiny-eyed and freaky. Clutching himself, rocking, gazing blindly out at the frosted streets. Occasionally, as if something snapped in his memory, he would begin to chant old marching ditties, calling cadence in a voice high and hollowed out. It worried all of them.

"Brains on a half-shell," Doc said. "I've seen it before . . . fever's fried the man's potatoes."

"That bad?"

Doc shrugged. "Not good, cowboy. Scrambled eggs an' hash browns. I seen it before, believe me, but never like this, never this bad."

Paul Berlin glanced over at the old man, who sat quietly in a chair before the parlor windows. Sarkin Aung Wan was feeding him soup.

"Maybe we should call in a doctor. If it's—"

"No," Doc said. "Doctors can't cure the LT's sickness. It doesn't go away after a shot of penicillin."

"No?"

Doc shook his head, taking off his glasses and wiping them with his shirttail.

"Nostalgia—that's the basic sickness, and I never heard of a doctor who can cure it."

"Nostalgia?"

"That's right. The old man's suffering from an advanced case. Nostalgia, it comes from the Greek. I researched it: straight from the Greek. *Algos* means pain. *Nostos* means to return home. Nostalgia: the pain of returning home. And the yearning, the ache that comes from thinking about it. See my drift? The old man's basic disease is homesickness. Nostalgia for the goddamned war, the army, the lifer's life. And the dysentery, the fever, it's just a symptom of the real sickness."

"So what do we do?"

184

"Time," Doc said. He put his glasses on. "It's the only anti-dote for nostalgia. Just give the man time."

So they waited it out in Tehran, passing without momentum into a new year. They made the usual inquiries about Cacciato, checked the hotels, kept an eye on the train and bus depots. But there were no signs of Cacciato, and the weather was too cold for sight-seeing. Except for one visit to the circus and a weekend excursion into the countryside, they stayed close to the boardinghouse. The days were gray and the nights seemed endless. More and more then men talked about moving on. Even Paul Berlin, who enjoyed the peace, felt a hankering for action.

Then they were arrested.

It happened only minutes after the beheading.

A mild winter's afternoon. They bundled the lieutenant up and led him through the city's narrow streets—a constitu-tional, Doc said, a chance for the old man to fill his lungs with clean air. Then it happened. They passed through an archway into a large brick plaza where a crowd had gathered around an elevated platform. The noise was fierce. People were shov-ing forward.

Using his elbows, Stink led them toward a roped-off area just below the platform. They stopped there.

"A spectacle," Doc said. "It's one of those true spectacles of civilization."

"What?"

"A show, man. Look there."

Along the rear of the platform colorful banners and flags had been strung up like party decorations. Beneath the bunting, a dozen military officers sat in a row of heavy leather chairs. The officers wore dress uniforms with medals and braiding and insignia. Some of them smiled and waved at people in the crowd.

185

"Can't get away from it," Doc mumbled. "You try, you run like hell, but you just can't get away."

"It's the truth."

"Look at them." Doc pointed at two of the officers who were sipping sherry and smoking. "Ringside seats. We should ship them to Nam, sell tickets. Try, but you just can't get away."

The noise was tremendous. A small boy in white shorts and sandals was knocked down, disappearing for a moment in a crowd of people shoving forward for a better view. Someone called out. Then the boy was there again, standing. A woman took him by the ear and pulled him away, and people laughed and applauded, and the woman shook her fist. Everywhere the noise was loud.

On the far side of the platform, police were using clubs to form an aisle through the mob. They would beat their way forward, hitting hard, but then the crowds would swell in again, closing the aisle, and the police would then holler and hit harder. Up on the platform the military officers paid no attention to this. They sat in their chairs and made jokes and sipped sherry.

"Here it comes," Doc said.

He pointed to a police van that had pulled up behind the platform. It inched forward a few meters at a time. The van's siren was wailing and a squad of police moved on foot to clear a path, but it made no difference. Immediately the crowd surrounded the van. Men were jumping onto the fenders and running boards; others piled on the hood and rear bumper. All the while martial music blared from loudspeakers at the rear of plaza.

"See?" Doc said. "What did I say? Isn't it a genuine spectacle?"

"It is."

"One of civilization's grandest offerings."

The lieutenant was sitting down now. His head was in his hands. He was rocking in time with the music.

When the van reached the roped-off area, more police came

to form a wedge up to the platform. The crowd turned quiet. There were nervous giggles, one far-off scream. The martial music ended.

For a moment there was absolute silence. Then the van doors opened, and a short, almost emaciated youth of about twenty stepped out. His hands were bound behind him.

Quietly, nodding once to a soldier beside him, the boy passed through the crowd and mounted the platform under his own power. If he was afraid, he showed no signs. His eyes were level. He kept his head and spine erect. After climbing to the platform he stood modestly near the backdrop of flags and banners. He smiled when a soldier came to untie his hands.

"Watch this," Doc said. He touched Paul Berlin's shoulder. "Your fine expedition to Paris, all the spectacular spectacles along the way. Civilization. You *watch* this shit."

"Let's go," Paul Berlin said quietly.

"No, man. No, I want you to *watch* this. Pay attention, look for all the pretty details."

So Paul Berlin watched as the slim, well-mannered boy was led to a chair at the front of the platform. The crowd remained quiet, but now the quiet had a hum inside it, a soft buzzing sound. Two soldiers guarded the youth, one on each side of the chair. After a brief delay another soldier climbed onto the platform. He carried a large white towel and a tray of silver instruments. The instruments sparkled in the bright winter sun. Seeing this, the crowd stirred and began pressing forward. The hum grew louder. Somewhere in the back a man whistled and shouted something that made the crowd titter.

Quickly, in brisk motions that showed he had expertise, the third soldier draped the towel around the boy's shoulders, clipped it, then selected an instrument from his tray.

"Jesus," Eddie whispered. He looked away, then looked back again.

"What is it?"

"Nothing, sir. Go to sleep."

"What?"

"A razor," Doc said. "I think it's a razor."

The crowd was clapping now. It was a peculiar sound, almost polite. The clapping ended when the soldier began lathering the boy's neck, using a brush that he dipped periodically into a shallow bowl on the tray. The youth said nothing. His eyes were open. He bent forward to give the soldier a better angle. The crowd applauded this. Steadily, with crisp professional strokes, the soldier shaved the boy's neck and a small area at the base of the skull. It took only a minute. Afterward the soldier bowed and offered a clean towel to the youth, who smiled and used it to wipe away the excess lather.

"Tip the fucker," Stink said. "Why don't he tip the dude?"

The loudspeakers played marching songs. One by one the officers seated at the rear of the stage got up and went to the boy, kissed his cheeks, then stepped back and saluted and returned to their chairs. An orderly poured more sherry. Later there were two speeches, then more music, and the boy waited patiently through all of it, looking out over the crowd as if searching out a familiar face. His expression was sober but not frightened.

The day seemed colder now. There was no wind, and the flags and bunting hung motionless at the rear of the platform.

Paul Berlin tried hard to be calm. Concentration, that was the answer—remember the details, store them up for future understanding.

Doc nudged him.

The boy was being led across the platform to a block of heavy wood. He stood at attention while an officer read a brief statement. Details, Paul Berlin kept thinking. He watched closely. There was a fly on the boy's nose. The dead of winter, but, yes, it was a fly. The boy kept shaking his head and blowing to get rid of it, but the fly stuck fast. He started to speak. Twisting his head, the youth tried to swat it away, but two soldiers had him by the arms.

"The fly!" Paul Berlin called. "Somebody—"

But the boy's head was already being pushed down. He

struggled to get at the fly, tongue flicking out, and there were tears in his eyes. It was not fear. It was shame. The youth tried desperately to shake off the fly, shivering now, his neck pressed down into the scooped groove of the wooden block. He swallowed once. Then he blinked. His attention was entirely on the fly. He did not look up when the hooded axeman stepped forward.

The boy's tongue was still groping toward his nose when the axe fell.

There was no basket beneath the block.

Detail, Paul Berlin thought. Small irritants: specks of lint, a piece of red clay, clumps of berries in foliage shooting flame, a wet leaking feeling that smothered fear in shame.

Eyes wet, tongue flapping, the youth's head dropped heavily.

"A spectacle," Doc whispered.

The crowd applauded. Then music played. Then the military officers saluted and moved off the platform.

The fly still perched on the boy's nose.

Afterward, with the afternoon still cold and sunny, Oscar led them through the crowd to a stand-up bar on the far side of the plaza. The bar was noisy and crowded, everyone discussing the execution with wide gestures and re-enactments.

They took a table near the windows and ordered drinks.

"So now we've seen it," Doc sighed. "Domestic tranquillity, the keeping of the peace. A real treat, wasn't it?"

Oscar Johnson's face was sweating. He wiped it with a napkin, then wiped his sunglasses. Behind him, a man was making funny twitching motions with his nose. Other men were laughing.

"Wasn't it a treat, Oscar?"

"It's the price," Oscar said. He wiped his forehead. "Sometimes there's a price."

"A murderer maybe," said Stink Harris. "I wouldn't doubt it. He looked like one . . . his eyes, I mean. His eyes looked just like Richard Widmark's eyes. You know? That real shiny look."

"He had blue eyes, for Chrissake."

"Who did?"

"Widmark. Widmark's got blue eyes. That boy, though—his eyes were brown."

"A murderer," Stink said. "I'll bet on it. You wanna bet, Doc."

"No, I want to drink."

"Let's drink then."

"A spectacle, all right. I told you it would be a spectacle, and wasn't I right?"

The lieutenant's face was crinkled up like old Kleenex. He didn't drink. He sat facing the plaza, looking out at where the platform stood. The crowd was mostly gone now.

They drank until dusk, then they left the bar and walked back through the plaza and up a narrow cobbled street that was enclosed on all sides by banks and government offices. They were drunk. Their singing bounced off the buildings. Clams, Stink Harris kept saying. He wanted clams for supper, so they went in search of clams. Instead they were arrested.

Again, no warning.

Oscar blamed it on Eddie, and Eddie blamed it on Stink, who kept insisting on clams.

"Look here," Eddie sputtered on the ride to police headquarters. "Clams, you kept asking for. Isn't that right? You wanted clams, so I asked where to find clams."

"You asked a *cop.*"

"Who else? A man wants directions, he asks a cop. That's all I did, I just asked."

At police headquarters they were led into a small lounge. Curtains partly hid the barred windows. The furniture was upholstered, the carpets new and deep-piled. The room smelled vaguely of fish. Clams, Eddie muttered.

They waited ten minutes, then a tall, gaunt man with a neat moustache and deeply tanned skin entered the room. He

190

shook hands with the lieutenant, smiled politely and asked them to be seated.

His name, he said, was Fahyi Rhallon, a captain in His Majesty's Royal Fusiliers. A soldier, he had been recently transferred to temporary duty with the *Savak*.

"The what?" Oscar said.

The officer smiled again. His teeth were smoke-stained.

"*Savak*," he said. "It is . . . how do you say it? Internal Security. Terrible duty for a man who would rather be killing Kurds."

"Yeah," Oscar said. "That's always more fun, ain't it?"

After dispatching an orderly for tea and sandwiches, the captain took out a pipe, filled it from a leather pouch, tamped it down and lit it. As if embarrassed to begin, he made courtly inquiries about their stay in Tehran. Had they visited the lovely mosques along the river? The museums? The ARAMCO Institute? A splendid city, he said, if you knew what to look for.

"All of it," Oscar said. "We seen it all."

The captain nodded. "I am pleased. You are tourists then."

It was a statement, not a question, but the man stopped for a moment to study his pipe. Then he smiled again, crossing his legs the way women do.

"Tourists," he said. "They have much to see in Tehran. In the mountains, too, if you wish to hunt the big Kopet Dagh ram. Do you hunt this ram?"

"No," Doc said.

"You only tour?"

"That's it," Doc said. "Seeing the sights."

The captain's pipe had gone out. Irritably, he put it down and lit a cigarette. "That is for the better, anyway. The big ram, it goes very fast. Not so many now, and not so big. So, yes, it is better that you do not hunt the ram." He shook his head apologetically. "Clearly it is a mistake then. You are only touring. I will tell this to Sergeant Ulam."

"Who?"

"Sergeant Ulam, the arresting officer. I will now tell him he is loco. He believes you are perhaps soldiers, American soldiers without passports, but now I will tell him you only tour. I say he is loco, yes?"

"Nutty," Doc said.

"Nutty!" Captain Rhallon clapped his leg. "Very good word —nutty!" He laughed and coughed and clapped his leg again. Then he smiled at Doc Peret. "So then it would not be an unsightly offense to see your passport? I do not wish to make offense, but rules—"

"It would be no offense," Doc said.

"I am much relieved."

"No offense in the least." Doc spoke solemnly. "In fact, sir, to show our passports would be a singular honor."

"I cannot say how gratified it makes me."

"Likewise, sir."

The officer smiled at each of them. "So many rules, you know. Rules and rules."

"Of course."

"So. You will honor me with passports?"

"Is it required?"

"Sadly."

Doc smiled back at him. "It is shared sadness, sir. Because, you see, it will not be possible to show you passports."

"It will not?"

"Unfortunately," Doc sighed. He glanced over at the lieutenant, whose eyes were closed. "At present, I fear, we are without passports. Otherwise it would be an honor to present them. A distinct honor."

Captain Fahyi Rhallon did not stop smiling. He gazed for a moment at the ash of his cigarette, then licked a fleck of tobacco from his upper lip.

"You are . . . you are without passports?"

"Unfortunately."

The man nodded, considering this. "I see. *Entirely* without passports?"

"That," Doc said graciously, "is the unfortunate state of things."

"Yes, I see."

Doc cleared his throat. When he spoke his voice was confidential. "The truth of the matter is that we . . . how should I express it? . . . we are traveling under certain military regulations. Mutual military travel pacts. Hence passports are unnecessary."

"Ah," the captain said. "Then you *are* soldiers?"

"Touring soldiers."

"Yes?"

"That's right," Doc said. His tone remained intimate, as if confiding a great secret. "Soldiers who tour, touring soldiers. In that sense, then, we are not strictly soldiers. There's a big difference."

"And passports are therefore unnecessary? Am I understanding correctly?"

"Perfectly," Doc said.

"But you are soldiers?"

"Of a sort."

"Soldiers on leave?"

Doc shrugged. "That's close enough. Touring soldiers."

Nodding, recrossing his legs and leaning back, the captain seemed troubled. He was not a handsome man, but there was dignity in the way he carried himself.

"It might have been better," he murmured, "if you had said this immediately."

"A mistake," Doc agreed. "We should have clarified the matter from the start."

"It is no shame to be soldiers."

"The contrary. Quite the contrary, sir—it is a privilege and honor."

Again there was a clumsy pause that was broken by an orderly who entered with a tray of tea and sandwiches. The captain seemed relieved. Getting up, he personally poured the tea and served the sandwiches on cloth napkins, smiling, scolding the orderly for forgetting cream and sugar, shaking his head as if to say the help wasn't what it used to be.

He watched with pleasure as Stink and Eddie and Oscar devoured the food.

"Your leader," he said. "He does not wish to eat?"

The lieutenant seemed to be dozing. His eyes were closed and his head rested on Sarkin Aung Wan's shoulder. She gently massaged his scalp.

"If he is ill," the captain said, his mouth showing concern, "we shall immediately call for a doctor. Is your leader sick?"

"Homesick," Doc said. "It happens to touring soldiers."

"Of course." The man sipped his tea, still looking at the lieutenant with a worried frown. "So then. You say you are without passports?"

"That's the nub of it," Doc said.

"And you say . . . you say you travel under the protection of certain other regulations. Is that the understanding?"

"Exactly. That's exactly it. We travel under certain mutual military agreements."

"Which do not require passports?"

"Exactly."

"I am stupid," the officer said. He tapped his skull. "I am a good soldier, and I study all regulations, but I fear I am stupid. I admit ignorance of these particular agreements."

"It's no dishonor," Doc said.

"But I should have known. My stupidity is embarrassing."

Stink Harris giggled and reached for another sandwich. He'd taken off his boots.

Doc glared at him, then turned back to the officer: "Again, sir, there are so many regulations. It's impossible to keep track. But, I assure you, the treaties exist and are presently honored by all signatories. The Mutual Military Travel Pact of 1965."

"Yes?"

"Ratified in 1956, reaffirmed in 1965. In Geneva."

"Geneva," the man murmured. He jotted this down on a piece of yellow paper. Then, stroking his moustache, he sighed. "Rules and more rules. Again, I am a stupid soldier who would rather be off fighting in the east. Rules! I study hard for the *Savak*. My wife tells me I am a bore. I study and study, but there are always more rules to study, and I am stupid. But yes, it is certainly a sensible treaty and I am ignorant not to know it."

"No harm."

"Harm? Oh, but it is always harm to detain the innocent. My stupidity, it has caused great harm and I must apologize." He struck his forehead with the palm of his hand. Then he looked at Sarkin Aung Wan. "And the young lady. Is she also a soldier?"

"No," Doc said. "The young lady, you might say, is under temporary escort—a matter of some delicacy. But of course she's subject to the same rules and privileges. It's covered in the treaties."

"Without question," said the captain. "In fact I now begin to recall the regulation. Geneva, yes?"

"That's the one, all right."

"Yes, I begin to remember. Regulations! They are like smoke in my stupid head, but, yes, I think I remember now. Geneva, 1965. I shall find this regulation and study it so that next time I do not let my stupidity cause pain. Rules and rules. Red tape like a pit of snakes! It is a genuine miracle that armies ever find their way to battle."

"True enough," Doc sighed. "A work of God."

The officer stood up and clapped his hands.

"So then. It is settled."

"We can go?"

"By all means! But I wonder—" The officer paused. "I wonder if I might apologize for this unseemly error. Yes? Perhaps I might make amends?"

"Not necessary, man. We—"

"But I insist. My stupidity must be paid for! No arguments . . . I shall buy drinks as penance for my ignorance. You will allow this?"

Doc shrugged. "An honor."

There was a short delay while the captain attended to his paperwork. Then he put on a high-peaked cap, buttoned his pockets, and led them out of the station. It was night now. Cold winds flushed the streets, driving huge drifts of snow up against the walls and windows of dark buildings. For a moment, Paul Berlin had a sense of being whisked backward in history: deserted streets, lampless and desolate and cruel. He remembered the beheading. The fly—dead of winter. He shivered and took Sarkin Aung Wan's arm.

Passing through a gloomy archway, the captain explained that a curfew had been recently imposed due to certain incidents of terrorism and sabotage. "No problem, though," he said, patting Doc's shoulder. "As soldiers we are exempt. In fact it is our solemn duty to enforce the curfew. One of the pleasures of soldiering, yes? We shall shall drink and enforce curfew till dawn!"

He led them into a bleak backstreet, through a series of alleys and archways, then down into a basement grotto. No lights or signs announced the place, but inside it was crowded with people dancing and singing and talking and drinking. The crowd was equally divided between soldiers and students. The students danced. The soldiers sat at tables along the walls.

"Now we enforce curfew," the officer smiled. He had to shout against the hard American music.

Waving at friends, he escorted them to a large round table near the bandstand and called for beer.

His name was Fahyi Rhallon, a captain in His Majesty's Royal Fusiliers, recently transferred to Internal Security. Over the sound of drums and guitars he spoke passionately of the fraternity and community of a field soldier's life, how battle made a man appreciate peace, how love and even God himself could be found in the meanest foxhole. This sort of talk never impressed Paul Berlin. He looked out at the students dancing fast to fast music. Flashing lights made the dancers look like fish

196

darting about in an aquarium. Along the walls, watching but pretending not to watch, many soldiers sat with their caps neatly folded in their laps. They, too, were enforcing curfew.

The dancers and the music made Paul Berlin think of home. He took Sarkin Aung Wan's hand under the table, squeezed it, and tried not to think.

"It is good to discuss these matters with the American soldier," said Captain Rhallon when the music ended. "One soldier can always learn from other soldiers, yes? But sometimes . . . sometimes I talk so much that I learn nothing. I must listen now. I will listen while you tell me things."

"What things?" Eddie said. "Rain and lice?"

"No, no! The war. I will listen while you tell me about your war."

Eddie laughed. "It was swell."

"You are fooling me."

"Honest. It was such a swell war they should make it a movie."

"A swell, wet war," Stink Harris said.

"I am being fooled. I see that."

"Just a war," Doc said. "There's nothing new to tell."

Captain Fahyi Rhallon smiled. "Not to contradict, but I must disagree."

"An honor."

"Each soldier, he has a different war. Even if it is the same war it is a different war. Do you see this?"

"Perceptual set," Doc Peret said.

The captain nodded. He was leaning forward over the table. His eyes were brilliant black. "Perceptual set! Yes, that is it. In battle, in a war, a soldier sees only a tiny fragment of what is available to be seen. The soldier is not a photographic machine. He is not a camera. He registers, so to speak, only those few items that he is predisposed to register and not a thing more. Do you understand this? So I am saying to you that after a battle each soldier will have different stories to tell, vastly

197

different stories, and that when a war is ended it is as if there have been a million wars, or as many wars as there were soldiers."

Doc Peret waited a moment. He glanced at Paul Berlin, then arranged his face in an expression of sober reflection. It was the way he looked before engaging in debate with Jim Pederson or Frenchie Tucker.

"I'll buy most of it," Doc said. "We're made differently, we see differently, we remember differently."

"Precisely."

"Right, and I guess I can accept most of that. Except for this: The war itself has an identity separate from perception."

"You are a realist," Captain Rhallon smiled. "An unpopular position."

Doc made a modest gesture with his hand. "Unpopularity is the price a good analyst pays. But anyway. The point is that war is war no matter how it's perceived. War has its own reality. War kills and maims and rips up the land and makes orphans and widows. These are the things of war. Any war. So when I say that there's nothing new to tell about Nam, I'm saying it was just a war like every war. Politics be damned. Sociology be damned. It pisses me off to hear everybody say how special Nam is, how it's a big aberration in the history of American wars—how for the soldier it's somehow different from Korea or World War Two. Follow me? I'm saying that the *feel* of war is the same in Nam or Okinawa—the emotions are the same, the same fundamental stuff is seen and remembered. That's what I'm saying."

"And what about purpose?" the captain said.

"Purpose? Same-same. The purposes are always the same."

"But . . . but I understand that one difficulty for you has been a lack of purpose. Is that not the case? An absence of aim and purpose, so that the foot soldier is left without the moral imperatives to fight hard and well and winningly. Am I wrong in this understanding?"

Doc Peret picked up his empty mug and filled it from the

pitcher. The musicians were moving back to the stage now. Students were getting up and moving to the dance floor.

"You're right," Doc said slowly, "and you're wrong. True, it's sometimes hard to figure out what the hell's going on, but I'll wager that troops at Hastings or the Bulge had the same problem. I mean, if they stopped to think about it—what the fuck am I fighting for?—if they did that, I'll bet they came up as confused and muddleheaded as anybody in Nam. And what about all the millions of soldiers who have fought bravely on behalf of bad purposes, evil aims? The Nazis, the Japs. They fought damned well."

"And they lost," said Captain Rhallon.

The lieutenant suddenly sat erect. "Tell him!" he said.

"You are feeling better, sir?"

"Better! Just tell 'em!"

The noise was building again. Doc Peret turned and glared at the musicians.

"Okay," Doc said. "Sure, they lost. But was it because they fought poorly? Hell, no. They lost because they couldn't build enough planes and trains and bullets and bombs. It wasn't *purpose* that lost it for them, it was *matériel*. They couldn't produce enough matériel."

Captain Rhallon considered this. "Yes. But . . . but in war one nation is able to make up for production insufficiencies by calling on the industrial capacity of allied nations. Is that not so? By citing a great moral purpose, Britain was able to generate American industrial aid to defeat the Germans. In comparison, Germany and Japan were left virtually without allies. Unable to summon other nations to their cause, because, in fact, they *had* no just cause. So in the end it was an absence of clear moral purpose that produced defeat."

"Tell it loud!" the lieutenant said. "You got him by the balls. Now squeeze!"

Music was playing. It was fierce, loud music. Colored lights were flashing, and the students were dancing in groups and pairs. The soldiers along the walls were singing.

"A nice trick," Doc said. "But you changed the subject. We're not talking about winning and losing. We're talking about how it *feels*. How it feels on the ground. And I'm saying the common grunt doesn't give a damn about purposes and justice. He doesn't even *think* about that shit. Not when he's out humping, getting his tail shot off. Purposes—bullshit! He's thinking about how to keep breathing. Or . . . or what it'll feel like when he hits that mine. Will he go nuts? Will he throw up all over himself, or will he cry, or pass out, or scream? What'll it look like—all bone and meat and pus? That's the stuff he thinks about, not purposes."

"And about running," the officer said softly, so softly he had to repeat it.

"What?"

"Running," Fahyi Rhallon said. "The soldier, he thinks about running. Will he run or will he stay and fight?"

Paul Berlin looked away. He watched the dancing students.

"Yes," the captain said, "running is also what the soldier thinks of, yes? He thinks of it often. He imagines himself running from battle. Dropping his weapon and turning and running and running, and never looking back, just running and running. Soldiers think of this. I know it. Yes? It is the soldier's thought above other thoughts."

"And?"

The man touched his moustache and smiled. "And purpose is what keeps him from running. Without purpose men will run. They will act out their dreams, and they will run and run, like animals in stampede. It is *purpose* that keeps men at their posts to fight. Only purpose."

The lieutenant cheered. Oscar Johnson muttered something, got up, and moved to a nearby table. He asked four girls to dance before one shrugged and followed him out onto the floor. She wore blue jeans and a polo shirt. She danced with her nose at the ceiling.

"Maybe so," Doc was saying. "Maybe purpose is part of it. But a bigger part is self-respect. And fear."

"For not running?"

"You bet. Self-respect and fear, that's why soldiers don't run."

"Fear?"

"Right on. We stick it out because we're afraid of what'll happen to our reputations. Our own egos. Self-respect, that's what keeps us on the line."

"But does not purpose reflect on self-respect?" the *Savak* officer said. "Does not the absence of good purpose jeopardize the soldier's own ego, thus making him less likely to fight well and bravely? If a war is without justice, the soldier knows that the sacrifice of life, his own valued life, is demeaned, and therefore his self-respect must likewise be demeaned. Is that not so?"

Eddie and Stink were now up and dancing. The clatter of drums and glasses made it hard to hear. The music kept making Paul Berlin think of home—dancing in the high school gym, Louise Wiertsma on his arm, and later going out to a big barn outside Fort Dodge, where there was more dancing and kids drinking, and the smell of hay in the lofts and cattle long butchered and sold and eaten, and Louise Wiertsma's hair, and home. He held tight to Sarkin Aung Wan's hand. She was young. They were all too young. Cacciato was young. Eddie and Stink and Oscar, dancing now, were young, and so were Pederson and Frenchie Tucker. Everyone was too young.

Fahyi Rhallon was asking now about their touring, and Doc said it was a magnificent tour. Tours of Laos and Burma and India and the highlands of Afghanistan, and now they were touring Tehran, and soon they would be touring all the way to Paris.

"Paris!" the captain cried. "You are fortunate. My best tour was to Damascus, but compared to Paris it was nothing. Paris! Is it a guided tour?"

"Yes," Doc said. "You might say that."

He went on to explain how it happened that Cacciato left the war in monsoon season, how they were dispatched to retrieve him, how they were determined to bring it to a rightful conclusion.

"Purpose," the officer smiled. "You have a mission with great purpose."

The lieutenant made a high scoffing sound.

Captain Rhallon looked concerned. "But he is a deserter, yes? This Cacciato? And your purpose is to stop him. Deserters, they must be pursued to the very ends of the earth. Hunted down like dogs. Otherwise—"

"Otherwise what?" the lieutenant said. "What difference does it make? One less soldier."

The officer hesitated.

"You are serious?"

"No," Lieutenant Corson sighed. "No, I'm just a sick fucker who don't know what's happening."

"But, sir. If this . . . this Cacciato is allow to run free, then the consequences—" Again the captain paused, glancing across at Doc Peret. "I can only speak of my own beliefs. My own country. Here, though, desertion is a most serious offense. Only this afternoon a boy was put to death for a similar crime."

"He was a deserter?"

"Oh, no," the captain said. "No, the boy had merely gone AWOL. For true deserters the punishment is not so kind."

"Thank God for mercy."

A waiter came and mopped up the table and put down three full pitchers. The music was slow now, aching, and the students danced close. Blurred, melancholy music. Listening, watching the dancers, Paul Berlin felt himself sliding through vanished moments: the high school gym decorated with lanterns and flowers; Louise Wiertsma's blond hair and curious smile; the way she hummed as she danced. This same song, the same ache. And in Chu Lai once, on stand-down, again it was this same swaying song, slow and powerful and sad, a Korean girl taking off her clothes to the song, and everyone singing and swaying and watching her strip, nobody thinking about the coming morning, everyone just singing and feeling sad and happy, Pederson and Bernie Lynn and Frenchie Tucker, everybody.

So the students danced slow, and Fahyi Rhallon was asking how the war went, what the strategies were, and Doc said it went very well on the good days and very badly on the bad days, but that in general it was hard to say, hard to know for sure, and the captain agreed with this, it was always hard to know how a war went. The music was low and loud and sad, and the students danced close. Some of them sang as they danced. And Eddie and Oscar and Stink were back at the table now, showing the captain how various ambush formations were set up, the classic X and L and O, and everyone agreed that the O was the best of the formations because it offered perimeter protection and a 360-degree killing circumference. Sad, throbbing music, and the students held tight to one another and danced to it, *don't be afraid, take a sad song and make it better, remember* . . . and Oscar was diagramming cordon and search tactics, showing how they worked in some situations and failed in many others, and the officer nodded and took notes.

The students danced until the song ended.

Then there was a new song, faster and not so melancholy, and the students separated and danced fast.

"Tripflares," Eddie was saying. "Now there's a useless—"

Paul Berlin took Sarkin Aung Wan's hand and led her to the floor. It wasn't easy. Even in the high school gym, even then he'd been a lousy dancer. "Like this," Louise Wiertsma kept saying, showing him the steps, but it was never easy. He danced cautiously. He liked the way Sarkin Aung Wan closed her eyes to the music, the way her chrome cross bounced on her sweater, her braided hair swishing so full. She smiled as she danced. He liked that, too. It was the way Louise Wiertsma smiled, guarding secrets. She smiled and danced with her mouth open and her eyes half-shut, her chrome cross swinging. He liked it.

"You are drunk, Spec Four," she said as she danced.

"No."

"Oh, yes. You are a very drunk Spec Four."

At the table again, Fahyi Rhallon was inquiring about sappers.

"Sleazy sons of bitches," Stink Harris said. "Up at Chu Lai they had these two converted sappers, Chieu Hoi types, and they was giving this demonstration on how they do it, gettin' through the wire and all that, and the bastards get all oiled up like fuckin grease, man, like fuckin ball bearings or something, and they just fuckin glide under the wire, glide. Isn't that right?"

"That's right," Eddie said.

"Fuckin-A, it's right. Unbelievable. Sleazy, oily little runts. Ugly."

"Stink speaks truth."

"Sure, it's the truth. They fuckin carry the charges strapped between their legs, right here, an' I swear they're no bigger than—"

"Stink's size."

"Eat it, man. No bigger than—"

"Stink, he'd make a swell sapper."

Paul Berlin drank beer and listened to the music and watched the dancing students. They all drank. Sarkin Aung Wan danced in her chair, swaying, and the soldiers watched from their tables along the walls, and the band was loud.

And later there were war stories.

All along it had been coming to this, and now the war stories started.

The students danced and the music was loud, and Eddie told the story about Pederson, then Oscar told about Big Buff. "You should've seen it," Eddie said when Oscar finished. "Old Buff, we found him just like Oscar says. Hunched up over his helmet like a prayin' Arab. No offense."

Fahyi Rhallon smiled and said there was no offense in the least, he was a practicing Christian. And then he told his own war story, one about a battle in the snow and how the snow looked afterward, and there was a respectful silence when the story was over, and then Oscar put his hand on Doc's shoulder: "Tell him," he said. "Tell the man the *best* story."

The music kept getting louder. The drummer was using iron pipes. The room moved under the music. The lights blinked white and yellow and black.

"Tell him," Oscar said. "Tell him the ultimate war story."

Paul Berlin was sick.

"Billy Boy. Tell him about Billy Boy Watkins."

Paul Berlin was sick. And when Doc began to tell the ultimate war story, starting with what a hot day it had been, how it was hot like never before, Paul Berlin got up and managed his way outside.

Cold now, very cold. His legs were weak. Cold and drunk, and his legs were weak, but not so cold and weak and drunk that he would listen to the ultimate war story. Not that drunk.

He buttoned his collar, leaning against a stone wall. The street was dark. He could hear the music inside, the drums and singing, but he did not hear the ultimate war story.

Sarkin Aung Wan came out.

"Yes," she smiled. "You are a very drunk Spec Four."

"Let's go."

"Very drunk. Am I safe with such a drunk?"

"Not that drunk. Not all that dumb drunk."

She took his hand. They walked up the street until the music was gone. They passed along an arcade, then through an alleyway, then across the deserted brick plaza where the platform looked frail and seedy in the moonlight, and where Sarkin Aung Wan's shoes made sharp clicking sounds that echoed off the banks and government offices. They stopped there for a time. Things were quiet. Then they turned onto a boulevard with statues and iron fences and winter shrubs.

"No," he said. "Drunk maybe, but not that crazy drunk."

Sarkin Aung Wan kissed him.

"Perhaps not," she said. "Anyway, it was such a silly story. So silly."

30
The
Observation
Post

FOUR O'CLOCK, HE THOUGHT. Ten minutes to four.
He bet himself twenty bucks on it, then knelt down
behind the wall of sandbags to check his watch. Eight
minutes to four. Twenty easy bucks—he should've joined the
circus, a time-teller.

It was colder now. The breeze had become a wind.

An hour till the first glistenings, an hour and a half until
dawn.

He could tell time by the way it came. By the cold and the
wind, and then later the growing gleaming in the tips of the
waves, then a spreading gleaming that would fill the wave
troughs and give them shape, wrinkles like the skin of boiled
milk, then the birds, then the breaking of the sky. He could tell
time by all of this, and by the rhyme of wind and sand, and by
the beat of his own heart.

It was a matter of hard observation. Separating illusion from
reality. What happened, and what might have happened?
Why, out of all that might have happened, did it lead to a
beheading in Tehran? Why not pretty things? Why not a
smooth, orderly arc from war to peace? These were the ques-

tions, and the answers could come only from hard observation. Doc was right about that. He was right, too, that observation requires inward-looking, a study of the very machinery of observation—the mirrors and filters and wiring and circuits of the observing instrument.

Insight, vision. What you remember is determined by what you see, and what you see depends on what you remember. A cycle, Doc Peret had said. A cycle that has to be broken. And this requires a fierce concentration on the process itself: Focus on the order of things, sort out the flow of events so as to understand how one thing led to another, search for that point at which what happened had been extended into a vision of what might have happened. Where was the fulcrum? Where did it tilt from fact to imagination? How far had Cacciato led them? How far might he lead them still?

Facing the night, he tried.

He tried again to order the known facts. Billy Boy was first. And then . . . then who? Then a long blank time along the Song Tra Bong, yes, and then Rudy Chassler, who broke the quiet. And then later Frenchie Tucker, followed in minutes by Bernie Lynn. Then lake country. World's Greatest Lake Country, where Ready Mix died on a charge toward the mountains. And then Sidney Martin. Then Buff. Then Pederson. Then Cacciato.

Yes, then Cacciato, who led them away in slow motion. But how far and why? Mandalay, Delhi, Tehran, and beyond? Order was the hard part. The facts even when beaded on a chain still did not have real order. Events did not flow. The facts were separate and haphazard and random, even as they happened, episodic, broken, no smooth transitions, no sense of events unfolding from prior events.

Moving to the south wall, he found the starlight scope under Eddie's poncho. He unscrewed the lens cap and placed the heavy instrument up on the sandbagged wall.

Observe, that was the trick: He put his eye to the scope's peephole and flicked on the battery switch.

The night was moving.

A bright green shimmering dazzle, and it was all moving. The countryside moved. The beach, the sea, everything. But he did not look away. He pressed his eye against the peephole and watched the moving night, turning the big plastic dial to full focus, high resolution, and he watched Quang Ngai move.

It was a trick of the machine, he knew this. So he concentrated.

He concentrated on the order of things, going back to the beginning. His first day at the war. How hot the day had been, and how on his very first day he had witnessed the ultimate war story.

31
Night
March

THE PLATOON OF THIRTY-TWO soldiers moved slowly in the dark, single file, not talking. One by one, like sheep in a dream, they passed through the hedgerow, crossed quietly over a meadow and came down to the paddy. There they stopped. Lieutenant Sidney Martin knelt down, motioning with his hand, and one by one the others squatted or knelt or sat in the shadows. For a long time they did not move. Except for the sounds of their breathing, and, once, a soft fluid trickle as one of them urinated, the thirty-two men were silent: some of them excited by the adventure, some afraid, some exhausted by the long march, some of them looking forward to reaching the sea where they would be safe. There was no talking now. No more jokes. At the rear of the column, Private First Class Paul Berlin lay quietly with his forehead resting on the black plastic stock of his rifle. His eyes were closed. He was pretending he was not in the war. Pretending he had not watched Billy Boy Watkins die of fright on the field of battle. He was pretending he was a boy again, camping with his father in the midnight summer along the Des Moines River. "Be calm," his father said. "Ignore the bad stuff, look for the good."

In the dark, eyes closed, he pretended. He pretended that when he opened his eyes his father would be there by the campfire and, father and son, they would begin to talk softly about whatever came to mind, minor things, trivial things, and then roll into their sleeping bags. And later, he pretended, it would be morning and there would not be a war.

In the morning, when they reached the sea, it would be better. He would bathe in the sea. He would shave. Clean his nails, work out the scum. In the morning he would wash himself and brush his teeth. He would forget the first day, and the second day would not be so bad. He would learn.

There was a sound beside him, a movement, then, "Hey," then louder, "Hey!"

He opened his eyes.

"Hey, we're movin'. Get up."

"Okay."

"You sleeping?"

"No, I was resting. Thinking." He could see only part of the soldier's face. It was a plump, round, child's face. The child was smiling.

"No problem," the soldier whispered. "Up an' at 'em."

And he followed the boy's shadow into the paddy, stumbling once, almost dropping his rifle, cutting his knee, but he followed the shadow and did not stop. The night was clear. Before him, strung out across the paddy, he could make out the black forms of the other soldiers, their silhouettes hard against the sky. Already the Southern Cross was out. And other stars he could not yet name. Soon, he thought, he would learn the names. And puffy night clouds. And a peculiar glow to the west. There was not yet a moon.

Wading through the paddy, listening to the lullaby sounds of his boots, and many other boots, he tried hard not to think. Dead of a heart attack, that was what Doc Peret had said. Only he did not know Doc Peret's name. All he knew was what Doc said, dead of a heart attack, but he tried hard not to think of this, and instead he thought about not thinking. The fear wasn't so bad now. Now, as he stepped out of the paddy and onto a narrow dirt path, now the fear was mostly the fear of being so dumbly afraid ever again.

So he tried not to think.

There were tricks to keep from thinking. Counting. He counted his steps along the dirt path, concentrating on the numbers, pretending that the steps were dollar bills and that each step through the night made him richer and richer, so that soon he would become a wealthy man, and he kept counting, considering the ways he might spend the wealth, what he would buy and do and acquire and own. He would look his father in the eye and shrug and say, "It was pretty bad at first, sure, but I learned a lot and I got used to it. I never joined them —not them—but I learned their names and I got along, I got used to it." Then he would tell his father the story of Billy Boy Watkins, only a story, just a story, and he would never let on about the fear. "Not so bad," he would say instead, making his father proud.

And songs, another trick to stop the thinking—*Where have you gone, Billy Boy, Billy Boy, oh, where have you gone, charming Billy?* and other songs, *I got a girl, her name is Jill, she won't do it but her sister will,* and *Sound Off!* and other songs that he sang in his head as he marched toward the sea. And when he reached the sea he would dig a hole in the sand and he would sleep like the high clouds, he would swim and dive into the breakers and hunt crayfish and smell the salt, and he would laugh when the others made jokes about Billy Boy, and he would not be afraid ever again.

He walked, and counted, and later the moon came out. Pale, shrunken to the size of a dime.

The helmet was heavy on his head. In the morning he would adjust the leather binding. In the morning, at the end of the long march, his boots would have lost their shiny black stiffness, turning red and clay-colored like all the other boots, and he would have a start on a beard, his clothes would begin to smell of the country, the mud and algae and cow manure and chlorophyll, decay, mosquitoes like mice, all this: He would begin to smell like the others, even look like them, but, by God, he would not join them. He would adjust. He would play the part. But he would not join them. He would shave, he would clean himself, he would clean his weapon and keep it clean. He would clean the breech and trigger assembly and muzzle and magazines, and later, next time, he would not be afraid to use it. In the morning, when he reached the sea, he would learn the soldiers' names and maybe laugh at their jokes. When they joked about Billy Boy he would laugh, pretending it was funny, and he would not let on.

Walking, counting in his walking, and pretending, he felt better. He watched the moon come higher.

The trick was not to take it personally. Stay aloof. Follow the herd but don't join it. That would be the real trick. The trick would be to keep himself separate. To watch things. "Keep an eye out for the good stuff," his father had said by the river. "Keep your eyes open and your ass low, that's my only advice." And he would do it. A low profile. Look for the beauties: the moon sliding higher now, the feeling of the march, all the ironies and truths, and don't take any of it seriously. That would be the trick.

Once, very late in the night, they skirted a sleeping village. The smells again—straw, cattle, mildew. The men were quiet. On the far side of the village, coming like light from the dark, a dog barked. The barking was fierce. Then, nearby, another dog took up the bark. The column stopped. They waited there until the barking died out, then, fast, they marched away from the village, through a graveyard with conical burial mounds and miniature stone altars. The place had a perfumy smell. His mother's dresser, rows of expensive lotions and colognes, *eau de bain:* She used to hide booze in the larger bottles, but his father found out and carried the whole load out back, started a fire, and, one by one, threw the bottles into the incinerator, where they made sharp exploding sounds like gunfire; a perfumy smell, yes; a nice spot to spend the night, to sleep in the

212

perfumery, the burial mounds making fine strong battlements, the great quiet of the place.

But they went on, passing through a hedgerow and across another paddy and east toward the sea.

He walked carefully. He remembered what he'd been taught. Billy Boy hadn't remembered. And so Billy died of fright, his face going pale and the veins in his arms and neck popping out, the crazy look in his eyes.

He walked carefully.

Stretching ahead of him in the night was the string of shadow-soldiers whose names he did not yet know. He knew some of the faces. And he knew their shapes, their heights and weights and builds, the way they carried themselves on the march. But he could not tell them apart. All alike in the night, a piece, all of them moving with the same sturdy silence and calm and steadiness.

So he walked carefully, counting his steps. And when he had counted to eight thousand and sixty, the column suddenly stopped. One by one the soldiers knelt or squatted down.

The grass along the path was wet. Private First Class Paul Berlin lay back and turned his head so he could lick at the dew with his eyes closed, another trick, closing his eyes. He might have slept. Eyes closed, pretending came easy . . . When he opened his eyes, the same child-faced soldier was sitting beside him, quietly chewing gum. The smell of Doublemint was clean in the night.

"Sleepin' again?" the boy said.

"No. Hell, no."

The boy laughed a little, very quietly, chewing on his gum. Then he twisted the cap off a canteen and took a swallow and handed it through the dark.

"Take some," he said. He didn't whisper. The voice was high, a child's voice, and there was no fear in it. A big blue baby. A genie's voice.

Paul Berlin drank and handed back the canteen. The boy pressed a stick of gum into his fingers.

"Chew it quiet, okay? Don't blow no bubbles or nothing."

It was impossible to make out the soldier's face. It was a huge face, almost perfectly round.

They sat still. Private First Class Paul Berlin chewed the gum until all the sugars were gone. Then in the dark beside him the boy began to whistle. There was no melody.

"You have to do that?"

"Do what?"

"Whistle like that."

"Geez, was I whistling?"

"Sort of."

The boy laughed. His teeth were big and even and white. "Sometimes I forget. Kinda dumb, isn't it?"

"Forget it."

"Whistling! Sometimes I just forget where I'm at. The guys, they get pissed at me, but I just forget. You're new here, right?"

"I guess I am."

"Weird."

"What's weird?"

"Weird," the boy said, "that's all. The way I forget. Whistling! Was I whistling?"

"If you call it that."

"Geez!"

They were quiet awhile. And the night was quiet, no crickets or birds, and it was hard to imagine it was truly a war. He searched again for the soldier's face, but there was just a soft fullness under the helmet. The white teeth: chewing, smiling. But it did not matter. Even if he saw the kid's face, he would not know the name; and if he knew the name, it would still not matter.

"Haven't got the time?"

"No."

"Rats." The boy popped the gum on his teeth, a sharp smacking sound. "Don't matter."

"How about—"

"Time goes faster when you don't know the time. That's why I never bought no watch. Oscar's got one, an' Billy . . . Billy, he's got *two* of 'em. Two watches, you believe that? I never bought none, though. Goes fast when you don't know the time."

And again they were quiet. They lay side by side in the grass. The moon was very high now, and very bright, and they were waiting for cloud cover. After a time there was the crinkling of tinfoil, then the sound of heavy chewing. A moist, loud sound.

"I hate it when the sugar's gone," the boy said. "You want more?"

"I'm okay."

"Just ask. I got about a zillion packs. Pretty weird, wasn't it?"

"What?"

"Today . . . it was pretty weird what Doc said. About Billy Boy."

"Yes, pretty weird."

The boy smiled his big smile. "You like that gum? I got other kinds if you don't like it. I got—"

"I like it."

"I got Black Jack here. You like Black Jack? Geez, I love it! Juicy Fruit's second, but Black Jack's first. I save it up for rainy days, so to speak. Know what I mean? What you got there is Doublemint."

"I like it."

"Sure," the round soldier said, the child, "except for Black Jack and Juicy Fruit it's my favorite. You like Black Jack gum?"

Paul Berlin said he'd never tried it. It scared him, the way the boy kept talking, too loud. He sat up and looked behind him. Everything was dark.

"Weird," the boy said.

"I guess so. Why don't we be a little quiet?"

"Weird. You never even *tried* it?"

"What?"

"Black Jack. You never even chewed it once?"

215

Someone up the trail hissed at them to shut up. The boy shook his head, put a finger to his lips, smiled, and lay back. Then a long blank silence. It lasted for perhaps an hour, maybe more, and then the boy was whistling again, softly at first but then louder, and Paul Berlin nudged him.

"Really weird," the soldier whispered. "About Billy Boy. What Doc said, wasn't that the weirdest thing you ever heard? You ever hear of such a thing?"

"What?"

"What Doc said."

"No, I never did."

"Me neither." The boy was chewing again, and the smell now was licorice. The moon was a bit lower. "Me neither. I never heard once of no such thing. But Doc, he's a pretty smart cookie. Pretty darned smart."

"Is he?"

"You bet he is. When he says something, man, you know he's tellin' the truth. You *know* it." The soldier turned, rolling onto his stomach, and began to whistle, drumming with his fingers. Then he caught himself. "Dang it!" He gave his cheek a sharp whack. "Whistling again! I got to stop that dang whistling." He smiled and thumped his mouth. "But, sure enough, Doc's a smart one. He knows stuff. You wouldn't believe the stuff Doc knows. A lot. He knows a lot."

Paul Berlin nodded. The boy was talking too loud again.

"Well, you'll find out yourself. Doc knows his stuff." Sitting up, the boy shook his head. "A heart attack!" He made a funny face, filling his cheeks like balloons, then letting them deflate. "A heart attack! You hear Doc say that? A heart attack on the field of battle, isn't that what Doc said?"

"Yes," Paul Berlin whispered. He couldn't help giggling.

"Can you believe it? Billy Boy getting heart attacked? Scared to death?"

Paul Berlin giggled, he couldn't help it.

"Can you imagine it?"

"Yes," Paul Berlin whispered, and he imagined it clearly. He couldn't stop giggling.

"Geez!"

He giggled. He couldn't stop it, so he giggled, and he imagined it clearly. He imagined the medic's report. He imagined Billy's surprise. He giggled, imagining Billy's father opening the telegram: SORRY TO INFORM YOU THAT YOUR SON BILLY BOY WAS YESTERDAY SCARED TO DEATH IN ACTION IN THE REPUBLIC OF VIETNAM. Yes, he could imagine it clearly.

He giggled. He rolled onto his belly and pressed his face in the wet grass and giggled, he couldn't help it.

"Not so loud," the boy said. But Paul Berlin was shaking with the giggles: scared to death on the field of battle, and he couldn't help it.

"Not so loud."

But he was coughing with the giggles, he couldn't stop. Giggling and remembering the hot afternoon, and poor Billy, how they'd been drinking Coke from bright aluminum cans, and how the men lined the cans up in a row and shot them full of practice holes, how funny it was and how dumb and how hot the day, and how they'd started on the march and how the war hadn't seemed so bad, and how a little while later Billy tripped the mine, and how it made a tinny little sound, unimportant, *poof,* that was all, just *poof,* and how Billy Boy stood there with his mouth open and grinning, sort of embarrassed and dumb-looking, how he just stood and stood there, looking down at where his foot had been, and then how he finally sat down, still grinning, not saying a word, his boot lying there with his foot still in it, just *poof,* nothing big or dramatic, and how hot and fine and clear the day had been.

"Hey," he heard the boy saying in the dark, "not so loud, okay?" But he kept giggling. He put his nose in the wet grass and he giggled, then he bit his arm, trying to stifle it, but remembering—"War's over, Billy," Doc Peret said, "that's a million-dollar wound."

"Hey, not so *loud.*"

But Billy was holding the boot now. Unlacing it, trying to force it back on, except it was already on, and he kept trying to tie the boot and foot on, working with the laces, but it wouldn't go, and how everyone kept saying, "The war's over, man, be cool." And Billy couldn't get the boot on, because it was already on: He kept trying but it wouldn't go. Then he got scared. "Fuckin boot won't go on," he said. And he got scared. His face went pale and the veins in his arms and neck popped out, and he was yanking at the boot to get it on, and then he was crying. "Bullshit," the medic said, Doc Peret, but Billy Boy kept bawling, tightening up, saying he was going to die, but the medic said, "Bullshit, that's a million-dollar wound you got there," but Billy went crazy, pulling at the boot with his foot still in it, crying, saying he was going to die. And even when Doc Peret stuck him with morphine, even then Billy kept crying and working at the boot.

"Shut up!" the soldier hissed, or seemed to, and the smell of licorice was all over him, and the smell made Paul Berlin giggle harder. His eyes stung. Giggling in the wet grass in the dark, he couldn't help it.

"Come on, man, be quiet."

But he couldn't stop. He heard the giggles in his stomach and tried to keep them there, but they were hard and hurting and he couldn't stop them; and he couldn't stop remembering how it was when Billy Boy Watkins died of fright on the field of battle.

Billy tugging away at the boot, rocking, and Doc Peret and two others holding him. "You're okay, man," Doc Peret said, but Billy wasn't hearing it, and he kept getting tighter, making fists, squeezing his eyes shut and teeth scraping, everything tight and squeezing.

Afterward Doc Peret explained that Billy Boy really died of a heart attack, scared to death. "No lie," Doc said, "I seen it before. The wound wasn't what killed him, it was the heart attack. No lie." So they wrapped Billy in a plastic poncho, his eyes still squeezed shut to make wrinkles in his cheeks, and they carried him over the meadow to a dried-up paddy, and they threw out yellow smoke for the chopper, and they put him aboard, and then Doc wrapped the boot in a towel and placed it next to Billy, and that was how it happened. The chopper took Billy away. Later, Eddie Lazzutti, who loved to sing, remembered the song, and the jokes started, and Eddie sang *where have you gone, Billy Boy, Billy Boy, oh, where have you gone, charming Billy?* They sang until dark, marching to the sea.

Giggling, lying now on his back, Paul Berlin saw the moon move. He could not stop. Was it the moon? Or the clouds moving, making the moon seem to move? Or the boy's round face, pressing him, forcing out the giggles. "It wasn't so bad," he would tell his father. "I was a man. I saw it the first day, the very first day at the war, I saw all of it from the start, I learned it, and it wasn't so bad, and later on, later on it got better, later on, once I learned the tricks, later on it wasn't so bad." He couldn't stop.

The soldier was on top of him.

"Okay, man, *okay.*"

He saw the face then, clearly, for the first time.

"It's okay."

The face of the moon, and later the moon went under clouds, and the column was moving.

The boy helped him up.

"Okay?"

"Sure, okay."

The boy gave him a stick of gum. It was Black Jack, the precious stuff. "You'll do fine," Cacciato said. "You will. You got a terrific sense of humor."

32
The
Observation
Post

STEADY NOW, AND UNMOVING.

Paul Berlin's eye came unstuck from the starlight scope. His vision squared itself. Steady now, and unmoving, the night was again held firmly by the eye. Solid things. The beach, the wire to the front, the moon and the brightest stars, the smooth line where Quang Ngai met the world, the physical place. Tips of waves flashed. Dark pigments separated from lighter pigments. Four thirty, he thought. No reason to check the wristwatch: He saw the first gleamings, and it was now four thirty.

He turned off the scope's power. He replaced the lens cap, returned the machine to its aluminum carrying case, then opened a can of pears. He ate slowly. Dawn, of course, would be a dangerous time, but he trusted his eyes, which now saw only steadiness and calm.

Billy Boy was dead.

Billy Boy Watkins, like the others, was among the dead. It

was the simple truth. It was not especially terrible, or hard to think about, or even sad. It was a fact. It was the first fact, and leading from it were other facts. Now it was merely a matter of following the facts to where they ended.

He ate the pears. When he was finished he dropped the can to the beach.

33
Outlawed on the Road to Paris

THEY WERE ARRESTED again on the tenth day of February. Roused from sleep, handcuffed to a broomstick, herded out of the boardinghouse to a waiting cattle truck. Swiftly, the truck took them through the streets of Tehran to a gray-stone jail where they were searched, fingerprinted, photographed, shaved, and then led to separate cells. For eight days, which Paul Berlin counted off on a pocket calendar, he saw nothing of Doc or Eddie or the others. He saw no one. There were no voices, no echoes, no doors opening or closing. His meals, delivered through a sliding panel, appeared as if wished for, when wished for, and the smell of dungeons made him blink with wonder. So he slept, and wondered, and listened to the sounds of stone on steel. Then deep in sleep he was awakened and blindfolded and led down a narrow corridor. He was pushed into a chair. Blindfolded, less afraid than awed, he felt moistness on his neck; he felt a hand touch him; his head was pressed forward, then there was a sharpness against his neck, a swift scraping followed by the chill of melting snow. He was being shaved. Eyes open beneath the blindfold, he shivered with each stroke. He swallowed and dreamed of the many things he had swallowed. The pleasure of swallowing.

When it ended he was led into another chamber where the blindfold was removed.

The room was yellow in floodlights. There was no furniture. At the center of the room, Stink and Eddie and Doc and Oscar and the lieutenant sat in a tight circle on the floor, their necks shaved, each of them handcuffed to a concrete pillar that rose to the ceiling. Sarkin Aung Wan, dressed in a pink *chador* and head cloth, was free to move about the cell. She kissed him on the throat, then moved aside as a soldier handcuffed him to the pillar. Two armed guards watched from the door.

"Welcome to the zoo," Oscar smiled. "Chimps an' teddy bears, we all say welcome."

"What's it about?"

"Evil. It has to do with wickedness."

The door swung open, and Captain Fahyi Rhallon hurried in. He was carrying his hat and a large leather briefcase.

"Gentlemen," he said quickly, "I must give many apologies. I do not know what to apologize first." He sat on the floor, opened the briefcase, and gazed at the contents. Then he sighed. "I learned this morning of your arrest. Immediately I rushed to headquarters. Innocent, I tell them. Yes, I tell them you are innocent touring soldiers. Very difficult. The *Savak*, it does not give answers easily."

"What were the questions?" Doc asked.

"Unfortunately," the captain said, "this is not the time for banter. Your situation is grave."

"Grave, like in shaved necks?"

"Sadly." Again Captain Rhallon stared into his briefcase. "Presently the charges are hard to ascertain. The specifics. Of course I shall continue my inquiries, but the *Savak* does not look kindly on inquiries. My own neck is at risk. But, still . . . I shall try to resolve this matter."

"What matter?" Doc said. "What *is* the matter?"

"Espionage."

"As in spying?"

The captain nodded. "Also conspiracy to commit sabotage, conspiracy to incite revolution, terrorism, unauthorized national entry, traveling without passports, the carrying of firearms without permit, failure to register said weapons, conspiracy to do harm to His Imperial Majesty the Shahanshah of Iran."

"That's all?"

"Sadly," Captain Rhallon said, "that is not all. There is another matter." The captain blushed and looked away. "Desertion," he said softly.

Oscar Johnson laughed.

"It is humorous?" asked the captain. "You find desertion humorous?"

"No," Oscar said, "but I find it kind of funny."

Captain Rhallon shrugged and pulled a portfolio from his briefcase. Opening it, he removed a sheaf of papers stapled together at the top corners.

He tapped the report.

"Personally," he said, "I do not believe a word of this. A gross mistake, I am certain. But still, I am sad to say that until it is settled your situation remains perilous." He turned to the second page of the report. "As it states here, initial inquiries at the United States embassy, Tehran, failed to produce verification that you travel under official auspices, either military or political. In fact . . . in fact, I fear that your own attaché's office had never heard of you. Further inquiries are now in progress, but, alas, without passports or other supporting documents—"

"Screwed," Oscar said softly.

Doc Peret tried to smile. "Look, haven't we been through this before? I explained it—we travel under authority of certain mutual military regulations. Remember? Geneva, 1965."

"It is a pity," said Captain Rhallon.

"Yes?"

"A terrible pity, but we cannot locate such regulations."

"Well, crap," Stink moaned. "Don't you got lawyers? A good lawyer can—"

The captain nodded soberly. "I assure you, we continue to examine the regulation books. The *Savak* is engaged at this very moment in an exhaustive search through the archives. Still, there are so many treaties, so much paperwork. It takes time. Alas, it does take time."

The officer cleared his throat and turned to the third page of the report. "Meanwhile, there remain the more serious substantive matters. The carrying of automatic firearms, explosives, fragmentation grenades, bayonets, knives, and flares. The inventory is exhaustive, to say the least. You will understand why there are certain suspicions."

"We're soldiers," Eddie said. "Combat soldiers, they always carry that stuff."

For the first time the captain smiled. He made a note. "Yes," he said, "that is certainly a fine argument. And I am sure the *Savak* will listen carefully." He smiled again, then clicked his teeth. "On the other hand, in a country like ours, where internal security is paramount, even soldiers must justify the possession of such immense quantities of firepower. You understand this? Why, even our own soldiers cannot—"

"Screwed," Oscar said.

"So perhaps you will now explain to me why you carry all this?"

"We been unjustly screwed."

Doc Peret, who had been studying his fingers, sat erect. "Listen up," he said. He gazed straight at the captain's eyes. "Ten days ago, without warning or warrants, we were dragged out of bed, arrested at gunpoint, thrown in the brig, kept incommunicado, left to rot. No lawyers. No warrants. No formal charges. No informal charges. No indictment, no arraignment. No *nothing*. Now . . . now, let's get this straight. What kind of shit is this?"

Captain Rhallon frowned. "Politics," he said.

225

"Politics? What sort of politics?"

"Alas," the captain sighed, "it is impolitic to talk politics."

"No kidding?"

"But, please. It is for your own well-being to explain. I implore you—"

Doc's voice was snow. "I told it before."

"Once more, then?"

Pausing, Doc let the silence work for him. "Okay, then. But this time get it straight. We're soldiers, American infantry. Third Squad, First Platoon, Alpha Company, First Battalion of the Forty-Sixth Infantry. Mission—to find and capture a runaway named Cacciato, to bring him back to face the music. All perfectly legitimate. And those are the facts."

"Cacciato," the officer murmured. He jotted it down. "First name, please?"

No one knew it.

Eddie and Stink offered a description, which Captain Rhallon painstakingly transcribed into his notebook.

"So, then," he said. "It is this Cacciato who is the deserter, yes? Who runs from civil and military obligation?"

"Hooray."

"And you do not run?"

"No," Doc said. "Cacciato runs. We chase."

"And you do not desert?"

"You're getting it," Doc said coldly. "Now you're catching on."

Nodding, the captain scribbled in his notebook then turned to the fourth page of the report. He examined it for a long time, tracing the sentences with his pencil, a ponderous reader whose thick black eyebrows kept bunching in the manner of a child having difficulty with a complex puzzle. His eyes were weary.

"I am stupid," he finally said. "I am just a stupid soldier. But to summarize. No passports. No authorization to pass through the territories of sovereign states. No verification by local U.S. officials. No written orders dispatching you on this . . . this

226

mission. No permits for carrying a small arsenal of firepower and war matériel. Will you agree with these facts?"

Doc shrugged. "Facts are one thing," he said slowly. "Interpretation is something else. Putting facts in the right framework. And we're counting on you to do that . . . to present the right interpretation to the authorities. To get us off the hook."

"The chopping block," Oscar said. "To get us off the big block."

The captain rubbed his eyes. He placed the report back in his briefcase and stood up.

"I shall try," he said. "I am not a lawyer. I am a poor man who understands nothing. But we are fellow soldiers and so I shall do what I can."

"And in the meantime?"

"In the meantime," Captain Rhallon said, "pray for comfort in the certainty of your innocence. In the purity of your own motives."

Paul Berlin's motives, as shapeless as water, washed through his imagination: a briny, sodden pressure that weighted him like gravity, layers of inclination pressing him deeper and deeper. His brain had the bends.

Things were out of control. Gone haywire. You could run, but you couldn't outrun the consequences of running. Not even in imagination.

Imagination—sometimes it seemed he'd wasted his whole life that way. Long summer afternoons as a kid, spinning out plans for a career in professional baseball. How he would practice hard, go to all the baseball clinics, take lessons, work his way into the minor leagues, up through Class A and Triple A, then finally up to the majors—the Twins or Cubs. Figuring how it could be done. Sometimes even writing down elaborate plans, working up a strategy, using his imagination as a kind of tool to shape the future. Not exactly daydreams, not exactly fantasies. Just a way of working out the possibilities. Controlling things, directing things. And always the endings were happy. Later, in high school, there had been new sorts of things to figure out. Whether to go to college or follow his father into the house-building business. As a stall, a way of keeping options open, he'd enrolled at Centerville Junior College. A long, fruitless two years. Oh, he'd done all right—good grades, some interesting books—and for a time he'd even considered heading down to the University of Iowa for a B.A. in education. He liked history and English, he liked kids, and maybe teaching was the answer. But by the end of his second year at Centerville he was back where he started. A feeling of vague restlessness. He remembered talking to the school counselor. "Drop out?" the man had said, a short little guy without humor. "Don't you know there's a war on?" And the truth was that he didn't. He *knew,* but not in any personal sense. He'd seen the fighting on TV, read about it, but never thought of it as real. So in the end, only four credits shy of graduation, he dropped out. It wasn't really a decision; just the opposite: an inability to decide. Drifting, letting himself drift, he spent the summer of 1967 working with his father in Fort Dodge, building two fine houses on the outskirts of town, long hot days, a good tan, a sleepwalking feeling. And when he was drafted it came as no great shock. Even then the war wasn't real. He let himself be herded through basic training, then AIT, and all the while there was no sense of reality: another daydream, a weird pretending . . . He was young. That was a big part of it. He was just too young. And then the following May, home on leave, he'd gone camping with his father along the Des Moines River. "It'll be all right," his father had said. "You'll see some terrible stuff, sure, but try to look for the good things. Try to learn." And that was what he did. Curling inside himself, keeping an eye peeled for the good things. What would happen when the war ended. What he would do. Where he would go to celebrate. Paris.

But this time something had gone wrong.

They were taken to a larger, more comfortable cell fur-

228

nished with sofas and rugs and upholstered chairs. A long, blank time. Hours or days, he couldn't be sure. Oscar and Doc talked vaguely about escape, tunnels and hacksaws, but it was hopeless. The floor was cement. The walls were stone. Stink Harris began whittling a toy gun—"Like Dillinger, we'll bluff our way out"—but the toy gun came out looking like a toy gun. So they waited. They slept and wrote letters. Each morning at dawn a barber came to shave their necks. One by one, they would sit on a stool while the barber did his work: lathering their necks, sharpening his blade on a wide leather strap, then shaving them with six efficient strokes.

"Ominous," Oscar would say afterward. "It looks evil."

Paul Berlin tried hard to figure a way out. A miracle, he kept thinking. Some saving grace. He lay with Sarkin Aung Wan at night, tracing the possibilities. Sometimes he would slip back to his observation post by the sea, looking down, and he would be struck by a vision of doom. Desertion—wasn't that what it really was? And in the end weren't there always conse-quences? A calling to account? Crazy from the start. None of the roads led to Paris.

Then, one morning while they were being shaved, Captain Fahyi Rhallon entered the cell. He glanced at the razors and began backing out, but Doc waved him in.

The captain managed a weak smile. He lit a cigarette and watched as the barber draped a towel around Doc's shoulders and went to work. The razor made sounds like a pencil being drawn over parchment.

"So," Doc said. "Do we have a verdict?"

The captain seemed fascinated by the shaving operations. He watched closely as the barber brought the razor up under Doc's ear, then sharply down, then up again and down, wiping the blade after each stroke.

"Sir?"

Captain Rhallon sighed. He touched his moustache.

"I did try," he said. "I presented your case to my superiors. Pled with them to grant the benefit of doubt. I did try."

"And the verdict?"

"I am sorry."

The razor nicked Doc's neck.

There was a long quiet.

"Well," Doc sighed.

"Yes?"

"It appears it's time for some diplomatic pressure. By Uncle Sam, I mean. Time for Sammy to step in on our behalf."

The captain shook his head. "Sadly," he said, "that will not be possible. Certainly not productive. As I say, your government does not know you. Or chooses not to. In either case, I fear the outcome is the same."

"Outcome?" Doc said.

Here the captain looked away. Ash fell from his cigarette.

"Outcome?"

The captain tried to smile. "Tomorrow," he said. "There are many hours until tomorrow. Anything might happen. Leniency, a pardon—"

What outcome?"

Captain Rhallon sighed. He left the cell. The barber's razor scraped steadily over Doc's bared neck.

Immediately another officer entered the cell. He might have been Fahyi Rhallon's twin: dark skin, a moustache, creased trousers. A colonel in the *Savak*, Internal Security, he wore polished black boots and white gloves.

The man stood near the door, looking at them with a kind of curious satisfaction. His gaze finally fastened on Oscar Johnson.

"Take them off," he said. He pointed at Oscar's eyes. "The sunglasses, take them off."

"These?"

The colonel nodded.

"But, man, I got this real bad eye problem. I can't—"

Something in the officer's gaze made Oscar stop. He removed the Polaroids.

"Now place them on the floor."

"My shades?"

"The floor. Place them on the floor."

Blinking, Oscar obliged. He glanced at Eddie and grinned.

"Now," the colonel said in the flat voice of a mechanic, "please step on them."

"Step on 'em?" Oscar was still grinning. "You sayin' to squash my shades?"

The *Savak* officer brought his teeth together. Two steps, and he was across the room. Heel only, he pivoted on the Polaroids, a snapping sound like twigs breaking. His elbow hit Oscar's nose with the sound of breaking bone. Oscar was grinning as he went down.

"Clowns," the colonel said.

"That wasn't—"

"Clowns, all of you." The man's voice was like lead. His eyes fell on Paul Berlin. "Another clown, yes?"

Paul Berlin got up. Incredibly, he was smiling. He couldn't help it.

"A jail full of clowns. Deserting clowns. Clowns pretending to be on a solemn mission. Clowns telling funny stories to the *Savak*, but the *Savak* does not laugh." The man reached out and put his gloved hand on Paul Berlin's forehead. "You smile. Am I funny to you?"

"No, sir. I was—" He couldn't finish. There was fire in his eyes. His nose seemed to slide into his brain, and he was falling, and he couldn't stop smiling. Then he stopped. The pain came, and he stopped.

Removing his left glove, the colonel stared indifferently at them, as if deciding whether it was worth his while to stay.

"So," he finally said. "You will confess now."

"To what?" Stink said. "You lousy Nazi, I wouldn't—"

But Stink was already squealing, clutching his nose and falling. Paul Berlin watched from the floor. He wondered how the man did it.

"Now you will confess. You will say to me, 'Yes, we ran from our duty; stupidly, we turned and ran.' You will say it. Say it now."

They said it.

"Louder," the colonel purred. "Say it loud. Confess so I can hear well."

"We ran," they said.

"Mean it. Say it with conviction. All of you together, tell me you ran like pigs. Confess it now. Deserters who ran like pigs."

"Like pigs," they all said.

"Without honor."

"We ran like pigs," they said, all of them. Paul Berlin said it with his nose covered, breathing blood, but he said it loud.

"Now tell me that this . . . this mission, this so-called *mission* . . . tell me it is fiction. Tell me it is a made-up story. Tell me it is an alibi to cover cowardice."

And they said it loudly. They confessed.

"Tell me it is impossible to march to Paris. Say it. Confess that it is stupid and impossible."

"Stupid," they said. "Impossible."

"But with conviction. Say it loud, with great conviction."

"Stupid," they said louder.

"Shout it. Shout to me that it is stupid and impossible to walk to Paris."

They shouted it. At the top of their lungs, so that it hurt, they screamed that it was stupid and impossible.

"Clowns," the colonel said softly. "Tell me you are clowns."

"Clowns," they said.

"Louder."

"Clowns!" they shouted.

34
Lake Country

"**B**LOW 'EM," OSCAR JOHNSON repeated. "Forget going down—just blow the fuckers an' let's move on."

Lieutenant Sidney Martin shook his head. "You've got it wrong," he said. "It's SOP to search the tunnels, *then* blow them. That's the procedure and that's how it will be done."

Oscar smiled. He had a way of smiling.

"You remember Frenchie Tucker, sir?"

"I remember," said the lieutenant.

"And Bernie?"

"Both of them. I remember both of them, but that doesn't change the SOPs." Sidney Martin folded his arms. He was not afraid. "This time," he said evenly, "we're going down."

Oscar smiled and glanced at Harold Murphy, who looked away.

"Sir," Oscar said, "I don't aim to be disagreeable. It's not my nature. But, honest, there's not a man here, not a single soul, who is gonna put hisself down in that hole."

Lieutenant Sidney Martin took a notebook from his pocket. "Go down," he said.

"No," Oscar smiled. "I don' believe I will."

Nodding, Sidney Martin carefully wrote Oscar Johnson's name in his notebook. Then he ordered each man down into the tunnel, and one by one, each refused.

Sidney Martin wrote in his notebook nine times.

"Cacciato?"

"Still out fishing, sir," Vaught said.

"Berlin?"

"No, sir," said Paul Berlin.

The lieutenant shrugged, wrote down Paul Berlin's name, then took off his boots and socks and flak jacket. He did not speak. He got out his flashlight and forty-five, and he crawled into the hole.

The men grouped around to wait.

"Maybe it'll just happen," Vaught said after a time.

Oscar spat into the dirt at the mouth of the tunnel.

"I'm only wishing," Vaught said.

The men were quiet, listening to Sidney Martin's movements in the tunnel. There was a sliding sound, then a hard thump, then what seemed to be the sound of breathing.

Spec Four Paul Berlin moved away. He sat on his rucksack and looked out on the mountains. Things were wet and still. No birds: that was one of the odd things—no birds and no trees. Once there had been plently of them, a green forest, but now the trees were stumps burned to the color of coal. No underbrush, no hedges, no grass. Everywhere the earth was scorched and mangled, bombed out into bowl-shaped craters full from a week of rain. The water was gray like the sky. Down the mountainside, beyond the squad's makeshift camp, Paul Berlin could make out the dim figure of a fisherman beside one of the craters. Cacciato, he thought. A dumb kid out fishing in Lake Country. This made Paul Berlin smile. He leaned backed and pretended it wasn't a war. It was Lake Country.

"Gospel truth," Oscar was saying. "The man's got us wrote down. Every name."

234

Stink and Harold Murphy murmured.

"Every name, an' next time man's gonna make us do it." Oscar gazed into the tunnel. He sighed and smiled. "Sidney don' ever learn. The dude just don' grasp facts."

"There it is, the whole truth."

"Sidney Martin seeks trouble, an' I believe he finally found it."

"You think so, Oscar?"

"I do. I think so."

Oscar lifted the grenade from his belt. It was the new kind, shaped like a baseball, seamless, easy to handle and easy to throw.

He held it as if judging its weight.

"See my point? It's preservation. That's all it is—it's self-fuckin-preservation."

Jim Pederson rubbed his nose, looked at a spot just beyond the tunnel. "We could wait, couldn't we? Talk to him. Explain the basic facts."

"I tol' you, the man don' *grasp* facts. All he grasps is SOPs."

"True, but we could . . . we could lay it on the line. Couldn't we? Tell him exactly how things stand?"

"Then what? Oscar said. "Same shit that happened to Frenchie Tucker?"

Pederson nodded. He was a quiet kid, a former missionary to Kenya, but he nodded and looked away.

"Preservation, " Oscar said. "The survival of the species, which is us."

Alone, sitting away from the tunnel, Spec Four Paul Berlin watched the fisherman out in Lake Country. He remembered how the bombers had come to bomb the mountains, making craters, and how the rains had come to fill the craters. Doc Peret was the one who had named it: *World's Greatest Lake Country*, Doc had said, and soon it had caught on. Everyone was saying it. "Casualties in Lake Country," they had said when Bernie Lynn and Frenchie Tucker died in the tunnels

—tunnels that led to tunnels, a whole complex through mountain rock—and in each case Lieutenant Sidney Martin had insisted that the tunnels be searched.

"Touch it, " Oscar said.

He held the grenade out. He pulled the pin and clamped the spoon with his thumb.

"Everyone," he said. "I want it unanimous."

Stink touched it first. Then Eddie, then Harold Murphy, then Buff and Vaught and Pederson and Ben Nystrom, then Doc Peret.

"Berlin."

Paul Berlin was pretending it was the Wisconsin woods. Indian Guides. Deep green forests, true wilderness.

He got up and moved to the tunnel and touched the grenade.

"That everybody?"

The men looked at one another, each counting. Someone whispered Cacciato's name.

"Where's he at?"

"Fishing," Vaught said. "Last I seen, he was out fishing."

"Jesus!"

"Fetch him," Oscar Johnson said. "Hustle it up."

"No time for that." Stink leaned into the hole, listened, then shook his head. "No way—the man'll be out any second."

"Fishing!"

"Do it," Stink said. His face was red. He was excited. "Drop the bugger. Right now, just drop it."

But Oscar Johnson backed away. He slipped in the pin, bent it hard to hold the spoon, then handed the grenade to Paul Berlin.

"Go talk to Cacciato," he said.

"Talk?"

"Explain the situation. Take the frag with you. Get him involved in some group rapport."

Then Lieutenant Sidney Martin's hands showed. He pulled himself out, put on his socks and boots and stood straight. He was not afraid. "That's how it'll be done from here on," he said. He patted his breast pocket, where the names were written. "First we search them, then we blow them. In that order."

"Blow it now, sir?" Vaught said.

"Yes," Sidney Martin said. "Now you can blow it."

It took four grenades to close the hole.

Afterward, Lieutenant Sidney Martin again touched his breast pocket. "And that's exactly how it'll be done from here on, " he said. "We follow the SOPs. I hope it's understood."

Oscar smiled and said he understood perfectly.

35
World's
Greatest
Lake
Country

"THERE'S NO FISH," Paul Berlin said, but Cacciato went fishing in Lake Country. He tied a paperclip to a length of string, baited it up with bits of ham, then attached a bobber fashioned out of an empty aerosol can labeled *Secret*. Cacciato moved down to the lip of the crater. He paused as if searching for proper waters, then flipped out the line. The bobber made a light splashing sound.

"There's no fish," Paul Berlin said. "It's hopeless . . . not a single fish."

Cacciato held a finger to his lips. Squatting down, he gave the line a tug and watched as the bobber fluttered in the mercury-colored waters. The rain made Lake Country bubble.

"Don't you see?" Paul Berlin said. "It's a joke. Lake Country, it's Doc's way of joking. Get it? Bomb craters filling up with rain, it's just comedy. No lakes, no fish."

But Cacciato only smiled and held his finger to his lips.

It was getting dark. Partly it was the rain, which gave the feeling of endless twilight, but partly it was the true coming of night. The sky was silver like the water. All day Cacciato had been fishing with the patience of a fisherman, changing baits, plumbing new depths and currents, using his thumb as a guide to keep the line from tangling. He was soaked through with the rain.

"You'll catch cold," Paul Berlin said.

"I'm all right."

"Maybe so."

"I'm fine."

"Yes, but you won't be fine with a cold. A cold is all you'll catch out here."

Cacciato gazed at the bobber. His fingers were raw. They were short, fat little fingers with chewed-down nails and deep red lines where the string had cut in. His face was pulpy. It was a face like wax, or like wet paper. Parts of the face, it seemed, could be scraped off and pressed to other parts.

When the bobber had drifted in close to the bank, Cacciato pulled out the paperclip and checked the bait and then cast it back into the water. The rain made pocked little holes that opened and closed like mouths.

"Give it up," Paul Berlin said gently. "It's for your own good."

Cacciato smiled. He moved his shoulders as if working out a knot, then he settled back and watched the bobbing *Secret*.

"Give it up."

"I had some nibbles."

"No."

"Little nibbles, but the real thing. You can always tell."

"It's impossible."

"Patience," Cacciato said. "That's what my dad told me. Have patience, he says. You can't catch fish without patience."

"You can't catch fish without fish. Did he tell you that?"

"Patience."

"It won't help. It won't change anything."

Paul Berlin laid his helmet down and sat on it. He felt the rain run down his collar. Thunder came from the mountains, making the crater water slosh like soup in a bowl. Beyond the crater were four smaller craters, all full of water, and beyond

239

the last crater was the stump of a large tree. Everything in Lake Country was dead.

"So it's for your own good," Paul Berlin said.

"Did they send you down here?"

"Yes, but for your own good."

"I won't do it."

"It'll happen anyway," Paul Berlin said. "All they want is for you to join in. They want it unanimous."

Cacciato worked the line with his fingers, fishing with exactness of a fly fisherman. He did not seem to mind the rain or cold. He wiped his nose with the back of his hand, then began winding in the line, jerking it to simulate the motions of a fly. The rain was steady.

"They're worried about you," Paul Berlin said. "Eddie and Oscar. Doc, too. Doc says you'll catch the flu if you don't quit."

"You're all swell buddies."

"It isn't like that."

"What's it like?"

"It's a thing that has to be done. That's all it is. It'll be done anyway."

Cacciato smiled again. He pulled out the paperclip, rebaited it, then tossed it far out into the crater.

"I had me some nibbles," Cacciato said. "You can tell them that. Just tell 'em I had some nibbles."

"And then what? What do I say then?"

"I won't do it."

"You think that'll stop them?"

Cacciato shrugged. "He's not all that bad. Once he let me carry the radio. Remember that? Along the river, Martin let me carry the radio. He's not all that bad."

"Maybe not." Paul Berlin watched the bobber shiver in the water. "But you think that'll stop it? Nothing will stop it. It'll happen anyway."

The water looked cold. It was clear, sterile water.

Paul Berlin took out Oscar's grenade.

"They want you to touch it," he said.

Cacciato was silent. His head turned, and he looked for a moment at the grenade, then he looked away.

"They say you better touch it. It's hopeless—it'll be done no matter what. And it's for your own good."

"What about you?"

"I'm a messenger."

Paul Berlin did not look at Cacciato. He looked out over the crater. The cold made his throat ache. It made his eyes sore.

"Touch it," he said.

"I got me a nibble."

"Touch it now."

Paul Berlin pried Cacciato's left hand from the line.

"A bite," Cacciato whispered. "I got one!"

Bringing up the grenade, Paul Berlin pressed it firmly into the boy's hand. The grenade was slippery and cold.

"I do! A real *strong* bite!"

"That's swell."

"Real strong!"

Cacciato's eyes never left the bobber in Lake Country. Releasing the boy's hand, Paul Berlin put the grenade away and watched as Cacciato played with the line as though feeling for weight, for life at the other end. He was smiling. His attention was entirely on the bobbing *Secret* in Lake Country.

For a long time Paul Berlin sat by as Cacciato fished the big crater. The mountains were full of thunder and soon the rain deepened. Dark came. The water seemed to blend with the land.

It was the same as Wisconsin. Paul Berlin closed his eyes. It was the same. Pines, campfire smoke, walleyes frying, his father's after-shave lotion. Big Bear and Little Bear, pals forever. Lake Country was always so sweet.

He opened his eyes and saw Cacciato working with the paperclip.

"Any luck?"

"Sucker took my bait." Cacciato winked. "But next time I'll nail him. Now that I got the technique."

"Be patient," Paul Berlin said.

He walked up the slope toward Oscar's lean-to. In the morning, he thought, he would have to eat a good breakfast. That would help. The woods were always good for the appetite.

Eddie and Oscar and Doc Peret sat around a can of Sterno, taking turns warming their hands.

"You talk to him?"

Paul Berlin put the grenade on the ground in front of them.

"You know how it is with a fisherman," said Paul Berlin. "Mind's a million miles away."

They were quiet until the flame died. Then Oscar picked up the grenade and hooked it to his belt. "So," he said. "That's everyone."

36
Flights
of
Imagination

A T MIDNIGHT THEIR NECKS were shaved for the final
time. They were led at gunpoint into a concrete shower
stall. Afterward they were photographed, given a
supper of turkey broth and bread, then locked in a large common cell. Stink Harris wept openly. Doc and Oscar wrote letters. The lieutenant slept. Eddie Lazzutti lay face-up on a cot,
hands linked behind his head, singing nursery ballads in a
voice like steel. The long vigil began. A miracle, Paul Berlin
kept thinking. It was all he wanted—a genuine miracle to
confound natural law, a baffling reversal of the inevitable
consequences. He thought of his father for a time, and of his
mother, and then he slept, dreaming of miracles. And deep in
the night, as the moon rose, Cacciato's round face appeared at
the window. The face seemed to float. Sarkin Aung Wan
gasped and shook Paul Berlin awake. A miracle, he kept
dreaming. But he blinked and reached out to grab the M-16
that came sliding through the bars. "Go," Cacciato whispered.
He smiled. "Go," he said. And then it started—an explosion,
the great iron door shattering like a shot melon, smoke, sirens,
and there was time only to snatch for their clothes and boots,

and then they were running. Running hard through a maze of bars and steel and floodlit hallways. Gunfire chased them, but they ran. They ran through the sweep of searchlights from a high watchtower. Doors broke open, concrete blew away. Panting, clutching Cacciato's M-16, Paul Berlin kept dreaming of miracles, and he ran hard. "Go," Cacciato was shouting now, leading them through the breaking maze and over the walls and away. Away, scampering through twists of street and alley, over walls, through moonlit courtyards and nighttime bazaars where donkeys brayed and flares opened high over blue-tile domes, flares and starbursts, guns rattling behind them, chased, and they caught a glimpse of Cacciato running flat-footed through the cobbled streets, and they took off after him. Paul Berlin ran wildly. He squeezed Cacciato's rifle and Sarkin Aung Wan's hand, and he ran. Fast, through midnight streets, running with his head down and lungs splitting. Then they came to the getaway car. Cacciato stopped for a moment, breathing heavily. He pointed at the car and shouted something, then disappeared.

Oscar drove. It was an Impala, 1964. Racing stripes sparkled on the body, sponge dice dangled from the rearview mirror. Fender skirts, mudflaps, chopped and channeled, leopard-skin upholstery. They piled in, and Oscar drove.

In the backseat, eyes closed, Paul Berlin could only think of miracles. Flee, fly, fled, he thought as Oscar drove fast through wee-hour Tehran. The tenses ran together, places blended; they passed the Shah's golden palace, through the arched gate of the old city and then into slums and filth and streets with no direction.

It was cold. Paul Berlin huddled against Sarkin Aung Wan, still clutching Cacciato's rifle.

They were on back streets now. Not even streets—gravel ruts. Dark buildings loomed like jungle. Searchlights swayed through the night, and the city was full of sirens.

Navigating, Doc directed them north through Ribiscu and Ebis, and Oscar wheeled the big car through vicious hairpin turns. No muffler, and the old Impala screamed in the night. Yellow headlights plucked out statues and frozen animals and sheets of winter ice. The sky kept opening with illumination. They were hunted now—planes and helicopters, sirens, search parties with guns and lanterns, floodlights swishing through the dark and soldiers silhouetted behind high barricades. Oscar drove fast.

Once they hit a dead end. The street simply stopped. Doc swore and jumped out and waved Oscar back with a flashlight, then pointed a new way north through chains of alleys and winding stone lanes.

Flight, Paul Berlin thought. Down the depths of Tehran, running.

He opened his eyes. The streets were wider now, the buildings better spaced. They were in the outskirts, it seemed, or in a section of the city that was mostly deserted. Fires burned in vacant lots. The sound of gunfire kept chasing them.

"Eisenhower Avenue," Oscar said, reading from a passing green sign. "They like Ike."

"Impossible," Doc said, but it was Eisenhower Avenue, all right, and when the lieutenant spotted a second sign he began chanting old war ditties. He was stunned. Spittle dribbled down his chin.

Speed, Paul Berlin was thinking. He felt giddy. Speed, sped, spent—watching flashing lights, sponge dice jiggling on the mirror.

Eisenhower Avenue emptied into a huge traffic circle.

Suddenly, as they entered the rotary, the sky ignited. There was a booming sound overhead, then light, then heat. Parachutes held flares high over the traffic circle. An ambush, Paul Berlin knew, and Oscar said it.

"Bushed," Oscar whispered.

He braked hard. The Impala skidded sideways into the rotary. Something exploded in the sky, a brilliant white light. Then the whole sky opened.

"Bushed," Oscar said.

245

Paul Berlin huddled deep in the back seat. He tried to close his eyes. He pressed hard, but the eyes would not shut. He could hear the sound of artillery, the crash of illumination, the lieutenant's singing.

"Bushed," Oscar shouted.

At the center of the rotary, as at the core of a merry-go-round, a dozen tanks and APCs were coming to life. Their turrets began swiveling like tracking radar. Soldiers knelt behind the tanks. They were firing. The sounds of the rifle fire were lost in the deeper sounds of artillery, but the soldiers were firing, and red tracers made pretty darts in the wind. The car bucked. There was the sudden smell of burning metal, then tearing sounds. The red darts made holes in the doors. A window crashed open and the wind sucked in.

"Bushed," Oscar kept saying. "Fuckin ambushed," he said, braking, then accelerating. They spun fast around the rotary. Slow motion, it seemed, but fast.

One of the tanks fired. The traffic circle turned a funny violet color. The Impala was picked up, held for an instant, then dropped. It came down hard, still going fast around the rotary. A second tank fired. The traffic circle glowed purple. The car staggered but kept going.

Stink's door had come open. He was weeping, hanging on to the elbow rest, but the spinning forces kept the door open, dragging Stink out. He screamed and clawed at the door.

"Bushed," Oscar was shouting. "Bushed, bushed, bushed!"

A third tank fired. There was the same purple light. A graystone building behind them lost its middle. The top floors dropped to the bottom floors. A mix of dust and smoke and bits of stone showered down.

Stink was screaming. The spinning forces had partly pulled him from the car. He held desperately to the elbow rest, bawling, then a fourth tank fired, and a fifth, and everything turned purple. The Impala was spun around backward, and Oscar pushed down hard. Holes kept opening in the doors and windows.

Paul Berlin tried to get his eyes to close. He leaned forward into Sarkin Aung Wan's lap.

Stink's screaming went higher. Eddie grabbed for him, caught him by the collar and held on. Stink squeezed the elbow rest. He wept and screamed, and round they went, weaving, braking hard, then speeding, and the firing continued.

Oscar hit the brakes.

"Reverse," someone hollered, but they were already in reverse, moving backward now as the fire turned to track them.

Then, fleeing backward, they were suddenly beyond the roadblock, outside the rotary, moving fast up a busy expressway, only backward, and Stink Harris was still bawling and clinging to the open door. The gunfire was behind them. Sirens wailed in the next block.

A mile up the road they stopped.

"Bushed," Oscar said softly. "I believe we been badly bushed."

They helped Stink in, locked the doors, then turned into the expressway's west-going traffic.

There was no talking. They rode along quietly, letting the flow of traffic carry them out of the city. Miracles, Paul Berlin thought. He watched the gentle evening traffic. Vacations ended, families going home. A smooth tar road that climbed out of Tehran, up a steep grade that finally leveled off on a plateau. Below and behind them, except for a sky still fuzzy with illumination, the city was already gone. Soon the traffic died away. A few incoming headlights, a stalled truck, and then darkness. Ahead was open road.

So straight on through the night, flat out through quarter-moon dark as in the steppes of the far Dakotas, wolf country, and the road was smooth and fast.

Paul Berlin drove now.

The others were sleeping. Sarkin Aung Wan slept with her

head in his lap. Oscar slept silently, Doc slept with his nose held high, the lieutenant slept with messy wet breathing.

And Paul Berlin drove. His eyelids hung on speed. Run, rush, recede—a rhyme to keep his eyes open, and he clutched the wheel the way he'd once clutched his rifle, unloving but fearful of losing it. The feeling of being flung over a waterfall, a landfall, spun out to the edge of the speeding dark. No control.

He thought of the sea. And for a time he was in two spots at once. He was there, speeding through zoo country, but he was also up in the sandbagged tower over the sea, where the tips of the farthest waves had turned pink like orchids and where, if he squinted to see, the coral of the shallow waters was beginning to glow the same sweet pink, and this dawned on him and made him hurry, made him press down hard, all the way, made him shove his foot to the floor and hold on tight. It was all he could do.

Out of control, and maybe it always had been. One thing leading to the next, and pretty soon there was no guiding it, and things happened out of other things. Like the time Cacciato went fishing in Lake Country. Raining like a bitch, the whole war sopped in rain, but there was old Cacciato, out fishing in Lake Country for perch and walleyes and bullheads. He remembered it. "Everybody has to touch it," was what Oscar Johnson had said. "He'll listen to you. Go talk to him." So, sure, he'd gone down to the crater to talk sense to the kid. "Hopeless," he'd said. "And it's for your own bloody good, and even if you don't join in, even so, it'll happen anyway, but, look, it's for your own good." So he'd pressed the grenade against Cacciato's limp hand. Was it touching? Was it volition? Maybe so, maybe not. "That's everybody," Oscar said afterward.

And then Lieutenant Corson came to replace Lieutenant Sidney Martin. The way events led to events, and the way they got out of human control.

"A sad thing," Cacciato had said on the day afterward.

"Accidents happen," said Paul Berlin.

And Cacciato had shrugged, then smiled, and kept fishing in Lake Country. He fished seriously. He fished without the least show of temper or fatigue. He fished the crater from all sides, shallow and deep, and he did not give up.

A very sad thing. Cacciato was dumb, but he was right. What happened to Lieutenant Sidney Martin was a very sad thing.

Paul Berlin squeezed the wheel and hung on.

Late in the night he crossed into Turkey. The border station was deserted. For an hour afterward the land was mostly flat. Then it began climbing, and to keep himself awake he did the old counting trick. He counted mesas. He counted flat-topped hills with sides dropping like the walls of skyscrapers. Buttes and summits and ridges as in Old Mexico, ravines cut by sheer cliffs, caverns, gullies and dried-up streams and land faults, lost sheep and wild dogs, dividing stripes flowing down the center of the road, howls behind him, beats of the heart, Tartars hunting him on horseback through canyoned country.

He drove hard across the moonscaped plains.

An hour before dawn he reached Ankara. The city lay in a gentle valley, sound asleep. He pulled off onto the shoulder, got out and rubbed his stiff thighs. The coming dawn was cold.

When he got back into the car Doc Peret was awake.

"Nomad land," Doc said. "You all right?"

"I guess."

"Not what you expected, is it?"

"No," Paul Berlin said. "It never is." He started the engine and pulled back onto the road.

It took nearly half an hour to circle the city and pick up the road to Izmir. Doc did his map reading in the hazardous light.

"Another two hours," Doc finally said. "Maybe less if you wing it."

So Paul Berlin winged it. Flat-out through the Anatolian

flatlands and down the townless, lightless country toward the sea, hell-bent for water, knowing now the full meaning of desperado.

Dawn came up in the rearview mirror.

It crept up slowly, pinkish and bright. The land descended, icy streams tracing slopes toward the sea. The streams came together into a large river that paralleled the road.

Late in the morning, in a village called Salihli, they stopped to take on gas, had breakfast, then continued along the river for fifty miles before turning south toward Izmir. The country was green again. There were farms along the road. The fields were cultivated, and goats and sheep grazed peacefully behind fences.

"Salt," Doc said. He touched his nose.

Stink rolled down his window and put his head out and shouted. The wind was warm.

Eddie sang sea chanties.

Then a last line of hills bulged up. They crossed the hills, and coming down they saw the sea.

They skimmed down from the hills. They passed across acres of flat white sand. Old olive trees stood in neat rows along the road, and sprinklers turned in the sun, and the countryside was brilliant with all the colors.

Paul Berlin drove fast. There were no speed limits. They were beyond the law. Soon they came down to the first low buildings of the city, white stone and white plaster, cool-looking. The streets were white. Things were bright and clean.

He drove straight to the harbor.

He parked on a side street. Oscar paid two boys to watch the car, then they hurried down to the water.

It was exactly as he imagined it.

Tubs of iced fish and vegetables lay in rows along the wharves. Boats and tugs and sailing ships, whitewashed buildings close in against the water, the smell of fish, the salt smell.

They walked to the tip of the longest pier. They shook hands all around. Oscar was grinning, even Oscar, and Eddie and Doc and Stink were laughing like kids, teary, and Sarkin Aung Wan kissed them, and the lieutenant sang *Blow the Man Down*. The sea stretched to the horizon.

"It can be done," Paul Berlin said. He pointed west to where the sky touched the sea.

"Yeah," Doc smiled. "Maybe so."

"It can be. By God, yes, it *can* be done."

37
How
the Land
Was

W HAT PAUL BERLIN KNEW best was the land. He did
not know the people who lived on the land, but the
land itself he knew well. He knew Quang Ngai the way
a hunter sometimes knows his favorite forest, or the way a
farmer knows his own acreage. He knew the dangerous places
and he knew the safe places. He did not hate the land. Digging
his holes in preparation for night, turning a spadeful of earth
and letting it fall, he sometimes felt fear, or curiosity, but he
never felt hate. Mostly he was struck with a powerful wonder-
ment about the physical place, the texture of the soil, the colors
and shadings, the slopes of countryside in relation to grander
slopes and higher angles of vision.

Quang Ngai was farm country. There was some fishing on
the coast—shrimps and red snapper and squid—and far to the
west there were mountains with rubber and fruit, but mostly
Quang Ngai was farm country.

The farms were rice farms. Village-owned and village-run,
the farms were worked not as private farms but as communi-
ties; the land was planted and tended by the people who lived
in the villages, and the harvest was placed in huge clay jugs,

some of which were buried, some of which were taken to market in larger villages. But he did not know the economics. What he knew was the land. He knew that the villages, at the center of the land, were part of the land. He knew that the commodity was rice, and that the rice was grown in paddies.

The paddies gave depth to the land. Depth that he'd never known before, not in Fort Dodge, where the land was smooth with corn in August, not in cities, where land was concrete. In Quang Ngai the land was deep. He knew from long days on the march that there was nothing loathsome about the smell of the paddies. The smell was alive: bacteria, fungus and algae, compounds that made and sustained life. It was not a pretty smell, but it was no more evil or rank than the smell of sweat. Sometimes, when there was no choice, he had slept in the paddies. He knew the softness and warmth, later the chill. He had spent whole nights that way, his back against a dike and his feet and legs and lap deep in the paddies. Once, on the very hottest day at the war, he had even taken a drink of paddy water, and he knew the taste. He'd swirled the water in his hands, letting the biggest chunks of filth settle, then, because his thirst had been greater than the fear of disease, he'd swallowed. He had done this knowing it was dangerous. "Don't never pee in a paddy," he was once told by a helpful PFC stateside. "You do, you'll get this sickness called elephantiasis. Real bad shit. The viruses live in the paddies, see, so when you pee the little buggers'll swim right up your urine stream, right up into your prick." But Paul Berlin peed when he had to pee, and sometimes he had to pee in paddies: standing knee-deep in the slime, imagining a billion brave viruses paddling hard in search of unpolluted waters.

Whenever he thought of the land, he thought first of the paddies. But next, almost in the same thought, he thought of the hedgerows. They were not the hedges found in museum gardens or on the front lawns of old Iowa houses. They were thick, unclipped, untended tangles. Twice the height of a tall man, the hedgerows served the function that fences serve in richer countries: They held some things in and other things out. But more than that, the hedges were a kind of clothing for the villages. From far off a village was not a village. From a distance, even seen through binoculars, a village was a thicket of vines and shrubs, and only behind the hedges did you see the true village. Guarding, but mostly concealing, the hedgerows in Quang Ngai sometimes seemed like a kind of smoked glass forever hiding whatever it was that was not meant to be seen. Like curtains, or like walls. Like camouflage. So where the paddies represented ripeness and age and depth, the hedgerows expressed the land's secret qualities: cut up, twisting, covert, chopped and mangled, blind corners leading to dead ends, short horizons always changing. It was only a feeling. A feeling of marching through a great maze, the feeling that mice must have as they run mazes. A sense of entrapment mixed with mystery. The hedgerows were like walls in old mansions: secret panels and trapdoors and portraits with moving eyes. That was the feeling the hedges always gave him, just a feeling.

The earth was red. He saw it first from the air, on the day he joined the war. A coral pink, brighter in some spots than in others, but always there. Later, as he looked closer, he saw it like film on the men's weapons and clothing and boots, under Stink's fingernails, on Vaught's sallow skin, clouding Doc Peret's glasses. The red, Doc explained, most likely came from a high ferric content in the soil, and from an oxidizing process, but for Paul Berlin the origins were unimportant.

The war was fought with the feet and legs, so he knew the trails. Dusty paths connecting one village to the next, or the pressed mud along paddy dikes, or the beaten-down grass of soldiers who had passed that way before. Sometimes the trails were roads, though never tar or concrete: The roads were called roads if they showed marks of cart traffic or the wear of wheeled artillery. It was best, of course, to stay off the trails. But often, when the men were tired or lazy or in a hurry, they used the trails despite the dangers. The trails, like the land, were red. They were narrow. They were often dark, or shaded, and they mostly wound through the low places, following the contours of the land, and for this reason they sometimes flooded out during the rainy season. They were dangerous. No one was ever killed by a land mine or booby trap unless it was along a trail. Exposed, always watched, the trails were the obvious spots for ambush. Still, there were many times when it was better to face these dangers than to face the wet of a paddy or the itch of deep brush. There were times when a fast march along a trail, however perilous, was preferable to a slow march through hostile country. There were times when mission required the use of trails. And there were times when it simply stopped mattering.

Small, unprofound things. The land's peculiar heaviness. The slowness with which things moved—days and nights, bullocks in the paddies, the Song Tra Bong. The squatness of the trees, the way foliage seemed to grow outward rather than upward. Few birds: It was one of those details that Paul Berlin noticed but never understood. "Where have the birds gone?" he asked Eddie Lazzutti one evening. Eddie stopped and listened. "What birds?" he said.

He had seen it in movies. He had read about poverty in magazines and newspapers, seen pictures of it on television. So when he saw the villages of Quang Ngai, he had seen it all before. He had seen, before seeing, hideous skin diseases, hunger, rotting animals, huts without furniture or plumbing or light. He had seen the shit-fields where villagers squatted. He had seen chickens roosting on babies. Misery and want, bloated bellies, scabs and pus-wounds, even death. All of it, he'd seen it before. So when he *saw* it—when he first entered a village south of Chu Lai—he felt a kind of mild surprise,

255

fleeting compassion, but not amazement. He knew what he would see and he saw it. He was not stricken by what he saw; he was not angered by it, or made to grieve. He felt no great horror. He felt some guilt, but that passed quickly. He had seen it all, before seeing it.

Quang Ngai started at the sea. The beaches were clean, white, beautiful. It was the sea that Paul Berlin liked best. Beyond the sea was paddy land. Beyond the paddies, going inland, was another kind of country altogether, meadows and uncut brush that climbed into foothills with few villages or people. Beyond the foothills were the mountains. Beyond the mountains, and beyond Quang Ngai, was Paris. He did not think beyond Paris.

38
On the Lam to Paris

ROM IZMIR THEY BOOKED a three-day passage to Athens. Oscar Johnson made the arrangements in a series of shady tavern dealings, and on a mild Sunday morning in March they boarded the *Andros,* an old freighter repainted and made over to accommodate thirty paying passengers. The decks were simple sheet steel. Rust covered the chain rigging and rails. Below, the passengers' quarters were cramped, dim lighting flickering in the companionways, but still it was a smooth and restful crossing. A true tourist feeling. Oscar and Eddie organized a shuffleboard tournament, Doc spent time reading, and Paul Berlin staked claim to a rattan recliner near the ship's bow. Sitting there through the warm afternoon hours, he watched the islands slide by like pictures in a travel magazine. He had a sense of immense calm. Pale Mediterranean waters, the sun's heat, mixed smells of oil and machinery and brine and fish.

A pleasant, leisurely passage: The first night they docked at the island of Psara, then in the morning they cruised southward past Khios and Ikaria, rounded the lower tip of Naxos and steamed straight west through the soft hours of late afternoon.

The lieutenant's health improved. The sun gave his face color. He resumed command. On the second day of the crossing, he ordered Eddie and Stink to see about getting haircuts; that same evening he sat down with Doc Peret for a conference about possible routes north after disembarking at Piraeus. He ate well and drank moderately.

Mostly this was Sarkin Aung Wan's doing. Like a daughter caring for an ailing father, she encouraged him to eat and exercise, coddled him, scolded him, gently coaxed him into showing some concern for his own welfare and that of his men. The lieutenant seemed deeply attached to her. It was an unspoken thing. They would sometimes spend whole days together, walking the decks or throwing darts or simply sitting in the sun. When the lieutenant showed signs of the old withdrawal, Sarkin Aung Wan reminded him of his responsibilities. "A leader must lead," she would say. "Without leadership, a leader is nothing." Then she would take the old man's hand and press it between hers, smile, and begin talking of the lovely things they would see in Paris. Her own motives were secret. What did she want? Refuge, as sought by refugees, or escape, as sought by victims? It was impossible to tell. Softly, effortlessly, she guided the old man toward recovery, and toward Paris, and through him she guided all of them.

So as the *Andros* made its way past Sífnos and Sérifos and Kíthnos, Paul Berlin let himself relax in his rattan recliner at the bow. The sea was calm, the air was sweet. They'd done it. The war was over. Ahead was Paris. "Make it to Athens," Cacciato had said, "and the rest is easy."

It was near midnight when they came in to Piraeus. Despite the late hour, the wharves were jammed with people milling in the light of torches and colored bulbs strung up along the piers and loading docks. Another tour ship had docked within the hour, and a swarm of customs agents and police moved through the crowd with sheathed bayonets. Clearly it was more than a routine customs check. Male passengers were being led off to one side, where they were thoroughly searched by a dozen white-helmeted policemen; baggage was dumped open on the spot; a loudspeaker blared out warnings for order in three languages. Each policeman carried a large poster of the sort that is tacked to post office bulletin boards, and the officers seemed to be trying to match faces to whatever was on the posters. The noise was fierce.

The ship turned in slowly toward the lighted docks.

"Us?" Stink said.

The others were silent. Eddie slumped over the railing, gazing listlessly down at the columns of police. His face was drained. Behind him, Sarkin Aung Wan and the lieutenant sat at a small table roofed by a red and green umbrella.

"Screwed and skewered," Oscar said. "Cops up the ass."

Doc Peret shrugged. "We almost made it."

"I can't—"

"So close," Doc sighed, "and yet so close."

Stink Harris was fidgeting. His tongue flicked out to lick sweat from his upper lip. He leaned over the railing, looked down, then quickly moved over to the lieutenant.

"Well, come on," he said, shaking the old man's shoulder. "Let's go. What's the plan?"

"Nothing I can do."

Stink's teeth rapped together. Again he shook Lieutenant Corson's shoulder, harder this time. The old man did not move. Stink hurried up to the bow, where the crew was making preparations for docking. He stood there a moment, his fingers twitching, then he turned on his heel and rushed back.

"Criminny! Think of something . . . What's the plan?"

Nobody answered. Eddie gazed straight ahead. Doc sat down Indian-style and put his head in his hands. Looking down on the wharves, Paul Berlin counted forty policemen before

259

he gave it up. Hopeless. The odds had been poison from the start.

Stink was frantic. He grabbed Oscar's arm.

"What we gonna do? Geez, I never . . . Jump! We could jump! Make a swim for it!"

"It's over, man."

"Bullshit it is! Disguises . . . That's it! We'll dress ourselves up. Like women or something. Couldn't we? Sure, we'll get disguised and slip by like smoke. Easy!"

Oscar pulled his arm free.

"What's wrong with you guys?" Stink shook his head violently, stepping back from them. His fingers kept twitching. "A joke, right? Right? Trying to fool me?"

Nobody spoke. The ship's foghorn made a loud rumbling sound as they slipped in toward the docks.

Stink smiled to show it was a fine joke. He touched Eddie's sleeve, then began tugging it, short jerking tugs.

"Quit?" Stink said. "Just quit?"

"Look, little man, you can't buck—"

"Bullshit!"

Stink's face collapsed. His fists clenched and he stepped back from them. His lips tightened. And for a moment, for the first and only time, Paul Berlin felt a measure of respect for Stink Harris. Not respect, exactly. Understanding, maybe—knowledge. The kid was a scrapper. Tough and unquitting.

Stink glared at them for a moment, then turned away.

Quickly, he stripped down to his underwear. He did not speak. He stuffed his shirt and trousers into his boots, tied the boots around his neck, and climbed over the railing. His skin was white. He held his wallet in one hand, his pocketknife in the other.

"Come on," Doc murmured. "It's not—"

Stink did not look back. "Fuck you fuckers," he said. That was all he said.

He jumped.

He pinched his nose, closed his eyes, and jumped.

There was no splash. They did not see him hit.

As the ship slipped cleanly into its moorings, and as the first ropes were cast off, Paul Berlin could make out the dim silver wake of a swimmer in the waters behind him. Silver, dark, silver, dark. Then the wake was gone. So was Stink Harris.

39
The
Things
They Didn't
Know

"LUI LAI, LUI LAI!" STINK would scream, pushing them back. *"Lui lai,* you dummies . . . Back up, move!" Teasing ribs with his rifle muzzle, he would force them back against a hootch wall or fence. *"Coi chung!"* he'd holler. Blinking, face white and teeth clicking, he would kick the stragglers, pivot, shove, thumb flicking the rifle's safety catch. "Move! *Lui lai* . . . Move it, go, go!" Herding them together, he would watch to be sure their hands were kept in the open, empty. Then he would open his dictionary. He would read slowly, retracing the words several times, then finally look up. *"Nam xuong dat,"* he'd say. Separating each word, trying for good diction, he would say it in a loud, level voice. "Everybody . . . *nam xuong dat."* The kids would just stare. The women might rock and moan, or begin chattering among themselves like caged squirrels, glancing up at Stink with frazzled eyes. "Now!" he'd shout. *"Nam xuong dat* . . . Do it!" Sometimes he would fire off a single shot, but this only made the villagers fidget and squirm. Puzzled, some of them would start to giggle. Others would cover their ears and yap with the stiff, short barking sounds of small dogs. It drove Stink wild. *"Nam xuong* the fuck down!" he'd snarl, his thin lips curling in a manner he practiced while shaving. "Lie down! *Man len,* mama-san! Now, goddamn it!" His eyes would bounce from his rifle to the dictionary to the cringing villagers. Behind him, Doc Peret and Oscar Johnson and Buff would be grinning at the show. They'd given the English-Vietnamese dictionary to Stink as a birthday present, and they loved watching him use it, the way he mixed languages in a kind of stew, ignoring pronunciation and grammar, turning angry when words failed to produce results. *"Nam thi xuong dat!"* he'd bellow, sweating now, his tongue sputtering over the impossible middle syllables. *"Man len,* pronto, you sons of bitches! Haul ass!" But the villagers would only shake their heads and cackle and mill uncertainly. This was too much for Stink Harris. Enraged, he'd throw away the dictionary and rattle off a whole magazine of ammunition. The women would moan. Kids would clutch their mothers, dogs would howl, chickens would scramble in their coops. *"Dong* fuckin *lat thit!"* Stink would be screaming, his eyes dusty and slit like a snake's. *"Nam xuong dat!* Do it, you ignorant bastards!" Reloading, he would keep firing and screaming, and the villagers would sprawl in the dust, arms wrapped helplessly around their heads. And when they were all down, Stink would stop firing. He would smile. He would glance at Doc Peret and nod. "See there? They understand me fine. *Nam xuong dat* . . . Lie down. I'm gettin' the hang of it. You just got to punctuate your sentences."

Not knowing the language, they did not know the people. They did not know what the people loved or respected or feared or hated. They did not recognize hostility unless it was patent, unless it came in a form other than language; the complexities of tone and tongue were beyond them. Dinkese, Stink Harris called it: monkey chatter, bird talk. Not knowing the language, the men did not know whom to trust. Trust was lethal. They did not know false smiles from true smiles, or if in Quang Ngai a smile had the same meaning it had in the

States. "Maybe the dinks got things mixed up," Eddie once said, after the time a friendly-looking farmer bowed and smiled and pointed them into a minefield. "Know what I mean? Maybe . . . well, maybe the gooks cry when they're happy and smile when they're sad. Who the hell knows? Maybe when you smile over here it means you're ready to cut the other guy's throat. I mean, hey . . . didn't they tell us way back in AIT that this here's a different culture?" Not knowing the people, they did not know friends from enemies. They did not know if it was a popular war, or, if popular, in what sense. They did not know if the people of Quang Ngai viewed the war stoically, as it sometimes seemed, or with grief, as it seemed other times, or with bewilderment or greed or partisan fury. It was impossible to know. They did not know religions or philosophies or theories of justice. More than that, they did not know how emotions worked in Quang Ngai. Twenty years of war had rotted away the ordinary reactions to death and disfigurement. Astonishment, the first response, was never there in the faces of Quang Ngai. Disguised, maybe. But who knew? Who ever knew? Emotions and beliefs and attitudes, motives and aims, hopes—these were unknown to the men in Alpha Company, and Quang Ngai told nothing. "Fuckin beasties," Stink would croak, mimicking the frenzied village speech. "No shit, I seen hamsters with more feelings."

But for Paul Berlin it was always a nagging question: Who were these skinny, blank-eyed people? What did they want? The kids especially—watching them, learning their names and faces, Paul Berlin couldn't help wondering. It was a ridiculous, impossible puzzle, but even so he wondered. Did the kids *like* him? A little girl with gold hoops in her ears and ugly scabs on her brow—did she feel, as he did, goodness and warmth and poignancy when he helped Doc dab iodine on her sores? Beyond that, though, did the girl *like* him? Lord knows, he had no villainy in his heart, no motive but kindness. He wanted health for her, and happiness. Did she know this? Did she sense his compassion? When she smiled, was it more than a token?

And . . . and what *did* she want? Any of them, what did they long for? Did they have secret hopes? His hopes? Could this little girl—her eyes squinting as Doc brushed the scabs with iodine, her lips sucked in, her nose puckering at the smell—could she somehow separate him from the war? Even for an instant? Could she see him as just a scared-silly boy from Iowa? Could she feel sympathy? In it together, trapped, you and me, all of us: Did she feel that? Could she understand his own fear, matching it with hers? Wondering, he put mercy in his eyes like lighted candles; he gazed at the girl, full-hearted, draining out suspicion, opening himself to whatever she might answer with. Did the girl see the love? Could she understand it, return it? But he didn't know. He did not know if love or its analogue even existed in the vocabulary of Quang Ngai, or if friendship could be translated. He simply did not know. He wanted to be liked. He wanted them to understand, all of them, that he felt no hate. It was all a sad accident, he would have told them—chance, high-level politics, confusion. He had no stake in the war beyond simple survival; he was there, in Quang Ngai, for the same reasons they were: the luck of the draw, bad fortune, forces beyond reckoning. His intentions were benign. By God, yes! He was snared in a web as powerful and tangled as any that victimized the people of My Khe or Pinkville. Sure, they were trapped. Sure, they suffered, sure. But, by God, he was just as trapped, just as injured. He would have told them that. He was no tyrant, no pig, no Yankee killer. He was innocent. Yes, he was. He was innocent. He would have told them that, the villagers, if he'd known the language, if there had been time to talk. He would have told them he wanted to harm no one. Not even the enemy. The enemy! A word, a crummy word. He *had* no enemies. He had wronged no one. If he'd known the language, he would have told them how he hated to see the villages burned. Hated to see the paddies trampled. How it made him angry and sad when . . . a million things, when women were frisked with free hands, when old men were made to drop their pants to be searched, when, in a ville called

Thin Mau, Oscar and Rudy Chassler shot down ten dogs for the sport of it. Sad and stupid. Crazy. Mean-spirited and self-defeating and wrong. Wrong! He would have told them this, the kids especially. But not me, he would have told them. The others, maybe, but not me. Guilty perhaps of hanging on, of letting myself be dragged along, of falling victim to gravity and obligation and events, but not—not!—guilty of wrong intentions.

After the war, perhaps, he might return to Quang Ngai. Years and years afterward. Return to track down the girl with gold hoops through her ears. Bring along an interpreter. And then, with the war ended, history decided, he would explain to her why he had let himself go to war. Not because of strong convictions, but because he didn't know. He didn't know who was right, or what was right; he didn't know if it was a war of self-determination or self-destruction, outright aggression or national liberation; he didn't know which speeches to believe, which books, which politicians; he didn't know if nations would topple like dominoes or stand separate like trees; he didn't know who really started the war, or why, or when, or with what motives; he didn't know if it mattered; he saw sense in both sides of the debate, but he did not know where truth lay; he didn't know if Communist tyranny would prove worse in the long run than the tyrannies of Ky or Thieu or Khanh—he simply didn't know. And who did? Who really did? He couldn't make up his mind. Oh, he had read the newspapers and magazines. He wasn't stupid. He wasn't uninformed. He just didn't know if the war was right or wrong. And who did? Who really *knew*? So he went to the war for reasons beyond knowledge. Because he believed in law, and law told him to go. Because it was a democracy, after all, and because LBJ and the others had rightful claim to their offices. He went to the war because it was expected. Because not to go was to risk censure, and to bring embarrassment on his father and his town. Because, not knowing, he saw no reason to distrust those with more experience. Because he loved his country and, more than that, because he trusted it. Yes, he did. Oh, he would rather have fought with his father in France, knowing certain things certainly, but he couldn't choose his war, nobody could. Was this so banal? Was this so unprofound and stupid? He would look the little girl with gold earrings straight in the eye. He would tell her these things. He would ask her to see the matter his way. What would *she* have done? What would *anyone* have done, not knowing? And then he would ask the girl questions. What did she want? How did she see the war? What were her aims—peace, any peace, peace with dignity? Did she refuse to run for the same reasons he refused—obligation, family, the land, friends, home? And now? Now, war ended, what did she want? Peace and quiet? Peace and pride? Peace with mashed potatoes and Swiss steak and vegetables, a full-tabled peace, indoor plumbing, a peace with Oldsmobiles and Hondas and skyscrapers climbing from the fields, a peace of order and harmony and murals on public buildings? Were her dreams the dreams of ordinary men and women? Quality-of-life dreams? Material dreams? Did she want a long life? Did she want medicine when she was sick, food on the table and reserves in the pantry? Religious dreams? What? What did she *aim* for? If a wish were to be granted by the war's winning army—any wish—what would she choose? Yes! If LBJ and Ho were to rub their magic lanterns at war's end, saying, "Here is what it was good for, here is the fruit," what would Quang Ngai demand? Justice? What sort? Reparations? What kind? Answers? What were the questions: What did Quang Ngai want to know?

In September, Paul Berlin was called before the battalion promotion board.

"You'll be asked some questions," the first sergeant said. "Answer them honestly. Don't for Chrissake make it complicated—just good, honest answers. And get a fuckin haircut."

It was a three-officer panel. They sat like squires behind a tin-topped table, two in sunglasses, the third in skintight tiger fatigues.

Saluting, reporting with his name and rank, Paul Berlin stood at attention until he was told to be seated.

"Berlin," said one of the officers in sunglasses. "That's a pretty fucked-up name, isn't it?"

Paul Berlin smiled and waited.

The officer licked his teeth. He was a plump, puffy-faced major with spotted skin. "No bull, that's got to be the weirdest name I ever run across. Don't sound American. You an American, soldier?"

"Yes, sir."

"Yeah? Then where'd you get such a screwy name?"

"I don't know, sir."

"Sheeet." The major looked at the captain in tiger fatigues. "You hear that? This trooper don't know where he got his own name. You ever promoted somebody who don't know how he got his own fuckin name?"

"Maybe he forgot," said the captain in tiger fatigues.

"Amnesia?"

"Could be. Or maybe shell shock or something. Better ask again."

The major sucked his dentures halfway out of his mouth, frowned, then let the teeth slide back into place. "Can't hurt nothin'. Okay, soldier, one more time—where'd you find that name of yours?"

"Inherited it, sir. From my father."

"You crappin' me?"

"No, sir."

"And just where the hell'd he come up with it . . . your ol' man?"

"I guess from his father, sir. It came down the line sort of." Paul Berlin hesitated. It was hard to tell if the man was serious.

"You a Jewboy, soldier?"

"No, sir."

"A Kraut! Berlin . . . by jiminy, that's a Jerry name if I ever heard one!"

"I'm mostly Dutch."

"The hell, you say."

"Yes, sir."

"Balls!"

"Sir, it's not—"

"Where's Berlin?"

"Sir?"

The major leaned forward, planting his elbows carefully on the table. He looked deadly serious. "I asked where Berlin is. You heard of fuckin Berlin, didn't you? Like in East Berlin, West Berlin?"

"Sure, sir. It's in Germany."

"Which one?"

"Which what, sir?"

The major moaned and leaned back. Beside him, indifferent to it all, the captain in tiger fatigues unwrapped a thin cigar and lit it with a kitchen match. Red acne covered his face like the measles. He winked quickly—maybe it wasn't even a wink —then gazed hard at a sheaf of papers. The third officer sat silently. He hadn't moved since the interview began.

"Look here," the major said. "I don't know if you're dumb or just stupid, but by God I aim to find out." He removed his sunglasses. Surprisingly, his eyes were almost jolly. "You're up for Spec Four, that right?"

"Yes, sir."

"You want it? The promotion?"

"Yes, sir, I do."

"Lots of responsibility."

Paul Berlin smiled. He couldn't help it.

"So we can't have shitheads leadin' men, can we? Takes some brains. You got brains, Berlin?"

"Yes, *sir.*"

"You know what a condom is?"

Paul Berlin nodded.

269

"A condom," the major intoned solemnly, "is a skullcap for us swingin' dicks. Am I right?"

"Yes, sir."

"And to lead men you got to be a swingin' fuckin dick."

"Right, sir."

"And is that you? You a swingin' dick, Berlin?"

"Yes, sir!"

"You got guts?"

"Yes, sir. I—"

"You 'fraid of gettin' zapped?"

"No, sir."

"Sheeet." The major grinned as if having scored an important victory. He used the tip of his pencil to pick a speck of food from between his teeth. "Dumb! Anybody not scared of gettin' his ass zapped is a dummy. You know what a dummy is?"

"Yes, sir."

"Spell it."

Paul Berlin spelled it.

The major rapped his pencil against the table, then glanced at his wristwatch. The captain in tiger fatigues was smoking with his eyes closed; the third officer, still silent, stared blankly ahead, arms folded tight against his chest.

"Okay," said the major, "we got a few standard-type questions for you. Just answer 'em truthfully, no bullshit. You don't know the answers, say so. One thing I can't stand is wishy-washy crap. Ready?"

"Yes, sir."

Pulling out a piece of yellow paper, the major put his pencil down and read slowly.

"How many stars we got in the flag?"

"Fifty," said Paul Berlin.

"How many stripes?"

"Thirteen."

"What's the muzzle velocity of a standard AR-15?"

"Two thousand feet a second."

"Who's Secretary of the Army?"

"Stanley Resor."

"Why we fightin' this war?"

"Sir?"

"I say, why we fightin' this fuckin-ass war?"

"I don't—"

"To win it," said the third, silent officer. He did not move. His arms remained flat across his chest, his eyes blank. "We fight this war to win it, that's why."

"Yes, sir."

"Again," the major said. "Why we fightin' this war?"

"To win it, sir."

"You sure of that?"

"Positive, sir." His arms were hot. He tried to hold his chin level.

"Tell it loud, trooper: Why we fightin' this war?"

"To win it."

"Yeah, but I mean *why*?"

"Just to win it," Paul Berlin said softly. "That's all. To win it."

"You know that for a fact?"

"Yes, sir. A fact."

The third officer made a soft, humming sound of satisfaction. The major grinned at the captain in tiger fatigues.

"All right," said the major. His eyes twinkled. "Maybe you aren't so dumb as you let on. *Maybe.* We got one last question. This here's a cultural-type matter . . . listen up close. What effect would the death of Ho Chi Minh have on the population of North Vietnam?"

"Sir?"

Reading slowly from his paper, the major repeated it. "What effect would the death of Ho Chi Minh have on the population of North Vietnam?"

Paul Berlin let his chin fall. He smiled.

"Reduce it by one, sir."

In Quang Ngai, they did not speak of politics. It wasn't taboo, or bad luck, it just wasn't talked about. Even when the Peace

Talks bogged down in endless bickering over the shape and size of the bargaining table, the men in Alpha Company took it as another bad joke—silly and sad—and there was no serious discussion about it, no sustained outrage. Diplomacy and morality were beyond them. Hardly anyone cared. Not even Doc Peret, who loved a good debate. Not even Jim Pederson, who believed in virtue. This dim-sighted attitude enraged Frenchie Tucker. "My God," he'd sometimes moan in exasperation, speaking to Paul Berlin but aiming at everyone, "it's your *ass* they're negotiating. Your ass, my ass . . . Do we live or die? That's the issue, by God, and you blockheads don't even talk about it. Not even a lousy *opinion*! Good Lord, doesn't it piss you off, all this Peace Talk crap? Round tables, square tables! Idiotic diplomatic etiquette, power plays, maneuvering! And here we sit, suckin' air while those mealy-mouthed sons of bitches can't even figure out what kind of table they're gonna sit at. Jesus!" But Frenchie's rage never caught on. Sometimes there were jokes, cynical and weary, but there was no serious discussion. No beliefs. They fought the war, but no one took sides.

They did not know even the simple things: a sense of victory, or satisfaction, or necessary sacrifice. They did not know the feeling of taking a place and keeping it, securing a village and then raising the flag and calling it a victory. No sense of order or momentum. No front, no rear, no trenches laid out in neat parallels. No Patton rushing for the Rhine, no beachheads to storm and win and hold for the duration. They did not have targets. They did not have a cause. They did not know if it was a war of ideology or economics or hegemony or spite. On a given day, they did know where they were in Quang Ngai, or how being there might influence larger outcomes. They did not know the names of most villages. They did not know which villages were critical. They did not know strategies. They did not know the terms of the war, its architecture, the rules of fair play. When they took prisoners, which was rare, they did not know the questions to ask, whether to release a suspect or beat on him. They did not know how to feel. Whether, when seeing a dead Vietnamese, to be happy or sad or relieved; whether, in times of quiet, to be apprehensive or content; whether to engage the enemy or elude him. They did not know how to feel when they saw villages burning. Revenge? Loss? Peace of mind or anguish? They did not know. They knew the old myths about Quang Ngai—tales passed down from old-timer to newcomer—but they did not know which stories to believe. Magic, mystery, ghosts and incense, whispers in the dark, strange tongues and strange smells, uncertainties never articulated in war stories, emotion squandered on ignorance. They did not know good from evil.

40
By a Stretch of the Imagination

I T WOULD NOT HAVE ENDED that way: cops and customs agents, defeat, arrested like wetbacks at the wharves of Western Civilization, captured within mindshot of the lighted Propylaea and Parthenon, nothing fulfilled, no answers, the whole expedition throttled just as it approached the promise of a rightful end. It wouldn't have happened that way. And it didn't. Again—back for an instant in his observation tower by the sea—again, this wasn't a madman's fantasy. Paul Berlin was awake and fully sane. Not a dream, he thought, nothing demented or unconscious or fanatic about it. He touched his left wrist. The pulse was firm. His brain tingled, his vision was twenty-twenty. Nothing nutty, nothing unusual. Leaning against the wall of sandbags, his back to the South China Sea, he was in full command of his faculties. He was speculating. Figuring the odds. Was this so crazy? Didn't everyone do it, one way or another, more or less? The pastime of whole armies—trench speculation, battlefield dreams, men figuring how, if suddenly free, they would deploy the rest of their lives. Everyone did it. Imagining how to spend freedom: squander it, invest it, use it like Monopoly money. Even Doc

Peret admitted to daydreams like that. Even Eddie Lazzutti liked to talk about how he'd use a million dollars if it came to him. After the war . . . that was how it always started. After the war: buy a car, travel, visit Disneyland, screw everything in sight, spend a year in the woods, never worry about trivial stuff, enjoy life, live. What if ? What then? That was all it was. It was speculation. A way of playing with the possibilities, figuring out step by step how it might be done.

So, no. No, it would not have ended at Piraeus. It didn't. They were not arrested. Coming down the gangplank, weary and expecting the worst, they filed through platoons of police and customs agents, eyes down, breath held, passing like magic through the main loading yard, through a gateway guarded by two cops who only nodded and waved them by, through a sea-smelling corridor that emptied at last into a dark street.

"So easy," Sarkin Aung Wan murmured. She hooked the lieutenant's arm and helped him toward a waiting taxi. "Like blinking, so easy. Like breathing."

The old man glanced behind him as if expecting pursuit. His uniform had the stale smell of sickness in it, an odor that couldn't be washed away. He walked with a slight limp. Eddie and Doc and Oscar followed, then Paul Berlin. Easy, he thought. No passports, no money, hunted down like common crooks, runaways. But, still, it was easy. His imagination, keen as a razor's edge, cut through the ordinary obstacles. He remembered what Cacciato had said on the morning he'd left the war: Make it to Athens and the rest is easy.

They spent two days there, or maybe a week. They rested, visited the Acropolis, made the usual inquiries about Cacciato. At first they hoped Stink might appear, wet and grinning and chastened, but as time passed so did their expectations. "He'll be here," Oscar kept saying. "The dude's got staying power, he'll make it." But there was nothing. Each day Doc checked the English newspapers for notices of drowning victims; Oscar and Eddie scoured the wharves and seedy back streets behind the Plaka, even went through a file of grisly photographs at the police morgue. But nothing. So with great misgivings the lieutenant decided there was no choice but to move on. "I don't like it either," he said, ignoring Oscar's steady stare. "But, look . . . we gave it our best, didn't we? We looked hard. Maybe—you know—maybe he'll show up along the way. Maybe he's waiting for us up the road."

They boarded a northbound bus for Zagreb.

"Foolishness," Oscar said, watching the city recede. "That's what I'm gonna miss. Stinko, the dude had loads of foolishness. No foolishness, no fun. No purchase on life's slippery runway."

"Sure."

"Dig my meaning?"

"Dig," Doc said. "Consider it dug."

In late afternoon they reached the border. The bus stopped outside a small wooden hut where six soldiers sat playing cards. The driver honked twice but none of the soldiers looked up. On the Yugoslav side it was the same smooth crossing, two honks and a wave, then the bus was moving fast again along the road to Zagreb.

Paul Berlin looked out on the dry, spare country. He could see mountains to the west, a long purply range that seemed endless. Behind the mountains was the sun. It was all so effortless. A matter of a few beginning steps, or a few thousand, and once started, it was as easy as sleep. Drowsy, listening to the sound of the tires on the road, Paul Berlin wondered why soldiers didn't desert by the millions.

They spent the night in Zagreb. In the morning they hiked out to a tar highway and hitched a ride north with a girl from California. It was a battered VW van that smelled of grease and orange peels. The girl was a revolutionary. Between Zagreb and the Austrian frontier she lectured Doc on the meaning of doom: assassinations, cities on fire, students swarming through Washington, universities under siege.

"It's coming down," she said. "It's happening."

276

Doc nodded. He lay back in a pile of blankets at the rear of the van. Slyly, still nodding, he winked at Paul Berlin.

Outside, tiny white flowers grew on the melting mountainsides.

"The thing I can't get over," the girl said, "is that you dudes actually were *there*. I mean, like, you saw evil firsthand. Saw it and smelled it. The evil. Children getting toasted, the orphans, atrocities. And you had the guts to walk away. That's courage."

"Well, it wasn't—"

"And the guilt." The girl wagged her head sadly. "God, the guilt must be awful."

"Guilt?" Oscar said.

"It must hurt badly."

Oscar looked at Eddie. "You got guilt, man?"

"All over," Eddie smiled.

The girl ignored them. From the shoulders up, she was all energy and motion, her eyes constantly flickering from the road to the mirror and back again. She wore a red bandana around her hair.

"Anyhow," she said, "I really admire you dudes. I do. There's so darned much rhetoric, hawks and doves, specialists and generalists . . . it drives you nuts. But . . . but you guys *did* something. You saw evil and you walked away."

"Not quite," Oscar said.

"No?"

"We nothin' but soldiers on the march."

The girl made a loud blowing sound through her teeth. "Cut it out. Look, I'm simpatico. We're brothers and sisters, right? I understand how it is."

"Yeah?"

"Sure, man. I'm a dropout myself. Two years at San Diego State, all the bullshit in the world. Couldn't hack it. So, bang, I quit. Sometimes you've just got to separate yourself off from evil."

Oscar stared at her. "You say it's same-same? Nam and fucking San Diego State?"

"Not exactly, maybe. But I can empathize. That's all . . . I can tell what it must be like. When you see evil you have to get away from it, right?"

"Evil?" Oscar tapped Doc's shoulder. "You ever see evil in Nam?"

"What's evil?" Doc said.

The girl smiled indulgently. They were passing through a small moated village full of spires and steeples. The van shimmied on the brick streets. When they were back in forest, Oscar removed Cacciato's rifle from its wrapping and began cleaning it.

"So all I'm saying," the girl continued, "is I'm behind you dudes all the way. You've got friends. All over the world, everywhere, there are people who'll be there to help. Sympathetic friends."

"No kidding?"

"Sure. These people can plug you into anything you need. Money, jobs, housing. Tickets to Sweden. Contacts. I mean, it's a whole underground network set up for guys like you. Resisters, deserters. Guys with the guts to say no."

Oscar let the rifle bolt fall.

"Stop," he said.

"And isn't that what friends are for? To help out when—"

Pausing, the girl glanced into the mirror. Oscar had the rifle against her ear. She pulled off onto the shoulder, stopped the van, and sat still while Oscar moved to the front seat.

She smiled at him. "Look, rape isn't necessary. I mean, hey, I really dig sex. Really. We can rig up a curtain or something."

"Out," Oscar said.

The girl kept smiling. She wore blue jeans and a sweater and a khaki jacket. "Outside?" she said.

"You got it."

"It'd be a lot more comfortable in back."

"Out."

Shrugging, glancing again into the mirror, the girl opened the door and stepped out. She watched while Oscar dumped out her suitcase and sleeping bag. She never stopped smiling.

Eddie drove, Oscar rode shotgun.

"You know," Doc grinned, "sometimes I do feel a little guilt."

It was springtime. The forests were wet. They saw lilacs and budding trees, melting snow high on the mountains, scrubbed villages, wide-open skies.

Through Graz and Linz, then northwest toward Passau, the Danube, through the dark, through Regensburg and midnight Nürnberg. It was easy.

In Fulda the van broke down. They left it behind, marched two miles to the railroad depot and boarded the next train west.

There was acceleration now. The nightlong rumbling of the train, crowded cars, the wind behind them.

Fast through the German heartland—Giessen, Herborn, Limburg—and at each stop Paul Berlin dashed for a window to watch as the conductor waved his lantern. There were streetlights in the towns, steeples over the churches, neon-lighted ads for Coke and Bromo-Seltzer. The end was coming. He could feel it. Already he anticipated the textures of things familiar: decency, cleanliness, high literacy and low mortality, the pursuit of learning in heated schools, science, art, industry bearing fruit through smokestacks. Wasn't this the purpose? The goal? Some vision of virtue? Weren't these the valued things? Wasn't freedom worth pursuing? If civilization had meaning, weren't these the reasons? Hadn't wars been fought for these very promises? Even in Vietnam—wasn't the intent to restrain forces of incivility? The *intent*. Wasn't it to impede tyranny, aggression, repression? To promote some vision of goodness? Oh, something had gone terribly wrong. But the aims, the purposes, the ends—weren't they right? Wasn't self-determination a proper aim of civilized man? Wasn't political freedom a part of justice? Wasn't military aggression, unrestrained, a threat to civilization and order? Oh, yes—something had gone wrong. Facts, circumstances, understanding. But had the error been wrong intention, wrong purpose?

Now, rushing through the German dark, Paul Berlin felt full of this same desire for order and harmony and justice and quiet. A craving. Good intention made good by good deeds. Civility on street corners and courtesy at the borders between nations. He could feel it coming.

At dawn the train crossed the Rhine.

There was a twenty-minute wait in Bonn—he considered getting off but decided against it—then they were moving again through the hilly country that rolled south toward Luxembourg. Things were familiar. Lightheaded and eager, he couldn't get over how easy it was. He felt he was riding on ice.

41
Getting Shot

THE BATTLE FLOWED DOWN the ditch. It turned into the village, through the eastern paddies, then north into the next village. It was a running battle. Gunfire came in bursts separated by long hollows of silence. There was no enemy. There were flashes, shreds of foliage, a bright glare. Heavy machine-gun fire rattled behind the hedges along the ditch, then later from a grove beyond the second village. Then it ended. It ended like the end of rain. There were dripping sounds succeeded by an immense silence.

Afterward, Paul Berlin and Cacciato and Eddie Lazzutti patrolled the ditch, slowly retracing the course of the battle. They moved carefully. It was a wide, shallow-cut ditch that during the rainy season overflowed to feed the paddies on either side. Now it was dry. Its bed was cracked with fissures deep enough to put a hand into, and along the banks elephant grass grew in crisp powdered tangles. Cacciato found Buff.

They dragged him from the ditch and laid him in the grass and covered him with a poncho, then Eddie used the radio to call in a dustoff.

Later Doc Peret came by.

"It's Buff," Eddie said.

He pulled back the poncho and Doc bent down to examine the body.

"We found him like that," Eddie said. "Unpretty."

Doc took the grenades and ammo off the body. Then he went through the pockets. He removed a pack of Luckies and a wallet and chewing gum and a penknife and the dog tags. He dropped everything into a plastic sack, clipped the sack shut, and tied it to Buff's wrist.

"You forgot something," Eddie said.

"Cover him up."

"Sure, but don't you want what's in his helmet?"

"Just cover him up," Doc said.

Behind them, Paul Berlin's eyes were closed. He sat with Cacciato at the lip of the ditch. Cacciato was opening a can of peaches. The peach smell was sweet. Eyes closed, Paul Berlin pretended he was at the bottom of a chlorinated pool. Pressing silence on his ears, breathing through a snorkle, fuzzy green images swimming in his head. He tried not to think. He concentrated on the silence, but then he was thinking. Buff's shirts —the way they stuck to his shoulders in the heat. Or when he wasn't wearing a shirt, the way his belly hung over his belt, jiggling as he walked. A big guy, Buff was. All that blood and flesh and fat. On hot days he would sweat and stink. They called him Buff, which was short for Buffalo, which was short for Water Buffalo. Paul Berlin tried not to think about it. When they died, they died. He pretended he was deep in a green pool in summertime.

"On his knees," Eddie was saying. "Cacciato found him like that, all hunched up on his knees, ass stickin' up in the air, and his face . . . you had to see it. Hunched up like the way Arabs pray, all tight, face down in his fuckin helmet. You had to see it."

"No I didn't."

"You did. Just like a prayin' Arab."

"Arabs don't pray that way," Doc said.

"Hell, they don't. I seen it on TV, man. Asses in the air, all hunched up like that."

"Okay."

"I seen it."

"I said *okay*."

There was a muffled explosion, a slight shaking of the earth. Two more explosions followed. In the village beyond the ditch the First and Second Platoons were blowing bunkers. Paul Berlin kept his eyes closed. What could you do? It wasn't really sadness. Or only partly sadness. Embarrassment, that was a big part of it. Noise and confusion, and then silence. You peek up. You feel the embarrassment.

He listened to Eddie and Doc talking softly behind him. Cacciato was still eating his peaches, and the smell mixed with the smells of the burning village.

He tried to concentrate on better things. His father raking leaves—red-gold piles to be jumped into, then taken to the incinerator behind the house, the smoke and bonfire smells, acorns popping. That was the smell. Bonfires and burning villages and dried crackling grass. It wasn't really sadness.

"Hey, man."

"Hey, Oscar."

Oscar Johnson dropped his pack. There was the sound of a canteen being opened, then quiet, then a rustling.

"Who is it?"

"Big Buff," Eddie said. "Who else?"

"Buff."

"There it is. You want to look?"

"No," Oscar said.

They were quiet for a time.

"Shot," Eddie said. "You had to see it . . . found him down there in the ditch. He was shot. Hunched up like a praying Arab in Mecca."

"Eddie's our Arab expert," Doc said. "And I wish to hell he'd shut up."

"I never said I was no expert."

"Then—"

"But I seen how Arabs pray, just like that. Like in *Lawrence of Arabia*."

"Yeah."

"A billion fuckin Arabs blowin' up trains."

"Buff. You wouldn't think it."

Paul Berlin listened with his eyes closed. Life after death, he thought. And what could you do? Beside him, Cacciato was opening a can of boned chicken. Brine smells, the click of the P-38, salt and fat. Cacciato, he'd eat anything. Ham and eggs from a can, tropical chocolate bars, anything. He'd eat it. Dumb, all right. Just dumb. You couldn't fake sadness. It had to be there. If it wasn't there you couldn't fake it. You were glad it wasn't you. There was relief—it was Buff and not you. You couldn't pretend away the relief. The salty smell of the chicken made him dizzy and he turned away.

The earth was shaking again. Two hundred meters up the ditch, the others were still blowing bunkers. The explosions came in groups of three. It was Stink's steady hand: tight, neat charges that left no stains against the sky. There was smoke, but the smoke came from the burning huts. Paul Berlin let himself slide to the bottom of his warm deep pool.

"Any kills?" Eddie asked.

There was silence. Paul Berlin could picture Oscar shaking his head.

"One-zip, huh? The gooks shut us out, one-zip."

"That's enough, man."

"I'm just—"

"Have some respect and shut the fuck up."

"What can you do? You can't—"

"You can have respect."

They were smoking now. Paul Berlin smelled it. He paid attention to the ritual. Quiet, then voices.

"He was okay."

"Sure, he was. I wish the hell they'd hurry."

"What time you got?"

"Noon," Doc said. "Almost noon. I wish they'd hurry."

"Buff don' care. He was always pretty slow anyhow. Jesus . . . that time in the mountains. Remember that?"

"What?"

"In the *mountains*."

"Oh, yeah."

"He was okay, though. He was—you know—he was okay."

"Pass the smoke, man."

"And, shoot, he was good with the gun, I'll say that. He knew that big gun."

"Pass it."

"He knew that M-6o like . . . like, he really knew it. Take it apart in twenty seconds, remember that? Twenty fuckin seconds."

"Sure."

"Zip, pow . . . just like that. Take it apart so fast you'd shit. I mean, he really knew that gun."

"I guess Murphy gets it now."

"I guess so," Eddie said.

"Unless Paul Berlin wants it." There was a pause. It was Oscar. "Hey, Berlin. You want the big gun now? You want it, it's yours."

Paul Berlin, whose eyes were closed, shook his head.

"He don' want it."

"I guess not."

"Maybe Cacciato wants it."

"No, Cacciato don't want it neither. Harold Murphy's elected."

"Thank God for democracy," said Doc Peret.

"Amen."

Oscar sighed. "Buff," he said. "No lie, the dude *was* good with that gun."

"Tell it."

"He was okay."

They waited another fifteen minutes.

When he heard the dustoff coming, Paul Berlin opened his

eyes. The day was bright without clouds. A single willow tree shaded part of the ditch. This surprised him. He hadn't noticed the tree before; in all these months, it was the first willow he'd seen. A fine white powder covered the tree and the grass beneath it. Maybe it was the powder that gave the air the smell of sulfur. It wasn't a pleasant smell, but it was pleasant to smell it. It was pleasant to see the bright light, and the tree, and the long shallow ditch.

No, he couldn't pretend to be sad.

He sat up and looked for the chopper. Eddie was on the radio now, talking to the pilot, and Doc and Oscar sat smoking beneath the willow.

"Yellow," Eddie said.

Doc threw out yellow smoke.

They didn't see the chopper until it was right on them, settling down in the brown grass beside the ditch, then there was a long blind struggle to get Buff aboard. The plastic sack fell off the wrist, and Doc swore and quickly tied it back on, and the noise was fierce, and white powder filled the air, and then it was done. The pilot held up two fingers; the chopper rose, dipped, and took Buff away.

"So," Doc said.

They smoked again, a serious and quiet smoke, then they stood up and put on their packs and pulled the straps tight. Cacciato was finishing a chocolate bar.

"So," Doc said. He tried to smile. "What about the helmet?"

It lay at the bottom of the ditch. They looked down on it, then looked away.

"We can't like—you know—just *leave* it there," Doc said. "It's not decent."

"True," Oscar said, but he did not move.

"Not decent."

"True enough."

Eddie knelt down, pretending to have trouble with his radio.

"And, look, the big gun's down there, too. We can't—"

"Yeah."

"Somebody's got to," Doc said softly. "It's not respectful to let it stay. Somebody's got to do it."

Cacciato did it.

He shrugged and smiled at Paul Berlin. There was chocolate all over his face. He dropped his pack and weapon, slid down the bank to the bed of the ditch, picked up the machine gun and carried it up to Oscar.

Then, again, he slid down into the ditch.

Very carefully, keeping it steady and close to his stomach, Cacciato picked up the helmet and carried it down the ditch to a patch of high grass.

Life after death, Paul Berlin thought. It was a stupid thought. How could it be? Eyes and nose, an expression of dumb surprise—how could this promise anything? He wanted to feel grief, or at least pity, but all he could feel was curiosity.

He watched as Cacciato stepped over a log, stopped, and then, like a woman emptying her wash basin, heaved Buff's face into the tall, crisp grass.

Then Cacciato climbed the bank. He rinsed the helmet under his canteen, wiped it with his shirt, and tied it to his rucksack. Smiling, he took out a stick of gum and unwrapped it and began chewing.

"That's better," Doc said.

"Sure, that's lots better." Oscar shouldered Buff's big gun, gripping the barrel with one hand. "Enough of this shit, let's go."

And they moved down the ditch toward the burning village. There were no more explosions. The battle was over, and the day was hot and bright, and white powder covered the land.

"There's a lesson in this," Oscar said. "The lesson's simple. Don' never get shot."

"There it is," said Eddie Lazzutti.

"Never. Don' never get shot."

"Tell it, man."

"I told it. Never."

42
The
Observation
Post

THAT WAS ALL OF THEM. Frenchie, Pederson, Rudy Chassler, Billy Boy Watkins, Bernie Lynn, Ready Mix, Sidney Martin, and Buff. Six months. A few half-remembered faces. That was the curious thing about it. Out of all that time, time aching itself away, his memory sputtered around those scant hours of horror. The real war was forgotten. The dullness, the heat, endless tracts of time, the tired villages and petty conversations and warmed-over jokes and rivalries and rumors and hole-digging and hole-filling, the long marches without incident or foul play—all fuzzy like summer days. Odd, because what he remembered was so trivial, so obvious and corny, that to speak of it was embarrassing. War stories. That was what remained: a few stupid war stories, hackneyed and unprofound. Even the lessons were commonplace. It hurts to be shot. Dead men are heavy. Don't seek trouble, it'll find you soon enough. You hear the shot that gets you. Scared to death on the field of battle. Life after death. These were hard lessons, true, but they were lessons of ignorance; ignorant men, trite truths. What remained was simple event. The facts, the physical things. A war like any war. No new messages.

Stories that began and ended without transition. No developing drama or tension or direction. No order.

Paul Berlin gazed down at the beach. There was enough light now to make out the contours of miniature sand dunes rolling inland like ripples in a pond. Squinting hard, he could see the iron posts that anchored the heavy concertina wire circling the tower. There were other shapes, still obscure, that would soon be turning solid and sharp.

He checked his wristwatch. Five o'clock. Barely half an hour until dawn.

Already he saw a spreading yellow glow at the horizon. The glow would turn pink. The pink would soften. The sea would run with color and the day would start. They would climb down from the tower. Breakfast would be eaten from cans, they would swim, they would bicker over bits of shade. Later in the day there would be patrols. Following the beach, they would trudge up to where the Batangan curved sharply eastward, then they would turn inland, circling, returning to the tower for lunch. If they were lucky, if the day went as most days went, there would be nothing but heat and flies and boredom.

But now, dawn still coming, Paul Berlin let himself wonder how things might have been: the ease of running, lightness of head and foot. How far could Cacciato take him? And what would he find?

Five o'clock sharp—he had to hurry.

43
The
Peace
of Paris

LUXEMBOURG, THE FIRST day of April. They board the *Train Rouge* for Paris. A four-hour ride. Four hours, Paul Berlin thinks—four hours out of . . . what? Six months on the march, eight thousand miles, continents piled on subcontinents. And now Paris. He wants to yell. Shatter the grimy windows, put his head out and open his eyes, let civilization suck him in, splash over him like a waterfall. Already he sees it coming. Paris, he feels it.

For two hours the train rattles south through a string of small towns, then crosses into France, then turns straight west at Metz.

The speed increases. He can feel it now. Greased tracks, a steady rumbling beneath the floor. He feels the acceleration.

He concentrates. He wants to see cleanly. Taking a handkerchief from his pocket, he spits into it and carefully wipes his window. It is not rich country. The farms are old and small and broken-looking; many villages still show the damage of a war twenty years over. Scars, pocked buildings. But what does it matter? He ignores it. He ignores the soot and coal dust, all the

artifacts of industry strewn like a child's toys along the tracks
—rusting flatbeds and switching gear, timbers, heaps of mangled iron, incinerators, tin cans, crushed old automobiles, tank
cars and abandoned warehouses and barbed wire. He sees
beyond this. The season is spring. The trees are making leaves,
and among all the junk he sees the blossoms of dainty white
flowers. And there is something else: To the north the sky is
swirling with a huge black thunderhead. Already dots of rain
splatter the windows. Just a sprinkle, but the promise is there.

He feels himself grinning. Glancing across the aisle, he winks
at Doc Peret, shakes his head as if baffled, tries to think of
something meaningful to say. Instead he just grins. Even the
lieutenant is smiling. The old man sits with Sarkin Aung Wan,
nodding and looking up when she points things out to him: a
passing bridge, a valley, a village. Behind them, Eddie and
Oscar are drinking wine, making toasts, joking, ogling a pair of
girls in the seat behind them. Paul Berlin wishes they would
quiet down. Sit still, watch the unfolding spectacle, pay attention.

Faster now. The train sweeps along the curve of a river,
rattles over an iron viaduct, through wet meadows and woods,
past an old farmhouse with a rolled red-tile roof and sagging
walls, past cattle herding together against the coming storm,
past flooded streams and graveyards and broken fences. It is a
blur. Speed pressing objects together, momentum turning everything slippery and gray. Detail, he keeps thinking. What
would Cacciato see? What would Cacciato want them to see?

"Boom!"

Eddie has crept up behind the two girls, jabs the point of his
finger into the air, pretends to execute them for their indiffer-
ence.

"Boom! Boom!"

Oscar laughs, claps him on the back. The two girls move to
another seat.

There is a new sound. Cannon? Artillery? Paul Berlin looks

out, wipes the steamed-up window. Lightning! Two jagged slashes to the north, then a third, then three rumbling bursts of thunder, then the rain.

The towns are close-spaced now—Château-Thierry and Meaux and then an unending chain of suburbs—and everything is tangled and fuzzy. Details flash by too slippery to hold. The window fogs up; he curses and wipes it with his sleeve. Outside, the rain is coming harder. He presses his nose against the window, wants to break through. His fingers tingle. He squeezes them into fists.

Then suddenly they are speeding through tunnels, lights flickering, and then out again into gray daylight. Things sparkle. The air is cold and he smells rain. He smells flowers. He hears thunder and church bells. He does! Deep bronze bells, chiming, he hears them. And the sky. Bruised and fat and tumbling, the sky seems to shiver, trembling, then letting loose. It is raining.

He forces the window open.

He hangs his head out, opens his eyes wide, and he sees Paris.

It comes like a ghost. First a swirling skyline, jagged Gothic towers touching the clouds, bridges and stone and yellow buildings, then a swirl of cement and brick, then things that appear and are snapped away like magic—a house with painted shutters, a bakery, a man walking his dog, warehouses, gleaming puddles, streets and parks and umbrellas.

The speed is incredible. Whistle hooting, a clatter, the city rushes at him.

He leans into the rain.

He opens his mouth and swallows. His teeth clatter like train wheels. His ears roar.

He feels himself start to smile.

"Paris," he murmurs.

The rain makes his eyes burn. He blinks and forces his nose straight into the wind. High spires sweep by. There is a long shudder of thunder, deep thunder rolling from horizon to horizon. The pealing of bells. Behind him, he hears Sarkin Aung Wan squealing, Oscar and Eddie and Doc cheering. But Paul Berlin wants this for himself. He pushes his face deeper into the rain. He spreads his hands out, wide open, watching them turn red and wet and raw. Far off, buried in the thunderhead, he sees for an instant the twin towers of Notre-Dame. He sees a gargoyle's wild eyes. The gargoyle is torn from its mount, wings flapping, and it flies—it does! Bat wings, screeching, caught up in the acceleration, picked up and flying. The thunderhead scoops up whole pieces of Paris: a great stone bridge, a bus, a cabbage from a lady's handbag, pennants and confetti. Real? He licks rain from his lips, he feels the wind, he gulps lungsful of rain and blinks and smiles, and it's real. Sure, it's real! Sidewalks now: gutters flowing like rivers, shops and galleries, bent trees, a green traffic light, horns blaring. And people. People huddled against storefronts and behind steamed shop windows, people cooking lunch and sleeping and holding hands. Sure, it's real.

The train seems to be slowing. A conductor's voice. Images clarify. In the railyard a man stands with a lantern, holding it loosely at his side, and behind him a massive heap of coal threatens an avalanche.

There is a braking sound. The train whines against its couplings. They glide into Gare du Nord.

Hissing, steaming, the train bucks and stops.

Rain pelts the station's huge vaulted roof.

"Paris," Paul Berlin says.

Then suddenly passengers are crowding the aisles, chattering and milling and reaching for parcels and luggage. Eddie and Doc and Oscar are shaking hands. Clapping shoulders, hugging, blinking in funny ways. The lieutenant's face is like wax. He keeps touching himself. He straightens his back, tugs down his fatigue jacket, carefully places his helmet on his head.

Then the old man nods.

"Look smart," he says, so softly he repeats himself: "Look smart, men. Show these folks some class."

So, yes: Oscar wraps up the M-16. Doc wipes his glasses. They move toward the doors.

Proudly, with all the dignity he can command, Paul Berlin is the first to step down. He helps Sarkin Aung Wan out. Then he waits as the others file off.

The station is dark and damp like a dirt cellar. Thunder rattles the glass roof panes.

They move boldly.

They march into the crowded lobby, down a flight of concrete stairs, through a turnstile and out the main doors. The rain is tropical.

They stop there. Across the street, the buildings are blurred as in a dream. But it is not a dream. Paul Berlin smiles and steps in a deep puddle. The water leaks through his boots. He stamps down. His eyes sting, and he blinks and hears himself laugh. For an instant he feels silly—a rucksack and canteens and combat fatigues. But Paris! He can't stop smiling. His face is wet and his eyes ache.

Doc claps him on the back. They hug. A taxi rushes by, spraying water, but it doesn't matter. They hug, everyone together, and they put their faces up, and the rain is cold and good. Oscar's face glistens. Eddie shakes his head and grins and licks his lips. Paul Berlin kisses Sarkin Aung Wan. She is crying. Crying and laughing.

Thunder booms through the city.

The lieutenant tilts his chin up. He seems proud. Solemnly, he reaches out to shake hands.

"We'll hump it," he says. He says this with dignity. "We'll end it right. On the march. Keep the column tight, no straggling, eyes straight ahead. Try to look like soldiers."

So they form up single file.

First the lieutenant. Next Sarkin Aung Wan, then Eddie and Oscar, then Doc Peret. Paul Berlin takes his spot at the rear. Proudly, proudly. Shoulders square and head erect. Route step up the gleaming streets. Cars and buses and honking horns, people gaping, but no matter. They march into Paris. The rain feels fine.

In the first week, they took rooms in a small brick hotel off St.-Germain, a block from the Italian embassy. The rooms were dimly lighted, the walls papered in brown and gold, the beds made of brass. Each morning they took breakfast together in a cramped sitting room full of antiques and stuffed couches, then, after two pots of coffee, they would split up to begin the search for Cacciato. It was sometimes hard for Paul Berlin to take this seriously, but Oscar would take great care to remind him of the stakes.

"Maybe everything seems sweet an' cozy," Oscar would say, his voice like silk, "but don't forget this ain't no pretty tourist visit. We're AWOL. Understand me? Absent without leave from a *war*, an' there ain't no way to explain unless we bring in the proof."

"Proof?" Paul Berlin would say, and Oscar would nod grimly.

"Catch the dude, hogtie him and bring him in. March him right into the U.S. embassy, plop him down on the bargainin' table. Then we got ourselves a negotiating position. Dig it? Then we got the physical evidence."

"And?"

Oscar would snort. "You don' see? We show 'em Cacciato an' we got a story that makes sense. How we kept chasin' him, all the way here, an' how we did our job and finally caught him, dragged him in. *Habeas* fuckin *corpus*."

They would listen to this quietly. Then Eddie would nod. "Us or him."

"That's it," Oscar would say. "That's the game. Us or him."

Even so, it was hard for Paul Berlin to see it Oscar's way. The rain ended. The streets were clean, flowers blossomed in public parks. Church bells chimed. Children slouched to school in blue coats, carrying their bags by long leather straps. On the warmest days, people sipped coffee at outdoor cafés, old women and pigeons sunned themselves on park benches, traffic snarled, sleek young girls showed their legs to businessmen hustling down St.-Germain. It was hard to think about Cacciato. Instead he found himself watching the fishermen fishing from bridges, the painters who painted them. In the museums there were pictures of jousting knights and harlequins with wooden swords: masked men, sad and funny. Pictures of ballerinas and castles and ladies on swings. Paul Berlin studied the pictures. He read the inscriptions on monuments. He climbed the city's hills. He learned the history of the bridges, which came first and which last, and what they were originally built for. He looked for detail. People chatting while infants slept in carriages, students reading under trees, the order of things. Simple courtesies. "Merci," people said. "Il n'y a pas de quoi," was the answer, and he learned these things. He looked for meanings. Peace was shy. That was one lesson: Peace never bragged. If you didn't look for it, it wasn't there.

The days were warm. Holding hands, he would stroll with Sarkin Aung Wan in the way he imagined lovers must stroll. They would follow the river to Pont du Carrousel, stopping there to watch the canal boats, then they would cross over to the Right Bank with its expensive-looking people browsing in expensive-looking shops and galleries. They would have a slow lunch, and he would watch her, noticing things he hadn't noticed before. The way she removed her sandals, curling her legs beneath her. The way her chrome cross bounced on her sweaters, or the way her hair, arranged differently each day, would shine like black silk. They touched in ways they hadn't touched before, and she would smile. He bought her flowers.

It was right. In Paris, where it ended, it seemed right to fall in love, and so he did.

"I'm in love," he told her.

She was walking barefoot along the river. "How lovely!" she said. "Isn't love nice?"

"It's true."

"I thought you only spoke of possibilities, Spec Four."

"No," he said firmly. "It's the truth."

They turned back to the hotel. Sunlight flowed through gauze curtains. He liked that. He liked the room's musty smell, a sparrow singing on the terrace, a vacuum cleaner purring down the hall. He liked it when she removed her gold hoop earrings.

"Such a wonderful possibility," she smiled. "How very lucky for you. How very fortunate."

"Don't make fun of it."

"Oh, no! No, I am very happy for you. To be in Paris and to be in love. How lucky!"

Details: the cool quiet he found in Place Dauphin on the Île de la Cité, where there were pigeons and old-fashioned lampposts and chestnut trees. Someone practicing the piano in a salon across the square. A dog frisking in new grass. All the simple, shy things. A black man in a checkered shirt and purple pants playing *La Rose de France* on his accordion.

Except for Oscar, no one mentioned Cacciato. The search was leisurely. There was no talk about mission or duty or responsibility.

At night they would go to one of the cheap sidewalk restaurants along Montparnasse. They would eat fried potatoes and drink wine, then afterward they would go to the dancing places. They would dance to Frank Zappa. Eddie would bring girls to the table, and everyone would have great fun with the helmets, pretending they were goblets, and then they would dance again. Strangers would buy drinks. Policemen would smile and shake their heads. Money was never a problem, passports were never required. There were always new places to dance.

"Spec Four?"

He kept his eyes closed. It was near dawn, and already there was traffic on the street outside. Below, in the tiny courtyard, he could hear crickets.

"Are you sleeping, Spec Four?"

"Yes."

"May I wake you?"

He heard a moth playing against a lampshade. His feet tickled. He tried to move away but the tickling continued.

"Am I being gentle, Spec Four?"

"What is it?"

"A feather," she said. She laughed, tickling his toes. "There is a duck in our bed."

"A yellow duck?"

"Heavens, no! A *red* duck. It will make us a fine supper."

He opened his eyes. She was kneeling at the foot of the bed. Her skin was dark, very smooth, and she did not look quite so young. There were feathers in her hair.

"Spec Four?"

"It's a wonderful name, isn't it?"

"Spec Four . . . do you think we might see about getting an apartment? Just for us? Nothing expensive, but—you know— a place to have for our own?"

"Isn't Spec Four a great name?"

"Yes," she said. She sat up, rubbing the feather against his knee. "Spec Four is my most favorite of all names. But—"

"I had it changed, you know."

"Yes, you told me."

"It used to be a very common name. I had it changed."

"I love your new name. But what about an apartment? Couldn't we find one?"

"Don't you like it here?"

"Oh, yes! I do. But this is a *hotel*. Hotels are for people visiting or passing through a place, but a real apartment . . . it would be permanent. Do you see the difference, Spec Four? If we could find a nice apartment, then we could be *settled*. It would be lovely, wouldn't it?"

"I suppose."

298

She looked at him.

"Then shall we do it? Shall we find an apartment?"

"I guess. Later, after—"

"After what?"

He sat up. "I can't just walk out. There's Eddie and Doc and the lieutenant, all of them."

"Your friends," she murmured.

"Sort of."

"Your great and wonderful and true friends."

"They're all right."

"Your sweet friends."

"That's not the point. We're still soldiers."

"Forget them," she said. She looked at him softly, curling her legs up. "Can't you simply forget them? We could find a splendid apartment. I would make curtains and we could . . . so many things. Be happy! Forget this silly hunt for Cacciato. Don't you see? This very instant, we could get dressed and be gone before the others are awake, and we could be *happy*. Do you understand, Spec Four? We can *do* it."

"That's running."

"Exactly!"

He shrugged. He fumbled for a cigarette, lit it, tried to think clearly.

"Maybe," he said.

"Just maybe?"

He tried to smile. "No, it's a real possibility."

She suddenly clapped a hand against her hip. It made a loud, spanking sound that startled him.

Glaring, she got up and went to the window. A large red welt spread across her hip.

"A possibility," she said. "Possibilities unending. Possibilities and possibilities."

"I've got to think."

"Thinking! Think and think and think! You are afraid to *do*. Afraid to break away. All your fine dreams and thinking and pretending . . . now you can *do* something, Spec Four. Don't you see? Why have we become refugees? To think? To make believe? To play games, chasing poor Cacciato? Is *that* why? Or did we come for better reasons? To be happy? To find peace and live good lives? No more thinking, Spec Four. Now we can make it permanent and real. We can find a place to live, and we can be happy. Now. We can do it now."

She turned from the window. Quietly, she crossed to the bed, held him, rocking, holding his head, swaying.

He closed his eyes. Soap and joss sticks, time spinning itself out in long yellow ribbons. Possible?

"Spec Four?"

He nodded. They would do it. Yes, they would: He would find a way to explain it to the others. He asked if she was happy.

"Yes," she whispered. "Now I am happy."

They rode the canal boats. They visited the Rodin Museum, sat through afternoon mass at Notre-Dame, took a bus out to Versailles. They had picnics in the Luxembourg gardens. They climbed the Eiffel Tower, where, at midnight, a tour guide looked out on the city lights and said to them, "Paris is not a place. It is a state of mind." Paul Berlin smiled, but secretly he hoped it was more than that.

They looked at four apartments. Two were impossible. One, only a block from the hotel, had a rose garden and shutters and oak floors, but Sarkin Aung Wan said she wanted something higher up. She wanted perspective. In the mornings, she said, she wanted to get up and go to the windows and be able to see rooftops and open spaces and even the river.

"Am I too hard to please?"

"No. We're doing it for pleasure. There'll be other places."

"I do so want it to be perfect," she said.

"It will be."

"I know that. I wanted to hear you say it."

"It will be perfect."

The fourth apartment was near the top of a steep hill behind

Invalides. A row of shops occupied the ground floor, and above them were a dentist's office and a small fabric store. The concierge's son showed them the way up. They were out of breath when they reached the sixth floor.

"Many stairs," the boy said. He seemed shy about using English. "The woman and gentleman are to be very strong, yes?"

The place was not much to look at. Three tiny rooms, a brown-painted floor of simple pine, a ceiling that gradually angled off so as to force Sarkin Aung Wan to stoop as she hurried toward the rear of the apartment. The boy smiled and shrugged apologetically. In the bedroom there were two old bureaus and a mirror and a dangerous-looking plank bed. The walls were badly cracked and everything had the strong smell of an exterminator's shop.

Sarkin Aung Wan loved it.

"A good scrubbing," she said. "Plenty of soap and water and paint."

They moved through the kitchen and out into a small sun porch that looked out on the belfry of a church. He could see a bronze bell and the eyes of a dozen pigeons roosting there. To the left, looking down the hill, there were narrow alleys and houses crowded close together, a small playground, laundry hanging to dry from rope pulleys.

"Isn't it splendid?" she said. "We shall have our breakfast here in the mornings. We shall drink coffee and—"

"And hear bells."

"You don't like bells?"

"Sure," he said. "Bells are swell. Especially big bells. Bells outside your window so close you can read the manufacturer's stamp on the clappers."

"You can't!"

"Made in Hong Kong."

She made a face, then turned to the boy and said something in French. The boy laughed. He spoke rapidly, pointing at his wristwatch.

"There," she said. "You see? He says the bells play only three times a day. Six times on Sunday."

"You like it, don't you?"

"I would like it if Spec Four Paul Berlin liked it."

He couldn't help smiling.

"All right. Ask the boy if we'd pay as much rent as the roaches."

She spoke to the boy.

"He says it is three hundred francs a month. The bugs pay only half that."

"A steal."

"And the boy says the bugs are exceptionally quiet. Only once in ten years has a bug been evicted for rowdiness."

"Tell him I find it hard to believe a bug was ever evicted."

She told him and the boy chuckled. He had shoulder-length brown hair that was held in place by a leather headband. "Connais pas," he said.

They stayed another ten minutes. Sarkin Aung Wan tested the faucets and oven and electricity, then she went back to the sun porch and stood with her hand shading her eyes. A strong afternoon sun made the room warm.

"May we take it?" she said. "I know we would be happy."

"I suppose. It's—"

"Are you backing out, Spec Four?"

"No. It's just that I keep thinking about Cacciato."

"Then it is time to stop."

"Sure."

"Will you smile?"

He smiled. "All right, we'll take it. But first I've got to tell the others. The LT, especially. He has a right to hear about it before everything's settled and done."

"Yes, I suppose he does."

"Do you mind?"

"Terribly." She kissed his cheek. "But we shall come back later, after you have had your talk."

"Soon."

"Very soon, I know. Should I leave a deposit?"

"Ask if it's necessary."

She asked the boy, who laughed and said the apartment had last been occupied in 1946. Deposits were not required. She took down the concierge's phone number and promised to call.

The sun was just over the rim of the city. They walked down the hill toward Invalides, circled around the broad cannon-studded lawns, cut through a park, then followed Rue de Varennes toward the hotel. The Italian embassy's flag was at half-mast. Things seemed very still.

"It is a lovely, lovely apartment," Sarkin Aung Wan said. "Isn't it better to hunt apartments than people?"

"Much better. Shall we stop for a drink?"

"To celebrate our apartment."

They had cognac in a small stand-up bar on Rue de Grenelle. A television was playing behind the bar, and there were pictures of students clashing with riot police. The police wore plastic face shields and armored vests. The students were running from gas. Then there were pictures of de Gaulle, hatless, sitting behind a microphone, then more pictures of students waving banners. There was no sound. No one in the bar paid attention.

Later they walked up to Rue St.-Simon. It was dark now, and the hotel's courtyard was quiet. They stopped and kissed.

Inside, Doc and Eddie and the lieutenant were playing canasta in the sitting room. The lieutenant was drunk.

"Easy does it," Eddie said. He motioned with his head toward the old man as if to signal something. "Eisenhower's dead."

"Ike?"

"It's in the papers."

"A chain-smoker," Doc said. "I keep telling people you can't smoke like that and expect anything else."

"Shut up."

"Sorry, sir. I was—"

"Just zip up."

It was no time to mention the apartment. Paul Berlin sat in for a few hands, then went up to the room. Sarkin Aung Wan was already asleep. He switched off the light, covered her, then took Eddie's *Herald Tribune* into the bathroom to read about Eisenhower. There were two pictures on the front page. One showed Ike as a cadet at West Point. The other showed him riding into Paris, the famous grin, his jeep swamped by happy Frenchmen. It was hard to feel much. A generational thing, he supposed. Maybe his father would feel the right things. He read the story—it was purely factual, stressing those aspects that related to France—then browsed through the rest of the paper, surprised to see how little things ever changed. The world went on. Old facts warmed over. Nixon was President. In Chicago, a federal grand jury had handed down indictments against eight demonstrators at the Democratic convention the previous summer. He'd missed that—the whole thing had happened while he was in basic training. Tear gas and cops, something like that. No matter: Dagwood still battled Mr. Dithers. What changed? The war went on. "In an effort to bring the Peace Talks to a higher level of dialogue, the Secretary of Defense has ordered the number of B-52 missions over the North be dropped from 1,800 to 1,600 a month; meanwhile, in the South, it was a quiet week, with sporadic and light action confined to the Central Highlands and Delta." Only 204 more dead men. And Ike. Ike was dead and an era had ended.

He folded the paper, leaving it on the stool so he could read the sports in the morning. He showered, smoked a cigarette, and got into bed.

He lay there a long time, thinking about a lot of things. Maybe in the morning he would try calling home. Explain things. Tell how it started as one thing and turned into something else. Get some advice. Whether to take the apartment. How to justify everything.

Sarkin Aung Wan turned and snuggled against him.

"Warm?" she said.

"I'm fine. Go back to sleep."

She curled closer. He could feel the small bones under her skin. It sometimes seemed he could break her like glass.

"I was dreaming, Spec Four."

"Really?"

"Don't you want to know the subject?"

"The apartment."

"And we had a puppy. A fuzzy little puppy with brown eyes, and . . . and we were lying on the floor, you and me, and we kept calling the puppy. And I had to train him not to . . . you know. But *such* a puppy! Wouldn't a puppy be nice?"

"Wonderful."

She was quiet awhile. He could hear her thinking.

"Are you all right?"

"Perfect."

"Spec Four?"

"Yes?"

"Who was Eisenhower?"

"Nobody," he said. "A hero."

When he knocked on the lieutenant's door the next morning the old man was still in bed. He was smoking. Bare-chested, wearing only his shorts, he looked almost ghostly in the pale light. His chest was sunken, the legs skinny and white, the ribs so prominent they could be counted.

"I can come back, sir. I didn't want to disturb you or anything."

"Who's disturbed? Do I look disturbed?" The lieutenant waved him in.

Paul Berlin lit his own cigarette and watched as the old man got up and began to dress. The room smelled of rubbing alcohol. There were other smells, hospital smells, that were harder to place.

"I'm sorry, sir."

"About what?"

"About—you know—Eisenhower. I'm sorry."

The lieutenant buttoned up his trousers. "Never knew the guy."

It was hard to find a way to begin. Paul Berlin went to the window and opened it by turning an iron crank. He stood there a moment, flipped his cigarette down to the courtyard, then turned and shook his head.

"Spill it," the lieutenant said.

"Sir?"

"Blurt it out. What's up?"

So Paul Berlin told him about the apartment and how Sarkin Aung Wan wanted to take it and how maybe it wasn't such a bad idea. Make things permanent. Settle down for a while.

"And the upshot is—?"

"No upshot."

"You're gonna split?"

"Sort of. I wanted to hear what you think."

"About splitting?"

"I guess."

The lieutenant smiled. It was a genuine smile, without irony. "She's a fine girl."

"I know that, sir."

"So what's the problem?"

"It's . . . you know. Just taking off. Leaving everything, ending it."

Shrugging, wagging his head, the lieutenant sat down to pull on his boots. "Water over the dam. Dam's busted. So why not make the most of it? Can't see what difference it makes if you go it alone or with your buddies or with some pretty little girl. Comes out the same."

"I'm not sure."

"No?"

Paul Berlin ran his tongue along his lips. "Well, it's just that so far we've been in it together, all of us. You know? I mean, we're a *squad*. Chasing down Cacciato, it's been sort of a mission. It's not like we just ran away."

"You really buy that shit?"

306

"Kind of. I don't know."

Lieutenant Corson pinched the corners of his eyes. He looked exhausted.

"What can I tell you?" he said. "I can't give no orders. Never could. I could play the game, make it look good, but now it'd just look silly. Far as I can tell, Oscar's running the show. And that's where I'd be careful."

"Can't you—?"

"Nope. Make up your own mind . . . either–or. Hell, maybe something good'll come out of all this shit."

"You mean it, sir?"

"Sure. Just watch out for Oscar."

"What about you?"

The old man sighed. He went to the wash basin and rinsed his face. "Who knows? Hang around for a while, I guess. Figure things out. I got this friend stationed over in Germany, so maybe I'll . . . I don't know. It wasn't my war."

"I wish I could help."

"Doesn't everybody?"

They had breakfast together, the two of them alone, then the lieutenant went out for a paper. Paul Berlin watched him move through the lobby, skinny and bloodshot and old, stiff, a lifer for life.

What could you do? The old man was right. Either you made the break or you didn't.

For a time he sat alone at the table. He felt sad. The old man, probably. But then he thought about Paris, all the things that could be done, the nice little apartment, fixing it up. He smiled.

Later Sarkin Aung Wan came down.

"It's done," he told her.

"Did he make a scene?"

"No. He said to do what's best."

"I wish he would—"

"I know. I know all about that."

That afternoon they leased the apartment. Afterward they

celebrated with a long lunch, then spent the rest of the day shopping. They bought a watercolor from an artist along the river, a rug, dishes and towels and place mats. At a small antique store near Invalides they found a bronze-cased clock. It didn't work, but that was fine.

"We're refugees," Paul Berlin said. "What does time mean to refugees? We'll buy a hundred broken clocks."

Instead they bought sheets and blankets and a radio, a chrome-framed mirror, silverware and a tablecloth and a geranium. They carted everything up to the apartment, piled it in the kitchen, swept down the floors, then went to the porch to watch the sunset. It was fine. They opened a bottle of wine and drank it slowly. The church's stained-glass windows glowed like gemstones. Then the bells began to chime.

"You see?" Sarkin Aung Wan said. "It isn't bad at all."

And it wasn't. The sound was rich. The pigeons were lined up in rows along the belfry.

"What do you think, Spec Four?"

"The bells are nice."

"Perhaps we could have a muffler installed. The pigeons are either very stupid or very deaf."

"And you're very pretty."

"I'm not too young for you? You keep saying I'm a child."

"You're fine."

They drank the wine and listened to the bells and watched the sun disappear. The porch captured the last light. Sarkin Aung Wan's cheeks glowed like new copper pennies. He kissed her.

"Are you pleased?" She looked at him closely.

"I'm pleased," he said. "I'm happy."

It was after midnight when they returned to the hotel. Oscar and Doc and Eddie were waiting in the lobby. They were sitting on their rucksacks, going over a street map. The lieutenant watched from the doorway.

"Pack up," Oscar said flatly. "Fast. You gon' wasted ten seconds."

"What?"

"No bullshit, just do it. Move out."

They looked shaken. Eddie's face was drawn. Doc kept rubbing his throat. On the floor beside them Cacciato's rifle was wrapped up in a poncho.

"*Do* it," Oscar said. "Now."

"Do what? We're—"

Doc stood up. "Oscar's right," he said softly. "You best hurry. We'll explain later."

"What happened? Everything was fine."

Oscar made a hard mocking sound. "Oh, yeah. Things was real sweet. Real cozy. Tourist shit an' apartments. An' sooner or later it catches up with you. Didn't I say that? Didn't I?"

"Sure."

"There it is. Sooner or later. Those is facts." Oscar went to a window, drew back the curtain and peered out. Then he turned and stared at them. "It's over. Good times are gone an' a billion fuckin chickens is comin' home to roost. Now get upstairs an' pack. We checkin' out."

44
The
End
of the Road
to Paris

EXCEPT FOR AN OCCASIONAL car or motorbike, the
streets were deserted. Hunted again, on the run, they
followed Rue de Grenelle to a large wooded park opposite Place Joffre. Oscar stopped there, signaling for them to
wait while he scouted out a spot to spend the night. The air was
damp.

"I don't get it," Paul Berlin whispered. "Things were fine, no
problem."

"Quiet."

"It doesn't make sense."

"Sense!" Doc laughed bitterly. He squatted in the grass, a
low fog wrapping him like a blanket. "Wonderful sense!"

"What—?"

Doc shrugged. "Same old tune. Hotel clerk gets suspicious,
calls in the gendarmes. One thing leads to the next . . . Where's
our passports, why all the military gear, who's our CO? Desertion, illegal entry."

Paul Berlin closed his eyes. Suddenly he wished it would all
end. Everything: the cold, the running, the war. He wanted to

go home. A clean bed, his mother and father, the town, every-thing in its place.

"Oscar's right," Doc sighed. "You can't get away with this shit. The realities always catch you."

"But maybe."

"No maybe's. Reality doesn't work that way."

Oscar crept out of the fog.

"Over there," he said. He pointed toward a clump of bushes beyond a statue of a man holding huge bronze scrolls. "We can set up the ponchos. Nothin' elaborate. Get some sleep an' then figure what to do."

"Jesus."

"You slept out before, man. Pretend it's Boy Scouts."

Doc and Sarkin Aung Wan helped the lieutenant into the bushes. They rolled out the ponchos and covered themselves with coats. Sleep was impossible. Impossible, Paul Berlin kept thinking. Impossible. Not this close to the end. A happy end. What was so wrong with that? He lay on his back, then his side, then he sat up.

Near dawn the fog turned into a steady drizzle.

They had coffee and rolls in a dingy café across from the park then wandered aimlessly up toward the river. The morning cold was amazing. It came in layers like frost. The lieutenant's cough was back and Sarkin Aung Wan helped him along, hold-ing his arm. The others were edgy.

"What happened to spring?" Doc muttered. "Flowers and sun and stuff? What happened to all the pretty things?"

"Be cool."

"April in Paris . . . what happened to it?"

They spent the morning on the move. When the rain got bad, or when the old man's cough worsened, they would duck into a museum or café, careful to avoid places where they might be conspicuous. At noon the rain let up. They decided to take a chance on the apartment.

It was midafternoon when they reached the building. They

waited outside for a time, watching for police, then they quickly crossed the street and climbed the six flights of stairs.

"This is it?" Oscar grinned. "Your swell apartment? The great escape?"

Rain had leaked through a ceiling fixture but otherwise things were exactly as they'd left them.

Doc got the lieutenant into the shower, then wrapped him in a blanket.

"So this is it," Oscar said. "Peace on earth."

"You can leave."

"Not 'less the rats start attackin'."

They waited until dark. Then Sarkin Aung Wan fixed a supper of cold meat and bread and wine. The lieutenant fell asleep on the floor.

"So what's the next move?" Eddie said. "I hear Sweden's real pretty in April."

"Shit."

"What's wrong with Sweden?"

Oscar shook his head. "Sweden's for candy-asses."

They waited. Oscar went to the window, stood there a moment, then turned. His sunglasses were tilted up on his forehead. When he spoke his voice was soft. It reminded Paul Berlin of lake country.

"Listen up real good." Oscar paused and removed Cacciato's rifle from the poncho. "Fact number one: We're in trouble. No papers, no orders. Far as law's concerned we nothin' but deserters. Fact number two: Sooner or later we're gonna be nailed. That's a fact of real life." He looked at Paul Berlin. "Fact number three: Some of you dudes been fuckin off. Pretendin' it's a lark, follow me? I ain't namin' no names, just telling facts. We got to get serious. No more dilly-dally shit, no more apartments or playin' house. You know what happens to deserters? You *know*?"

"They burn," Eddie said.

"There it is."

"Maybe we could explain it," Paul Berlin said. He felt a little embarrassed. "Couldn't we? Tell them how Cacciato—"

"Get off it, man."

"I mean . . . maybe we should just turn ourselves in. Go over to the U.S. embassy tomorrow, walk right in. Explain exactly what happened. How we started after Cacciato, and how . . . you know. Maybe they'd go easy on us."

Oscar was quiet. He looked at Eddie, then at Doc. He sighed. He walked across and put his finger against Paul Berlin's chest.

"You know somethin'?"

"What?"

"I pity you."

Paul Berlin smiled.

"I do, man. I pity your sorry ass. You don' dig the basic game, do you? The game's set up, all the pieces out on the board, an' either we play or we fry. Burn. No choice. Dig it? You don' amble nice an' polite into Uncle Sam's embassy and blush an' tell some crazy story like that. The game, it ain't played by those rules. You got to have proof. Evidence."

They were quiet. Sarkin Aung Wan sat with the lieutenant's head in her lap, gently stroking his forehead. Doc seemed to be concentrating on something in another room.

"Understand me? We either keep runnin' or we do somethin' positive."

"Like what?" Paul Berlin asked, but he knew the answer.

Oscar grinned. "Like we go huntin'. That's what . . . We put on our huntin' threads an' we do it right. We catch the dude an' we bring him in and we drop him on the bargaining table."

"Back to the beginning."

"There it is," Oscar smiled. "There it is."

In the morning they began the search. Oscar took charge, handing out maps and search sectors, reminding them of the stakes. "He wins, we lose. No screw-ups." Sarkin Aung Wan moved out to the sun porch. She watered the geranium, put

313

it up to catch the sun, then gazed across at the church belfry. Paul Berlin stayed away. He couldn't explain it, and she couldn't understand. It was more than skin-saving. It was responsibility. Either you understood responsibility or you didn't, and she didn't. The lieutenant, too. The old man didn't even listen when Doc tried to explain things. He coughed, blinked, then looked away.

"Mercy," he mumbled.

"What?"

"Nothing. Leave me be."

So they began without him. Paul Berlin was assigned to the tourist and commercial areas in the first arrondissement, and he spent the day working his way up and down a hundred unfamiliar streets. It seemed impossible. He tried hard to inspect each face, each building or park bench, but in the end he only walked, letting his feet do the looking. He spent two hours in the Louvre, then wandered up through the open gardens to Rue de Rivoli, then followed a chain of twisting streets to Place Vendôme. After lunch he doubled back toward the east, using the sun as a guide, ignoring his maps. His feet ached. He'd forgotten how it was.

Paris, he kept thinking. Peace and quiet and happiness. And now it was gone. He stopped once for a Coke, sipping it slowly and watching the late afternoon crowds make their way home, then he joined the flow across Pont Royal and returned to the apartment. Doc and Eddie were already there, soaking their feet. They didn't look up. "Nothing," Eddie said.

It went that way for days: avoiding police, worrying that the apartment might be discovered, long hours on the streets, fatigue that produced crazy dreams at night. With the lieutenant still sullen and withdrawn, Oscar took firm command. "The dude's out there," he kept saying. "He's hidin' out like a skunk an' I smell him." At night they took turns staking out the major railway and Metro stops. They adjusted the daily search sectors, combed through the visitor rolls at the Palais

Royal, checked the hotels. But they found nothing. It was as if Cacciato, if he existed at all, had somehow torn himself free of physical fact.

"He's got to eat," Oscar would say. "Don' he? He's got to eat an' sleep and wash his undies like the rest of us."

But there was nothing.

Walking the streets, Paul Berlin tried to make a game out of it. A puzzle. What had brought Cacciato here? Why Paris? Why not Madrid or Brussels or New York? Details: the density of the city, gray and brown and yellow stone, the temper of things, rubbish in the river, but still an oddly beautiful river, the things seen and heard and felt. What was Cacciato after?

Paul Berlin looked hard, paying close attention, but the details only looked back at him.

At the apartment, Sarkin Aung Wan and the lieutenant refused to have any part in it. They spent their time together, talking softly, avoiding the others. Paul Berlin tried not to look at her. Partly it was guilt. Guilty if you fulfilled old obligations, guilty if you abandoned them. Sometimes he would catch her gazing at him, her eyes full of pity—not quite pity, not exactly, but something very close.

"We'll still do it," he told her one evening. The others were asleep. "I swear, as soon as this thing is ended."

She tried to slide away but he grabbed her wrist.

"Can't you understand that? Just give me a chance to finish all this."

"No."

"What? No what?"

She pulled her arm free. "Spec Four, you have the alternatives. It is time to choose."

"But, look, it's not realistic to just run off."

"Realistic! Is it *realistic* to make our apartment into a military headquarters? To chase a poor simple boy . . . Is that *realistic*? I would rather be unrealistic."

"But I promise—"

"Oh, I know about promises," she said. "Spec Four, you are full of such promise. Promise and promise. Promise unending."

He watched her move away. He tried to imagine it differently, he tried hard, but the power to make a wish was no longer the power to make it happen. It was a failure of imagination.

The next morning he found Cacciato.

It was . . . oh, it was in Les Halles. Among the oranges and turbot and baby pigs dangling from their hocks, among bins of celery and pushcarts piled high with spring turnips; there, where hawkers shouted out prices and come-ons and where women scrambled for freshness in their daily bread; amid the fruit wagons and rows of neck-wrung chickens, halves of warm beef open to flies, clogged gutters and garbage, crowds pushing through troughs of grapes and melons and string beans—there, in midmorning market on a spring day.

Cacciato, no question.

He was alone. Rosy cheeks and a happy smile. A wicker basket on one elbow. Still chubby, still pink, still young and healthy and scrubbed.

It was Cacciato.

Stepping back, then freezing, Paul Berlin felt no surprise. No great emotion. It happened as it should have happened—a simple, easy thing.

Cacciato: the same pink spot at the crown of the skull. A little bigger than he remembered him. Sparrow-eyed. Munching on gum, roundfaced, misshapen.

Pausing now and then to squeeze a melon or a head of lettuce, Cacciato moved easily through the crowd. People smiled and nodded at him. He seemed in no hurry, stopping once to buy bananas, another time to buy fish and sausage. At each booth the hawkers would have pleasant words for him, and Cacciato would smile and wave and continue on. He might have been a boy sent by his mother to do the day's shopping.

Paul Berlin followed at a distance.

Staying with the crowds, he tracked him through a huge iron pavilion and then down Rue Baltard to the Fontaine des Innocents. Cacciato stopped there, pulled out a loaf of bread, broke it in half and began feeding the pigeons. Methodically, as though it were a job to be done, he threw out crumbs until the entire loaf was gone, then he picked up his basket and moved down a chain of winding streets into a part of Paris that Paul Berlin had never seen. It was poverty. Thickset roofs clung to one another as if designed to block out sunlight; everywhere there were tenements running in bleak rows like barracks, one to the next. There was no beauty in it, no elegance or charm.

But Cacciato didn't notice. Whistling now, he turned into a narrow cobbled lane roofed with drying laundry. He paused a moment, half turning, then he shifted the wicker basket to his left elbow and entered an old stucco building.

Paul Berlin felt calm. The road ended where it surely would have ended, a dead-end alley. No exits and no tricks.

Without hesitation, he followed the lane to its end. It was an old hotel. A faded blue and white sign gave the rates and the proprietor's name.

He rang the bell, waited, rang it again, then tried the door. It was unlocked.

Inside, the lobby had the smell of dust. There were a few tattered chairs, a sofa, a stained rug and broken windows. The place was abandoned.

He waited a moment, listening, then he heard the whistling again. It came from the ceiling. An old, familiar song. Climbing the stairs, Paul Berlin found himself humming. The words to the song wouldn't quite come. What was it? He tried for silence, a light foot, steadiness. *Billy Boy, Billy Boy* he found himself humming, climbing, *where have you gone, charming Billy?*

The stairs ended in a long hallway. There were no windows or carpets. No lighting except for what came from the lobby below.

The whistling was closer now. He followed it, humming along, stopping to listen at the numbered doors. At the end of the hallway he found it. The door was painted bright green.

He pushed the door open and stepped in.

Cacciato smiled. He was in his underwear, sitting on a cot, peeling carrots into a metal pan. Like a baby, clean and smooth and plump.

He smiled.

He put the knife down, and the carrot, and got up and put his hand out. The hand was soft. The smile was immaculate. A baby's smile, beguiling and meaningless. "Hi," he said.

"You found him?" Doc said. "Cacciato?"

Paul Berlin, who discovered the truth was simple, handed Oscar a slip of paper with the hotel's name and address. The lieutenant covered his eyes.

"You *found* him?"

"Simple."

Doc laughed. "What . . . what'd he say? Cacciato."

"Nothing."

"I mean, how did he explain it? Didn't he—?"

"Nothing," Paul Berlin said. He felt himself shaking. "Not a thing."

"Leaving, walking away? Didn't he say why? Why he did it?"

"Nothing!"

"Take it easy, man."

"Nothing," Paul Berlin murmured. "A dummy. No reasons, no answers. Nothing. Just a baby."

"Easy."

"A big dumb baby."

"Relax. What'd you expect?"

"Nothing."

Imagine it: The Majestic Hotel is darkened like a theater stage. In the Salle des Fêtes, the hotel's old conference room, there is the sound of an audience that isn't there. Feet shuffling, a cough, the murmur of voices. Somewhere a champagne bottle is opened. Light applause. Then trumpets and drums, a diplomatic flourish.

Spotlight: It falls on a large circular table topped with green baize and rimmed with chrome. The table is just over thirteen feet in diameter, one hundred and thirty-five feet in circumference. An invisible line divides the table into two precise halves. Around each of these halves there are eight leather armchairs. Sixteen chairs in all. On the table before each chair is a microphone and headset. There are no flags, no nameplates or other identifying symbols.

Spotlight expands: Imagine marble floors and marble pillars, glided ornamentation, drapes descending forty-foot walls, an arched ceiling, an enormous Louis XIV tapestry depicting birds in flight.

Paul Berlin enters from the right, Sarkin Aung Wan from the left.

Spotlight contracts: a narrow beam focusing on the green circular table.

Paul Berlin takes a seat at the giant table, on the half closest to the tapestry; Sarkin Aung Wan walks to the far side, bows, then sits. They put on the headsets. There is a squeak, the sound of amplification, as each of them tests a microphone.

Then a pause. The parties do not look at each other. The conference hall is hushed—the echo of an audience no longer present.

Without pleasantries, Sarkin Aung Wan unfolds a piece of parchment paper and begins to read.

"During the many months it has taken us to reach this table" —but it is not her voice, it is the voice of translation, a man's voice, precise and unaccented and impersonal—"we have traveled some eight thousand American miles. As irony will have it, this number has its exact complement in American lives lost over that same period. I find no humor in this. I find it sad. But this sadness is neither inevitable nor unending; we might still develop a common vision of happiness, and by our action here we might begin the realization of that vision.

"It is easy, of course, to fear happiness. There is often complacency in the acceptance of misery. We fear parting from our familiar roles. We fear the consequences of such a parting. We fear happiness because we fear failure. But we must overcome these fears. We must be brave. It is one thing to speculate about what might be. It is quite another to act in behalf of our dreams, to treat them as objectives that are achievable and worth achieving. It is one thing to run from unhappiness; it is another to take action to realize those qualities of dignity and well-being that are the true standards of the human spirit.

"Spec Four Paul Berlin: I am asking for a break from violence. But I am also asking for a positive commitment. You yearn for normality—an average house in an average town, a garden, perhaps a wife, the chance to grow old. Realize these things. Give up this fruitless pursuit of Cacciato. Forget him. Live now the dream you have dreamed. See Paris and enjoy it. Be happy. It is possible. It is within reach of a single decision.

"This is not a plea for placidness of mind or feebleness of spirit. It is a plea for the opposite: that, like your father, you would build fine houses; that, like your town, you would endure and grow and produce good things; that you would live well. For just as happiness is more than the absence of sadness, so is peace infinitely more than the absence of war. Even the refugee must do more than flee. He must arrive. He must return at last to a world as it is, however much in conflict with his hopes, and he must then do what he can to edge reality toward what he has dreamed, to change what he can change, to go beyond the wish or the fantasy. 'We had fed the heart on fantasies,' says the poet, 'the heart's grown brutal from the fare.' Spec Four Paul Berlin, I urge you to act. Having dreamed a marvelous dream, I urge you to step boldly into it, to join your own dream and to live it. Do not be deceived by false obligation. You are obliged, by all that is just and good, to pursue only the felicity that you yourself have imagined. Do not let fear stop you. Do not be frightened by ridicule or censure or embarrassment, do not fear name-calling, do not fear the scorn of others. For what is true obligation? Is it not the obligation to pursue a life at peace with itself?

"You have come far. The journey to this table has been dangerous. You have taken many risks. You have been brave beyond your wildest expectations. And now it is time for a final act of courage. I urge you: March proudly into your own dream."

Silence, a murmur of assenting voices.

Spotlight shifts: across the green-topped table, a narrowing of the beam. Paul Berlin waits, then gently taps the microphone. His face is tanned and takes the light well. It is an angular, handsome face. The brow drops flat and solid. The nose is distinguished. The lips, slightly parted, seem on the verge of a shy smile, but his manner is not shy. Reserved, perhaps, but still confident. There is grace in the way he lights his cigarette, holding it as if it isn't there, adjusting his papers, glancing up for a moment, nodding politely, barely, a diplomatic courtesy. He wears a blue suit with the most subtle pinstripes. His tie is gray, his shirt is white. In the spotlight, his light brown hair seems almost blond. His hands are steady. His eyes, set wide, are equally steady. No signs of timidity or bashfulness.

And when he speaks, leaning into the microphone, his voice is resonant and firm. A diplomat's voice.

"Friends," he begins. The amplification system whines, and he moves back slightly: "Friends, I don't pretend to be expert on matters of obligation, either moral or contractual, but I do know when I *feel* obliged. Obligation is more than a claim imposed on us; it is a personal sense of indebtedness. It is a feeling, an acknowledgment, that through many prior acts of consent we have agreed to perform certain future acts. I have that feeling. I make that acknowledgment. By my prior acts— acts of consent—I have bound myself to performing subsequent acts. I put on a uniform. I boarded a plane. I accepted a promotion and the responsibilities that went with it. I joined in the pursuit of Cacciato. I marched. I voted once to continue the pursuit. I persisted. I urged the others to persist. I tied myself to this mission, promising to see it to its end. These were explicit consents. But beyond them were many tacit promises: to my family, my friends, my town, my country, my fellow soldiers. These promises, too, accumulated. I was not misled. I was not gulled. On the contrary, I believe . . . I *feel* . . . that I am being asked to perform a final service that is entirely compatible with what I had promised earlier. A debt, a legitimate debt, is being called in. No trickery, no change in terms. I knew what I was getting into. I knew it might be unpleasant. And I made promises with that full understanding. The promises were made freely. True, the moral climate was imperfect; there were pressures, constraints, but nonetheless I made binding choices. Again, this has nothing whatever to do with politics or principle or matters of justice. My obligation is to people, not to principle or politics or justice."

Paul Berlin pauses here, clears his throat, reaches for a glass of water.

"But, please . . . I don't want to overemphasize all this. More than any positive sense of obligation, I confess that what dominates is the dread of abandoning all that I hold dear. I am afraid of running away. I am afraid of exile. I fear what might be thought of me by those I love. I fear the loss of their respect. I fear the loss of my own reputation. Reputation, as read in the eyes of my father and mother, the people in my hometown, my friends. I fear being an outcast. I fear being thought of as a coward. I fear that even more than cowardice itself.

"Are these fears wrong? Are they stupid? Or are they healthy and right? I have been told to ignore my fear of censure and embarrassment and loss of reputation. But would it not be better to accept those fears? To yield to them? If inner peace is the true objective, would I win it in exile?

"Perhaps now you can see why I stress the importance of

322

viewing obligation as a relationship between people, not between one person and some impersonal idea or principle. An idea, when violated, cannot make reprisals. A principle cannot refuse to shake my hand. Only people can do that. And it is this social power, the threat of social consequences, that stops me from making a full and complete break. Peace of mind is not a simple matter of pursuing one's own pleasure; rather, it is inextricably linked to the attitudes of other human beings, to what they want, to what they expect. The real issue is how to find felicity within limits. Within the context of our obligations to other people. We all want peace. We all want dignity and domestic tranquillity. But we want these to be honorable and lasting. We want a peace that endures. We want a peace we can live with. We want a peace we can be proud of. Even in imagination we must obey the logic of what we started. Even in imagination we must be true to our obligations, for, even in imagination, obligation cannot be outrun. Imagination, like reality, has its limits."

Full spotlight: Sarkin Aung Wan and Paul Berlin stand, stack their papers, then wait. They do not look at each other. There is no true negotiation. There is only the statement of positions.

Footsteps click in the great conference hall. The lieutenant enters. He wears his helmet and rucksack. He shakes hands with Paul Berlin; they exchange a few quiet words. The old man then crosses to Sarkin Aung Wan. He offers his arm, she takes it, and they move away. A moment later Paul Berlin leaves by a separate exit.

Spotlight dims: An electric hum fills the Salle des Fêtes. The amplification system buzzes indifferently.

Spotlight off.

Imagine it.

45
The
Observation
Post

ALREADY THE FLIES WERE awake. Two sea gulls perched on the tower's south wall. The night was over. The sea was blue. Soon the others would be awake. The day would start. They would roll up the ponchos. Doc would shave. Eddie and Oscar would go in for a swim, then they would eat breakfast, then swim again, then sit in the shade beneath the tower to wait for resupply. Later they would go out on patrol. There would be no battles, no terror, and the day would be long and calm and hot.

Those were the coming facts, as nearly as he could guess.

The war was still a war, and he was still a soldier. He hadn't run. The issue was courage, and courage was will power, and this was his failing.

"Facts," Doc Peret liked to say. "Face facts."

Six o'clock now. He rubbed his face.

The facts were not disputed. Facts did not bother him. Billy Boy had died of fright. Buff was dead, Frenchie was dead. Pederson was dead. Sidney Martin and Bernie Lynn had died in tunnels. Those were all facts, and he could face them squarely. The order of facts—which facts came first and which came last, the relations among facts—here he had trouble, but it was not the trouble of facing facts. It was the trouble of understanding them, keeping them straight.

Even Cacciato. It was a fact that one day in the rain, during a bad time, the dummy had packed up and walked away, a poor kid who wanted to see Paris, no mysterious motives or ambitions. A simple kid who ran away. There was no use toying with the truth. It couldn't be colored or altered or made into more than it was. So the facts were simple: They went after Cacciato, they chased him into the mountains, they tried hard. They cornered him on a small grassy hill. They surrounded the hill. They waited through the night. And at dawn they shot the sky full of flares and then they moved in. "Go," Paul Berlin said. He shouted it—"Go!"

That was the end of it. The last known fact.

What remained were possibilities. With courage it might have been done.

46

Going
After
Cacciato

"**H**E'S GONE," Doc said. "Split."

"Gone where?"

"Who knows where? Him and his gear, everything. Just gone."

Paul Berlin shook his head. "Impossible. He wouldn't do it."

"No? Go look for yourself. The man's gone, flown the coop. Appears he's taken the girl with him."

The apartment had been cleaned out. The rugs, the clock, the watercolor, Sarkin Aung Wan's geranium and new curtains —all gone. The floors were swept. The bed was made up in crisp forty-five-degree angles. The closets were bare. In the kitchen a single joss stick smouldered on the counter.

"Believe it now?" Doc said. "Not even a lousy fare-thee-well. Right when things come together, right at the buzzer, the old fart takes off without even a salute."

Paul Berlin's eyes burned. It was the joss smoke. He went to the stick and squeezed it until the burning stopped.

"Gone," Doc sighed. "Both of them. Makes you wonder, doesn't it? Makes you faithless."

"Maybe they just—"

Doc wagged his head. "Face it, they deserted like rats. Must've been planning it all along. Everything so neat and tidy, all the loose ends tied up . . . not even a good-bye."

Paul Berlin's eyes were stinging. Her smile when she first saw the place. Her excitement, the way she took his arm. The way she called him Spec Four, thinking it was his name. Clipping his nails. Long sunny days on the march. Refugees. The apartment, the whole idea of refuge. Such a fine idea.

He went out to the sun porch. For a time he stood alone, looking out on the church belfry. He wished the bell would chime—something. He closed his eyes and made the wish. Doc put a hand on his shoulder and led him inside.

"My condolences. Honest, it's a tough piece of luck."

"She was right."

"What can I say, pal? What can I say?"

Later they found the note. It was tacked to the bathroom door: "Heading east. A long walk but we'll make it. Affection."

Doc read it over twice, then three times, shaking his head.

"East?"

"The Far East."

"Don't even say it, man."

"Maybe—"

"Too simple, too slick. A sick old man, a girl. It can't be done."

Oscar Johnson took command. The final operation, he said: Stake out Cacciato's hotel, plug up the exits, wait, and, when the kid showed himself, move in to end it.

It was Oscar's game.

"No waffling," he said. "No pitty-pat shit. Tonight we do it right."

There were no arguments. Oscar unwrapped Cacciato's M-16 and held it out. Doc touched it. Eddie touched it. Paul Berlin touched it.

"Done," Oscar said.

They showered, changed into fresh uniforms, then met for a final strategy session.

At dusk they moved out.

Single file, Oscar leading, they marched down St.-Germain to St.-Michel. The night was warm. The café awnings along St.-Michel were held full by a breeze. Girls sat at the sidewalk tables, legs carefully folded, smoking cigarettes and watching the passing crowds. Paul Berlin tilted his helmet down. He concentrated on the march.

They crossed the river at Cité. Immediately the lights and traffic were gone. They circled the massive Palais de Justice, moved across Pont au Change, then turned in toward Les Halles.

No one spoke.

Oscar took the rifle from its blanket and carried it openly, patrol style, the barrel off to one side. No more pretense. Lead-colored turrets stood bare against the sky. Silhouettes, statues, and gargoyles. The night seemed to move. Paris, Paul Berlin was thinking, but the feeling was Quang Ngai. He told himself to be brave.

Counting: That was one answer. He counted his steps, watched the others move in front of him.

They crossed the square at Fontaine des Innocents and moved into the huge deserted market area. Smells of clotted sewage, algae, rotting vegetables, animal fat, the paddies. Moonlight played on the high iron-latticed pavilions. Once, when Oscar spotted a policeman, they stopped and waited in the shadows of an abandoned store front; otherwise it was just a march.

It was past midnight when they found the dead-end alley.

There were no lights. The hotel looked old and forlorn and empty, like an abandoned farmhouse outside Fort Dodge.

"You're sure?" Oscar whispered.

Paul Berlin nodded. "Up there. Second from the right." He pointed to Cacciato's second-story window. Two panes were missing.

They listened, letting their eyes adjust. There were no lights or signs of life in the building. Doc took off his glasses, spat on the lenses, wiped them, put them on again. He managed a nervous little laugh.

"Think he's up there?"

Oscar shrugged, cradling the rifle against his stomach. "Wait here. I'll see what there is to see. Keep alert."

He trotted down the alley, stopping once to test the front door, then he circled behind the building. When he was gone, Doc moved into the shadows of a cluster of garbage cans. Eddie chuckled and whispered something obscene, and Doc laughed, and they sat down to wait. It was the wound-tight feel of an ambush. Partly hidden, partly exposed. The wondering and the waiting. Paul Berlin felt a little guilt. Not much, but enough to think about. Mostly it was an eagerness to have it over and finished.

Oscar was gone nearly twenty minutes.

Then Paul Berlin felt a cold tickle on his ear.

"Swell lookout," Oscar purred. "Real alert."

The tickle was painful. He tried to move. It was the pain ice gives when it sticks to flesh. Without looking, Paul Berlin knew it was the rifle muzzle.

"I was Charlie, what would you be?"

"Dead," Paul Berlin whispered. "I'd be dead."

"God's own truth," Oscar said. "A dead lookout."

"Sorry. I was—"

"Pitiful." Oscar lifted the rifle. The cold tickle persisted. "You guys . . . you're genuine yo-yos, aren't you? Aren't you?"

"I guess."

"I guess, I guess. Fuckups. Dipsticks in the overall slime."

"We try," Doc murmured. "We do try."

Oscar smiled coldly. "Tryin' don't cut it. Honest, I pity you. Battin' in the wrong fuckin league. I just got pity."

No one answered him. Paul Berlin scratched the tickle on his ear.

"No more tryin'," Oscar said. "Tonight you pitiful mothers

is gonna do. Tonight I teach the basic difference between fuckup tryin' and doing. Understand that? I say it, you do it. Real simple like."

Even in the alley's thick dark Oscar wore sunglasses. Paul Berlin wondered for a moment about the miracles of vision. He scratched his ear and wondered.

Oscar waited a moment.

"So. We got ourselves an understanding? Follow your friendly leader, that's all."

Paul Berlin started to speak, then thought better of it.

"Words?" Oscar smiled.

Paul Berlin shook his head.

"Good. An improvement. A definite betterment." He glanced at his wristwatch. "Listen up. I got the place scouted. No back doors. Only other way out is them two fire escapes. See 'em?"

Doc and Eddie nodded.

"All right, then. What you're gonna do is this. You're gonna climb up there an' you're gonna sit an' you ain't gonna let nothin' in and nothin' out. Think you can manage?"

"Sure," Eddie said. He looked at Doc and grinned. "We can do that easy."

"Splendid. Real progress."

"Nothing to it," Eddie said.

"When you're set, give me a wave. I'll do the messy shit. If Cacciato's inside . . . if he's there, then we got his ass. Fini. If he's not, we hold positions an' wait. When he shows we nail him."

"What about me?" Paul Berlin said. "Where you want me?"

Oscar made a wide, mocking gesture with his hands. "I don't," he said.

"Say again?"

"I don' want you. You're a fuckup. Man, you're the worst."

"Hey, don't—"

"You heard me. Go home. Go hide your head."

Paul Berlin backed off a step. Then he swallowed. "I'm going along, Oscar."

"Shit."

"I am. I'm going."

"The messiness?" Oscar grinned. "You want in on the real nasty stuff?"

"I'm going, that's all."

"Brand-new balls?"

"I'm going."

Oscar studied him, then shrugged. "Okay, man. Even yo-yos got to get their brand-new rocks off. See if they work, right?" He let the rifle bolt fall. "So what's the delay?"

They filed up the alley.

Climbing slowly, Doc and Eddie made their way up the two fire escapes, testing the steps as they went. Paul Berlin tried not to think. He made his thoughts into a revolving sphere, a tiny marble, and he concentrated on the marble. He watched it turn. A silver, shining marble. He could feel the fear coming, but he kept his attention on the marble. Focus on it, watch it spin in the dark, a brilliant glowing sphere. Like a star. Be brave, watch the silver star.

When Doc and Eddie reached the second story, they crouched down and waved.

Oscar raised the rifle.

"Ready, Deputy? Showdown time."

Oscar led the way inside. The doors were unlocked. Lighting a match, Oscar moved slowly across the lobby to the staircase. He stopped there. He listened, then lit a second match, then tested the stairs. The place smelled old. It smelled of dust and mildew and age. Damp, like lake country. Like the smell of old canvas. When the match went out Oscar did not light another.

Eyes firmly on the spinning silver star, Paul Berlin followed Oscar up the stairs. He tried for silence. Stealth, cunning. He listened for telltale sounds. The hotel was quiet.

At the top of the stairs Oscar paused again, shifting the rifle, turning, feeling for the walls. A window at the end of the hallway let in a pale path of moonlight.

Oscar began moving up the hallway. His shoulders were rolled forward. He stepped lightly, carefully, but there was no tension in the way he carried himself. He seemed loose and ready.

At the end of the hallway, Paul Berlin pointed to the green door. Then he stepped back.

Oscar grinned. "No, man."

"What?"

"Heroes first." Oscar pressed the rifle into Paul Berlin's hands. "You dig this shit so much . . . here, take it. Go ahead."

"I don't—"

"Take the weapon. It's your move."

The rifle was incredibly light. Paul Berlin had to squeeze to keep it from drifting away. The shining silver star was gone.

"Go!"

Oscar used his shoulder to drive the door open.

The room was empty. Paul Berlin felt the emptiness before he saw it.

Then he felt the fear.

A monstrous sound hit him. It jerked him back.

"Jesus," someone was saying, loud. Oscar, maybe.

The sound spun him around. His ears exploded. Suddenly he was on his knees. He couldn't stop shaking. He squeezed the rifle. He held on tight, but the shaking wouldn't stop.

Someone was whimpering. A pitiful, silly sound. Behind him in the dark there were shouts, voices calling, the sound of someone running.

Red tracers made darts that stuck to the far walls. A smouldering smell. Burning. Holes opened like magic in the walls. The plaster turned crisp and black.

Shaking, shaking—he couldn't stop it. He tried to drop the weapon. He tried to throw it, but it kept shaking him.

He heard himself whinny.

A dozen rounds were off in the time it took to squeal. Glass was breaking, windows popping. He squeezed the weapon and held on and whinnied.

"Jesus," a soft voice kept saying, far off. "Jesus, Jesus."

The noise ended. There was a click, then echoes, then quiet.

He was on his knees. His eyes were closed. Rocking, swaying, eyes closed tight, but even so he kept seeing red tracers, slim and sharp, brilliant red threads in the dark. The shaking feeling was gone. He smelled the burning.

"Jesus, Jesus," he moaned.

He let the rifle fall. He put a hand to his lips and held it there, not quite touching. He felt the breath on his hand, felt himself swallow. Somewhere a fire was burning. It was a hot blazing fire, a bonfire. He heard people talking. Then there was a floating feeling, then a swelling in his stomach, then a wet releasing feeling. He tried to stop it. He squeezed his thighs together and tightened his belly, but it came anyway. He sat back. He shivered and wondered what had gone wrong.

"It's okay," Doc murmured. "All over, all over. Fine now."

Paul Berlin sat cross-legged to hide his folly. His arms and hands and feet weren't working right. First the shaking feeling, next the numbness, next the swelling in his belly and next the wetness and next the folly and humiliation.

"No sweat," Doc was purring. "You hear me? It's all over."

The fire blazed away.

He smelled the grass. He heard them talking, very softly. There was the breeze and the grass and the fire.

"Just the biles," Doc said. "Right? It's just the pitter-patter of the biles. Just the tinkle of the biles, no sweat."

The shaking was back. Doc helped him lie in the deep grass. He lay there, letting the weapon shake him, and when the shaking ended he watched how the grass waved with the breeze. Like spring wheat. He wished he could cover himself. Maybe he could sleep. Sleep away the rest of the war. He closed his eyes and listened to the soft voices and the breeze against the grass, then he opened his eyes, very slowly, seeing first his own eyelashes, then light, then the dawn sky.

"Dumb," Oscar said.

Stink giggled. It was Stink's high giggle.

There was the heavy sound of something being dropped, someone grunting, and the brittle sound of the fire.

Lieutenant Corson bent over him.

"Better now?"

Paul Berlin nodded.

The old man winked and made a comforting gesture with his hand, a kind of affectionate pat.

"It happens, kid. Sometimes it happens. You got to—" The words trailed off. The lieutenant winked again and moved away.

Folly, that was all it was.

The fire was very hot. He sat up, crossing his legs, watching the fire. He tried for control. He didn't look at the others. Later he would have to look at them.

"Dumb," Oscar said. "Stupidest thing I ever seen."

Stink laughed.

Harold Murphy said something to them, then he turned and went over to his gun. He seemed angry. He kicked the gun, then kicked it again, then picked it up and moved away.

Doc Peret was back again.

"See, man? Everything's real cool." He held up a canteen. "So what's your poison? I got Beaujolais, Pouilly Fuissé, and this one last magnum of 1914 Goofy Grape. Which'll it be?"

"I didn't mean to."

"Sure."

"I was tense. I didn't mean it."

Doc kept smiling. His eyes wandered. "So place your order, cowboy. Chablis? Or this real saucy Spanish number? Both vintage years, I swear. Or if you're on a budget I can recommend this special—"

334

"It just started. You know? It was like the gun just started . . . I didn't mean to."

"Sure, man. No harm."

Doc unscrewed the canteen lid and sniffed it.

"Drink up," he said. "You lucked out . . . a terrific nose. Real sweet stuff."

"It just happened."

"No harm. Come on now, take a swig. Isn't that vintage stuff?"

The Kool-Aid was warm. The taste was between strawberry and lemon.

"What about Cacciato?"

Doc's eyes kept roving. He smiled. "It's over. Tell me if that isn't the sweetest stuff you ever swallowed."

The big breakfast fire burned hot. Near the lip of the hill, where the land dropped off sharply to the west, the lieutenant and Eddie Lazzutti were taking turns with the binoculars. They stood knee-deep in the grass, neither of them speaking. Eddie handed the glasses to the lieutenant, who held them to his eyes for a long time, swiveling, scanning the jungle below, then shaking his head.

"Dumbo," Oscar said. He glanced over at Paul Berlin and shook his head. "I never seen nothin' like it. Never once."

Dawn had become morning. Paul Berlin got up. He heard birds in the trees. He stood very still for a moment, feeling the men watching, then he turned away.

He followed the hill's eastern slope to the place where the grass was matted. He remembered crouching there, poised and waiting for what would happen next. How did it start? A kind of trembling, maybe. He remembered the fear coming, but he did not remember why. Then the shaking feeling. The enormous noise, shaken by his own weapon, the way he'd squeezed to keep it from jerking away from him. Simple folly, that was all.

He picked up the rifle.

Gold cartridges sparkled where they had fallen, strewn in the grass like spilt pennies.

He broke the weapon open, checked the barrel for dirt, then closed it up again. The magazine was empty. Removing it, he replaced it with another from his bandolier, then, very carefully, he pushed the safety switch from automatic to safe.

Farther down the hill he found his pack. It had started there. Dropping the rucksack, lightening himself for the final climb, the last hundred meters. He remembered following Stink up the hill. He remembered the smell of the fire, the sense of something hidden. He remembered the lightness of the rifle. Floating, seeming to float.

He opened the rucksack. Near the bottom he found a fresh pair of trousers. He changed quickly. He rolled up the wet pair, carried them to a clump of bushes, dropped them in and pressed them down with his boot. He tried to do this with dignity.

What else?

He shouldered the pack and climbed back up the hill.

Later, after Oscar doused the fire, the lieutenant went to the western lip of the hill for a final look. He covered his eyes with one hand, shading them, and he gazed west for a long time. He did not move. When he came back he was smiling. "That's it," he said. "Finished." He winked at Paul Berlin as if to relay some secret.

"We had him," Stink said.

"Did we?"

"Sure, we had him good."

"Who knows?" The lieutenant was smiling broadly now. He looked happy. "Maybe so, maybe not."

"Ready, sir?"

Harold Murphy heaved the big gun to his shoulder.

Doc gathered up the things Cacciato had left behind—some Hershey bars, two signal flares, the dog tags. Oscar strapped Cacciato's weapon to his pack.

Then, when they were formed up, the lieutenant motioned with his hand and led them away.

It was the march again.

They found the old path and followed it through the morning, backtracking. At dusk they camped at one of the old sites. And in the morning they continued east. They marched hard. It was the old order restored. Stink at point, Oscar at slack, next the lieutenant and Eddie and Harold Murphy, then Doc Peret, then Paul Berlin.

The country was familiar. On the evening of the second day the mountains began falling toward the paddies. Below, the land stretched eastward for many miles, flat and green, ending at the sea.

They came down from the mountains.

The next afternoon they stopped at a hamlet, resting and taking on water, then continued on. It was the war again. They spaced themselves ten meters apart, avoided paths, sent out flank security when it was necessary.

Late that day they were within radio range. The lieutenant made the call. Missing in action, he said. He spelled out Cacciato's name phonetically, repeated it, his voice calm. He smiled when it was done. Then they were moving again, down from the mountains, through the rough country, into the paddies.

Flat, hot farm country. The march was easy now.

At suppertime they made camp along a narrow irrigation ditch. They dug their holes and set out the tripflares and prepared for night. In the morning, with luck, they would reach the sea.

Night spread up the ditch and passed over them and rolled toward the mountains.

They talked softly. They talked of rumors. An observation post by the sea, easy duty, a place to swim and get solid tans and fish for red snapper. Later they talked about going home. It would become a war story. People would laugh and shake their heads, nobody would believe a word. Just one more war story. Then Oscar talked about two women he knew, and how, when he got home, he would choose the one who most hated war stories. This made Harold Murphy talk quietly about his wife. The lieutenant did not talk at all.

When full dark came, they moved to their separate holes along the ditch. The stars were out. And soon the moon appeared, very pale at first, but then turning bright as it passed over the mountains.

Paul Berlin slept. There were no dreams. When he awoke he saw that the lieutenant was sitting with him.

Together they kept the guard.

They watched the immense stillness of the paddies, the serenity of things, the moon climbing beyond the mountains. Sometimes it was hard to believe it was a war.

"I guess it's better this way," the old man finally said. "There's worse things can happen. There's plenty of worse things."

"True enough, sir."

"And who knows? He might make it. He might do all right." The lieutenant's voice was flat like the land. "Miserable odds, but—"

"But maybe."

"Yes," the lieutenant said. "Maybe so."